The Manuscript

MICHAEL STEPHEN FUCHS

PAN BOOKS

For Mr Huckabloon

First published 2006 by Macmillan
an imprint of Pan Macmillan Ltd

This edition published 2008 by Pan Books
an imprint of Pan Macmillan Ltd
Pan Macmillan, 20 New Wharf Road, London N1 9RR
Basingstoke and Oxford
Associated companies throughout the world
www.panmacmillan.com

ISBN 978-0-330-45257-1

9 8 7 6 5 4 3 2 1

A CIP catalogue record for this book is available from the British Library.

Printed and bound in Great Britain by
Mackays of Chatham plc, Chatham, Kent

The Manuscript

Michael Stephen Fuchs has a degree in philosophy from the University of Virginia, many years of experience working in technology, and a keen and abiding interest in evolutionary psychology, cognitive neuroscience, genetics/genomics and artificial intelligence – as well as what these new discoveries have to tell us about timeless human questions. His second novel, *Pandora's Sisters*, is published by Macmillan New Writing. He lives in London and out on the wild web.

With boundless thanks to:

My aunt Valerie Sayers (the real writer in the family), for warm-hearted support and free professional advice; my amazing and adored sister Sara, for single-handedly resurrecting a deceased project; all of my other family members for, basically, ruling the universe; Mike Barnard, for fearlessly championing new writing, for liking mine in particular, and for being unrelentingly spectacularly nice to me; Mary Chamberlain, for skilfully massaging the text (while still letting me keep my Fuchsisms); and Mark Pitely, for getting dragged right into the trenches, for helping teach me how to tell stories, and for the AYT bit (among many others).

This novel was made with:

Bailey's "The Original" Irish Cream, Anderson Valley Boont Amber Ale, Blue Moon Belgian White and Harvest Pumpkin Ales, Hacker Pschorr Weiss, Franziskaner Hefe-Weiss, Gorden Biersch Marzen, Alaska Pale Ale, and Motherlode Golden Ale; Djarum Super 'class A' cigarettes; the fine espresso drinks of Cafe Mocha (Virginia Highlands, Atlanta), Torefazzione Italia (Palo Alto), and Cafe Borrone (Menlo Park); Apple PowerBook, Power Macintosh, and G3 computers; Alice in Chains *Dirt*, Public Enemy *Fear of a Black Planet*, Yello *Stella*, Metallica *And Justice For All*, everything by Machines of Loving Grace, White Zombie *Astro-Creep 2000*, everything by Live, William S. Burroughs *Spare Ass Annie and Other Tales* (rest in peace, Uncle Bill), Eric Serra *The Professional Soundtrack*, James Newton Howard *Grand Canyon Soundtrack*, Moby *I Like To Score*, Tori Amos *From the Choirgirl Hotel*, and Tool *Aenima* (though this last got me evicted); the films of John Woo and Luc Besson; ass-kicking exploits of Captain Sir R. F. Burton; encouragement and advice of Lawrence Block; revealed wisdom of Lao Tzu and Steve Pinker; world-class firearms from Bersa and Sturm Ruger & Co.; Alex Garland (who always got younger, while I didn't); US Interstate 40 (nearly two thousand plot-prodding miles of it); Webster's New World Dictionary (2nd) and Thesaurus (thanks, Mom and Pops); all the real, fragile, and wonderful people to whom the resemblance of characters in this book is purely coincidental; and the Internet, without which.

Prologue

In a small hut filled with oily candlelight shadows, a man toils at a page. The curve of his back arches over paper, quill, and inkpot, tendons in his neck taut with concentration and questionable posture. He drives his stylus to the edge of the desk, pressing a stack of rough-edged paper with bloodless fingers. He stabs out for fresh ink, then resumes inscribing.

His upper body sways from side to side, a tense keeping of time. His palsied movements mirror the spread of wet scratches across the page. Sweat droplets arc from his body, melting into the dirt floor. He inhabits a fevered dream – or, rather, he is reaching out to something within a dream, frantic to pull it into this world.

Later, a few hours before dawn, the man emerges from the hut. He wears a cured leather satchel slung over his shoulder; a revolver and a knife nestle on his belt. He clutches the sheaf of pages, ink now dry, rolled tightly in one fist. Stepping from the shadow of the doorway into a clearing, his face is caught by moonlight: deeply tanned and lined, with glinting and fierce black eyes. A ragged scar traces one cheek, above and to the side of a sinuous forked moustache.

Another man, white-haired, fully bearded, and wearing robes, waits for him in the near-darkness. They exchange a few whispered words, and embrace. Then the first man departs, trotting down the path and beyond the ring of huts. Soon, he is clambering through the thick underbrush of the mountainside, scrabbling in the dark; descending, and still descending.

When he reaches the base of the mountain, the sun peeks over the grass plains to the east, glinting off the mountains behind him. Another man waits for him by the circular embers of a fire.

"Dick, you're back! I've been up in the Sierra de San Luis . . . My God, Dick. You look as though you've just seen a ghost."

"What day is today?"

"What?"

"The date. The day of the week, of the year. I . . . I've lost track of the date."

"Why, it's Friday, Dick – the 25th. It's Christmas. Christmas Day, 1868."

Part One

The universe we observe has precisely the properties we should expect if there is, at bottom, no design, no purpose, no evil, no good, nothing but blind, pitiless indifference.

— CHARLES DARWIN

Miles to Go

A square bar dominated the center of the 14th Street Pub, the watering hole at the edge of Thomas Jefferson College, in Hookeville, Virginia. A harried barkeep hopped around the square's interior, mixing drinks in a fine alcoholic mist. A man named Miles Darken, in company with other 14th Street regulars, slumped on the other side of the bar, emptying mugs of draught beer and nursing the week's indignities.

Miles had slouched into the bar just after 8pm, topcoat billowing around his tall, slim build and clunky boots. It was Friday night and a crowd had already filled the room. Swiveling on his stool, he looked for familiar faces. He couldn't make out the back corner through the throng.

Dana Steckler sat in the corner booth, shouting over the tumult with her friend Paulina. Dana pulled her chin-length red hair behind her ears, lit a cigarette, and leaned in.

"Isn't that your friend Miles, at the bar?" Paulina asked.

"That is him."

"Why don't you go say hi, and introduce me properly?"

"Give me a minute."

"Sure. While we're waiting: what's it like sleeping with Professor Castrolang?" Dana looked scandalized. "I saw you sneaking into his office three times last week. You can see his door from the student lounge. Well, if you crane your neck, you can see it." They both laughed.

"He's my new advisor," Dana answered. "I'm obligated to sleep with him."

"I thought you might be doing research for him. That's what you said earlier."

"Okay, you got me. It's a research project." She sighed. "One I don't feel like talking about right now. Let's go introduce you to Miles." Dana palmed her cigarette and the two squeezed out of the booth and across the crowded floor.

"Hiya, handsome." Dana nuzzled Miles' ear, distracting him while she swiped his mug from his other side. As he swiveled left, and then right, Dana helped herself to a sip.

"Hey there, doll," Miles said, not commenting on the purloined beer. "Who's this?"

"Miles, this is Paulina. She just transferred into the philosophy department as a sophomore." In a mock aside, she added, "And she's nineteen." Turning to Paulina, she said, "He likes nineteen-year-olds. Cradle robber."

Miles made claws and growled. "That's cradle-robber *baron*, thanks very much." He turned back to Dana. "So what's up? Moreover, where have you been lately? The disappearing act have to do with your big, mysterious research project?"

"Goddammit," said Dana. "Can't a person do graduate work in peace around here without a constant public inquiry? Anyway, it's not 'big and mysterious.'"

"Then why the big mystery?"

"Okay, that's it, buster. Now we're going to talk about your vanity web page."

Miles piped down and looked nervously about the room.

"That's right," Dana said, pressing her attack. "Paulina, you can now look up all your favorite facts about Miles at boatanchor.tjc.edu."

"What's a boatanchor?" asked Paulina blankly.

"It's Miles' personal workstation," Dana answered. "Now Miles' personal web server."

"I'd planned to name it cracksmoker," Miles said blithely. "But that got vetoed by the people who paid for it. Anyway, I had to put some documentation online; a web page seemed to be the place for it." Miles shifted slightly. "But honestly, I don't care that much for the web. It has no interaction or community. On Usenet, on the other hand, I can jump into a discussion group and instantly connect with thousands of people who know what they're talking about."

Dana threw a crumpled bar napkin at him. "You mean thousands of people who happen to agree with you." The other two looked at her inquiringly. "Miles thinks he's old school with his Usenet groups. But I think it's dangerous being surrounded by people who think just like you do. *You start to believe all your prejudices are right.*" Dana stubbed out her cigarette and helped herself to another sip of Miles' beer. "I've got to get back to the computer lab. I've got work to do."

"On a Friday night?"

"Thesis advisors are unfamiliar with the category. Paulina, are you leaving?"

"I think I'll stay awhile," she said, eyeing Miles.

"All right. Miles, let's have brunch. Call me, okay?"

Miles started to answer, but Dana had already pushed her way through the shifting mob to the door. He looked back at Paulina and shrugged.

Outside the bar, Dana paused and pressed her back to the brick wall of the alley. She produced another cigarette, but merely held it in front of her, regarding it. She really did need to get back to work. But given that she was not convinced the subject of her search existed, she doubly resented having to go look for it on a Friday night. She sighed, put the cigarette away, and began the walk back toward the darkened campus.

"So," Miles asked Paulina, "why'd you transfer?"

"I don't know," she answered. "What I was doing before didn't seem to me to be right. So I thought I'd try something else. Or at least somewhere else."

"Ah," said Miles, smiling down at his beer. "Another seeker. Do you think you will find the answers that have eluded you in the philosophy department of Thomas Jefferson College?"

Paulina stiffened slightly. "Well, maybe I will. What is it you do at TJC, by the way? Dana told me you're not a grad student."

"Merely a graduated student. Now I work here, in the Academic Computing Center."

"And does that make you a graduated seeker as well?" Paulina asked. "You're now doing just what you're meant to be doing in the universe?"

"I have no idea," confessed Miles. "But I do think that's turned out to be the central question of our generation: 'Is this right? Is this what I'm meant to be doing?' I keep waiting to run into someone with a satisfactory answer." Miles paused to sip. "How did you meet Dana?"

"In the department. She's taken me under her wing, I suppose. I think she's made it her mission to try and make my transition more comfortable."

"Oh, yeah?" Miles asked instantly. "We'll have to put a stop to that dastardly scheme."

"What?" Paulina appeared flustered again.

"Making you more comfortable. How nefarious. I mean, if there was one thing you were trying to accomplish in transferring, it was to flee from comfort, right? That was the whole point."

Paulina kept her silence for a moment, then asked, "How do *you* know Dana?"

"Actually, we dated in undergrad," Miles said quietly. "It was a long time ago."

Paulina sized him up again. "What you said about comfort just now. Comfort's so bad?"

"Take it from me," Miles answered with an easy authority. "You know what still being in your college town three years after graduation is like? It's a lot like being in bed, sleeping in late. Very warm, and pleasant, and comfy. But now and again, you stir a bit and you think, 'Jesus, I can't believe I'm still in bed.' But then you roll over and drift back off."

He shrugged, smiled resignedly, and called for the bill.

Miles' walk home from the pub took him past the main computer lab. Within, Dana sat in silence, entering very dramatic search terms into the library database system, LexisNexis and, finally, a number of web search engines. The latter kept alternately returning zero or thirty thousand hits.

She was beginning to have grave and debilitating doubts that the thing she'd been charged with finding was out there at all. If such a thing existed, why wouldn't the world know about it? But neither could she still her fascination with the idea. *So tempting*, she mused to herself. *It is very human to imagine that there really might be final answers. Out there just waiting for us to find them.*

"Waiting for *me* to find them," she amended out loud.

She looked out the window, which rose to the ceiling. In the reflected light of the thick glass, she saw only her own bright and puzzled reflection. Beyond its surface, Miles passed into the shadows of the lane behind the building, which led to his empty apartment.

Great Secrets

In the late morning, twisting on his futon, Miles booted up leisurely.

First his eyes flickered and lit up. Then various mental processes hummed to life, starting with the operating system – rough knowledge of who and where he was. The OS did a few quick hardware diagnostics: stomach empty, bladder full, head throbbing just a little. He then fired up pointers to long-term memory volumes; he could now call up such data as his parents' birthdays, or the Independent presidential candidate in 1980, if he really needed to.

Happy with his Sunday morning start-up, Miles tried some network activity: he trundled out of the bedroom in his boxers and picked up the phone.

"Hey. It's me. Brunch invitation still good?" He held the phone with one hand, and scratched his back with the other. "Yeah, sure, bring her. Pick you up in half an hour."

Miles rolled his Datsun to a stop in the parking lot of Dana's apartment complex. Dana and Paulina appeared from the stairwell and wordlessly took their seats in the car. They all sighed expressively at the late morning air – bright, clear, and cool.

Miles rolled out of the lot and descended the broad sweep of a partitioned boulevard, the car idling low and easy, sunglasses and chrome glinting wildly. They negotiated a few other cars and the odd pedestrian, cutting a loop around the campus and toward downtown. Miles eased the car regally into a shadow-speckled gravel parking lot. He smiled as he pulled on the parking brake.

"I hope Cafe B is okay," he said.

As they clambered out of the car, Dana said, "Miles is being ironic, Paulina. Cafe B is the best brunch for five thousand miles in any direction."

"Gimme the Sunday Number Three," Miles instructed the waiter, salivating, "with both the bacon and the sausage."

Dana: "I'll have the Number Three, too. Vegetarian version, though, please."

Miles to Paulina: "Dana has some kind of problem with devouring innocent creatures to give ourselves cancer and heart disease. But that's nit-picking, isn't it? She should live a little."

"Vegetarians live six years longer," said Dana. "I'll make sure there's bacon at your wake."

"Thanks," said Miles. "By the way, how went your Friday night research-athon?"

"Like a well-oiled machine."

"So, are you going to tell us what you're researching now?"

"If that's the only way to make y'all stop asking." Dana let her bangs swing in front of her face, then brushed them away again. "It's more silly than anything. I feel silly talking about it."

"That would explain," drawled Miles, "your elaborate silence."

"Well, it's this. My new academic advisor has got me on a scavenger hunt for a lost document. I happen to think it's just a rumor, a myth. If it does even exist at all, it's going to turn out to be another discredited scrap on the tall historical pile of 'revealed religious truths.'"

"Goddamn, Dana," Miles said, "will you please tell me what you're babbling about?"

She shook her head and drew breath before speaking carefully. "It's a religious text. Or a philosophical one, maybe. It dates from 1868 or 1869. It was written by one Sir Richard Francis Burton. And it was lost – if it ever existed at all." She paused. "Do you know who Burton was?"

Miles squinted as if trying to recall. Paulina shook her head blankly.

"In a small nutshell, he was a nineteenth-century explorer, soldier, writer, translator, and a lot of other things. He discovered the source of the Nile, translated the *1001 Arabian Nights*, and snuck into Mecca disguised as an Arab, among many other exploits."

Dana paused as food began to hit the table. Between greedy gulps of coffee, she continued. "Burton spent several years in South America in the 1860s. For about six months of that, he disappeared into the highlands of Brazil and Argentina. There was no record of what he did on this trip. Just a lot of rumors. Wild stories about running gunfights with bandits in the mountains."

"Cool," said Miles. He tucked into his eggs, keeping a half an eye on Dana.

"There's one story that's wilder yet," she continued. "His discovery of the lost tribe, and the manuscript he produced describing them. As the story goes, somewhere up in the mountains which divide Argentina and Chile, sometime around the end of 1868, Burton stumbled into a remote and unmapped village, populated by an isolated tribe. Racially, they were not related to either the indigenous Indians, nor the conquering Spaniards. And, moreover, they were a very serene and wise bunch of people." Dana paused. "People who understood things the rest of us do not."

"Things like what?" asked Miles.

Dana paused before speaking down at her plate. "The nature of consciousness. Free will and morality. The shape of the universe, and time's arrow. How to access the Godhead; where the soul goes after death. Past lives, maybe." She looked up at the other two again. "'Meaning of life' stuff, for lack of a less dramatic way to put it."

"Wow." Miles pushed his plate away from him and gave Dana his full attention.

"Anyway, as the story goes, these people showed Burton all of their secrets – showed him in a way that left no question of their truth – and he wrote a first-person account of everything he saw."

"And this record was lost somehow?" asked Paulina.

"His wife burnt all of his papers on his death. The notion is – again, if you buy into any of this – that Burton never dared publish what he learned in South America. And it went up in flames."

Miles sipped from his coffee cup. "If it was destroyed, then why are you looking for it now?"

"That's what I keep asking myself." Dana exhaled and pushed back from the table. "But I actually want to turn the tables and ask *you* a couple of questions in your field of expertise."

"Sure, shoot." Miles replaced his coffee cup and looked expectantly across the table.

"If something is somewhere out on the Net, web search

engines will always be able to find it? They know about everything that's out there?"

"Not precisely." Miles shifted in his seat, clunkily shifting mental gears. "In order for a document to be in a web search index, generally some other document has to link to it. Search engine spiders just follow links, one after another, page to page, indexing everything they find on the way."

"So if something wasn't linked to anything, it wouldn't get indexed?"

"Not unless someone specifically registered it with the search engines." He pinned her with his squint. "I'm guessing this question is not *totally* unrelated to the earlier topic?"

"Not totally." But just then their waiter appeared with a check and an unsubtle intimation that they should pay it and clear out. They could see the line of aspiring breakfasters snaking out the front door. "I need to get back to work, anyway," noted Dana.

After dropping off the other two where he'd found them, Miles rolled the Datsun into the circular drive in front of his building. Inside, he puttered around in the vaguely menacing shadow of a coming Monday morning. He went to bed early; but later, in the night, he dreamt of Dana's young friend Paulina shouting to him from South American mountain tops, trying to tell him she had found the Great Secret. In the dream, Miles struggled to remember what that was supposed to be.

Things Fall Apart

Tides of quiet starlight pooled into the dim living room as Dana entered, coming home late again, on Sunday night. She stepped through the blackness of her little off-campus apartment, then pulled open the drapes, and the sliding glass door behind it.

She stood at the suddenly bright edge of the main room,

tired and all alone, a crisp breeze kicking the corner of the drape around her ankle. She let her satchel slip from her shoulder to the half-shadowed living-room floor and stepped out onto the balcony.

Dana's building sat on a rise, a half-mile from the center of campus. The distance and the elevation provided a lovely, quiet view of the twinkily lit-up buildings of the college – close enough that each backlit windowpane glinted at her, but too far for drunken reveling or other noise to carry.

Dana stood in the breeze and monitored the distant lights. She thought about Paulina, and what TJC and Hookeville might look like through new eyes. Dana thought of her life as a graduate student in the field of medical ethics, and she worried that all of her reading and writing and research – all very intent, all concerned with the life of the mind – might have caused her to go a little bit blind to the world. Paulina seemed more prone to questioning where she was in the larger scheme, what the point of all this was.

She thought about Miles, and how he worked so hard to be a good friend to her, and that perhaps she didn't do as much as she could to reciprocate. There was so much work to do, and so few hours. Outside of 9 to 5 – actually, more like 11 to 5 – Miles' time was his own, and he seemed to have forgotten what it was like to be a full-time student. Still, Dana wondered if she didn't take him for granted, assuming he would always be around for her, whenever she got around to taking him up on it.

Ever since their romantic dissolution four years earlier, Miles had been the soul of solicitousness. She attributed it to guilt. There had been no real reason for their break-up; Miles had simply felt a sudden and irrepressible desire to get out, and nothing Dana said could change his mind.

She sighed, and patted herself down for cigarettes. She got one lit despite the breeze and fumed serenely into the darkness.

Because she was south of campus and elevated, Campbell Hall, home of the Philosophy Department, dominated her view.

Dana could see light leaking out of the windows on its south face. One of them could be her advisor's office, though she could not tell for sure.

But she could well picture the scene within that tiny room, having spent so many afternoons there. Especially the one day in August, when Professor Jim Castrolang had related to her an unlikely tale of enlightenment found, and lost, and – maybe, if they were on the ball – found again.

"Sir Richard Francis Burton," James Castrolang had recited on that day, two months earlier, seemingly casually, "1821 to 1890. English explorer, soldier, anthropologist, eroticist, swordsman, linguist, translator, writer – but you can get the biographical sketch from any of a number of sources." Jim paused to pace the tiny office. "Which I suggest you might do, when you get a chance."

Dana crossed her legs, sitting in the lone chair before the cluttered desk. She nodded at his suggestion, which she did take to heart a few minutes later, making a beeline for the main library.

Before that night ended, Dana knew that Richard Burton had been all of the things Castrolang had ticked off, and also many more: inventor, scholar, geographer, surveyor, naturalist, student of the world's religions, skilled mesmerist, member of the Royal Geographical Society, co-founder of the Anthropological Society of London, discoverer of Lake Tanganyika in Africa, and prolific writer, poet, and translator of such works as the *Arabian Nights* and the *Kama Sutra*. And, despite being a brawler and political lightning rod (known to many as "Ruffian Dick"), he had ultimately been knighted.

Sitting in a shadowed study cubby, buried in a remote corner of the hulking library, Dana had pressed a Burton biography into her lap – the first of several books on the man she would read, or skim, in the weeks to follow. She stared transfixed at Burton's fierce, angry-eyed, brow-shadowed image on the slick paper insert of the book. His visage was unlike any other she had seen: ugly and handsome, captivating and terrifying.

Turning back to the front of the book, she ran though the details of Burton's early life.

Born in England in 1821, raised in France (where he picked up French as well as Spanish, Portuguese, Italian, German, and Greek), he later returned to England, only to get expelled from Oxford for brawling, drunkenness, and disrespect. He signed on with the British Army in India and, with a Bombay teacher, took up the study of Hindustani, hoping for a staff appointment as a translator. He also studied Gujarati and Sanskrit, in which he absorbed himself so much that his fellow officers bequeathed him the not-entirely-affectionate nickname, "white nigger". Despite that, he continued with his language studies, learning Persian, Sindhi, Punjabi, Pashto, Multani, Armenian, and Turkish. In the end, he mastered twenty-nine languages and a number of dialects.

Under the command of Sir Charles Napier, conqueror of the Sindh, Burton worked as an intelligence officer in the British Indian Army, often going in disguise, dressing as a wealthy half-Arab and half-Iranian merchant. He rented a shop and sat in the market asking questions; his disguise allowed him the opportunity to observe daily Indian life as no other foreigner could.

Ruminating on these arresting details, Dana laid herself out straight and diagonal in her rough wooden chair, steepled the scuffed volume in her lap, and rubbed the bridge of her nose. She had already spent more than two hours in the library, and Burton hadn't yet turned twenty-eight, though he'd accomplished more than Dana thought she might ever aspire to.

Burton was most famous, even in his own day, for two exploits. The first was smuggling himself into the holy and forbidden Arab cities of Medina and Mecca, making the sacred *hajj* disguised as an Arab physician. For months he maintained the ruse, aware that if he were found out he'd be torn limb from limb in Mecca, where infidels were forbidden to set foot. The second was his discovery, with John Hanning Speke, of the source of the Nile in the middle of Africa. This capped a months-long overland expedition, which involved hundreds of men and beasts, and which nearly killed him and Speke both.

These were only the most renowned of his exploits. "Much like Jefferson," Castrolang had told Dana, back in his office, "he was engaged by everything. Nothing was uninteresting to him, or foreign to his mind. However, our interest is in one discovery of Burton's which appears not to have made it into the official record at all." Castrolang paused there.

"So you're telling me," Dana said, "Burton discovered some people who no one else ever had, and who claimed to have some esoteric knowledge." She paused to gather the flapping threads of her thought. "And these people ostensibly shared these answers of theirs with Burton, in person, in 1868 or 1869. And he wrote down everything he learned from them."

"Right," agreed Castrolang. "We think. Possibly."

"I guess I still don't understand," Dana ventured, "exactly what you're saying Burton discovered. What 'questions' does this document answer?"

"The intractable ones," Castrolang answered unemotionally, and without hesitation. "The nature of consciousness – does it come from a soul, or simply a very complex brain? Which is true of our fate – free will, or determinism? What's the truth about morality? Are some things really right, and others always wrong? Why we have been put on this planet, if we have been put here." He paused, looking her in the eye. "And God. Yes or no?"

Dana found she could formulate no response to this.

In 1865 Burton was appointed Her Majesty's consul to Santos, Brazil. During his three years there, he wrote three books, invented a new kind of carbine pistol, explored the provinces, and led an expedition to inspect the gold and silver mines in the interior. He took a 1,300-mile float down the São Francisco

River on a raft, most of it alone. "This was typical of Burton," Castrolang had said. "Interested in everything but his job. For three years, the consulate languished."

In the middle of 1867, Burton left for Rio, and an exploration of the highlands of Brazil. About that region, he wrote, "It was a dangerous and lawless place, and a revolver at night is as necessary as shoes. If a strange person asks you for a light, you stick your cigar in the barrel of your gun, and politely offer it to him, without offence being given or taken."

This cavalier attitude to danger partly explained Burton's enjoyment of his tour of the US territories: he could carry a Colt revolver and a Bowie knife without drawing attention. He was also one of the best swordsmen of his day, having studied from his youth under a number of masters. He fought in the war in the Crimea, and survived an ambush in the Arabian desert. ("I was never more flattered in my life," Burton wrote, "than to think that it would take three hundred men to kill me.") He was wounded on several occasions, most notably on an early expedition in Africa, in Berbera: he awoke in the middle of the night to find the camp under attack by Somali warriors. While fighting them off with a sword, he took a spear through both cheeks; it knocked out several teeth and left a prominent, and frightening, lifelong scar.

"When he did get back to Buenos Aires, that's when the screen goes black," Castrolang had said, pausing in his pacing. "To this day, no one knows exactly how long Burton was there. And this was a man who took meticulous notes about everything: flora, fauna, minerals, native cultures, geography. He turned almost every trip he took into a book, over forty volumes. He was recognized as one of the leading anthropologists, and geographers, of his day.

"From September 1868 until the end of March of the next year, it is unknown exactly what Burton was doing; no record exists. During this time, he took the only unrecorded trip of his life. Only an outline of this expedition can be pieced together.

He had met a man named William Maxwell on his passage to South America. They later set out together, overland across Argentina, and explored the Sierra de San Luiz mountain range. Burton was the first person in history to map those mountains.

"Burton and Maxwell crossed through a pass in the Andes into Chile. Years later, a friend said that Burton claimed to have killed four men on this trip – most likely not true. Burton habitually made himself out to be even worse than he was. He loved to shock, and counted enemies as badges of honor.

"After resting in Santiago de Chile, they caught ship for Peru and left the South American interior behind.

"By the evidence, his wife Isabel had no idea where he had been," Castrolang had said. "Also, he'd been drinking heavily. His career was in tatters, all the promise of his youth ended in an unprestigious appointment to a backwater consulate. And he was about to turn fifty. Shortly after he had returned, in a cafe in Lima a stranger congratulated Burton on his appointment to the consular post at Damascus, the job he'd jockeyed for his whole life. Tramping in the jungle, he had not heard that he'd gotten it.

"So he left," Castrolang had concluded. "His mysterious time in the jungle was soon forgotten. Many of the areas he passed through – the mountains of Chile, the Uspallata Pass – were unexplored then, and remain largely unexplored today. Very rough country, and nothing to go there for."

"Sorry," Dana had ventured. "If he did write something about his time in Argentina, what happened to it?"

"Isabel," Castrolang exhaled heavily. "It seems likely that Burton concluded this work could never be published. After his death, Isabel burned his papers, all his unpublished works. She spent sixteen days in his study with twenty-seven years' worth of notebooks." Castrolang turned his back to her, and poked his fingers in the blinds, beyond which the darkness had gotten worked up.

"The Manuscript is said to be only one or two dozen pages. I would wager she never saw it. I would wager that it was buried in something else, and that's how it went up. But there are ideas floating around about how a copy could have survived."

"So," Dana whispered, her throat catching. "Do you have any ideas about where we should start looking for this thing?"

Castrolang turned from the blinds, facing her again with a boyish and pinch-lipped smile, but his eyes betrayed his solemnity. "Online," he said simply.

Machines of Loving Grace

Monday morning, and Miles Darken lay back in his comfy ergonomic rolling chair, pulled his keyboard into his lap, and resumed typing. His fingers a blur, dark eyes squinting seriously through thick lashes, he paused to sweep his black, straight hair back from his high forehead. Locked up with the machines, buried alive in the basement complex that housed Academic Computing, Miles monitored and manipulated the digital pulse of the entire campus. Miles was a member of an elite technical order, the Priesthood of Unix Systems Administrators. Miles made the machines run.

Day after day, time out of mind, Father Miles sat in his cubicle, headphones on, listening to some Frank Sinatra or Public Enemy, earning his pay without being hassled too much. When he did have to deal with human beings, it was almost always through electronic mail. It helped very much to put a clean, digital face on the intractable vagaries of people and personal interaction. But of course, behind the e-mail was always some bozo user – maybe an undergrad, maybe a professor – with way too much time and not nearly enough common sense.

But today, digging himself out from under the hill of work-related mail, Miles came up with this unexpected gem:

From: Paulina <pop3b@doorstop.tjc.edu>
To: darken@boatanchor.tjc.edu
Subject: From Paulina
Date: Mon, 18 Oct 2004 08:59:00 -0500 (EST)

Dear Miles,

I hope you don't mind me looking you up and writing unbidden. But I've been thinking about your comments from the weekend -- particularly the one about "having no idea what you're doing"; no answer to the question "Is this right?" Maybe I'm being presumptuous, but afterwards I started to have a strange feeling that you have a better idea of what you're doing than you let on. Or that you knew something you were holding out. I guess you just seemed awful sanguine for a guy claiming to be totally lost in the world. Any confessions?

Sincerely,
Paulina

Miles leaned toward the bright wash of the monitor surface. He paused for a moment, trying to decide whether to respond just now, but his fingers took off without him.

From: darken@boatanchor.tjc.edu
To: Paulina <pop3b@doorstop.tjc.edu>
Subject: re: From Paulina
Date: Mon, 18 Oct 2004 09:47:47 -0500 (EST)

So -- you've come to the Old Man on the Mountaintop, beseeching for the Great Secret, eh? Well, I'm actually in a basement. But you're so earnest (not to mention so cute), that I will go ahead and give up the goods. Here it is: The secret of life is learned solely through working with computers. Bet you wouldn't have guessed that.

The very first thing the computer industry teaches you is: "Whatever It Is, You Can Learn How To Do It." The computer world changes so rapidly, and so regularly, that the only real job skill is being able to pick up new skills quickly. And the nice thing is that this gives you a lot of confidence with things *outside* the computer world. After you've given yourself a crash course in your 9th programming language, or 5th operating system . . . suddenly a leaking faucet, or a foreign language, or a thorny interpersonal problem, just doesn't look that intimidating anymore. You think, "Hell, it can't be any harder than C++."

It took me about two years to really master most aspects of Unix (my main job). Using that as a benchmark, I should get this Living As An Adult In The World thing nailed in about 6 more years, give or take.

Life: Hack It.

Miles

Miles stretched his legs out into the gloom under the desk. He shook his head and grinned. Nothing like a little unsolicited idolatry from a cute nineteen-year-old co-ed to ease you into the week.

Shaking some fog off the tip of his nose, he saw his oversized coffee flagon lying cold and empty on his desk, keening sweet little solicitations at him. On site and plugged in before 10am on a Monday, he didn't really care to attempt this feat without the aid of chemicals. Though, speaking of Great Secrets, he remembered a particular question of his own, one that he wanted to lodge before he forgot about it. So he fired off a quick one—

From: Miles Darken <darken@boatanchor.tjc.edu>
To: steckler_d@tjc.edu
Subject: Followup to Sunday
Date: Mon, 18 Oct 2004 09:56:05 (EST)

Dana - Hey, doll, happy Monday. Needless to say, it was great to see so much of you this weekend. Though, erm -- could you explain to me again (okay, for the first time) why you're looking for this lost document online (if that's what you're doing)? - M

—then reverently lifted the mammoth, ceramic vessel with both hands and padded out of his cube, squinting. Gunning for coffee. Finding the day's first pot brewing, he leaned in and attempted to administer some caffeine to himself nasally.

* * *

One source of succor for those imprisoned in computer labs all day is the flow of e-mail, coming up in real time. When mail came in from Miles at the beginning of another frustrating day at the machine, Dana jumped on it like a castaway on a bottled message.

From: steckler_d@tjc.edu
To: Miles Darken <darken@boatanchor.tjc.edu>
Subject: Re: Followup to Sunday
Date: Mon, 18 Oct 2004 10:01:04 (EST)

Hi, Miles. It was grand to see you as well.

Miles Darken wrote:
>
> Erm -- could you explain to me again (okay, for the first time)
> why you're looking for this lost document online (if that's
> what you're doing)?

I guess I wasn't any too subtle with my transition from telling you about the document to asking about web search engines. Jim, my advisor, has been looking for the Burton manuscript since 1996. Last year, he heard a twist on the rumor -- that it was hidden out on the Internet somewhere. I do know where he heard this: on one of the religion groups on usenet.

Anyway, that's it. 1) Hear rumor about revealed wisdom. 2) Fail to find a trace of it for years. 3) Go out and dig up urban myth that it is cleverly hidden in a remote corner of the Net. 4) Recruit hapless and naive grad student into looking for it (ie looking for something which most likely doesn't exist, and never did).

Love,
Dana

Dana stared over the top of her monitor, the message she'd composed going slowly out of focus. Looking across the empty air of the high-ceilinged and drafty lab, she could picture Miles at his post, squinting into his monitor, his window on the world. She tried to decide if she would prefer to inhabit his shoes rather than her own. Right now, and lately, her feelings seemed to trip on each other as they ran by in different directions. She clicked on Send.

* * *

Miles decided that while he might send Dana his reactions to this a little later in the day, at the moment he had an overdue date with his discussion groups. He slipped into his headphones, leaned back, and dropped into alt.quotations, the forum devoted to "great things we wish we had said ourselves". He scanned the list of topics.

Group alt.quotations . . .
112 messages unread
1 "Better to keep you mouth shut ..." 1 Yossef
2 Zen & Etc.; Pirsig Quotes 1 The Reeds
3 Who said this? Trivia Question Tom
4 Looking for Government quote David A. Lyons
u 5 Star Trek quotes 6 Bill Gascoyne
u 6 QUOTE Re NEW YEARS OR THE HO Alex A. Buonsante
7 Nixon's speech, I think. 3 G. MANFREDI
u 8 work quotations 1 Tom
9 Identity quotations Morgan Lewis
u 10 attribution sought celeste@gloac.com
->98 more topics

Hmm, "attribution sought". A common enough inquiry on alt.quotes – everyone forever wanting to know who said what. But then again, Celeste was a cute name. He tabbed through.

Article 36515 attribution sought
C. Browning
<celeste@gloac.com>

"It is not important what you believe, only that you believe."

I've seen this twice now -- both times unattributed. Any clues?

Thanks,

Celeste Browning
GA, LLC.
celeste@gloac.com

Holy shit, hilarious. Miles grinned broadly, tapping one foot to the music mainlining into his head via headphones, feeling the caffeine singing in his veins. He stared at that hauntingly familiar string of eleven words and thought, *Net.fame is such a rush.*

Even at the end of the day, walking home alone in the dusk, Miles still glowed. It wasn't every day you got asked to provide an attribution to *your own quotation.*

He had come up with that quote around age nineteen, during long years spent reading philosophical novelists, exploring various flavors of Eastern mysticism, interpreting art-rock lyrics and, of course, participating in the obligatory late-night dorm-room bull sessions.

In large part, he had been trying to understand how so many millions of people, some of them surely sensible, could believe so fiercely in such divergent philosophies, religions, and mythologies. Finally, Miles had concluded perhaps it wasn't all that important one find just the right belief system. His theory, as he had briefly held it, was that the simple act of faith, of any kind, transcended the details: "It's not important what you believe, only that you believe."

This pithy notion had come back looking for him today because, a couple of years earlier, Miles happened to put the quote into his e-mail signature for a few weeks. Out of some vestige of modesty, he did refrain from attributing it to himself.

Imagine his surprise and frustration when he saw that quote reappear on two subsequent occasions: once in a collection of motivational quotes on some guy's web page, and later in somebody *else's* signature. (Both times unattributed, of course.) Today, however, for the first time, someone had been so stirred by his aphorism as to go looking for its source.

Miles crossed the avenue, boots crackling in the dry grass of the median, nearly home.

The Net

Article 36559 attribution sought response 1 of 3
Dante at aol.com

Celeste <celeste@gloac.com> wrote:
> "It is not important what you believe, only that you believe."
>
> I've seen this twice now -- both times unattributed. Any clues?

I'm thinking that's Nietzsche. I don't have a source, and don't remember where I saw it. But I'm pretty sure it's Nietzsche.

_____
Dante
dante@aol.com
Roller Hockey God

Article 36560 attribution sought response 2 of 3
soozie@outsight.com

Celeste <celeste@gloac.com> wrote:
> "It is not important what you believe, only that you believe."
>
> I've seen this twice now -- both times unattributed. Any clues?

Sounds like Emerson to me.

Hope that helps,
Sue

Article 36561 attribution sought response 3 of 3
Miles Darken at TJC ACC

Celeste <celeste@gloac.com> wrote:
> "It is not important what you believe, only that you believe."
>
> I've seen this twice now -- both times unattributed. Any clues?

Actually, I said that.

Miles Darken

At home now, sitting before a laptop on his living-room floor, Miles surveyed his handiwork with no little glee. He looked around the room, lit by a single candle and the glowing butt of a clove cigarette. He didn't feel like drinking anymore, nor quite wanted to be sober. Back in his misspent youth, Miles' friends had referred to cloves as "buzz enhancers", for their uncanny ability to bring a fading buzz back to life. This was useful if you were at a club and couldn't drink, because, maybe, you were nineteen or something. On the downside, cloves were also rumored to make your lungs bleed.

Miles blew a smoke ring, shifted his hunch over the keyboard, and checked mail again. Listless, finished with his immediate task, still not tired, Miles watched his clove burn cracklingly.

He wouldn't mind catching up on a few other newsgroups. Rec.guns, for starters. Like a lot of technocrats, Miles tended toward flaming civil libertarianism, and also liked to advocate, and exercise, his Second Amendment rights whenever possible.

On rec.guns he need never apologize for keeping at hand the capacity for deadly force. He need not recount the fairly acute moral agonizing he had undergone before deciding to purchase a handgun. He certainly needn't ever belabor the fact, not to anyone in this particular group, that the fundamental, inalienable human rights to self-defense and freedom from tyranny in government are recognized and protected (not granted) by the Second Amendment to the Constitution of the United States of America, which says nothing about hunting, sporting purposes, or the National Guard (he'd checked twice). He took a deep breath.

It's dangerous to be surrounded by people who think just like you do.

He turned off the voice in his head and maximized his newsreader. He scanned the topics, then grepped (searched by keyword) for any reference to the handgun he owned – a Bersa autoloader in .380.

His screen jumped and the cursor landed at line 70.

Group rec.guns...
141 Articles Unread
u 67 Concealed Carry in Texas Billy J. Beckworth
u 68 [WTB] SIG 225 mags and H&K P7M8 Julian Hsiang
u 69 Rules of a Gunfight 162 Joe Chew
u 70 Bersa .380 – Opinions? 1 Bob Colvin
u 71 How do I get a full-auto in CA? 4 Ely Kumli
u 72 ~~ Have you ever used your handgun 5 Steve Dunham
->66 more topics

Article 110392 Bersa .380 -- Opinions
Bob Colvin, <colvinb@ibm.net>

Since the liberalization of concealed weapons laws here (here being North Carolina) I'm looking for a carry gun. Pretty set on a high capacity .380. (No lectures on stopping power, please. A .380 in the pocket beats a .44 in the closet.) I saw a reference to a high-cap .380 made by Bersa, but I've never run into one in person.

Opinions from folks who've owned or shot one muchly appreciated.

Thanks in advance,

____
Bob Colvin
colvinb@ibm.net

Article 110395 Bersa .380 -- Opinions Resp 2 of 2
Miles Darken at TJC ACC, <darken@boatanchor.tjc.edu>

I've owned that model Bersa for over a year and adore it. It's compact, sleek, and feels great in the hand. High visibility 3-dot combat sights, push-button mag release. Very sexy. ;^) It's very accurate, and I've never been able to make it jam. Only $330, too. Happy to answer any other questions; good luck with your decision.

Miles Darken

As he posted this response, Miles noticed that another response had already flitted in over the wire. Had that been there? Or had it come in while he was typing? He tabbed through.

Article 110394 Bersa .380 -- Opinions Resp 1 of 2
C. Browning, <celeste@gloac.com>

I've owned the Model 86 Undercover for over a year. It's compact, light, and very comfortable to shoot. It's never done anything but discharge, no matter what I feed into it. And it's awfully accurate.

I could afford a much more expensive pistol (and in fact own several). But the Bersa is what I carry. I love and depend on it.

Hope that helps.

Celeste Browning
GA, LLC.
celeste@gloac.com

"Whoah, that was trippy," Miles muttered into his thin halo of sweet smoke.

The message came from the same chick who had posted about his belief quote in alt.quotations. The *very same* chick. What, Miles couldn't help wondering, were the odds? Moreover, who reads alt.quotes and rec.guns? Nobody's that eclectic.

Correction: nobody else is that eclectic.

The Expediter

Up north, although the air was colder, the Internet traffic flowed briskly right along. Out in the corporeal world, a woman navigated the Upper West Side of Manhattan like a brilliant fish in brackish water. She wore a long coat over smart business attire, boots, hair down. And not to forget the gun – the little .380, a small but very serious high-capacity autoloader, tucked in there under the suit jacket.

She paused at a building front, beneath the letters GA. The smaller plaque in the doorway read, "GA, LLC. Import\Export\Manufacturing". The lines of business listed on the plaque were profoundly misleading, but also in a sense accurate. The firm known to some as Global Acumen did engage in importing, exporting, and manufacture – of information. Principally a private intelligence agency, GA worked for certain multinational corporations, wealthy individuals and families, opposition governments in exile, and others who found it necessary or preferable to outsource the function of intelligence gathering. Often highly demanding, dangerous, and/or illegal sorts of intelligence gathering.

Celeste Browning, the woman in the doorway, excelled at expediting these sorts of things – coordinating the activities of dark, dangerous, and ragged edge-traversing field agents, data-triturating computer jockeys, wonkish industry analysts, and of course the ever-present coltish clients. She had the rare ability to ensure, reliably and repeatedly, that a mob of this sort kept moving toward a completed project, a happy client, a cleared wire transfer, and nobody dead or in a third-world jail.

On her good days, Celeste considered this a pretty cool gig for a twenty-eight-year-old female person. She tried to bear this boon in mind as she swiped her security card for the fourth time. She restrained herself from audibly cursing the machine, which would get recorded.

Finally, blessedly in her office, fingers steepled stilly, Celeste leveled her gaze on the Young Turk on the other side of her desk – her first appointment of the day. She said, "Welcome to Global Acumen. You won't be working under me, but our employer felt you might benefit from hearing how I came here, that it might put the circumstances of your employment into context." She smiled thinly.

"In 1996, I was an undergraduate at Columbia University, just up the road. I didn't know then that I would never finish that degree. I spent most of my time, anyway, in various extracurricular diversions – not all of them innocuous. For instance, I picked up the questionable habit of poking around, sans permission, in other people's computer systems."

Celeste settled into her swivel chair as she narrated. "Perhaps you can picture me, twenty years old, sitting in a darkened, cramped dormitory room, bathed in the pale glow of the monitor. Buffeted by the clacking of the keyboard," she continued, accenting with narrative abandon, "soothed by the solitude of the early morning. Thrilled with the power and naughtiness of it all. It was very exciting to be young, talented, and criminal. Except that, one night, I finally went poking around in the wrong system."

* * *

ENTER LOGON ID: guest
ENTER PASSWORD: •••••••••
ANONYMOUS LOGON DENIED
PASSCODE ROUTINE INITIATED. PLEASE WAIT....

ENTER LOGON ID: expdtr1024@gloac.com
ENTER PASSWORD: •••••••••••

WELCOME TO GA INFO SERVICES MAIN MENU
ACCESS LEVEL 3
03:22:19 11\30\96

"Cool beans." The machine and the hacker glowed at each other. The young Celeste Browning – tall, smooth-skinned, classically beautiful – tossed her chestnut curls over her shoulder. She hunched over the desk, chin on one knee, the characters on the screen reflecting on her round-framed glasses.

Menu after menu sped by, the first few unremarkable: Airbills – Domestic\Foreign, Breakbulk Commissions, Agency Directories. But soon she turned up Financial Disbursements – OFF BOOK, Operative Manifest – by Continent, Expedition Database – by Threat Scenario, and Contractors – Clean\Wet. She couldn't get access to these areas, but the headings alone made her mouth go dry.

She moved through this terrain, slowly getting a picture of the sort of individuals whose privacy she was violating. The clock marched toward dawn, her 8am class forgotten – which was just as well, as she would not be attending it ever again. Shortly before the sun rose, she heard scratching in the lock of her door. Panic enveloped her, but she did think to log off before doing anything else. The heavy door swung open – and none of the hall lights beyond were lit.

Two figures slipped inside, crossed each other, and moved to opposite ends of the room. They walked with both arms extended stiffly forward. More Celeste could not make out through the darkness, peering through the cracked doors of her wardrobe. She heard whispering and the faint crackle of radio static. Her hands trembled on the surface of the swing-out doors. *What the fuck?* she asked herself. *What have I done?*

The figure on the opposite end of the room gestured and took hold of the bed in the corner. The second figure moved directly in front of the wardrobe doors and pointed what now appeared to be a pistol toward the bed. The noise of the mattress and frame overturning covered the sound of the wardrobe door rushing open and by the time the one at the bed turned around again, Celeste had already whacked his companion with a wooden shoe tree and recovered his handgun.

There followed a silent moment of extreme tension, and no movement. Then the man by the bed slowly and daintily pulled the chain on a bed-table lamp, illuminating the unlikely scene. At one end of the room, a husky middle-aged man in dark attire crouched behind an overturned bed pointing a 9mm automatic at a slim young woman who, at the other end of the room, crouched over an unconscious figure, pointing another 9mm automatic right back at him. Both the man and the woman had their lips slightly parted. Neither breathed.

"Team Zero, advise current status. Clear." A short burst of static followed, all of this leaking faintly out of a little earpiece dislodged from the ear of the man on the floor. It was evident that no one in the room had any very good ideas about what should happen next.

* * *

"Again, Team Zero, please advise status. Clear." The Situation Room chief cocked one eye toward the man at the radio desk and took a big bite of coffee while the operator paused. "Holy shit. Stand by, Team Zero. Uh, Chief – we've got a little miscue here. Is Mr. White in the building?"

"So there we were," Celeste said to the young man, "the two of us, sharing a moment, our own little 'Mexican standoff' – there in student housing, on the campus of an Ivy League school. I don't suppose you've ever been in a situation like that, have you?" Celeste glanced at the prompt on the flat computer screen to her left: New Mail.

"So," she went on, not waiting for a reply, "there sits this gorilla, peering over my upended bed, exchanging niceties with whoever's on the other end of the line. That was when the phone on the desk rang. I nearly laughed out loud when the guy looked at me seriously and said:

"It's for you."

"You're kidding," young Celeste intoned. The man's expression didn't change in any way that would indicate jocularity. Celeste stared wide-eyed from behind her spectacles. The heady combination of sleep deprivation, tremendous adrenaline flows, and this impossible, surreal situation were causing her to entertain some very unlikely thoughts. *What the hell*, she mused. *I've been waiting twenty years for something interesting to happen.*

Like she'd done it her whole life, she shifted the gun to her left hand and scooped up the phone from its cradle.

"I assume you're the one who sent these punks that I am currently manhandling," she said sweetly into the mouthpiece. A distinct pause followed from the other end.

"Ms. Browning, I gather. Pleased to make your acquaintance. My name is Mr. White – and I would be very grateful if you would be so kind as to return my employees to me in one piece."

* * *

"He asked me to come to work for him on the spot," concluded the twenty-eight-year-old Celeste. "I didn't even ask for details, I just said yes. Such was my state of mind then. As it turned out, I proved well-suited to making a strong contribution here at GA. Mr. White has quite the gift for knowing such things about people. And I do believe, that night, somehow I knew it about myself as well. So, do you feel like you're ready to become part of the team?"

As the young man exited, Celeste skimmed her incoming mail from the last ten hours. She responded to a query from the boss, providing a brief summary of the meeting just ended. "His background looks okay," she noted, clacking away. "But I wouldn't put him into anything sensitive too soon." She clicked on Send, then checked the clock on the corner of her desktop.

Cool. Just time for a little Usenet.

The Dealer

Elsewhere in that same singular city, a man was being serenaded inside of a helmet. The man, who was called FreeBSD, had rigged up the stereophonic helmet because no one manufactured one. It didn't much mitigate the fantastic danger already inherent in riding a motorcycle to have raucous music pounding straight into the ears of the rider; so headphones in motorcycle helmets were an unavailable option. It had been a fairly modest engineering problem to solve on his own, though. And so here he was zipping back to Manhattan on the Long Island Expressway, deep in the aural bliss of edgy – and exceedingly loud – modern rock.

In a past life – prior to his reincarnation as a high-volume New York City narcotics dealer – this man FreeBSD had held the job of lead systems administrator at the MIT New Media

Lab. That gig had left him a lot of time for personal projects. Like patching his MP3 player into his head protection.

The type of music FreeBSD favored tended to impart substantial energy, and a certain blissful state of – not to put too fine a point on it – *not giving a fuck*. By no means could one embody not giving a fuck quite so forcefully as by willfully failing to hear car horns, police sirens, and indeed noise of any sort on the road while on a motorcycle – a mode of transportation that was, even under ideal conditions, one of the most direct routes to death and dismemberment still common in our society since coal mining, stage coach robbery, and frontier homesteading all went out of style.

But FreeBSD didn't tend to think all that far into the future. When he did think ahead, he was mainly focused on pulling off early retirement. In his line of work, it was axiomatic that an early retirement was one you were more likely to live to see.

But today was stretching his cognitive horizons.

Today he had gotten mail from his bot.

He had been battling an install problem on a new Linux machine out at the warehouse on Long Island. (FreeBSD kept a lot of computers both at that location and at the Crib, his front office, in Manhattan. His operation was seriously digital; and emphatically online.) He had paused to catch his breath, wipe his forehead, and check mail.

And that's when he found the mail from his bot. He hadn't heard from the bot in five months – and hadn't expected to ever again. In fact, he'd completely forgotten it was still running at all, and it was only doing so because he had forgotten to turn the thing off on his way out the door.

Now the bot was back. And it appeared to have found for FreeBSD something that a whole lot of other folks were avidly searching for, and which he himself had long given up hope of ever finding. Now he raced home on the bike to find out if it was really, genuinely, *the thing* – and what that might mean if it was.

The Thinker

TJC Professor James Castrolang: wispy bearded, gray crewcutted, with angular features. Speaking into his office phone, between the walls of books, behind the desk, before a patient and bright-eyed undergrad. Talking about a gig.

"Mostly classics. Yes, we do a couple of Monk pieces. Yes, I'll hold." He covered the mouthpiece with thin fingers. "I'm sorry, I don't normally do this kind of business here."

"No, hey, that's fine. I'm done for the day." The nineteen-year-old undergrad on the other side of the desk flashed an amused grin from beneath a flop of hair. "What do you play, Mr. Castrolang?"

"Uh, tenor sax. We have a little jazz combo, do the odd wedding and party. I'll try to wind thi— Yes, hi. Four hundred dollars." Just perceptibly, he winced across the desk. "We don't like to go much over three hours, including set breaks, or we're scraping for material. Yes, great. I'll give you a call over the weekend to set the logistics. You don't take e-mail, do you? No, I'll call. Yes, we're looking forward to it as well. Yes. Thank you."

The amused youngster had recently enrolled in Mr. Castrolang's hugely popular PHIL 332 Epistemology class. Now he had turned up at office hours, gunning for additional discussion of the fundamental questions of whether we can actually know anything about ourselves or the world.

Castrolang replaced the phone. "Sorry. Now, we were speaking of brains in vats . . ."

The youth nodded.

The basic "brain in the vat" premise is that there's really no good way to know for sure that you are not actually a disembodied brain suspended in a vat of goop, with malign scientists pumping in all of your sensory experiences via electrodes. This old epistemological standby had gained an awful lot of currency since the *Matrix* films.

Before either the teacher or the student could address the topic, the door, half-open, knocked.

"Oh, my," hemmed Castrolang, visibly pained. "I see Miss Steckler is queuing up outside, and I've been rather keen to see her. I don't suppose I could put you off until next week?"

"No problem at all," answered the undergrad. "For all I know, I'm not even here in the first place. Happy to come back later." He smiled and exited.

Dana waited until he had gone and said, "You know, I don't mind if you call me Dana."

"Thank you, and come in, Miss Steckler." Castrolang smiled at her, showing a perfect absence of irony. Irony was kind of frowned on in the pedagogy business. "How is the research coming along? Any further clues on the digital trail?"

At that moment, just outside of Campbell Hall, Miles walked briskly by, his friend Cal in the lead. Cal was thin and jittery and intelligent and had graduated from TJC the same year Miles had. Where Miles had stayed to work, Cal had stayed for grad school. Today, the two were meeting for lunch, but first they had gone by the computer lab, where Miles hoped to dig up Dana.

Now they made a beeline for 14th Street, where Miles intended to buy Cal a pint to make amends for dragging him all the way across campus in a futile Dana hunt. And he intended to buy himself one, as well, just for the goddamned hell of it.

Ten minutes behind them, Dana charted the same stretch of sidewalk on the edge of the quad; but it was back to the lab for her. Castrolang hadn't seemed knocked out by the progress of her research. Dana had carefully presented a number of printouts at their meeting, representing some tantalizing historical/theological tidbits. Some stuff about Burton. And some stuff about rare, lost, or forgotten religious texts. But nothing at the intersection of those topics.

And definitely not the thing itself.

Castrolang turned out to have that most devastating method of registering disappointment: looking vaguely hurt. Which sucked for Dana. She held onto this thought as she walked.

She liked the man very much and wanted to please him, to contribute to his work. But lately she'd thought that maybe she wasn't just exactly the right person for this project. She felt she had been picked to help him on the basis of her membership in a particular generation; and that maybe she lacked certain more important characteristics that would make her successful in this arena.

She wasn't sure what these characteristics were exactly. But they might have something to do with doggedness, curiosity, or unflagging focus. And better Internet search skills.

She entertained these vague notions as she tromped up the steps to the microlab. The heavy door swung out under the pull of her spare arm; her wool cape billowed back in the outdraft. Dana spared a glance and a half for the room and zeroed in on an empty seat at the end of the first row. She dropped her satchel, dog-eared papers peeking around the flap, and shook the mouse to kill the screensaver. She pulled a sheaf of printouts from the bag.

She logged in.

"I guess she only said she'd *probably* be in the microlab at lunch time," allowed Miles, over a foamy beer head. He and Cal were on their second round, while the menus lay cold and neglected. "As you get older, you have to, you know, make an effort to get together. Otherwise, jobs, and lives, and research projects come between people."

"'Research projects'?" asked Cal. "Since when are research projects, like, major life fixtures?"

"Hell, you're the perpetual grad student."

"Never let academics interfere with life. First rule. But Dana's been blowing you off?"

"Well, she's been ducking out early a lot. And I'm worried she's been working too hard."

"Oh yeah? What is she working on?"

"Dude, do not even ask." Head lowered, rolling his eyes, Miles twisted at the waist and gestured impotently at the passing server for another round.

Back in the lab, Dana slumped against her terminal. She felt thwarted more quickly every time she tried this. She hissed aloud, her throat thick with frustration, drawing curt looks from up the aisle, "If this fucking thing existed, *somebody* else, *somewhere*, would have found it already."

The Dealer][

FreeBSD chirped the bike to a stop in the alley, by the back entrance to the Crib, thinking his helmet might take itself off from the sheer pounding pressure of the music blasting inside. He swung his bent right knee over the seat, pressed his gloved hands and helmeted forehead to the alley wall, and rolled his eyes back behind the black visor.

He was just really addicted to this shit.

He shook off both the rush of the aural stimulant and his nappy dreadlocks as he removed his helmet, swiped his keycard, kicked open the heavy steel door, and guided his mind back to current events. In the back room of the complex, the server room, he sat down at the console of a Unix box. His fingers worked to sort through the issues on the screen as his mind recounted the events that had led to today's shocker of a mail message.

For three years prior to his arrival in New York, Paul Lineberry – the future FreeBSD – had toiled, as noted, in the hallowed halls of the New Media Lab of the Massachusetts Institute of Technology (Cambridge, Mass). He had come to that storied place because a job there, which had come upon him at just the right time, had struck him as a markedly better deal than what he'd been doing prior to that: namely, studying chemistry at graduate level at Dartmouth College, confecting unprofitable potions on the crumbly frozen shores of the Connecticut River.

He'd fallen into working toward a master's in chemistry by way of having successfully acquired a bachelor's in chemistry, and, well, it was a slippery slope. At the time (graduation), it had seemed like the thing to do. Little had Paul realized that the life of a science graduate student tended toward such activities as begging favor of academic advisors, working depressingly late nights in dangerous-smelling labs, and liturgically bouncing basic concepts off of the nice haircuts and poor attitudes of insufferable undergraduates. Paul had somehow imagined that grad school would be much like undergrad, which for him had largely involved a lot of Frisbee tossing on the grass, witty banter with cute co-eds over aromatic coffee and unsubtle sexual subtexts and, of course, life-threatening alcohol consumption. It had also involved exceedingly minimal academic exertion, the young Paul Lineberry having quickly and propitiously adopted the comfortable habit of blowing off his studies mightily and relying on his superior intellect to pull him through in the end.

Sadly, such tactics had gone over like a lead zeppelin in the upper echelons of the department, where brilliance was not rewarded nearly so much as obeisance. Not surprisingly to anyone who knew him, Paul Lineberry unfailingly found groveling at the feet of wizened academic chemists to be a great big drag. He had already gone a fair distance down the garden path of getting drummed out of the program when he took the initiative himself and declared, "Fuck y'all motherfuckers" to an office full of stunned faculty members. He cleaned his cigarettes and his coffee mug out of his desk and popped off for a bit of Frisbee in the last light of that fateful day. After a few pleasant and deeply idle weeks he dropped a note to his buddy at the New Media Lab, who had been begging him, on and off for a number of months, to come fix their network for them. The offer was a late bloomer, only finding its full blossom in Paul's eyes after a month or so of unemployment. It also had no competing suitors.

Moving from Hanover to Cambridge hadn't caused any major cultural shock, and the sysadmin job hadn't been taxing for any longer than it had been novel, which worked out pretty well. That is to say, the machines and network stuff weren't anything he hadn't played around with on and off for fun anyway, and – once he got everything straightened out, automated, and humming along on autopilot – the workload went way down. Unfortunately, he knew exactly one person in the Boston area, and his friend at the Lab was far too busy fiddling around with neural networks to do more for Paul socially than go out for the odd beer after work. Needless to say his friend didn't know any women, so – after getting Paul the job – that was as far as his usefulness went. And so it went.

So the ex-academic wandered the wet, stone streets of the town, the bellowing of drunken, migrating college students, suddenly so foreign, ringing in his ears. He stared at the water and drove his motorcycle across the bridges, and in and out of the hillocks of the various campuses. And he wandered back to his building in the late morning to twiddle the bits and kill another day. But the bits only bore so much twiddling, and the days got longer, and his instrument of deliverance from the spinning gears of academia started looking more and more like just another bleak machine.

He took up various pursuits to battle the encroaching boredom: free computer science classes at MIT; boning up on Perl, awk, sed, and other cryptic lingua franca of the Unix world; writing some games, and playing them, which never managed to be interesting for long (it was a bit like doing your own crossword puzzles). He tuned up the bike and built the headphone system for it. He spent late nights in dim espresso joints, reading all those things he'd always meant to read, while exchanging coy glances with the coffee wenches. Pondering, occasionally and briefly, if this is what he was supposed to be doing. If this was what one did.

In the end, though, the technical puttering, loud music, and caffeine palpitations were only more drugs to distract him from the fundamental, underlying, and ultimately unavoidable meaninglessness of things in his new world (as in the old one). It was this lingering sense of meaninglessness – that he had always sensed vaguely and was coming to apprehend distinctly – coupled with further and somewhat more novel attempts at distraction, which led Paul Lineberry, by and by, to Plan C. To his next reincarnation – as FreeBSD.

Web Images Groups News Froggle New! **more»**
"meaning of life" Search Advanced Search Preferences

Results **1 - 10** of about **776,000** for "meaning of life". (0.36 seconds)

The **Meaning of Life** (1983)
The **Meaning of Life** - Cast, Crew, Reviews, Plot Summary, Comments, Discussion, Taglines, Trailers, Posters, Photos, Showtimes, Link to Official Site, ...
www.imdb.com/title/tt0085959/ - 48k - Cached - Similar pages

The idea of looking on the Net for meaning in life was hardly a new one, but there was still some novelty in using a web search engine to find it directly, immediately, and literally. By name. Paul had been searching, via the web's winning search engine, for some info on an obscure aspect of Sun's NIS+ system, when it occurred to him to launch his frivolous query. Searching for the "meaning of life" online, on that otherwise unremarkable evening, had been apropos of nothing. It was a throwaway idea, as evidenced by the first hit he got back: a web site devoted to Monty Python, and their movie of the same name. Happily, things picked up a bit from there:

FAQ about the **Meaning of Life**
Real, non-cryptic, intelligent, satisfying answers you haven't

heard. Our place in the cosmos, our successors, AI goal systems, and why to get up in the ...
yudkowsky.net/tmol-faq/meaningoflife.html - 15k -
Cached - Similar pages

The Meaning of Life
Provides advice for those who want to know the meaning of life.
www.aristotle.net\~diogenes/meaning1.htm - 3k -
Cached - Similar pages

EAWC Essay: Storytelling, the **Meaning of Life**, and The Epic of ...
Article by Arthur A. Brown discussing the literary development in the several versions of the epic of Gilgamesh.
eawc.evansville.edu/essays/brown.htm - 19k - Cached - Similar pages

The Real **Meaning of Life**
Looking for the meaning of life? This web site presents several hundred points of view. Find purpose.
life.shutterline.com/ - 7k - Cached - Similar pages

What is the **meaning of life**?
The meaning of life is to increase fitness. ... "personal choice", "to be found within oneself", or even "to ask the question 'What is the meaning of life?'"...
pespmc1.vub.ac.be/MEANLIFE.html - 18k - Cached - Similar pages

The web's first few hundred offerings on this subject consisted mostly of banal reflections by amateur web authors with existential unease and time on their hands; technical philosophical treatises; and, of course, more Monty Python fan pages. Brushing back the nappy locks that had grown long, but which he had not yet twisted, Paul gurgled with dismay, feeling that he had come no closer to apprehending significance – but, even worse, he hadn't killed more than ninety minutes. He'd had no expectation of the former, but some hope for the latter. So he cranked open his trusty newsreader, latching, for some reason, onto this odd mission.

After four hours of browsing and grepping through the alt.religion.* and alt.philosophy.* hierarchies, and related FAQs (frequently asked questions lists), he was no closer to enlightenment. But it was, at least, time to go home.

He distracted himself with more workaday and less quixotic pursuits for the next week, and the whole hopeless and desultory project would have ended there, except he belatedly remembered he didn't have to limit himself to the current Usenet feed. A few years earlier, a service had appeared called Deja News, and had begun archiving all newsgroup postings and making them searchable. Google had bought the service, allowing Paul to take his digital dumpster dive historical.

Results 1 - 10 of about 122,000 for "meaning of life". (2.71 seconds)

Related groups: sci.philosophy.meta
talk.origins
talk.philosophy.humanism

Re: The **Meaning of Life**
The Meaning of Life As I write this document, let me tell you first that I seriously doubt my sanity. Then a voice from the past ...
talk.origins - 17 Apr 2002 by Aron-Ra - View Thread (36 articles)

Purpose and **Meaning of Life**?
Nyob zoo, What is the Purpose of Life? What is the Meaning of Life? What is the purpose of life? The ... time. What is the meaning of life? ...
soc.culture.hmong - 17 Apr 2002 by Tham - View Thread (1 article)

The **Meaning of Life**, Summary!
Dear Reader: The meaning of life has always been interesting to me. Sometimes we can get bogged down with stream of consciousness ...
talk.philosophy.humanism - 23 Jan 1997 by Richard F. Hall - View Thread (18 articles)

Re: Answers In Evolution - **Meaning of Life**
In answer to one of the most searching questions in biology, "What is the meaning of Life?" The answer from evolution is, Duh... ...
talk.origins - 13 Jun 2004 by David Mills - View Thread (42 articles)

Re: What is the **meaning of life**
Ian and Alice in their answers to the question, what is the meaning

of life, are focusing on two levels of analysis. Ian has an ...
humanities.philosophy.objectivism - 29 Jan 2003 by kym -
View Thread (77 articles)

Re: Creativity and **Meaning of Life**?
MC.Harrison wrote: – snip – Do you think there is a possibility that they will all agree on a common meaning of life? No. Many people ...
misc.creativity - 11 Nov 1998 by Horace Confab -
View Thread (6 articles)

Re: The **meaning of life**
... diagrams. It works with this question too. I did ask for the meaning of life in general as a goal, but not as a starting point. Nobody ...
mensa.talk.misc - 27 Oct 1998 by Roger Burks -
View Thread (15 articles)

Re: **The meaning of life**
... Very general questions, such as "what is the meaning of life" can be approached in the same way, but do not admit of a simple answer. ...
sci.philosophy.meta - 28 Jan 1999 by VERDIGRIS -
View Thread (30 articles)

He clicked through, one link after another, world without end. As usual, Usenet did provide more interesting – certainly more colorful – grist for the mill. And while there were only a fraction as many hits as on the web, there were still north of one hundred thousand, providing Paul with great time-wasting opportunity. But something funny happened on the way to the forum, at around about the thirtieth page of search returns.

Re: **Manuscript**
... The final secrets of the meaning of life on earth. Reincarnation. God. Heaven, hell. Space-time, ...
alt.religion.taoism.angry - 22 Jan 2003 by Abhijit -
View Thread (3 articles)

That was grabby. In his survey of religion groups, Paul had come across one or two relating to Taoism; but he'd never seen alt.

religion.taoism.angry. Moreover, though he knew little about this creed, he knew enough to be puzzled by the name of this group. Wasn't Taoism pacifistic? What could be meant by "angry" Taoism?

From: Abhijit <ARC94001@jarmon-ins.com>
Subject: Re: Manuscript
Newsgroups: alt.religion.taoism.angry
Date: 2003/01/22

Heh heh. As to speculation about this aboriginal, desert island manuscript of enlightenment: I too have heard reference to it, floating out through smoke and drunkenness in the Village. But here's something of which you may not know: THERE'S A COPY OUT THERE SOMEWHERE. Hidden online. "How does one *hide* a document online?" you might ask. Simple. Step 1: Put a machine on the net with an IP address, but no name. Don't register it with InterNIC. Step 2: Put it in a protocol no one uses. Gopher. Or finger. Or switch it back and forth amongst scores of TCP/IP methods. Step 3: Run the service on an obscure and unreserved port number. Voila. No one will ever find it.

Why would anyone do such a thing? I have no idea. But I heard someone did just this.

So, that's it: Just find the IP address; the service; and the port; and all will be revealed: The final secrets of the meaning of life on earth. Reincarnation. God. Heaven, hell. Space-time, made comprehensible. The final morality. The big ball of wax. Straight from the horse's mouth; the folks bred to be in the know; the spear-chuckers with the inside line.

If you happen to believe that this manuscript exists - or that some Cyber-Paul was perverse and cryptic enough to bury his Gospel out online somewhere. Who knows? Stranger things have happened.

Abhijit
The Only White Man The Natives Trust

It all would have ended right here, too. Except that Paul had strange dreams that night about revelatory gospels floating adrift in uncharted seas out at the edge of the Internet map. And he got bored again, the next day. And he was fucking around with network sockets in Perl, anyway.

It didn't even prove a difficult coding project, merely a novel one. So Paul Lineberry (in his last few weeks as such) created, not the first, but certainly the hardest-working and most intriguing search engine spider anywhere on the Net.

Though in many ways he was jaded, there still lurked a little techno-utopian in this chemist turned sysadmin and, deep down, he knew the Internet was commoditizing the world's most valuable resource, that which had allowed Homo sapiens to utterly dominate the planet: information. He knew too that, for the first time, we had a universal, collective human memory – that the Net was wiring together into one sprawling, distributed archive everything that had ever been learned by anyone. And he was intrigued by the notion that there might be some revealed spiritual wisdom tucked amidst the travel advisories, restaurant reviews, and investing tips. But, as with everything you heard online, it was a good idea to look for some corroboration, or at least some background on the source.

First he tried to subscribe to alt.religion.taoism.angry, but it didn't exist anymore. The MIT newsfeed didn't have it, and neither did Dartmouth's. He inquired upstream to UUNet; they had carried the group until a few months earlier, when it disappeared, cancelled.

He sent mail to this Abhijit, <ARC94001@jarmon-ins.com>. It promptly bounced back: account terminated. He went back to Google Groups, searching for any other posts to that group, but found only a handful. The last few posts on record talked vaguely about moving the group to a private server. After that, only silence.

Needless to say, this only contributed to the air of mystery and conspiracy. Neither Paul, nor anyone else he could find, had ever even seen the original post, only the response. But, if he had read it right – and he had no great faith that he had – then some kind of religious text had been hidden somewhere out there on the Net. And, more, it was *the* religious text, the one with actual answers, presumably verifiable in some way. Again, his hunt for "the meaning of life" on the Net had been only, and intentionally, a tongue-in-cheek distraction. He never anticipated finding anything enlightening, and still didn't. He doubted this document existed or, if it did, that it would have any palliative effect on his particular existential ache. But he was fascinated by the sort of bottle in which the message was said to be adrift. In security circles, this was called "security by obscurity". Don't lock the door – just put it in a room no one would think to enter.

So Paul started coding. If the truth, as they say, is out there, then his creation would find it. He programmed his bot, or intelligent agent, to go out and traverse the entire space of 2,113,929,216 possible Internet IP addresses, looking for stuff. IP addresses look like 208.48.26.200 or 198.137.240.91, with one bound to every site name, like www.nytimes.com, or www.whitehouse.gov. Moreover, this space of theoretical addresses is well-defined, as IP numbers only go so high. They consist of four octets in binary notation: 256 × 256 × 256 × 256, or 2 to the 32nd power, with about half those numbers ruled out for various reasons.

Port numbers were a different story. Most every machine on the Net could provide multiple services at the same IP address, but on different ports. While ports 1–255 were used for the most common Internet services, there was no theoretical limit to how high they could go. And what Paul was looking for here was hardly a commonly used service. He decided to put in a floor of 256, essentially starting in unexplored territory, and an arbitrary ceiling of 10,000. This opened the possibility of missing something on a higher port, but increased the likelihood that the job would finish running before his natural death.

There were a lot of variables: network latency, machine

response time, how long the bot "let the phone ring". But he could do some of the math. Essentially, this program was going to try to connect to over two billion machines (some of which might exist) in almost ten thousand subtly different ways.

And on top of that, one last multiplier remained: which services to try, if you happened to get a connection. HTTP (web), FTP (file transfer protocol), gopher, NNTP (Usenet), and finger were the obvious ones. Each of these services could return a large text document, and were commonly used to do so. And while they usually ran on standard ports (HTTP on 80, FTP on 20 and 21), they could theoretically be run on any port you liked; people just wouldn't tend to find them – which, in this case, was the point. In addition to these usual suspects, Paul also threw in such protocols as timed, name, whois, hostnames, who, syslog, echo, netstat, qotd, domain, dictionary, X400, and POP3, just for the goddamn hell of it. Paul planned to run the entire laundry basket up the flagpole, just to see if anyone would salute.

The salutes he ultimately got back involved every finger combination on the hand, and some appendages he'd never heard of. He quickly realized an entire hidden Internet lay out there, an uncharted space five hundred times as large as the known and populated territories. A virtual underworld.

He programmed what he hoped was the right amount of intelligence into the system, such that he wouldn't be hassled by it thirty times a day – but wouldn't miss anything good, either. The bot ran through a series of comparison operations when it happened upon a document in the near-vacuum of this vast, out-of-bounds space.

When the bot – which Paul named Bob – snared something vaguely document-like in its trawling, it first did a spot-check of the major web search engines. If Google had it, it was probably just a misplaced web page, and was discarded. Items that passed the no-indexing test were then grepped for a long series of keywords. Some of the terms (enlightenment, desert island, reincarnation, God, heaven, hell, space-time, final morality) came straight from the alt.religion.taoism.angry post. Others (meaning, consciousness, life in the world, love) Paul personally felt should be telltales for any meaning of life worthy of the name. The remainder (fertilizer bomb, fissile material, semtex, assassination, one million kilos, etc.) were a stock group of hot-button terms that wags occasionally included in their signatures to annoy federal agents snooping for terrorists and drug kingpins.

Paul thought these were always interesting things to grep for.

So did Bob, as it turned out.

And, needless to point out, poor Dana Steckler might as well have been rifling newspaper at the bottoms of birdcages, for all the chance she ever realistically had of finding this thing.

Webcams; String

Miles nursed his three-pint-lunch mini-hangover and queried himself about what the fuck he was doing. This sort of internal dialog seemed to take place with increasing frequency as he grew older. Not only did the boundaries of appropriate behavior shrink as he crept up on his quarter-century mark, but some mad nineteen-year-old inside his brain seemed determined to act out – act out even more egregiously than had the genuine nineteen-year-old Miles back in the day.

As a result, at such times as in the aftermath of three-pint weekday lunches, Miles not infrequently experienced a certain sense that he was *not really going about things in the right way.* That his behavior patterns were not appropriate, nor sustainable, nor salutary to his professional or personal success. And that some rogue segment of his volition was leading him forcefully down some embarrassing garden path.

No one had appeared near his cube to notice any such thing.

But he nursed his solitary shame all the same. The shame, and the keen oblongotal throb. He figured there had to be some Tylenol somewhere and he ventured out to look for it, stepping gingerly and trying to keep the physical pain and mental fog off of his face.

He also figured there had to be some way to make better sense of things. His parents' answers to the question of how one should live – Christianity, marriage and children, small-town life – he had tossed right out the window onto the blurring tarmac, and not glanced back. Most of the people he had graduated with had moved off to big cities, started careers, and basically worn the mantle of the young adult out in the world. This, for better or worse, Miles had not done; and he didn't regret it – none of those people, when he heard from them, seemed to be floating on clouds of bliss. That seemed to leave what he was doing; which was starting to look more questionable with every year that went by.

"You poor dear, it was right in this box, a full bottle of fifty."

"Hmm."

"You can't believe the crud you accumulate in three years."

"Hmm. Say. Are those webcams?"

"These? Someone just dumped them in my area. Why? Do you know what they're for?"

When you got right down to it, Miles' multitasking capabilities were not always all that stellar. Yeah, frequently he could pull a few stunning parallel processes out of his ass. Conducting two totally coherent conversations simultaneously, one with his mouth inside his cube, another with his keyboard across the globe. (This always drove the support guys unhinged when they came to talk to him.) Debugging a couple dozen lines of code while installing some software and checking voicemail. Etcetera.

But at least as frequently, he got tremendously fixated on

some one damn thing, rendering him useless to every other task until further notice.

On this particular morning, his fixation was in regard to a certain <celeste@gloac.com>, late of alt.quotations, and rec.guns. Miles very much hoped to hear back from her, though he could not say why this was so important to him. Probably something to do with the ego-fluffing of seeing himself quoted and, of course, with the incredible oddity of running into the person who quoted him, twice in the same day. Whatever the reason, Miles had kept checking alt.quotes, and of course checking mail, from 10am until lunch. But there was nothing.

After lunch – and after undertaking pain relief – his fixation shifted its object to another project. He had already written off the day. Between his morning, waiting around single-mindedly for mail, and his debilitated state in the afternoon, nothing useful was going to happen this day as a result of anything he might do.

So when Cal dropped by Miles' desk, around 4pm, he almost tripped on a length of string – with his neck. Miles had erected a fairly elaborate apparatus, and part of it hung at head height.

"What's all this?"

"I found some webcams. And some string. Little cardboard."

"Cool." Cal stepped gingerly inside. "Are these on the Net?"

"Yeah." Miles flipped over from the shareware application that drove all the suspended webcams, to his mailer and newsreader. Still nothing.

He'd been hard pressed to resist the urge to write to this woman Celeste after seeing her post in rec.guns. But he had resolved to play it cool – the Miles Darken cool had taken some heavy maintenance over time, so he felt disinclined to blow it now – and let her write him if she was going to.

Cal twisted around one of the tiny, spherical digital cameras, on its jerry-rigged cardboard and twine cradle. He then sat down on the desk so Miles could show him the web page and the automated image capture software. His web page on boatanchor displayed three distinct views of his cube to the web, updated every minute. On the minute.

Celeste watched the picture refresh, the man's back still turned. She could see him talking to someone, barely visible, in the entrance to his cubicle. She had considered it a shot in the dark to try to connect with her web browser to the machine in the address of the guy with the Bersa, the same guy who had taken credit for the quote about belief. So she had been surprised to find, not merely a digital picture of the fellow, but a whole live-action series of them.

She flipped back to her mailer and began typing, wearing a suspicious, but amused, expression. She spared one last glance at the web browser, as the picture refreshed. Miles Darken, the guy, now looked right at the camera. His eyes were pitch black, his hair dramatically swept, and his face mostly in shadow.

To: Miles Darken <darken@boatanchor.tjc.edu>
From: C. Browning <celeste@gloac.com>
Subject: re: attribution sought
Date: Tues, 19 Oct 2004 17:38:42 (EST)

In alt.quotations Miles Darken at TJC ACC wrote:
>Actually, I said that.

I'd been given to understand this forum was for appreciating others' quotes, not promoting your own. Nevertheless -- you really said this? First? I do think it's a very interesting sentiment. I've got to go now, the office cleaning crew is here and they have an armed escort.

Regards,

Celeste Browning
GA, LLC.
celeste@gloac.com

Important Problems

From: Miles Darken <darken@boatanchor.tjc.edu>
To: Dana <steckler_d@tjc.edu>
Subject: Re: Followup to Sunday
Date: Tues, 19 Oct 2004 17:56:48 (EST)

Hey Doll,

I've got to get out from behind this monitor, or my eyes are going to burn into my skull. Up for coffee? Or do I have to come physically pry you out of that microlab?

M

From: Dana <steckler_d@tjc.edu>
To: Miles <darken@boatanchor.tjc.edu>
Subject: Re: Followup to Sunday
Date: Tues, 19 Oct 2004 17:58:03 (EST)

You could pretty much just drop some bread crumbs at this point. I'm starting to really not like being here. Meet you at Espresso Hovel?

D

A half hour later, Miles found Dana in the back corner, holding down the couch, comfy chair, and unfinished knee-high table. Espresso Hovel had local art, scratchy classic jazz, threadbare couches, cigarette smoke, pastries under glass, snorting-and-steaming steel machines, fliers noting the dates of upcoming poetry slams, and sartorially eclectic and serious-miened people mostly sitting alone with really thick books – all the key stereotypes one expects from a college-town coffee joint.

Miles went for comestibles. He returned shortly with a "ginormous" coffee, an Italian soda, and a cranberry muffin. He planted himself in the deep chair. It was well-suited to his trademark slouch, though it left his tanker of coffee slightly out of reach.

"So, how you holdin' up?" asked Miles, looking tired. He held the edge of his hand to his forehead. One of the overhead track lights was trained a little too nearly on his position.

"Oh, life could be worse. As someone I know is always saying."

They smiled at each other.

"That sounds very philosophical," allowed Miles, reaching across to put a small dent in his coffee. "Maybe I need some of what you're studying." Miles knew well that Dana's studies, in medical ethics, were comprised mainly of classes in two departments: religious studies and philosophy. Putatively, these disciplines would help her become wise on issues such as the Hippocratic Oath, cloning, euthanasia, abortion, malpractice. Eventually, with luck, she would have an office in a medical center somewhere with a "Medical Ethicist" name plate on the door.

"Perhaps you do," Dana said, slightly defensively. "You're constantly asking big questions. I can tell you, you're not going to get any answers from your beloved computers."

Miles looked at her wryly. "Well, at least we computer people can justify our salaries. I mean, we're making progress – faster machines, more complex software, better artificial intelligence." He paused for effect, and coffee. "But what new startling breakthroughs have there been in metaphysics in the last two thousand years? Or in logic? Nothing's changed! Physical reality is just exactly the same as it was in Ancient Greece. Haven't they solved all these problems in all this time? Shouldn't the philosophers all be getting real jobs by now?"

Dana leaned back, looking down and shaking her head slightly. "Well, you know what, you've come to the wrong place for an argument. I actually agree with you. No one's made any major progress on any of the important problems in philosophy. And I don't personally have any hope they ever will."

"Oh really?" Miles seemed genuinely surprised.

"Yep. But I'm different from the people you'll find in the philosophy department, in large part because I spend half my time in the religion department. Because I have a foot in both camps, I can see that the philosophers – the rationalists – have been pounding away at the same problems as the theists – the mystics. And despite diametrically opposed approaches, both groups have failed just the same."

"You say 'important problems' . . ."

Dana smiled and twirled an unlit cigarette. "You want a rundown?"

"Yeah, I've got all night."

"Don't worry, it shouldn't take that long. Let's see . . . um, consciousness, for one thing. Consciousness, or sentience. How did we come to have self-awareness? Is it just from having a really complex brain? And does that mean computers will become sentient any year now? Or is it because of a God-granted soul, something only people get? And how do we get immediate experience as part of the deal? How can I actually *feel* a toothache, or have the immediate experience of seeing a patch of purple? Can a computer have a toothache? Can a worm?"

"It's all about complexity," answered Miles. "My machines get toothaches all the time."

"Then you're misunderstanding what an immediate sensation is."

Miles left that untouched. Instead, he asked, "What else?"

"Next is probably the self, or seat of identity. Where is this thing I think of as me? Is it in my brain-pan? In some invisible aura that floats over my head? Where does it go when I'm blown up in a bizarre gardening accident? What happens to it if my body's destroyed, then rebuilt exactly – say, when I beam up to the *Enterprise*? Can it still possibly be me? When does a sperm inside an egg acquire a self? At the first mitosis?"

"I'm pretty sure you're just in your brain-pan," Miles ventured.

"So if we duplicated my brain-pan, and the body around it, down to the atom, there'd be two of me? What would that be like?"

Dana was beginning to make Miles feel a bit like a third-rate thinker, with this polished litany. Maybe formal philosophical training was worth something after all.

"Temporality's another tricky one," Dana continued. "How does time actually work? Is it like the commonsense view – the present the only reality, the past only memories, the future just hopes and fears? Or is it like Einstein said, a four-dimensional matrix with all times always present and real and us just moving through them, down the time axis? If so, where does that leave free will if everything that's to happen is already all laid out for us?" Dana paused to light her cigarette.

"Free will's a huge issue whichever way you deal with time. How can I be responsible for my actions, legally and ethically, when they are presumably caused by my genes, and my parents, and the arrangement of atoms in my brain-pan, if that's what you think it is? If I choose to do something, what does it mean to say I could have done something else? For whatever reasons, I *didn't* do something else – and in this world, events only unfold one time. No, I *couldn't* have done something else, because I *didn't*. I only did the one thing, presumably for some sufficient reason. And if the circumstances were the same again, I'd do the same thing again."

Dana hunched over the muffin, pinching at it. "Morality. That's a big one. Whatever I just did, say it was the 'wrong' thing. Say it was recreational torture."

"'Recreational torture'? What are they teaching you kids?"

"That's one of my advisor's pet examples. In philosophy, you're often examining gray areas. It helps to have clear examples on either end of the spectrum, something everyone agrees on, as a starting point. Recreational torture is supposed to be something everyone agrees is wrong no matter what."

"Ah. Gotcha."

"But *why* is it always wrong? Who says? What does it mean to say I 'ought' not to have done it? Where's 'ought' in a universe of particles and brain-pans? If you believe in ethical utilitarianism, where the goal is the greatest happiness for the greatest number, is recreational torture okay if it makes me happier than it makes my victims sad?"

Miles felt his inner libertarian yearning to answer that you can swing your recreational torture device just as far as the next guy's nose, but no further. But he was feeling somewhat awed by Dana's impressive parade of conundrums.

"So . . . you're saying they don't have any solutions to these problems?"

"They have tons of them. But none are any good. Or, not good enough."

"What are they?"

"Well, we would be here all night if I tried to recount the history of philosophy. But the important thing is: someone comes up with a very detailed, and usually very convincing, solution to one of these problems; and then the next guy comes along and refutes the first one, just as convincingly. That's what the philosophy journals are full of, every month, every quarter. It's great fun to read. But the next refutation is always just around the corner. And nothing ever gets put to bed, as you've noticed." She paused and drew a deep breath.

"But so, this one contemporary philosopher, Colin McGinn, has put forth a fairly radical explanation about why these questions echo, answerless, through the ages. He says, maybe we just don't have the kinds of brains you need to solve these kinds of problems. It's not very human to think that there are things we can't figure out. But maybe that's our problem. Monkeys can't do calculus, and never will, no matter how long they think about it. Why do we think we can figure out anything if we think long enough? Our minds evolved, just like our bodies. And our bodies can't do everything, like split in two parts, or jump a hundred feet."

"Interesting point."

"And kind of humbling, isn't it? On the other hand, maybe the Martians have better brains, and can understand free will and sentience and whatnot."

"If humans are just whistling in the dark . . . Then why do you keep studying this stuff?"

"Good question. Just pigheaded, I suppose."

Dana closed down the symposium by noting that she had to get back to the lab, a familiar refrain. But she and Miles stood together another moment, alone in the shadows outside the cafe.

"Thanks for a needed distraction, Miles."

"Hey, thank *you* – for the free Big Questions lecture."

"There's probably a cubby in hell reserved for me, for going on with all that."

"Not at all. And you were right, I have been thinking similar thoughts myself lately. Just without all the words to describe them. One question that's burning a hole in my head, though. This lost text you've been looking for. What's it called?"

"Jim just called it the Manuscript. Capital M."

"This Manuscript. If it existed, and you found it, is the notion that it would answer the questions we've talked about tonight?"

"Bingo." She shrugged. "That and a couple on the religion side of the house."

"Such as?"

"Nature of the soul," Dana answered casually. "Existence of God. Those are the big ones."

"This is working out to be quite a document," Miles said quietly.

"And so you see why, deep down, I don't really believe it exists."

"I see your point. Still, that would be awfully cool." He looked at her seriously. "If you found it, I mean. The endless philosophical-circle jerk would be over. And the endless beseeching of the heavens, trying to make sense out of things."

"You mean *you* would be able to make sense of things."

"Maybe."

"Don't worry, you're not alone. But do me a favor and don't hold your breath, okay, Darken?"

"Didn't say I'd hold my breath. Might hold out hope, though . . . I have faith in you."

"Thanks, dearheart. Now I've got to get back to it. I'll see you Friday."

Day at the Office

If you could follow a whole burst of IP packets, a group of IP packets, that cohered on reassembly into something like an e-mail message . . . But you can't, because not cohering is what IP packets do. On their way from – to pick a couple of spots entirely at random – Hookeville, Virginia, to New York City, New York, basically the job of these data packets, as dictated by the odd magic of the Internet Protocol, is to swarm across the Internet willy-nilly, each trying to find a good route to, not even their final destination, but just a next destination that might get them, not even necessarily closer to, but just still moving on toward, their final destination. Still, it's possible, probably not even uncommon, for all the packets that make up an e-mail message to traverse the same route, all side by side in formation, like sea horses riding into battle.

People commonly point out – and it is not true, but it is still illustrative – that the progenitor of the Internet, namely the US Department of Defense's ARPANet, was specifically designed with redundancy in mind, so as to function after a nuclear attack, even with big pieces of it wiped out. Again, in point of fact, it was not designed for this reason, but the Internet looks and works precisely as we would expect it to had it been.

Also illustrative is the fact that fifty per cent of all global Internet traffic – including, sometimes, mail from, say, Kuala Lumpur to Beijing – goes through Northern California. Out of the way? Sure. Efficient? Not really. But all told, just amazingly reliable. The mail always gets where it's going, even if pieces of it have to go halfway around the world first.

So, if you could follow a burst of IP packets, say from Hookeville, Virginia, to New York, New York – if you were to piggyback on one of those hundreds of little blips, firing staccato out the back of a machine, tumbling through a local hub and router, sluicing onto some optical fiber strung hill over dale, zipping swarms of oscillating light, splaying outward in pulses much too fast to consider, broken apart and reassembled a dozen times while tumbling through a dozen more routers, darting stealthily through the wall of a nondescript office building in midtown Manhattan, reassembled a last time, all the parts accounted for and in just the right place, turned into magnetism on the shiny copper plate of a hard drive, where to wait faithfully and patiently all the night through to be read by just one person, to be turned into a file, and into pixels, and into light, and into optical pulses, and into ideas, and into someone else's mind . . . is this what genuine and meaningful contact between two human beings might look like?

Is this what falling in love might look like?

Probably.

* * *

From: Miles Darken <darken@boatanchor.tjc.edu>
To: C. Browning <celeste@gloac.com>
Subject: Armed custodial engineers (was re: attribution sought)
Date: Weds, 20 Oct 2004 10:18:42 (EST)

On Tuesday, C. Browning wrote:
> I've got to go now, the office cleaning crew is here and
> they have an armed escort.

I have a friend with an armed Escort. At the moment he just keeps a canister of mace in it, but he keeps talking about installing fore and aft mounted machine guns, to better deal with the aggressive drivers around here. We all just laugh at him for driving that Ford.

And, it's funny you bring up armaments. More on that later, maybe.

>you really said this? First?

Not sure about first, but I did say it recently. And a few people have echoed it since. If I had known it was going to catch on, I would have put my name on it -- and avoided contributing to the immortal body of work of Anon. He and Ibid must be making a killing.

L8r,
Miles

But of course Miles' comment about armaments was a wasted attempt at foreshadowing, for Celeste had already seen his post in rec.guns, right beneath hers, ten minutes after writing to him personally last night, and was this morning still not a little freaked out about it. You would be, too, triply so if you happened to be in Celeste's line. That's why she felt very jumpy when her boss broke the plane of her office, while she was still giggling, despite herself, at the armed Escort quip.

"Good morning, Celeste. Catch you at a bad time?"

"No." Celeste swallowed her laughter. "No. I was just writing to you, actually, with regard to the biotech project."

"Have you decided to fire the client?"

Celeste laughed, then softened.

The client in question was a huge multinational, one which had been working on a new type of medical imaging system. Of course, it was likely that others were working on such a technology as well, and this company wasn't too keen on dropping millions of dollars on R&D if they were going to get beaten to the patent. So they had hired GA to gather and analyze large volumes of data from sources public and, ahem, private, about where their main competitor stood in the research race. The hard part – coaxing the target firm into giving up the informational goods – had gotten done over a month ago. All that remained was crunching the numbers and extrapolating from them when the competitor would likely get to market.

But the biotech people had gotten fussy about some of the assumptions GA had made, as well as some of the equations they had developed. To compound matters, the longer they all spent futzing around with the weighting of the data, the staler it got. Celeste had to keep going back to the surveillance team and asking them to redo work, which of course they just loved. Soon, she'd have to go back to the insertion team to redo work – a prospect she didn't even remotely want to think about.

At the end of the day, management was something of a burden to Celeste – always requiring more effort to delegate, review, and fix (and smooth egos) than it would have just to do it herself.

But, of course, her role was no longer to do the work; rather, it was to ensure that work the other employees did didn't get them arrested, killed, or deposed – or, worse, get the company fired, federally investigated under RICO, or fire-bombed.

"No," Celeste answered, smiling. "Nothing so drastic as firing the client. But I may need your sign-off on staging another on-site op."

"Hmm," Mr. White considered, scratching his chin. He had angular features, framed by close-cropped, straight, and nearly gray hair. A bit over six feet, and slim, he stood inside a dark gray suit. His appearance was crisp; and he smelled nice (Celeste thought). He also wore an expression of inquisitiveness, respect, and a lack of presumption – which was basically how he dealt with his staff. His employees appreciated that; though most who had been around awhile figured the boyish manner to be an artifice. If one believed half of the rumors about Mr. White's professional background, he was certainly four times as jaded, grizzled, and dangerous as he seemed.

"If it's okay with you," he answered, "it's okay with me."

She must have betrayed disappointment, because he added, "All the necks involved are your necks. So it's your decision."

Celeste said, merely, "Understood."

Mr. White turned and left. Celeste turned back to her

machine, to get back to work. Right after responding to this one piece of mail . . .

> From: C. Browning <celeste@gloac.com
> To: Miles Darken <darken@boatanchor.tjc.edu>
> Subject: re: Armed custodial engineers (was re: attribution sought)
> Date: Weds, 20 Oct 2004 10:36:00 (EST)
>
> Thanks for the attribution. I would have felt silly thinking I had an authentic F.W. Nietzsche or R.W. Emerson, when it was really an undiscovered early M. Darken.
>
> Must go back to breaking rocks for The Man, now. Without the rocks, life has no meaning.
>
> Celeste Browning
> GA, LLC.
> celeste@gloac.com

She clicked on Send, and a whole new swarm of IP packets spurted out of the back of the building, heading south. On their way out of the city, in the next few minutes, they would brush elbows with some other unlikely packets, headed in the same direction.

Forty-some blocks south of the bustling GA offices, FreeBSD's offices were empty and dark. The Crib was always empty in the morning. Only FreeBSD was there – and had been all night. He was a sweaty, awful wreck. He'd been reading the Manuscript again. In the server room . . . in the main room . . . with a laptop out on the stoop . . . with the same laptop, sitting on the can, splashingly expelling the espresso and mangos which had been his sole sustenance for the last almost twenty-four hours – since the evening he'd received the mail from the bot.

The long-lost bot, Bob, had come waltzing in with its arms waving – and with something unspeakable and singular in hand. Hometown bot makes good. FreeBSD hadn't had time to be amazed or impressed that Bob had actually found the goddamn thing, because as soon as he read it, he could no longer think of anything else. And he couldn't stop rereading it.

He'd stopped only briefly, when he went back on to the Net – the regular, out-in-the-daylight Net – to look again for references to the Manuscript. These would be easier to spot now that he actually knew what the Manuscript looked like. Remarkably, after hitting Google, and Google Groups, he did a grep of the *current* newsfeed. And, sure enough, there he found a reference. A conspicuous one, and in alt.religion.misc – right back, more or less, where he'd started.

And this was what prompted him sending off some packets which ran into Celeste's.

Both swarms went out on the same line, New York to Hookeville – the express. This route, of course, passed through MAE-East, the principal network access point on the East Coast. Interestingly, though, the two swarms met up earlier, because both Global Acumen, LLC, and FreeBSD contracted with the same Internet service provider in New York.

FreeBSD made use of stolen, hijacked, and forged accounts, anonymous remailers, anonymizing web-client software, and lots of creative routing and forwarding for his online communication. Still, someone had to fit a pipe to the back of his building. He'd gone with the company he had because they were established enough to provide reliable service, but had grown too quickly to have time for getting inquisitive about any one customer. He could kind of get lost.

GA's network engineers had felt the same way; and used the same provider for the same reasons.

So FreeBSD's and Celeste's packets actually queued up in the very same router at the local exchange point, for a few minutes on Wednesday morning.

Neither had any way of knowing this, of course.

Miles spent Wednesday afternoon breaking rocks, in the form of doing overdue upgrades. This involved more waiting than work, when things went right, and so he sat in his cube wearing headphones, air-drumming wildly, and glancing intermittently at his screen. When bits of software finished installing, he started the next bit. When intriguing mail came in, he responded:

From: Miles Darken <darken@boatanchor.tjc.edu>
To: C. Browning <celeste@gloac.com>
Subject: re: Armed custodial engineers
Date: Weds, 20 Oct 2004 12:08:42 (EST)

>Without the rocks, life has no meaning.

Rocks? I'd been given to understand that everyone in New York City is out patronizing the arts every night; and by day filled with life and energy by their lucrative careers in publishing and finance.

Miles

The Fun Lovin' Criminals

From: Dana <steckler_d@tjc.edu>
To: Miles <darken@boatanchor.tjc.edu>
Subject: newsgroup
Date: Weds, 20 Oct 2004 15:38:42 (EST)

Miles,

Have you ever heard of alt.religion.taoism.angry? I was trying to subscribe, but it's not on the subscription menu. What do I do?

Dana

From: Miles Darken <darken@boatanchor.tjc.edu>
To: Dana <steckler_d@tjc.edu>
Subject: Re: newsgroup
Date: Weds, 20 Oct 2004 16:39:58 (EST)

We don't have it. Unfortunately, I also went ahead and checked our upstream provider -- and it's not in their newsfeed either.

Before you ask: no, if our isp doesn't carry it, we can't get it. So, you're out of luck, unless you want to try and find another isp around here who *does* carry it.

This also have to do with the Manuscript?

M

alt.religion.misc Topic 99 of 222
Article 40985 missing newsgroup? 0 Responses
Dana, <steckler_d@tjc.edu>

I've gone through all the alt.religion faqs, and I don't see any reference to alt.religion.taoism.angry. Also, my ISP claims they've never carried it. The only way I know it exists is from some archived posts in Google Groups. Does anyone know what happened to this newsgroup -- or how I can subscribe?

Thanks for any help,

Dana Steckler

Back in New York, though of course geography is a null issue online, two guys watched Dana's Usenet post as it came across the wire. Two New Yorkers, neither of them Celeste Browning or FreeBSD, two totally other New Yorkers, were online right at that moment, and highly interested in what was happening online, and down in Hookeville.

"Holy sheet. Have a look."

"Another post in a.r.m?"

"Not only that. Another post in a.r.m from Thomas Jefferson College."

"Wow. 'Dana', huh? Is she cute?"

"How do I know? Planning a trip to Virginia?"

"All I know is," said the pale man with the shaggy hair and the oval glasses, as he turned away from the other's desk, "this organization needs more members of the opposite sex."

The second man, in the chair, swiveled away from his machine. A washed-out slash of light from the picture window, causing him to blink, caught his black ponytail and well-trimmed beard, over very dark brown skin. "Members of the *appropriate sex*," he corrected.

"Fuck it," the other said. "Chicks. This gang needs more chicks."

"Should I write her back?" the bearded one asked. He spoke in peremptory tones with a clipped Indian accent.

"Prolly not," the white man said, scratching his light stubble and pulling open a mini-fridge on the floor. He extracted a can of Guinness. "Just grep the newsfeed for her. We'll keep an eye out and throw a line in newsmonitor.pl."

"So? Someone took away your write permission to newsmonitor.pl, Shan?"

"No. Your Perl's just a lot stronger than mine, Abhijit."

"Yeah, right."

While the two sparred, a response to the first post flitted onto the screen:

alt.religion.misc Topic 99 of 222
Article 40995 Re: missing newsgroup? 1 Responses
Bob Roberts <bob_roberts@best.com>

> I've gone through all the alt.religion faqs, and I don't
> see any reference to alt.religion.taoism.angry.

I think it got cancelled. I used to subscribe (not that I ever read it, like 38 of the 40 groups I subscribe to). A few months ago it wasn't on my menu anymore. Must have gone away.

HTH,
Bob Roberts

As Abhijit reached to swivel the monitor for Shan's benefit, his cuff crept up his forearm, revealing a tattoo on the inside of his wrist: a pictograph in white ink. While the two stuck their faces up to the monitor, someone walked in behind them.

"Heads up, gentlemen," she sang. The two turned to face a female of the species, who appeared to be about fourteen, though actually twenty-four. Small, of African descent and pleasingly shaped in a nonsexual sort of way, with straight hair pulled back, she wielded an indulgently disapproving expression. From Abhijit and Shan's frozen response, one would have thought Sergeant Rock had just waded into the room loosing his sidearm from leather.

"Hey, Naja," Shan managed guiltily.

"Time to put away your toys," Naja hummed in a lilting falsetto, smiling and flashing huge eyes, "and come play with the others." She turned on her heel and exited.

Abhijit logged out and the pair stumbled over his chair following her, both cursing quietly. They groused their way down the hallway, which ended at a door to a small conference room. The two tumbled in, squeezed around a boat-shaped table, and found seats. Four others were already seated; Naja stood schoolmarmish at the fore. An LCD display of prodigious dimensions filled the wall behind her. Before her she held a small electronic device, a palmtop computer.

The others at the table included a short, full-figured woman who only looked Hispanic when you knew that she was; a thin, pale man in blockish attire with a Calvin Klein manner of neat haircut, glasses with thick black plastic frames, and no discernible expression; a chiseled Asian with curly bangs, oval wire-rimmed glasses, sharp lapels, and a book hidden under the lip of the table; and a tall, medium-skinned black man with a flat-top fade (a Marine's haircut) and a close-lipped grin.

"Attendance is poor tonight," Naja sang. "And so we will begin with commitments for upcoming events." She consulted her palmtop without moving her head. "Investment bank hardware liberation on Friday?" Everyone raised their hands, and she smiled approvingly. "How *nice*! But you must have already heard we have security codes and an inside friend." She nodded back and forth.

"Raid on Councilman van Bakel, the twenty-fifth?" Only the other woman raised her hand. "Okay," Naja scolded, "we need at least two more to make that happen." She pouted and did tricks with her eyebrows. "I nominate Abhijit and Shan," she said, looking back to the palmtop screen.

"No good," clipped Abhijit. "I have a security gig that day. Get Snitch."

"If I can reach him at the flophouse, you're off the hook. But not Shan." Before Shan could protest, she danced into her next number, lilting and pouting. "And we're going to visit a lovely sexual predator on the twenty-eighth. Independent confirmation from two victims. No legal action pending." She paused and smiled. "And *no* security." All hands went up.

"*Good!*" Her voice lowered, and became almost gravelly. "That one will be fun."

Naja continued through items of business and points of order. The conference room had dim lighting, dark walls, and no windows. A perpetual quiet hum droned on. Distraction, and napping, prevailed during meetings. The minds gathered there began slipping discreetly out of the cracked door, and drifting away, down the dark hall.

The mind belonging to Angelo, the black man with the neat haircut, drifted back to northern Kuwait, spring of 2002. He often returned to that time and place, always feeling the same insistent sun on his shoulders, through his thin shirt; sand irrepressibly making its way into his boots; the weight of a double apportionment of thirty-round magazines strapped to his torso. He turned his face to a little merciful breeze. Angelo got to visit many of the very few high places in the desert, where his boss would scan the horizon with binoculars and make matter-of-fact observations. Angelo kept his gaze on the closer stretches of sand, and occasionally on his boss, a Marine infantry colonel who would, in a few days, lead a regiment of Angelo's peers in an efficient and irresistible sprint across the desert.

Angelo's job was security detail for the colonel, which is why he went around so heavily strapped. Angelo held the rank of corporal in one of the few Marine Reserve companies initially called up for the Iraq invasion. In real life, Angelo was a student first, reservist second. Here he was, missing classes, and women, and lazy warm evenings drinking pitchers and shooting pool at Southern University in Baton Rouge. He never asked why a college boy had been picked to safeguard one of the top field commanders in the theatre; but he could speculate. Working one's way through school instilled responsibility, for starters. Also, Angelo had never let down a friend, family member, or colleague in his life – and almost certainly never would. His squad mates were of like character, and many also held responsible positions in the forces massing on the border.

On his return, nearly a year later, Angelo would have enough hazardous-duty pay to buy a new car, two full terms to make up toward his degree, and a lifetime's worth of daydream footage.

But then he thought of the little weapons locker that sat on the other side of the conference room wall behind him. He tipped his chair back, and returned from the desert.

"Someone *else* looking for the newsgroup!" Naja chirped in amazement. Shan had reported their findings from alt.religion.misc. "Did he mention the Manuscript?"

"It was a 'she'," corrected Shan. "She didn't mention it."

"And where did she *hear* about our little Usenet misadventure? And where was she *writing* from?" Abhijit started to answer, but she cut him off: "No, I'm going to die from any more piecemeal intelligence. Just forward me the post and any responses. Then grep the newsfeed for her; probe her account gently, and do however much of a profile you can for free. I'll take a look after the gig tonight. God, running that newsgroup was such a mistake. But," and she looked tired and resigned, "I guess we didn't really know what we were doing back then."

The group remained silent. Naja picked up her place: "Speaking of 'profiling', I'd like to see people taking a *li-ttle* more responsibility when using the targets database . . ."

* * *

T'ien Ken, the curly-haired Asian man, was deep in his book. Inside the book, Stanford economist Brian Arthur genially lectured. "As we begin to understand complex systems," Arthur said, "we begin to understand that we're part of an ever-changing, interlocking, nonlinear, kaleidoscopic world." T'ien Ken scanned the pages from under lowered lids, through thin-rimmed oval spectacles. He appeared serene, almost noble, his muscular body tilted back from the table at an angle. He wasn't hiding the book, he just wasn't being any more obtrusive with it than necessary. No one at the table would ask him to stop reading. They all knew that later, if they asked him to, he would recite the proceedings of the meeting almost verbatim; and then quote a passage from the book. Or work them in together, if he needed to, commenting on any similarities between the text and the discussion. His multi-tasking capabilities were stunning. He read on:

> "So the question is how you maneuver in a world like that. And the answer is that you want to keep as many options open as possible. You go for viability, something that's workable, rather than what's 'optimal.' A lot of people say to that, 'Aren't you then accepting second best?' No, you're not, because optimization isn't well defined anymore. What you're trying to do is maximize robustness, or survivability, in the face of an ill-defined future. And that, in turn, puts a premium on becoming aware of nonlinear relationships and causal pathways as best we can. You observe the world very, very carefully, and you don't expect circumstances to last."

Ken showed a thin smile. He knew Arthur had taught at Stanford University. Similar thoughts to these, not fully realized, had caused Ken to leave that place after only five quarters of study in computer science. From there he had gone to work for a nano-technology firm in Silicon Valley, one of those start-ups continually on the verge of a major round of venture financing. After four months of working in what turned out to be a volunteer capacity – he never did get paid – he had lighted out for the East. On reflection, some kind of seeking after viability (as well as grocery money) had driven him from there – and probably driven his parents from Revolutionary mainland China, years earlier.

Now, money was rarely a problem. Later tonight he'd go home and pick up a few hours of contract programming work, which would keep him in groceries and books for the next month. He reached to turn the page, scraping it on the edge of the table, one ear on the meeting.

"Is this going to go late? *The Wild Bunch* is on at Radio City Music Hall at ten thirty."

Naja frowned.

"Wow," said Shan, "world's largest screen, that could be good. Is it the director's cut?"

"Pipe down, you." Naja dragged her non-existent nails across the smooth glossy surface of the LCD. The effect was purely symbolic, but not lost. She paused to poke at her palmtop with a stylus, lamenting the delay; but at least they were moving forward.

"Tonight is a hard entry as well," she intoned, looking up as a detailed floor plan flickered to life on the screen behind her (transmitted wirelessly from the device in her hand). She turned in profile and pointed out a room, a series of rooms, an entry route, escape routes. "Yes, I know, we've been going in hard an awful lot. Let's all pay attention, and we'll get out easy again."

Laylah, the young Hispanic woman, sank into her own daydream. There she zipped through the fast traffic of the Rickenbacker Causeway, fleeing the throng of downtown Miami for the open spaces and relative placidity of Key Biscayne. She drove her new Mercury Capri, a high school graduation gift from her father, her best friend beside her. The third passenger was the wind, all around them with its noise, ubiquitous. It was early spring, they nosed out onto the second stretch of bridge, the chill Atlantic glinting again beneath them. Glamorous music shredded into the wind; they knew the songs well enough to fill in the gaps that got sucked over the windowsills, over the seat backs.

Dad had owed her a good graduation gift. Dad worked as an "independent businessman", in the nebulous sense of being involved in various ventures that made money. In Laylah's early teen years, he'd mostly done arms dealing, typically to both sides in small regional conflicts, as Laylah would later gleefully recount to her blanching JAP friends at Barnard.

In Laylah's household, at the heart of the Cuban émigré community in Miami, two languages were spoken. She grew up fluent in both, and with a knack for tongues that would ease her into near-fluency with French, Italian, Portuguese, Russian, and Arabic by the end of college. But home was also a place where startlingly seedy-looking Latinos in military fatigues would ring the bell and ask for her father by his industry nickname. "Eh, ees 'Snake' een?" they would inquire of the pubescent Laylah, at the door of the house in Coconut Grove.

Laylah drove her recompense for indignities suffered over the flat and extended stretch of the South Florida bridge, and back into the little room in Manhattan to rejoin the other equally unlikely characters with whom she'd cast her lot in later days.

"This guy is *so* dirty, I can't even quite bear to handle his file." Naja bobbled the palmtop on her fingertips, by way of illustration. "He's been with the DEA more than twenty years, and is one of the top-ranking agents in the city. Meanwhile, he's been dealing drugs himself through a dozen different outlets, using guys on the agency payroll to make his drops." She clenched her teeth. "Not to mention using agency guns and muscle to do his enforcing. Hate to say it, but this guy has played very rough with the *honest* drug dealers in Manhattan."

"So we're sticking up," grinned Abhijit, "for the hometown dealer."

"Mom 'n' Pop," underscored Shan.

She smiled. "No, really we're just cashing in. We have reason to believe he's got at least a hundred thousand in cash in his apartment, and no one he can report to if we happen to liberate it."

"I love that word, 'liberate'," smiled Shan. "But I thought we couldn't get through security at his building."

"We can't, by ourselves. First we pick him up at a buy in Chinatown, and then he takes us up to his apartment. In and out."

"How exactly do we know about this guy?"

"From one of our friends amongst the 'hometown dealers'. She was very forthcoming and helpful."

Mike worried about tonight. He sat expressionless and pasty, fingers steepled in his lap. His sculpted hair, obelisk-like eyeglass frames, pale skin, and stony expression made his head akin to a piece of modern sculpture. Or an ad in GQ.

He frowned deeply, the lines in his cheeks flexing. He let his head run, spooked. As far as he was concerned, they *had* been going in hard – and in person – too often lately. There were easier ways to distribute comeuppance and gather cash. Usually it could be done from a stolen laptop, through a hijacked WiFi connection, in an anonymous public area somewhere. Then you threw the laptop in a dumpster and walked away, without ever having set foot anywhere in the first place. The group had come to rely too much on their balls and guns, and not nearly enough on their brains and technology.

To eschew hip-leather was an odd position for a young man who had come here straight from Texas. But possibly, the Lone Star State – with its highest per capita rate of firearms ownership – had made him jaded by, or at least frightened of, the cool iron.

In Texas, he had worked for EDS, a firm where brain power was held in high esteem. He'd landed there after earning a BS in Systems Engineering from Ohio Tech, and after having grown up on the clean, white-bread streets of Shaker Heights, Ohio.

Mike looked at least as white as he'd been raised. But he also had a coolness, reserve, and evenness of speech that did not exactly bespeak color or ethnicity, but which belied the suburbs. In a sense, he was *too* controlled and self-possessed to fit into white stereotypes. Whites were never so set-upon as to require such self-possession. Except, perhaps, young intellectual whites in white-bread middle America.

But his nerves and sensibilities never got used to the armed stuff. His blood ran thin. Or, as he insisted, he just preferred to get paid for being smart, rather than for working hard, or for risking his hide. *Work smarter, not harder* had been the mantra at EDS.

He touched his fingertips to his collarbone and shook his head. But there was really nothing for it; they went where their mistress told them. Paying attention again, Mike realized she had wound down the briefing. They were ready to go. He knew it for sure when he heard, "Let's fuck it up," T'ien Ken's usual pre-action mantra. As he said it, Ken pushed himself away from the table, biceps looming large. Everyone else then stood and filed out, moving to the room next door – the weapons locker. A hardwood plaque above the doorway proclaimed:

Be like an uncarved block of wood –
So you can beat the shit out of people

* * *

In a back room in Chinatown, three Chinese and a white guy, with wispy stubble and an open collar under his suit jacket, sat at a table, negotiating over currently illicit drugs. The four sat in a clearing of palettes, shelves, and sprawling piles of consumer goods. The crap was piled to the high ceiling, and several crooked paths through the merchandise forest led away from their little crate of a table to the storefront on the street, and further into the bowels of the warehouse.

The negotiations had gone long. DEA Agent Poplawski rubbed his temples tiredly, turned his head to the left, and raised his eyebrows. A black girl with an unlit cigarette in her mouth was walking up the aisle right toward them. She wore baggy clothing, all black. Her hands hung by her side, empty.

This struck Poplawski as more than odd. From his vantage, he caught sight of her a few seconds before the Chinamen. She stepped right up to the table. "Trouble you for a light?" she asked pleasantly. Everyone else seemed to move in slow motion.

Reacting automatically, from long practice, Poplawski produced his Zippo.

Her expression unchanging, the girl flashed out, grabbing the hand with the lighter and locking the wrist. Pulling him off balance, she dragged him from his chair, and onto his knees.

Agent Poplawski's eyes went wide, but not so wide as those of the three Chinamen who at that moment felt the touch of high voltage stun devices in the backs of their necks. The rows of merchandise were lousy with young, sleek, black-clad intruders.

Mike sat behind the desk in the front of the warehouse. The previous clerk lay tied up at his feet, underneath the desk. The small man was squirming quite a bit, causing Mike to shift his feet to get them arranged comfortably. Out on the street, the pedestrian and motor traffic was light at this hour. And they had locked the front door, in any case.

Mike looked over his shoulder at the sound of cursing. It came from far down the dim hallway – but was growing closer.

"Fine! You assholes will be *shot* at my building!"

T'ien Ken now held the bellowing man's wrist locked, as the group marched into the brighter light of the front area. Angelo and Laylah brought up the rear.

When no one commented, and their pace did not slow, Poplawski shouted, "*Who the fuck are you people?*"

Naja nodded and said, "Kenny," and he broke the man's wrist. Poplawski crumpled to his knees, which Naja kicked out from under him; she then put her heel into the pit of his stomach. Flat on the cold floor, he looked up into her cool, white eyes. Shan's face peeked over Naja's shoulder, with the ceiling as backdrop. He answered quietly and unsmilingly, "We're the Angry Young Taoists."

The whole parade marched past Mike's station at the front counter. He hopped up, unlocking the glass door for them. As the others filed out, he glanced worriedly back into the dark interior of the building, and at the edge of the counter, where he half-expected the clerk to appear, Houdini-like.

Though tense, he couldn't help but grin at the furious and impotent expression on the man they trundled out the door. *The more you know*, he thought, reciting in his head now an AYT mantra, *the less likely you are to try and fuck with us.*

Locking the door behind him, he dog-trotted up to the side of their van and climbed in.

The Fed

One hundred and thirty miles northeast of Hookeville, on the beltway that rings Washington DC, a gray Toyota Camry skimmed by a line of cars, passing on the right, then zipping down an off ramp – the Fort Meade exit, halfway between DC and Baltimore.

Parking sixty yards from the main building, nodding and snorting to find such a close space at at the tail-end of the morning rush-hour, a husky, blond, fortyish man in a woolen jacket and open collar lumbered from the car and jogged across the lot. He swiped an electronic smart card to open the glass front doors and entered a wide lobby. In its center, a lone receptionist sat on a podium, surrounded by a chest-high, circular desk.

"Good morning, Mr. Luther," said the crewcutted man behind the desk.

Stanley Luther flashed an ID absently as he strode to the single door in the room, set in the back wall. It clicked faintly, and he gave it a solid yank. Beyond the embrasure lay a ten-foot hallway and another, identical door, which emitted another click. In the small room beyond, another receptionist sat before a door with biometric access controls (a configurable combination of voice, thumb print, retinal, and skin current), and two unblinking black-clad twenty-two-year-old men with submachine guns standing behind a pane of glass.

This last gave Stanley the howling fantods every single time he passed it. He couldn't bring himself to meet the matching, disapproving gazes of the lethal mannequins inside.

Today the biometrics combo was thumbprint and skin, a quick and complementary pair; he was in the complex in a few seconds. *Hate this fucking place*, he thought, as he often did, regardless of the vicissitudes of the access control mechanisms.

He thought about contract work. But then cut himself off quickly – he did not even want to bring that forbidden thought into this sacrosanct and terrible place. Sensibly enough, he worried that wandering thoughts could precipitate a verbal slip-up. Another part of him, however, feared that his thoughts might literally be read out of his head in some way, a level of paranoia to which he had not previously subscribed. However, as he had now actually taken on some contract side work (utterly forbidden, under pain of he cared not to think what), no level of anxiety or caution could really be considered excessive.

He nodded at a few familiar colleagues, ignored the rest. He came on-site only rarely. He ducked into his uncluttered and sterile cube. The building kept dust out of the air, or there would be plenty on his terminal. An assignment awaited him on the pristine machine.

He settled down to read it, not missing the days when he had to speak with a supervisor for routine gigs.

He struggled to master his thoughts. He exhaled.

He logged in.

The Correspondence

"Shut up, you crack-smokers." A small crowd of junior coworkers had flooded into Miles' cube, biting at his ankles, screaming that something or other had blown up, and supplicating for him to lay his hands on it and fix it. But Miles was trying to read mail here.

> From: C. Browning <celeste@gloac.com>
> To: Miles Darken <darken@boatanchor.tjc.edu>
> Subject: re: Armed custodial engineers (was re: attribution sought)
> Date: Thur, 21 Oct 2004 13:22:21 (EST)
>
> >I'd been given to understand that everyone in New York City is out
> >patronizing the arts every night; and by day filled with life and
> >energy by their lucrative careers in publishing and finance.
>
> *I* thought genteel Virginians minded their own affairs. Anyway, everyone knows that New Yorkers are only filled with life and energy by two things: eating out and redecorating their apartments.
>
> As long as we're prying, what exactly do you do at Thomas Jefferson College that's so glamorous? Working on that 3rd liberal arts degree?
>
> Celeste Browning
> GA, LLC.
> celeste@gloac.com

"*Please* help, Miles." A female undergrad, a student employee, shook his shoulders. Miles tried to shrug her off. Failing that, he exhaled prodigiously and finally deigned to address them.

"What."

"All the CGI scripts on www.tjc.edu," they shouted in squeaky chorus. "They're all giving '500 Server Error' messages! They're all broken!"

Miles wistfully minimized his mail reader, pushed back from

the desk, and allowed the lynch mob of munchkins to escort him out of his cube. But not before firing off one message:

From: Miles Darken <darken@boatanchor.tjc.edu>
To: C. Browning <celeste@gloac.com>
Subject: re: Armed custodial engineers
Date: Thur, 21 Oct 2004 13:28:04 (EST)

>As long as we're prying, what exactly do you do at
>Thomas Jefferson College that's so glamorous?

Actually, I work here. I fiddle around with machines for Academic Computing. I'm a systems administrator.

Miles

Miles then spent three minutes over on the web side of the house, the time it took him to figure out that someone had moved sendmail without telling the mail-to scripts. He fixed it, then shook his head in a manner meant to convey bottomless disdain, and trundled back to his cube. And it was pretty much just pretending to work, and writing mail, after that, for all the day long.

* * *

From: C. Browning <celeste@gloac.com>
To: Miles Darken <darken@boatanchor.tjc.edu>
Subject: re: Armed custodial engineers
Date: Thur, 21 Oct 2004 14:02:42 (EST)

>I'm a systems administrator.

Unix geek, eh? I've been thinking lately how nice it would be to just work with computers all day. The more I have to deal with cranky clients and clueless coworkers... the more I feel like just curling up with the machines.

Not sure why I'm confiding all this in you. I guess I don't meet many Unix people anymore.

Celeste

From: Miles Darken <darken@boatanchor.tjc.edu>
To: C. Browning <celeste@gloac.com>
Subject: Unix (was re: Armed Custodial Engineers)
Date: Thur, 21 Oct 2004 14:48:55 (EST)

Hey -- you've come to the right place for Unix. Heck, I almost only *speak* in Unix anymore. I find myself saying shit like "Hey, Bill, just diff the 2 versions of this report; cat the results together; and pipe it to the boss. But if something more important comes up, you can just background that process."

Miles

From: C. Browning <celeste@gloac.com>
To: Miles Darken <darken@boatanchor.tjc.edu>
Subject: re: Unix?
Date: Thur, 21 Oct 2004 15:20:42 (EST)

<grin>. If only people took commands the way Unix does, following a neat set of rules! I've dealt with a lot of people, and a fair number of computers, and one thing I've learned is that the computers are relatively very, very predictable. When you say something to a computer, there's a limited range of responses you might get back; with people, virtually anything can happen.

Celeste

From: Miles Darken <darken@boatanchor.tjc.edu>
To: C. Browning <celeste@gloac.com>
Subject: re: Unix?
Date: Thur, 21 Oct 2004 15:26:20 (EST)

Man, you said it. And with computer programs, you even get to compile them before you run them -- which is basically a process of the computer *telling you* beforehand if you're about to say something it might react badly to. I've always thought it would be fantastic to have English language compilers, for our messages to people.

I'm sure you've noticed how easily, and frequently, e-mail gets misinterpreted, misconstrued, taken in totally the wrong spirit. Wouldn't it be great if you could run messages through a compiler before you sent them? It could alert you to improper syntax . . . undeclared variable feelings . . . unsupported literary methods . . . malformed expressions of love . . . infinite emotional loops . . . uncaught taking of exception. Then you could at least be reasonably sure that your message would run well on the target platform. I think run-time errors would be greatly reduced.

And that's what I think.

Miles

From: C. Browning <celeste@gloac.com>
To: Miles Darken <darken@boatanchor.tjc.edu>
Subject: re: Unix?
Date: Thur, 21 Oct 2004 15:37:01 (EST)

That was a very pretty formulation, Miles. You must have *some* sort of a poet's soul underneath the computer mercenary armor -- as well as time on your hands to think about all this stuff. ;^) And while we're on the subject of your job, tell me this: Did you always want to do what you're doing? Did you plan it?

Celeste

From: Miles Darken <darken@boatanchor.tjc.edu>
To: C. Browning <celeste@gloac.com>
Subject: re: Unix?
Date: Thur, 21 Oct 2004 15:48:40 (EST)

Did I plan to get into Unix systems administration? Not really. Most people don't. It all starts innocently enough: "Hey, Miles, can you fix some permissions problems for us?" "Hey, Miles, why don't you take next week, and help mount those new disks?" Once people know you know how to do Unix stuff, it's pretty much all over.

But the checks keep clearing, so I try not to think about it too much.

Miles

From: C. Browning <celeste@gloac.com>
To: Miles Darken <darken@boatanchor.tjc.edu>
Subject: You too, eh?
Date: Thur, 21 Oct 2004 16:01:50 (EST)

Miles,

Ow. Thanks for your honesty. I didn't mean the Unix stuff, so much -- just where you are in life in general. It's probably a long way from New York to Hookeville. But guess what? I'm still in my college town, too. (I went to Columbia.) Albeit there's a little more room to hide in New York. Though sometimes it doesn't feel like it.

I guess the question I'm asking myself a lot is, "Self, do you have ANY sense of how you got to where you are?"

Celeste

From: Miles Darken <darken@boatanchor.tjc.edu>
To: C. Browning <celeste@gloac.com>
Subject: re: You too, eh?
Date: Thur, 21 Oct 2004 16:15:39 (EST)

Celeste,

The other parts of my life have proceeded in no more orderly fashion than my so-called career. I think I got where I am mainly by taking one level step after another, and carefully avoiding the hills. And staring at my feet.

Life could definitely be a hell of lot worse than having to get up 5 days a week and fiddle around with computers. I've got plenty of money. My job's easy at this point. Hookeville's nice. And I've got a lot of friends here.

Still, I can't help feeling a little under-utilized. It just feels . . . like I'm waiting for something.

Miles

From: C. Browning <celeste@gloac.com>
To: Miles Darken <darken@boatanchor.tjc.edu>
Subject: re: You too, eh?
Date: Thur, 21 Oct 2004 16:51:42 (EST)

Small Internet.

Celeste

Drama Management

Dana spent three dazed hours in the lab that morning, twenty surprising minutes in Castrolang's office, and the rest of the afternoon lying in the quad, trying to figure out if all her problems had just been solved, or had just begun.

"You've found it? The Manuscript?" she had asked, wide eyed. Sitting on the business end of the big desk, she felt torn between delight that their quest, and her torment, might be at an end, and chagrin, or perhaps indignation, that the old man had succeeded where she had not.

"Not precisely. I've found someone who claims to have it."

"That's wonderful." Dana kept her smile unequivocal, a skill she had refined.

"Yes, let's hope so," Jim agreed. "That it is what we've been looking for," he added, with a glance at his computer monitor.

"I'm sorry I wasn't able to find it for you," Dana ventured.

"Oh, not at all, not at all. You've been very helpful." As usual, he went to lengths to put her at her ease. "Very helpful. Also . . . there is one last thing you could do to facilitate this."

"Of course."

"Do you happen to know the Alpha Beta Tau fraternity house?"

Now, sitting in the quad, feeling the rough grass stalks on her ankles and contemplating a gray sky, Dana recounted the end of the conversation. For some reason he would not explain, James Castrolang needed Dana to pick this thing up for him, in person. And the person he asked her to pick it up from did not sound like the kind of character she really wanted to meet – particularly at the odd hour, and the odd place, she had been asked to do so. Why couldn't he just try to seduce her like a normal male faculty member?

She got up as the sky turned black and the rain started to fall in sheets. One could be forgiven for believing, as Dana had previously, that sheets of rain were the telltales of Hollywood rain-making machines. But now, Dana saw the rain strafe the grass and the pebbles in rolling slices, tides and waves of the sky, movements of the aerial ocean. It looked like she was in for a stormy weekend.

In the Crib, it was raining understatement.

"What all this, boss?"

"It's your gig for the weekend," FreeBSD answered, so flatly that defibrillators were indicated.

"For down Hookeville way?"

FreeBSD nodded, just visibly, purse-lipped.

"What up with all this coke, then."

"*It's your gig for the weekend.*" Elaboration was clearly not forthcoming.

"Right." The very young, light-skinned black man stared at FreeBSD across the bar top, skeptical, but still deferential. He began to zip up the bag. FreeBSD's hand came down on his.

"Mark your calendar. You meet midnight Friday."

"With my usual guy."

"With your fraternity boy. Right." FreeBSD cleared his throat lightly. "But that's not who you're doing the deal with. There'll be a girl there."

FreeBSD slid a printout across the bar top. It had text at the top – a time, a date, and directions – and a color laser-printed photograph below. A headshot, pixilated and grainy.

"Redheaded party girl, right? She must have a lot of friends, want this much coke."

FreeBSD turned and walked out of the room. "Call me, you run into any problems."

* * *

From: Dana Steckler <steckler_d@tjc.edu>
To: Miles <darken@boatanchor.tjc.edu>
Subject: End of Days!
Date: Thur, 21 Oct 2004 17:09:32 (EST)

Hi, Miles,

I'm writing for 3 reasons.

1 is that I think I've been walking around feeling sorry for myself -- all because of this research project. But, really, it was stupid and short-sighted of me. As you have sagely noted, 'life could be a hell of a lot worse.'

2 is that I soon will have no cause for self-pity! You may not believe it -- I don't really myself -- but my search may be at an end. 'You've found the Manuscript!?' you ask? Not precisely. But we have found someone who claims to have it -- and is willing to part with it, for a price. I'm afraid it's going to turn out to be nothing, a fool's gold. And I'm a little worried about the fact that I have to go pick it up. But I have gotten my hopes up; and Jim's convinced. And I'm determined to put this to bed. Whatever it is on offer, I'm not coming back without it. And then I'm finished with this thing, one way or another.

3 is that when I am finished, I'd like for us to spend more time together. I do need you in my life, to believe in me . . . to remind me of the person I always thought I was. Somehow, lately, I feel smaller than I used to be, and you're still just as big.

Love as ever,
Dana

Miles paused to absorb all this. But not for real long. He began typing:

From: Miles <darken@boatanchor.tjc.edu>
To: Dana Steckler <steckler_d@tjc.edu>
Subject: re: End of Days!
Date: Thur, 21 Oct 2004 17:34:11 -0500 (EST)

At Thur, 21 Oct 2004 17:09:32 (EST) steckler_d@tjc.edu wrote:
> As you have sagely noted, 'life could be a hell of a lot worse'.

That's right. Checklist: arms and legs, all attached; food in belly, that's good; not wasting away from any unspeakable diseases (at least, none that you've told me about); not being sued, deposed, or sought by the authorities in connection with anything illicit or murderous (again, at least nothing that you've told me about).

>Somehow, lately, I feel smaller than I used to be, and you're
>still just as big.

It's the duster, babe. I'm a small man in a big coat.

Everything will be fine; you'll see. Congratulations on being done.

M

Miles tapped his cube wall and looked through it to an image of the woman on the other end of Ariadne's electronic thread. Dana had so many layers of self-protection: her focus on her studies and fast-approaching career; her powerful sarcasm; the little girlishness she would retreat to, and from which she couldn't be assailed by adult ideas of rationality or responsibility. Underneath all this, though, Miles well knew, hid an immense self-doubt. It was this core of her which engaged Miles' concern, and over which he felt so protective – or, maybe, responsible. He squinted at the monitor, trying to gauge again his responsibility for Dana's happiness. It was a tough one.

"Fuck it, I'm going home," he informed boatanchor. He gathered keys from the desk drawer and coat from the corner of the cube wall. He kissed his hand and planted it on the monitor, then turned and treaded through corridors that had already gone dark, and quiet but for the hum of the machines.

Bad Mojo (The Fed][)

Stanley Luther, mercurial and sulking federal agent, denied the luxury of heading home just yet, tabbed through screens of text, chin on his left fist, right fingers on the space bar, lips parted. Reading, at long last, his assignment.

Issue Record # 028942AB
Agent: S. Luther
Issue Cat: Surveil

Subject: James Edison Castrolang, ContactDB# : 249395

Issue Background: Regard to tracking interest in historical textual document, whereabouts unknown (possibly destroyed), possibly apocryphal, reportedly authored by 19th-century English explorer Sir R.F. Burton; doc describing a So. American aboriginal tribe; Agency interest in particular regard to interest from such sectors, globally, as [suppressed] and [suppressed]. Undocumented (possibly apocryphal) aborigines said to have genetic (/mystical) capacity for:

- [suppressed]
- [suppressed]
- [suppressed]
- telepathy
- astral transport
- germline genetic manipulation
- [suppressed]

Myth, and Issue history, documented in Agency docs dating to 1973. See:
\\Minerva\Archive\Field_Docs\1973\rathkopf\debriefs\42
\\Minerva\Archive\Field_Docs\1973\rathkopf\debriefs\44
\\Minerva\Archive\Field_Docs\1979\mcclure\debriefs\101
\\Minerva\Archive\Field_Docs\1996\edmund\1

Stanley popped a new window, logged into the case document server, skimmed the first four docs – which made no sense – and checked the last to get an ID on this "Edmund" character. The folder was a symbolic link to a folder on a remote machine named "[suppressed]". It figured; "Edmund" was one of a number of regularly used opaque names – it had no meaning attached to it, and that was the point. They may as well have named the directory "bob" or "foo". *This agency*, he shook his head, *really needs a few new opaque names.*

Scattered intel of doc considered insubstantial, discounted, until [suppressed], at which time reports from Xanadu Group indicate spike in intelligence activity and inquiries, global, on Issue.

Xanadu Group, Stanley knew – though he was not really authorized to know this – was the stable of geeks (twenty of them? four hundred? that he didn't know) who sat in a shielded barn at a satellite campus out in Loudoun County. There, they tirelessly and meticulously gathered publicly available, intercepted, and otherwise-acquired data from computers, networks, and, principally, Internet traffic. They then scoured this for tidbits relevant to national security, or to Agency interests (overlap here was imperfect).

Xanadu was a splinter operation of the much larger, and longer-standing, Echelon Project. Echelon had been in business possibly since as early as 1948, charged with collecting, decrypting, and analyzing virtually every communication sent anywhere in the world – via satellite, microwave, telex, cellular, cable, and fiber optic. The rise of the Internet, however, had created special challenges, and special opportunities, in over-the-wire snooping. Sometime between 1979 and 1993 (depending on which rumors you listened to) Xanadu sprang up to address them.

> Issue Objective: Acquire subject, surveil for 36 hours. Record subject movements, activities, and contacts. Acquire subject local databases -- including online accounts, directories, and archives; compile and include in Issue report.
> Details ContactDB.

Stanley flipped windows again to check the details on this subject. Sure enough, he saw all the info and resources needed to get into the subject's accounts: usernames, passwords, directory structures, as well as floor plans with home and office computers circled and starred. James Edison Castrolang's interior life had become an open book. Stanley decided this stuff had Xanadu Group written all over it, with the big red crayon. He did not have leisure to be surprised by this fact, though. He was too busy being surprised by the subject's location: Hookeville, VA.

For fuck's sake.

Stanley Luther's disciplined thought control could not keep him from recalling the fact that he had already made travel plans to Hookeville.

* * *

Striding smoothly into the cold glare of dusk in the Agency parking lot, Stanley wondered if he had been too assiduous in avoiding the gaze of the receptionist on his way out. Bobbling his keys, he concluded it didn't matter. Gaze avoidance was his most standard maneuver in the Agency building.

He tossed a thumb-sized memory stick onto the car's dash. One couldn't do that with the big accordion files that mission details used to come in. But then, those wouldn't melt in the car, either. Stanley pulled the door shut behind him, dug out his Blackberry, and fired it up. Back in the building, a few minutes earlier, he'd had to brace his body against the shock of recognition, the uneasy déjà vu that hit him on reading his assignment. He'd also had to resist the temptation to look at his personal mail account from his desk. Logging in from the car was safer, but still reckless.

The details of his contract job had come via e-mail, as well, beamed down from his faceless overseers in New York. He logged in and scrolled down hastily:

> Proceed to 321 Quadrangle Lane, ground floor, SE corner room, Hookeville VA (the Alpha Beta Tau house). Using a law enforcement persona and credentials, interdict a narcotics transaction. Acquire the target item, and withdraw. Details for delivery will be provided after acquisition. Advise with any questions.

Hookeville, VA. The big man exhaled heavily, then laughed. Both his current Agency assignment, and the strictly forbidden and dicey contract work he had picked up, had him traveling, inexplicably, to Hookeville, Virginia. *Great – save myself a trip*, he thought, shaking his head. *With possible detours through Leavenworth, or the bottom of a dumpster.*

He pulled out and gassed up the Camry. Driving southwest into the coldly metallic sunset, he admitted that stranger things had happened. But probably not to living agents.

* * *

From: an8465407@anon.penet.fi
To: <castrolang_j@tjc.edu>
Subject: Re:
Date: Thurs, 21 Oct 2004 12:08:55 (EST)

<castrolang_j@tjc.edu> wrote:
> I appreciate your willingness to deliver it in person, very
> kind of you. I'll be sending an assistant to meet with you
<snip>

Great, so we are good to go for this weekend. Tell your girl to be at the frat house at midnight, and to have the money handy -- and to not make too much of a scene, if she can manage it.

Pleasure doing business with you.

F

The desk lamp ripped a white streak through the middle of the message on the screen, and Jim Castrolang pivoted forward the better to make it out. His movement sent a short stack of books on the desk toppling, causing him to startle. It had gotten very late, and the building was empty. He had only the desk lamp lit, and his cracked door was letting in some of the darkness from the hallway.

Reaching to toggle the desk lamp up a notch, Jim spared another glance at the screen, and considered how the electronic missive there might represent an end to his search, maybe even to his much longer and abiding search, the one around which his whole career revolved: the search for things that were true. He sighed and shook his fingers out of his lap.

His Miss Steckler would be reliable in bringing back . . . well, whatever it turned out he was buying. *But it must be the Manuscript, simply must.* This man who had written, calling himself only "F", was uncannily detailed in describing the document's contents. He either had the document, or he knew enough about it to front a good forgery. Either way, it was worth the money. It was only money.

Settling his fingers on his keyboard to compose his response

– just to confirm the arrangement, one more time – Jim looked again at the time-stamp on the mail. His anonymous correspondent had replied to his last mail less than one minute after receiving his.

Home is the Place

The raindrops fired out of the clouds in parallel lines, the splashes of their misty termini speckling Miles, who leaned against the wooden railing of his patio and daydreamed.

He was home early tonight. He'd stripped off his cuffed cotton trousers, and black boots, and everything down to his cotton boxers; and then he'd put on some music, cracked a frosty one, and turned on the laptop. It sat on the living-room floor and glowed in the premature darkness of the storm.

The patio, facing the parking lot, bordered by the railing which supported his elbows and beer, seemed a sort of womb to Miles. He had been getting quite comfy when, through the amniotic storm noise, he heard his phone, still on his belt, chirp its text beep. That would only be one thing: work.

He retreated indoors, leaving the door open, and scooped up the phone without looking at it. Settling himself on the floor, he brushed the laptop's touchpad, bringing the screen to life. He logged in. And then the head Unix geek proceeded to make the machines work, again.

When he had finished saving the day – a peremptory reboot of an aging and cranky SCO box fixed the "emergency" – he leaned back and sighed heavily. He looked again out at the storm, and then glanced at the clock on his desktop. *That killed four minutes*, he thought.

He decided to write Celeste again. *What the hell.* It compromised his dignity a little to write her twice in a row. But he was intrigued. And deeply bored.

The Grind (Drama Management Part 2)

Celeste studied the droplets on the window, wondering how she had become a passenger in the back seat of an automobile. It wasn't the ride that took her to the edge of panic – though driving in Manhattan was often an exercise in taking one's life in one's hands. It was the company.

It was generally the company.

The sleek and silver Pontiac Trans Am wiggled its fins and tail and cut through the narrow channel of Broadway, leaving a wake of pedestrians, slower vessels, street garbage, and dank air. In its belly were three sailors in suits, and Celeste. The latter listened to the former, blustering:

"I took the letter into his office and put it on his desk, just sat the fuck down. Not a word."

"That's cold, Dodge. Are you promoted, or fired?"

"Hang on. So White says, 'Maybe you'd be better off working for NSA. This looks like a good offer.' I told him I'd either be working for NSA on Monday, or I'd be heading up operations in London. One of the two, I didn't care which."

"You're so full of shit, Dodge. But we're sad to see you go. When do you ship?"

"Next month. Get my stuff in order. I've needed to get overseas for some time."

"Yeah."

"Where'd that asshole learn to drive? Watch out."

The car ramped over a slick hump of an intersection; Celeste slumped in the velour seat. She didn't know which would kill her first, the driving or the conversation, but she prayed one would finish her off quick. One day soon, she promised herself, she would learn to turn down office lunches, and theater invitations, and walks in Central Park, and stay in her apartment instead – enjoy the misery of solitude, avoid this more maddening sort. *Avoid being annoyed.*

Sometimes she felt it just wasn't her lot to get on with other human beings. Surely she would end up as one of those bitter old witches living in the big house on the mountainside (what was she doing in Manhattan?), with a pointy fence guarding 120 desolate acres. Or on a little patch of desert island real estate, perhaps. She'd heard such castaway havens were for sale in the Caribbean. She'd read *Tar Baby*. She could dream.

More than her future, though, Celeste pondered her past. She had long ago figured out that Darwinism handily explained most important human behavior. The inexorable sociability of humans was an easy one to pin down in evolutionary terms: the raging individualists amongst our ancestors, the ones who trekked out into the jungle on their own, eschewing the comfort and safety of the tribe – those guys all got eaten by sabertooth tigers, or stomped by mammoths. They didn't stay alive long enough to procreate and spawn us (or anybody else). We descended from the ones back in the clearing, holding hands and singing songs around the campfire.

All of which led Celeste to wonder which genus of lizards, or tribe of Atlantis, or interstellar raiding party, had spawned her seed.

Even more depressingly, the question was neither fair nor accurate. She had gone to dinner with these guys, hadn't she? And she'd do so again, despite her hundredth petulant pledge to stop subjecting herself to this. Over and again, people proved more trouble than they were worth. Except for – *bzzz* – except for people who were God knows how many thousands of miles – *bzzz* – God knows how many thousands of miles physically removed. She tilted her phone out from between the velour and denim – incoming e-mail. She meant the people she met online, those few she could deal with, scattered haphazardly around the globe, loosely connected by 45 megabit per second Ariadne's threads.

Chin on chest, she gazed down at her waist: "From <darken@

boatanchor.tjc.edu> Subject: Very Non-Urgent." Celeste used a filter that forwarded to her phone any incoming mail with the word "urgent" in the subject line. *Hmm, looks like I'd better rethink that heuristic.*

"Celeste, are you going home, or back to the office?"

"Wha—? Home, please. Just drop me home, thanks."

Back to the keyboard. Back to the physical solitude, and the virtual camaraderie. Back to the interactions that don't annoy – or, at least, are easily terminated when they do.

* * *

From: Miles <darken@boatanchor.tjc.edu>
To: celeste@gloac.com
Subject: Very Non-Urgent
Date: Thu, 21 Oct 2004 19:14:11 -0500 (EST)

Hey, again. Speaking of jobs -- what exactly is a "Global Acumen"? Sounds like, maybe, some kind of consulting? What do you do there?

Earlier you mentioned your annoying coworkers. Here's something that might help. We were having a similar discussion a couple of months back, and somebody posted a typo: "cow orkers".

"*Cow orking?*" the cry went up. "Is that even legal in this state?!" Ever since, people in the workplace are always referred to as cow orkers. Particularly when you're not getting along with them.

I tell you, I've had the oddest week – and that's even on top of my correspondence with you. It started on Sunday, with a friend of mine telling me that her masters research project is, basically, to discover the fundamental secrets of the universe. Tall order, huh? Don't ask me to explain – I don't understand it myself. But then again, I can't seem to stop having weird dreams about it either. I hope she finds what she's looking for – I for one could use some answers right about now. Do you ever have those weeks where each little act of the cosmos seems to be demanding some explanation from you about what you're doing? And why?

I don't know, it's strange. You go through life thinking you're making the right decisions for yourself, odd though they may seem to everyone else. But you like them -- right up until something goes wrong. Then, first bit of trouble, you immediately chastize yourself for not having taken the better traveled path.

You think you're making compassionate decisions, as well. You like to think that you can protect everyone, save everyone, be there for everyone. But one day, you try to do something for yourself -- and find you've trespassed against someone terribly.

Shit, I don't know what I'm babbling about, sorry. It's been an odd week. I hope you're doing well.

Miles

Celeste watched the lights come up on the little cityscape on her monitor. The default module of her now-ancient screen saver, "Starry Night", depicted a minimalist urban skyline after dark. Celeste had never felt any need to install anything more elaborate. This one had a spare beauty to it.

When she left the mouse and keyboard idle for ten minutes – as she had while staring at Miles' message – the monitor faded quickly to black, then relit slowly and delicately, individual pixels firing up one by one. In the bottom third of the screen, little window rectangles of lights formed into larger rectangles, buildings, and groups of buildings. In the upper portion of the screen, lit pixels impersonated stars and constellations. A single, desolate, flashing beacon sat atop the tallest building, warning off little screen-saver jetliners that would never come.

The best part of the module had, unfortunately, been lost to advancing technology. Every five seconds or so, a shooting star would arc ephemerally across the starry dome. The program had been written, however, years before Celeste's computer was manufactured, before clock speeds of 2.4 gigahertz were dreamt of. So Celeste never saw the shooting star. It moved too fast for the human eye now. *Another melancholy sacrifice on the altar of progress.*

She swiveled in her chair, and decided to take herself out. Not for the disturbing, comforting warmth of other bodies, she told herself, merely for the frothed espresso drinks.

She tucked the Bersa, slipped on her topcoat, and locked the apartment smoothly.

She arrived at her destination, just three blocks over, before the cold penetrated her coat pockets, going for her gloveless hands. At the familiar counter, she ordered her quad non-fat latte, and pulled off her coat as she waited.

Celeste looked up to see the girl behind the counter holding her drink, gripping the cash register, and staring stunned at Celeste's waist. *Oh shit* – she'd taken off her coat, revealing the butt of her pistol thrusting out of her waistband. *How stupid was that?* She pulled out her shirt-tails and shrugged meekly. She paid, took her drink, and ascended the narrow staircase to the loft.

At the top, she paused as multiple pairs of chess players turned to assess the beautiful newcomer. She grabbed a seat, tossed her hair off of herself, and raised her head on her slender neck, scanning the two rooms, one above, one below. She drank deeply from her tall glass and contemplated the other people.

She felt the caffeine hit her bloodstream, and thought about this Miles Darken character, and his questions. Another nice thing about Net friends, they were more easily lied to. She could claim to be in "sales" or "brokerage" or whatever, without ever having to explain 4am phone calls, trips to the office on major holidays, and unscheduled fifteen-day overseas trips. She considered the oddity of finding herself in two newsgroups with the same guy. She didn't do a great deal of Usenet, and the groups she did read reflected her fairly eclectic interests. So, with many millions of people on 20,000 groups, the odds were against her running into the same person twice. Unless, of course, that person had been specifically looking for her . . .

What if someone had staked out her online hang-outs? Maybe her habit of posting to Usenet was a liability. Doing so sent her name and e-mail address, as well as information about her habits that could be used to profile her, shooting around the globe. Maybe the company needed an Internet usage policy. Maybe they needed to change their provider, get everyone a new user identity. Maybe—

Then she remembered *she* had initiated the correspondence with Miles Darken, after seeing his post in rec.guns. Just as he had seen her question on alt.quotes. Still, she knew that a clever competitor, or government agency type, someone with good moves, might post something he knew would interest her, try to draw her out. Maybe he didn't own a Bersa at all.

And how did she know he had really authored the quote? He could have just made that up!

And what kind of a name was "Miles Darken"?

Oh, fuck it, she was never supposed to be underground, anyway. If she got made online, that compounded an existing hazard. It didn't create a new one.

With that thought she finished her drink and exited, glowing slightly.

Stepping onto the walk, Celeste scanned the street, and remembered an acute need for shampoo. Turning left rather than right, she headed toward the ole corner store. Bell ringing on the glass doorway, the narrow entrance gave way to a candy rack on the left, counter on the right. She squeezed by a fuzzy-faced, ponytailed, thirtyish white man with a six-pack; a young, overweight black woman with a jumbo bag of chips, a six-pack of Pepsi, two plastic-wrapped sandwiches, and a fistful of food stamps; and a woman her own age with two large bags, cat food and cat litter. She surveyed the group, carefully not looking at them as she brushed by. An Hispanic couple debated cookies in the left-most of three aisles. A fat man in a hat stood at the magazine rack in the right-most aisle, debating adult magazines with himself.

Assessing none of these people as a likely threat, Celeste let her guard down to "condition yellow", as relaxed as she ever got in public after dark. She took three steps up the middle aisle, selected a bottle of White Rain, and turned back to the people in the front of the store. *Don't hate me because I'm beautiful.* The words ran through her head as if spoken by someone else. She squinted at the white man, Hispanic couple, black woman.

And then, in that small space of time, the light in her field of vision went inexplicably thick and white. Shapes blurred, lines softened. Sound fuzzed. Motion wound down. And everything, and every*one* she saw seemed unexpectedly vulnerable, and sympathetic, and just numbingly, unbelievably sad. For no reason she could grasp, suddenly Celeste knew that these other human beings were the farthest thing from "threatening" one could dream up. Their flesh was hers.

And she could feel in her bones, as if she had lived their trials, how difficult and dangerous and hopeless and burdensome life must be to all the *other* people. She saw the history of Life on Earth laid out before her, there in the store, and she could see what an awfully bad deal it was for all the humans not endowed with her gifts and charms and health and money and blessings and intelligence – the 99.995 per cent of humanity, across the planet, and across time, who didn't have it nearly as good as she did. She suddenly realized she had hit the jackpot in the Karmic Super Grand Sweepstakes.

And she didn't deserve a whit of it. She didn't even appreciate it.

Holy Shit, she thought, tearing up, marveling that none of this had ever occurred to her in her twenty-eight oblivious, pretentious years on this lonely, orbiting stone. What a strange revelation to come to her, totally outside of any context. What a stupid thing to be thinking now.

And as she collected her change, only one thought remained: that she would never silently curse her cow orkers again. Her animosity from the car went up like ignited gasoline vapor.

By the time she hit the sidewalk, the light had just about gone back to its normal color.

The Cleaner

Twenty-five blocks north of the ole corner store, in a twenty-four-hour gym, late-night basketball held thrall. On the sidelines of a clean and well-maintained court – rubber floors, good lighting, all four nets intact – several young spectators watched a one-on-one game. Two youths, both black, both wearing shorts to their knees and two-hundred-dollar high-top sneakers, faced each other on the court. Neither had yet seen his twentieth birthday.

"I'm goin' to da tenth floor, and droppin' you off at da eighth," taunted one.

"Bring that shit, black," replied the other gamely. He spread his feet, guarding the basket.

The man with the ball head-faked right, then crossed over his dribble and drove left. The defender stayed with him, but found himself backed up a half step too far when his man pulled up for the bank shot, which rattled in.

The crowd went wild, a half dozen youngsters on the sideline hooting appreciatively. Gold chains rattled around their necks, and their nylon tracksuits rustled. White teeth shone through dark lips. Fans high up in the walls, six feet wide, thrummed to life. The basketball rolled straight and patient out of bounds, and one of the spectators stooped, smiling, to retrieve it.

The two players bumped fists, top to bottom, grinning and shaking their heads.

Somebody whistled appreciatively.

And then the muted sound of gunshots – five of them, at even intervals – zipped into the gym.

The eight youths, suddenly very small in the large room, paused for a very heavy heartbeat. And then each of the eight, boys and girls together, dropped their grins and reached for their guns.

"Uh oh," said the man holding the basketball in one hand, a pistol in the other.

"I heard that, G. Sounds like game time."

Riiiinngggg.

"Hello."

"Hello, Noel. It's Anthony. Have I caught you at a bad time, Noel?"

"No, Anthony. No, it's not a bad time."

"That's good, Noel. So. I have work for you. The job would be for this evening. Do you think you will be interested in working this evening?"

"Yes, this evening is fine."

"Fine, that's fine. The client is a young man, a young Negro, and he will be playing basketball at a health club uptown. It's a nice place, the BodyWorks, at 90th Street on the East Side. Do you know where that is?"

"I know where 90th Street is."

"Fine, Noel, fine. I'll be sending a courier over with our client's portfolio in a few minutes."

"Okay, Anthony."

"Good, Noel, good. Take good care. Goodbye."

Click.

"Motherfucker! Motherfuck—"

Slap, slap, slap, slap.

The force of the four rounds knocked the young man over hard, and his body slid ten feet, painting a bright red streak across the white locker-room floor. He slid past the last locker in the row and into the open area of the showers. Beneath the first shower nozzle, another youth – the one who had gotten taken to the hole a few minutes earlier – stood frozen, holding a large automatic handgun, directing the barrel toward the corpse at his feet. The wide, dead eyes of his friend stared up at him.

He stood frozen with parted lips, feeling the silence return. He tried to blink the fog of shock from his head. A young life filled with violent episodes had not inured him to seeing his whole crew wiped out, or prepared him for being stalked through his own health club by some motherfucker he hadn't even seen yet. *Well,* he thought, *I'm going to put out some fucking rounds, at least. I paid enough for this gun.*

He stepped over the corpse and rounded the corner, swinging his arms and gun straight down the direction of the blood trail. *Pow, pow, pow!* Chips of cement sprayed from the wall opposite him as he fired, and a shadow crossed the edge of his vision. He stopped firing, his instinct telling him to move. Wherever the shadow had gone, it wasn't in front of him, where he was shooting. He leaned forward and sprinted down the aisle, and sprawled headlong in the blood slick. *Oh, fuck . . .*

A foot came down on his right wrist, his gun hand, and he felt something hard in the back of his neck. Noel leaned over him and listened to the ragged breathing of the young man, stared at the back of his glistening neck.

Riiiinngggg.

"Hello."

"Hello, Noel. It's Anthony. How was work tonight?"

"Work was fine. I'm done."

"Good. I'm glad you're done so quickly. Because there's new work. Some very important customers have asked for you by name. You remember the Christmas job last year?"

"I remember."

"Same people. Same compensation. New work. It's only that . . ."

". . ."

"Well, there's travel involved. I told them that you don't like to travel, that you don't leave the city. But they're such good customers . . . I told them I would ask you."

". . ."

"It's not far, Noel. A few hours by car. Down south. Virginia. They'd provide a car."

". . ."

"Think about it, Noel. Can we at least block your calendar for the next couple of weeks?"

"Yeah, okay, Anthony."

Craters on the Moon

Miles rolled the car through the semicircular drive in front of his building, Dana riding shotgun. The branches of the hard-woods reached down to caress them, and the moon sat fat and brilliant over the row of houses. They were back from a last-minute run for costume accessories for the evening's coming debauch.

Dana looked across at Miles' angular profile, while Miles looked skyward at the lunar orb. "And, see, here's the thing that gets me," he segued from nothing, squinting up at the heavens. "Like, twelve billion of us, give or take, have walked around down here. Guys like Plato, Alexander the Great, that frozen Cro-Magnon dude. Cleopatra, Mayan priestesses, Jesus the Nazarene, serving wenches in eighteenth-century East End London . . . your Richard Burton guy. Twelve billion of us. And you see that thing up there?" He pointed at the glowing disc overhead. "Every one of us has looked up at that. That very physical object. That. *That.*" Miles jabbed emphatically.

"I see it," Dana assured him.

"But do you?" Miles went silent, looking down at the dash.

"What's wrong, honey?"

Miles paused before answering. "I don't know. I never know." He looked up and down the street, deserted and quiet. "Usually it's just this sort of low-grade uneasiness – about this job of mine, about living in Hookeville, being single, childless, all these little decisions that have added up to a life, as it's termed. And I think this specific, everyday disquiet is maybe overlaid on top of a much deeper, more generalized existential unease. And so these two quiet rumblings sit on top of each other, one in a high frequency, the other low, and they sometimes create big harmonics. Of course I ask myself, 'What am I still doing in this sleepy little town?' But the scary part is the way that question rhymes with, 'What am I doing on this whirling, wet rock?'"

"That's been everyone's question, Miles," Dana said, giving his arm a squeeze. "That's why religion is Earth's number one industry. Thus the appeal of philosophy, as well. Maybe even art."

Miles arched his brows and stared into the middle distance. "Well, none of those three have answered the question. Not for me, at any rate."

"Which question, Miles?" She could see his jaw clenching in the dimness.

"'How do I live?'" he whispered. "The question is 'How do I live?' It's as if something is missing. Like a pattern I can't quite make out. Something that I don't know its name."

Dana stretched her legs out in front of her and looked down at her lap. She said, "Don't get too down for being confused, Miles. It's natural enough to feel that way. You know, to an extent, we just have the wrong evolutionary makeup for the lives we find ourselves leading."

Miles looked across at her, expectantly.

"You want to know why you feel out of sorts? Like something's missing? Well, think about it: for ninety-nine per cent of human evolution, we lived in small nomadic bands, hunting and gathering on the African Savannah. And we haven't evolved any since then. This blip of agricultural society has not had time to register, much less the little sliver of the industrial revolution on top of that. And the information age? Please. Miles, you sit in a beige cube and stare into a liquid crystal display for eight hours a day. You walk amongst anonymous crowds and send *e-mail* to keep in touch with your family and lifelong friends. You think your brain has any hardwiring to cope with any of that?"

Miles kept silent.

"The whole fabric of modernity is foreign. And so, ever since the Greeks, we've been trying to figure out what's wrong. What's missing. And trying to figure out, as you say, 'how to live.'"

"Plus, as you said the other night . . . the big questions don't even have answers."

"No, they seem not to."

Miles twisted around, retrieving a bag from the back seat. "Come on. We've got to get ready."

Dana paused and frowned a little. Miles worried her when he got like this. She thought maybe he made life harder than it needed to be, which of course was already plenty hard enough.

Miles, for his part, had already moved on to thinking there was no way he could possibly conceal a firearm in his outfit for the party.

Pimps and Hos

Rate Sheet

Service	*Hourly Rate*
1. Gazing fondly and telling convincing lies	$20
2. Foot massage/tickling	$25
3. World-Class Cuddling™	$50

Miles' fingers danced across the keyboard. "Can you give me a hand with this?" he shouted into the next room. "Or are you still painting yourself?"

"I'm still working. I want to be a presentable pimp for you. You know appearance means a lot."

4. Manual stimulation $75
   Up to 3 orgasms included free.
5. Full cunnilingus service $100
   Unlimited orgasms. Wandering hands, add $25.
6. Tongue bath, full body $100

"Okay, take your time. No problem." Miles grinned, fingers darting expertly, creative juices glistening on his eyeballs.

7. Intercourse $200
   Choose from 5 standard positions, Western techniques only.
8. Full-service intercourse $500
   Unlimited positions, all esoteric techniques, pick and choose from our extensive menu – best sex of your life or full refund guaranteed.
9. Custom fantasies *call for price quote*
   Complete seduction package tailored to your specifications, including exotic locales, the best in romance, exquisite foreplay, and mind-blowing sex – even convincing pillow talk. No fetish or fantasy too bland or bizarre.

"Well, could you maybe just sign off on this before I print it? You're going to be the one handing these puppies out."

"Sure. I'm done." Dana walked in. "You get ready while I proofread."

Miles went for the Print button, but pulled up short as a window scrolled from underneath his rate sheets. The electronic mail slot was flapping, and Miles felt the same little surge of delight that always came in this moment, never dimming even after thousands of such moments. New mail.

From: C. Browning <celeste@gloac.com>
To: Miles Darken <darken@boatanchor.tjc.edu>
Subject: re: Very Non-Urgent:
Date: Fri, 22 Oct 2004 20:14:11 -0500 (EST)

>You like to think that you can protect everyone, save everyone,
>be there for everyone.

Well . . . say the words, break the spell.

Thank you, by the way, for your messages from yesterday. I confess that, somehow, your words (and jokes) have made me feel less alone. I also wonder if our somewhat uncanny connection online hasn't prompted a bit of a mystical experience I seem to have had. I won't get too Carlos Castaneda on you; but suffice it to say, in a single strange moment, I found myself feeling a lot more one with all of the other people on this planet – the ones who are normally annoying the crap out of me. It was striking – so much so that I feel as if I need to do something to honor it. Something . . . ennobling. I don't know what.

Ah, well. I hope your weekend brings you peace.

Fondly,
Celeste

Dana's arm snaked around his neck and her perfume settled around him.

"What's this?" She gestured at the mail message on the screen.

"Somebody I met online."

"Well, flirt later. You're late for work. Remember who works for whom, please."

"Yah, boss." Miles slipped his T-shirt off. Dana stood close before him, looped a black silk bow tie around his neck, and began tying.

"Where'd you learn how to do this?" he asked, watching her intently.

"From the ho before you." She gave him a little slap to shut him up.

The two followed each other up the stairwell out of the basement apartment and into the still night. Dana wore a charcoal pinstripe suit and tortoiseshell eyeglass frames. She'd pulled her chin-length hair back into an efficient knot and carried a fountain pen and a black business binder stuffed full of the rate sheets Miles had printed on glaring yellow paper. Miles wore tight black trousers, clunky black boots (the same ones he wore every other evening of the year) and the bow tie. His black hair, growing long, swept back from his forehead and hung on his neck. Thirty push-ups before departure had swelled up his biceps a bit.

"I'm freezing," Miles said, hugging himself.

"You're the one who refused to wear a coat. Even for the walk over." She pivoted her torso and rubbed his arms vigorously. The phosphorescent lamplight glinted off of his shoulders and Dana's hair. It was cold and quiet.

It was hot and loud when they arrived at the 14th Street Pub, for the annual (regulars-by-invite-only) Pimps & Hos Party. Good thing it was private, as the crowd was by no means fit to appear in public: leather miniskirts and leather vests, lace garters and leisure suits; quite a lot of bare flesh. Miles maneuvered to the bar for drinks, making a channel for Dana.

"Hi, kids," grinned the barkeep. "What can I pour you?"

"A big nubile blonde, with thighs like an iron vise." Dana pinched Miles' arm for that comment and handed the bartender a rate sheet. He laid it on the bar in a puddle and read as he poured, roaring with laughter a few seconds later, as the meaning of the document registered.

A bearded man in a terry-cloth bathrobe brushed by them, following on the four-inch razor heels of a woman on a leash. Aside from the heels, the woman wore only a black thong bikini bottom and fluffy nipple tassels. Both of them got rate sheets.

"Hi," Miles breathed, as the pair brushed past.

"Hey, there," said the Bathrobe Guy and the Nipple Tassel Woman in unison, as they submerged into the crowd, laughing aloud as they read. Miles and Dana's gender inversion of the sex worker relationship seemed to be going over well.

Miles felt a tug on the hair on the back of his head and craned his neck back, of necessity. Looking over his own shoulder, he saw a cascade of loose brown hair, a hesitant smile, and a great deal of very smooth, white skin. It was Paulina, wearing a lingerie ensemble – bustier, camisole, and garters. Her figure was wonderful.

"Hey there, you," Miles managed.

"Hi, Paulina," Dana said. She handed her a rate sheet. "Of course, you get friend prices."

As they dawdled at the front of the line, the bartender shouted at them to "take your damned drinks, you sex industry gougers".

The Buy (Dana)

Cold and clear – a perfect central Virginia late autumn night, blocks of illumination from above falling metallic, still, and heavy; the crystalline wash of human breath picking up some of the glare, before flaring and speckling out, firework-like, into the darkness.

Only a couple of hours after arriving at 14th Street, Dana had slipped out of it, alone. Now she moved through this night, across a landscape picked out by heatless street lights. She ascended stone steps, skirted the corners of a looming Jeffersonian building, and was startled when she caught her own reflection in a double-paned window. Trapezoids of light from the building anointed her in turn as she sloped onward, hands in pockets, wordless, head shrouded in the halo of her breath.

Fraternity row lay just ahead.

Miles and Paulina stood close in a corner of the pub, just outside of range of the makeshift dance floor. Occasional limbs, cats o' nine tails, and other appendages and appurtenances slapped into them, as the dancing throng swayed. For a half hour, the two chatted about the sort of forgettable things one chats about when one is really thinking about romance. After a while, Miles thought to ask, "Where did Dana get off to anyway? Have you seen her?"

"She said she had to run out for a bit."

"What for?" Miles asked, looking concerned.

"She didn't say. But I did get the impression she didn't want you to know about it."

"Why not?"

"She thought you'd be worried about her."

"Smart girl," Miles said. "But very stupid of her going out alone at this hour."

"Don't worry. She said she's just going across campus. Want to go for a walk outside?" With that, Paulina gave Miles an unmistakable smile. He smiled in return, forgetting for the moment to worry about Dana's safety.

Dana picked up her pace as the cold began to seep in. She moved from a narrow sidewalk into an ill-lit parking lot. Light from two windows spilled out of a large house; faint music leaked from somewhere deeper inside. She picked her way up the winding foot-stones and mounted the porch. She thumped on the letters ABT, which peeled off the door in red flecks.

Creeaaakkkk.

"Hey. You must be Dana . . . Nice suit you got there."

Miles and Paulina strolled their second lap around the block, arm-in-arm. Miles continued to make suitably witty comments, and Paulina continued to be charmed by them. When their humor had turned almost completely to sexual double entendres, she stopped and turned to face him. Putting on her best naughty vixen expression, she asked him, "So, are you really the cradle robber Dana makes you out to be? Or is it just the reputation you like to keep up?"

Miles laughed. "Oh, I haven't dated anyone too young for me in, oh, it's been days."

Paulina smiled. "How old is too young for you?"

"Nineteen's about right."

"And how old are you?"

"Twenty-four."

"Okay," admitted Paulina, grudgingly. "I suppose that's a decent enough indecent gap. And one last question: don't you live near here?"

Miles issued a silent promise to himself to stop complaining about living in a college town.

The man facing Dana in the fraternity house doorway wore a sparse Van Dyke beard, flannel, and a bandana over messy blond hair. He projected a spittly lower lip, a red-limned squint, and a slightly suspicious expression. After he had scanned the horizon to its left- and right-most edges, his face reflected a favorable decision and he gestured toward the interior.

"Well, y'all come on in."

And then he led the refugee from the Pimps & Hos Party around the perimeter of the ground floor, past some desultory partying, and down a cluttered and nearly dark corridor. The two then ducked into a bedroom that was awfully tiny to be cluttered with so much crap.

It was also cluttered, Dana saw, with two separate, magnificently slouching, black guys.

"Hey," the fraternity guy drawled smilingly as he pulled the door closed. "Dana, this is my man T-Bone. T-Bone, this is Dana." Dana struggled to make out the first figure in the dimness. She saw a twentyish black man wearing jeans, a too-large pullover sweatshirt, another Van Dyke beard, and an expression of partial ease. He raised his chin at Dana and issued a solemn "'Sup?"

At first Dana thought T-Bone was the one she'd been instructed to meet. But then she saw a droopy and scowling puddle of dreadlocks and baggy jeans in the far corner of the room. This one was dressed as Dana had been told to expect. The fraternity guy turned theatrically in his direction, rubbed his scruff significantly, and introduced, "Jean-Michel. *The man with your bag.*"

In the glare from the one bulb in the room, which generated more shadows than light, Dana could just see the cappuccino-skinned youth with dark rope for hair, poor posture, and a red duffel bag under his chair. The bag; her bag. He, and it, sat in the small space on the other side of the waterbed.

"Well," said Dana, trying to smile, "I'm the girl with the envelope." She reached into her inside jacket pocket and removed a thick tan package.

Wordlessly scanning faces in the room, Jean-Michel gingerly laid the duffel on the ululating surface of the bed and eased the zipper open. Dana could not yet make out the contents. She stepped forward, holding the envelope before her.

Then, without preamble, the door blasted in powerfully behind her, knocking her to the floor. A voice shouted something over her head. And then gunfire erupted very, very close to her, a sound like trains. Glass crashed. Dana clutched the floor.

Miles held Paulina's hand as they walked, perhaps a little too tightly.

"I'm a little worried," he said, "about leaving without telling Dana."

"You," said Paulina, smiling up and across at him, "should cut that umbilical cord. You two haven't been together for four years."

Miles sighed. "It's not like that," he said. "But we're still very close. And I worry."

"Then it *is* like that," Paulina riposted, reaching up and running a hand through his loose hair.

"Okay, you're right. Guilty as charged. Anyway, I'm sure she'll manage to get home safely by herself, one night out of the year."

"She manages it most nights, coming home from the computer lab. Is this your building?"

* * *

More hollering; Dana thought she heard the word "police". She'd only just dared to peek over her own forearm, and then the gunfire began again, like cold hands, three feet away, violence displacing the air of the room, pressing her down with an evil weight. Her mind overloaded and shorted out, she focused on the feel of the cool wood floor against her cheek.

Then a single beat of silence. She opened her eyes, and a body hit the floor in front of her face. Dana sprang to her feet, away, in horror, as if fired from a gun. Nothing else in the room moved. A night breeze came in through the empty window pane.

Miles turned the bolt-lock behind them, drew breath, and rubbed his shirtless torso. He looked toward the kitchen, thinking about a nightcap; and toward his laptop, thinking about maybe quickly checking mail. He told Paulina to make herself at home – which she did, in the bedroom – and that he'd be back in a minute or two.

He logged in quickly. No mail; including no mail from Dana. He stared at the screen for a few seconds, wearing a vaguely hurt expression. A distant but distinct popping sound drew him out of his seat and to the window.

"That's gunfire," he announced, still shirtless, striding into the bedroom.

"Or frat boys with fireworks," countered Paulina, undoing buttons and lowering herself to the futon on the floor. "Now come to bed. That is, if you're quite done with e-mail." Her brown hair spilled over a pale shoulder as she shrugged out of her coat.

"No, that was a nine millimeter and, maybe . . . a forty-five," Miles insisted, reaching into the night stand. He removed and opened a small plastic box.

"My God. Is that a real gun?" Paulina asked. But Miles had already padded into the living room, flicking off lights in his path. Paulina sat stilly, legs tucked beneath her.

Returning to the bedroom, Miles peeked out through the

blinds, then laid the gun on the night stand. He went down to his knees on the futon, reached out, and brushed Paulina's bangs behind her ear. Holding his gaze, she asked, "Are you going to leave that thing out?"

"Does it bother you?"

"I don't know. I've never seen one in person before. Actually, I guess it's a bit of a turn-on."

"My kind of gal." Forgetting again about Dana, Miles lay down on the futon and moved close to her. He reached up to kill the last light – and to give the gun a little nudge where it rested.

Part Two

"Close! stand close to me, Starbuck; let me look into a human eye; it is better than to gaze into sea or sky; better than to gaze upon God."

— HERMAN MELVILLE

The Buy (T-Bone)

"My mother was a beat cop in New York," said Theron "T-Bone" Johnson, stroking his Van Dyke beard and pulling at the gun under his baggy sweatshirt. "I grew up in Harlem, took the train to the Bronx High School of Science. The thing was, it wasn't exactly easy to be an *inconspicuous* Bronx Science student. It was like, every other day, guys on the next platform going, 'Oh, look, Bronx Science motherfuckers. Let's fuck those boys up.' It wasn't me so much, I was just the only brother for like forty blocks in any direction riding the train with a white boy and a Chinese boy. So, I knew those train tunnels, 'cause it was like, if you *didn't*, and found yourself at the end of some tube, and no train coming just then, you got your ass beat.

"Of course, that was in the good ole days, back when you just got your ass beat, but walked away from it. What you want to know all this about me for?"

"'Good ole days'? How are you, T? What, like, twenty-two years old, you went to school like in the late nineties or something?"

"I'm twenty-five, smart guy, and yeah, I went to high school in the nineties. So? What's up? Your wizened, Geritol-taking, slow-moving ass got a *problem* with that?"

"No, T, I got no problem," answered James, Theron's partner, from the driver's seat of the sedan they shared, parked just out of view of the fraternity house. "I'm glad you're here, and I'm glad to be here *with* you – and I'm glad it's your GenX ass who's going into that building and not me."

"Yeah, well, it's going to be your Boomer ass what's gonna

have to come in and back me up. You got that earplug in good, right? *You can hear me, right?*" Theron shouted into his cuff: "*Hep! Come get me! These drug dealers are fuckin' me all up!*"

"Yeah, I can hear you just fine. You just keep your shit tight in there, okay?"

Theron exhaled. "Yeah. I've got to get to the gig. Back in a flash." He slid out of the seat and pressed the car door closed behind him.

The clean moon peaked around the steeple of the house, and Theron's breath glowed around him. He walked briskly fifty yards down the dark curve of the road, rounded the corner of the structure, then stopped in the shadows and the gravel. He took a chill breath, patted himself here and there, and put his hand to the colorless door on the side of the house, above the letters *ABT* painted in red. He knocked five times.

"T-Bone! What up, brother?" Theron turned a wry smile on the white face that greeted him. The youth wore the same beard as him, tracing the mouth with a fine light fuzz. He ushered Theron in with an understated excitement. Theron twisted his neck left and right as he entered.

Theron'd had to shoot the shit for three games of foosball before the connection finally showed. Foosball was preferable to pool, as it didn't involve leaning over a table, a dicey maneuver for a guy with one handgun in his waistband and another in an ankle holster. And a badge in his pocket.

The connection had finally come in the back door, to much clandestine aplomb, and Theron recognized him from surveillance photos. It was the connection that Theron wanted. Not even the connection; the connection's boss. And that guy's boss. Always up the food chain.

The three now sat in the fraternity guy's shithouse bedroom, only one of them talking.

"Yeah, man. She'll be here. Midnight. Any second." The fraternity guy shifted on the edge of his waterbed. "Y'all want a beer?"

"No, man, thanks," Theron answered.

"I'm gonna, I'm gonna go out to the door. She should be here any second."

"Right. Cool," said Theron.

The connection sort of nodded, from underneath his dreadlocks. He and Theron sat looking in other directions for about two minutes, at which time the fraternity guy slipped back in. He had a chick with him. He introduced the chick to Theron and the connection. Theron didn't know the chick.

She and the connection started to do a deal on the bed. Theron could just make out white stuff; that was good.

Somebody kicked in the door, somebody shouting, "Federal agent! On the floor!"

Federal agent? What the fuck federal agent? Theron moved his hands toward his head, having no desire to get shot by interloping feds. His eyes stayed on the door, which was bouncing off the chick's ass and slamming closed again. The guy outside was still outside. Then the door lit all up, gunfire behind Theron, loud as fuck, ten rounds in a row, splintering the wood of the door jamb. The connection was blazing away, not an instant's hesitation. Then, after the ten, five more rounds – Theron watched these ones slap into the fraternity guy, and the fraternity guy go backwards out his own bedroom window, as if yanked on a rope.

Theron pulled his gun from his belt holster and pivoted. Before him was the connection, hunching and scowling, the magazine from his nine hitting the floor, and another one slapping in. Theron pulled his hammer back and shouted one shout, "Police!" But the connection's slide just dropped forward with a crisp crack, good to go. So Theron pulled his trigger, opening up, as did the connection. They sat eight feet away from each other, blasting away.

Theron felt a weight on his thorax like a half dozen vises, his vest squeezing the life out of him. His breath went away and he tumbled off the edge of the bed, onto the floor. Twitching, he looked down his body and saw a splash of blood on his arm. And just beyond that: the face of the girl.

He passed out.

"*What happened here, Theron?*"

Theron rolled his head from left to right. He recognized his partner's voice, through cotton.

"What happened, T-Bone?"

"Dreadlocks dead?" Theron whispered, trying to look to the other end of the room.

"Yeah, man." Again, urgently, "What happened?"

Theron snorted. "Yo, I have no idea. Where's the chick . . . ?"

With that Theron passed out again. James held one palm clamped on the young man's wound – north of the seven slugs in his vest, where one high shot had hit him in the collarbone – as he waved in the EMT crew with their gurney.

How did this happen? he thought dazedly. *And what chick*?

The Wake-up Call

"Good morning, Miles."

"Is it morning . . . ?"

"In some cultures. Not yours, I gather."

Paulina gazed glowingly into Miles' slowly opening eyes from a few inches away. Then she put her head into his chest and snuggled against him. He traversed her bare skin beneath the sheet with his fingertips.

"I think I'm young again," he declared.

Paulina was still spluttering her laughter when the phone rang out shrilly from the next room. And again, and again, and again, and then there was a *boop* and then Miles' hissy voice said, *Hello, you've failed to reach Miles Darken, as will often happen when using a primitive communications technology like telephony . . .*

"Who would be calling at this hour?" As Miles rose from the bed, Paulina threw him his boxer shorts, which landed on his head. Shrugging them off, then on, he tromped out.

. . . Feel free to leave a recorded message, but if you're serious about reaching me, you'll send e-mail instead. Send it to—

"Hello?"

"Just take it easy, doll. I'm not getting any of this. You were where? You don't really mean 'dead'? . . . Oh, Jesus. Fuck."

Paulina leaned around the corner of the living room, wrapped in a sheet, sporting concern. She had a guess about whom Miles was speaking with in such frightening terms. He seemed to call every woman "doll" at intervals, but he always called Dana that. She snuggled up to the wall and listened as calmly as she might.

"Jesus. What are you going to do? Where are you now? I'll be there in fourteen minutes. Don't move, don't go anywhere. I'm coming right now, okay? Okay, bye."

Miles looked up at Paulina. He was too adrenalized to look or feel affectionate, even under the expectancy of her gaze. She wondered if Miles' devotion to Dana, his tendency to take personal ownership for her happiness, was ill-afforded. From her first impressions, he seemed to be teetering on his own perfectly crumbly brink half the time already.

She did smile at that thought, and Miles grinned back at her, misunderstanding. He was dressed in a minute.

"You don't mind letting yourself out, do you?" he asked.

"That's fine. Are you going to tell me what's happened to Dana?"

"As soon as I get the details, you'll be the first to know." Miles kissed her on the forehead, which made him seem old to both of them. And then he was gone.

The Buy (The Fed)

In a darkened gravel parking lot, federal agent Stanley Luther rolled his car to a quiet stop. He shifted in his seat, unsnapped the seat belt, and adjusted a handgun tucked in his waistband. Opening his laptop on the seat beside him, he woke it up and watched approvingly as a video window, and other digital telltales, came to life. He scanned the empty parking lot and listened to a prop plane buzz by in the night. He checked his wristwatch.

Moving light from the video display drew his gaze down again. In a crowded room, replicated in fish-eye grayscale and shadow, figures stepped in from the edge of the frame. "Showtime," Stanley whispered to no one.

He turned the door handle and swung out onto the asphalt, the overhead bulb from his car spilling an irregular yellow shape onto the gravel. He pressed the door closed behind him, then trotted two hundred yards down the lane, finally disappearing into the shadow of the fraternity house. He opened a side door and slipped inside.

Navigating from memory, he found the room at the end of the hallway, the door closed. He put an ear to the wood: voices. He pulled his piece with one hand, and an ID with the other. He took a deep breath. And he put his foot into the door, just beside the handle, his full weight behind it.

The door gave way, and Stanley followed it in, shouting, "Federal agent! On the floor!" But the door only flew two feet before banging into something solid, and swinging back at him, knocking him back into the hallway. He paused and shook his head, dazed. As he stood there regrouping, shots blasted out, rounds tearing through the wood of the door. Stanley closed his eyes against flying splinters and thought, *Whoa, guess that saved my sorry ass . . .*

He retreated six steps down the hallway and went into a

crouch, head cocked. The shooting had stopped, but then resumed, two guns this time, in different calibers. Then it was over again. Stanley didn't move for a full minute, considering the advisability of going into that room.

Figures appeared at the end of the hall, unspeaking and wide-eyed: fraternity guys.

"Stay back, police," Stanley growled, waving his ID vaguely. Faced with this audience, squirming, Stanley finally moved into the room, gun held stiffly forward.

A sulfur and cordite stench washed over him, and he found himself standing directly over a body. A black guy, one he didn't recognize, with a big Colt auto near his outstretched hand. Then Stanley saw an arm poking up from the other side of the waterbed. He rounded on it, and found another black guy, very pulpy-chested, wedged between the bed and the wall. This would be the traveling drug salesman. Movement drew him back toward the door. Passing by the window, he looked out and saw the white kid lying on his back in a pile of glass shards, his chest also a big pulpy mess, his expression betraying belated confusion.

Turning back to the first prone figure, by the door, Stanley saw him lolling as if trying to come to. He leaned over and examined him more closely. In addition to the auto, he had a snub .357 on his ankle. He'd also been shot through the collarbone, and – what's this? – several times in a nice Kevlar vest under his pullover.

Sonuvabitch. Stanley dug in the man's back pocket and fished out a leather fold-over, keeping one eye on the unconscious figure. He flipped it open.

"Johnson, T., Narcotics." *Fuck.*

Well, that explained the shoot-out, of all the rotten fucking luck, but where was the bag? He began tossing the room. Hidden under the blood-flecked folds of the blanket he found a single brick of cocaine. *Must have gotten lost in the shuffle.* He picked it up and spun it in his palm. On the opposite side he saw masking tape and drawing in greasepaint, unfamiliar symbols. He peered intently in the dim light, making out writing of some sort, in some unknown language. He pocketed the brick.

Now figures appeared in the doorway, crowding in. Stanley flashed his ID again, said, "Get the fuck out, police," and finished his sweep of the room. No trace of the bag, nothing on the courier but his piece, which he wouldn't be needing, and the cop still comatose. He found the tiny cylindrical camera on the bookshelf where he'd left it, and dropped it smoothly into his coat pocket. "Nine one one," he offered to the slack-jawed crowd, on his way out the door, starting the jog back to his car.

He emerged onto the street, tucked his piece in his belt, and darted between two squad cars zipping into the fraternity house parking lot, lights and sirens whumping away. He regained his car, pulled out smoothly, and accelerated out of town.

One good thing about this backwater, he considered. *I can be in a nice deserted horse pasture in five minutes, and look at this tape.* If the bag was gone, there must have been someone else in the room at some point. And Stanley almost certainly had that person on candid camera.

He picked a desolate field, killed the lights, and rolled off of the rural route. He yanked the laptop off of the floor where it had fallen, and repositioned it on the seat beside him. He rewound to the last point he'd seen, that of figures entering the room, then played it forward at half speed. He could see the courier, the cop, and the kid, sitting, doing nothing. He sped it up, until the kid rose and left the room. Stanley slowed it down again as he re-entered – with someone in tow.

A slight woman, or girl, with short, light hair stepped into the frame. Some gesturing went on, and then there was the bag, laid on the bed by the courier. The mystery girl produced an envelope. And then the door flew open. In a flash, the courier had a piece in his hand, blasting away at the entrance. (Stanley thought how odd it was to be watching the other side of the scene he'd lived through only a few minutes earlier.) The girl hit the deck, electrically. The white kid, though, raised his hands in front of him, palms out; the courier pivoted and fired on him, and he went out the window, ass first.

Now the cop was armed, and the courier was reloading. (Magazines in and out, nice moves.) And then the pair blazed away at each other, both of them going over on their backs.

And finally . . . the girl sprang to her feet. She stepped tremblingly toward the window. She paused, and looked back at the bed where the bag lay. She grabbed it by one strap, and turned – and with that she, and it, darted out the window.

Damn. Stanley rewound a few seconds, then went through the next frames one at a time. *C'mon babe, show me a little smile* . . . Sure enough, the girl looked at the camera as she turned back to the window, giving Stanley exactly two frames of her face, one blurred, one okay. He grabbed a screen shot and, while the GPRS modem connected, he typed out a mail message:

From: SLuther <sluther@remote1.dct.nsa.gov>
Subject: ID
To: r-lab@dct.nsa.gov
Date: Sat. 23 Oct 2004 03:09:32 -0500 (EST)

Need an immediate id on this woman, residence Hookeville VA, probably an enrolled student at Thomas Jefferson College.

Thanks,
S. Luther

He attached the image file to the message, clicked on Send, and disconnected.

After that, there was only quiet and dark and fogging windows. Shifting in his seat, he felt the pressure of the squishy brick in his coat pocket. He removed it and held the writing up to the dash light. He did not find it any more intelligible than before.

The Bag

Miles shot a look at his watch, not breaking stride. The watch face glinted at him in the thin and slanting 6am light. He winced and kept moving through the cold, quiet morning. He focused not on his discomfort – he'd never seen 6am before and didn't like the look of it so far – but on making good time, as he walked briskly to the rescue. His destination: the TJC Philosophy Department.

Miles topped the last rise and rounded on the hulking building. The morning sky began to blanch and a few creatures, mostly the flying variety, chirped a small welcome. To Miles, it seemed a morose overture.

He pushed through the swinging doors and took the stairs two at a time. He found the Philosophy Department lounge, which contained a wall of cubby-holes, a rack of journals, and two couches – one of them with Dana on it.

Dana was all knees and chin and bangs and burning cigarette. And a little smeared mascara and blood. Small and unmoving, still she stood out in her suit, and mop of red hair, and small palpable halo of tiredness and tragedy.

Miles knelt before her, and she drooped onto his shoulder.

Miles held up a hand to stop Dana's verbal torrent. He took a measured sip of coffee. He said, "One thing at a time. Just start from the party." Dana's voice caught in her throat, and she turned away, looking out a window.

The two sat hunched over coffee cups in a twenty-four-hour diner. Miles had steered them there mainly because he direly needed caffeine, and because they obviously had some debriefing to do. And because it was the only place Miles figured to be open.

Miles reached across the table to dab at the red and black stains on Dana's face, while she gathered herself. And then she did her best to explain to him what seemed to have happened to her.

The two ventured back to Miles' apartment an hour or so later, by which time, mercifully, Paulina had left. Miles did not relish trying to explain to her what Dana had just explained to him, any more than he wanted to explain to Dana why Paulina was at his place at that hour.

In the diner, Dana had told her tale, and fielded Miles' questions as best she could. But Miles hadn't found her answers hugely helpful. He attributed the gaps in her narrative to shock. Despite Dana's phlegmatic manner, Miles had managed to learn that she had been on an errand to pick up a copy of her Manuscript thingy at the ABT house, and that something deadly had transpired there. Something with gunfire, and with the police; and with a dead body. And with a bag of something that was not remotely the something Dana had gone there for.

Now they sat quietly in Miles' living room. "The bag, please," Miles directed. Dana loosed her grip on the duffel – which she had been clutching under her arm since Miles found her – and passed it across, her hand shaking. Miles pulled on the zipper.

"Well, fuck me right in the ear," he managed. He reached in and produced a taped-up, plastic-wrapped brick of white powder. It weighed maybe two pounds. There were four or five of these inside the bag. Miles shook his head and exhaled. "I, um, I don't believe these here are your religious document. Do you think?" Dana monitored her feet in silence. "Dana, you have *got* to explain to me how you ended up with this."

She sat hunched over, still not meeting his gaze. "I don't know. I . . . I thought it was the bag I was supposed to be picking up. It was red, with white straps. After all the shooting, when I got up, it was just sitting there on the bed. And I'd been thinking so much about how I wanted this whole thing over. I couldn't leave without it. Other than that, I wasn't thinking, not at all. I couldn't."

Miles went to the couch and sat down beside her. "Okay, that makes sense. But I still don't understand how the bag could turn out to be full of drugs, like, this trust fund of cocaine – instead of a twelve-page document, which is what you were supposed to be picking up."

Dana shook her head. "I don't know . . . Some kind of mix-up, maybe, something . . ."

"We'll sort it out." Miles touched Dana's shoulder. "Everything's going to be okay."

"I'm not sure it is," Dana said, and with this she choked on a sob. "There's something else," she managed. "Something I didn't tell you before."

"Well," sighed Miles, "it can't be a whole lot worse than everything so far."

"After I grabbed the bag and went out the window," she managed, "I ran, just ran, flat out. I found myself on the quad. I sat down beneath some trees, just to catch my breath. But I didn't get up for an hour. When my strength finally came back, I made my way home. Inside, I saw my computer across the room, and I realized something was wrong with it. The screen was on. That is, the screen saver *wasn't* on. It turns on after thirty minutes. Someone had to have touched the mouse or the keyboard since the night before. Someone had been there in the last thirty minutes."

Miles' brow now started going for his chin, dire concern sitting all over him like a shroud.

"So I turned right around," Dana continued, "and went to the department lounge in Campbell. I knew I could get in, and it was the only place I could think to go. I crashed on the couch for about five hours. And then I called you."

Miles agonized acutely at the thought of intruders in Dana's apartment. But he was very clear about one thing, given that fact. "This has to go back," he said, touching the bag.

Dana looked up at him. "Back to who?"

"To whoever was supposed to be selling you the Manuscript. That person almost certainly owns this stuff. Or knows who does. And we need to find him. Ideally, before he finds us."

"I don't know who he is," Dana said. "I was never in contact. Only Jim was. By e-mail."

Miles perked up. "It was arranged by e-mail?"

"Yes."

"And Castrolang is a faculty member?" Miles rose and disappeared, returning with his laptop. Dana looked meekly on. "Guess who's got root on the server with his mail on it."

"You mean you can read his mail?" Dana asked. But Miles only typed, furiously, in response. Dana added, "Why is it so important to return this? Do we have to?"

This got Miles' attention. He paused in his typing and turned to face her with a patient and concerned look. He said carefully, "Yes, Dana. Yes, we do." If she was a little confused about why they had to return this bag, Miles was painfully clear on the subject. "I expect it's worth a fortune. And whoever owns it knows you've got it." He refrained from adding that, only an hour after she took it, someone had come looking for her in her apartment – and only by luck hadn't found her there.

Dana sat quietly while Miles interfaced with the machine. He logged into the primary mail server, changed to root, then changed to user castrolang_j and opened a mailer. There wasn't much there, so he found the relevant correspondence quickly. Mainly, he was looking for an e-mail address. It turned out to be an address at an anonymous remailer, a service located in Finland that forwarded mail, stripping it of all identifying information. Miles shook his head, switched back to himself on the system, and pasted the address into a new message. And he began composing a carefully worded message. The basic theme was: *Oops, our bad – now, how do we get your property back to you?*

He launched the mail and leaned back on the couch. He took a deep breath, then looked across at Dana. She still sat motionless, staring blankly. Miles watched her, worried, for thirty seconds or so, before looking back to the screen. A response had come in. "Holy shit," Miles breathed. "This guy is on." He moved his hands back to the keyboard and responded to the response.

From: <darken@boatanchor.tjc.edu>
To: an8465407@anon.penet.fi
Subject: Re: returning the goods
Date: Sat, 23 Oct 2004 09:09:23 -0500 (EST)

an8465407@anon.penet.fi wrote:
> How do you propose to return this "property" to me?
> I've found the USPS often has issues with delivering
> these sorts of materials.

Heck, we'd be happy to bring it right to you, if it will get this settled. Just tell us where to go.

Miles

When another response came back, a minute later, Miles turned to Dana and he asked her, "So – how would you feel about getting out of town for a day or two?"

"Sounds fine," she answered dully.

To Miles, they had every reason in the world to be somewhere other than Hookeville right then. Firstly, to return the bag. Secondly, to get Dana far away from whomever was out prowling around for her. At first, Miles had thought about going to the police. But he quickly remembered they were already involved – they'd been at the fraternity house. And so had Dana, looking for all the world as if she were buying a large supply of drugs. To Miles, ducking out for a few days while things cooled off seemed a markedly better plan than trying to explain that one away . . .

Flight

Miles emerged from his apartment into the late morning, two bags slung over his shoulder. He let Dana out and patted himself down for keys. He found them in his jacket pocket, along with one of Paulina's undergarments. Someone had a real sense of humor. He shoved the bit of silk and frill back in before Dana caught sight of it. But she seemed to be in her own world anyway.

Miles figured it to be about seven hours from Hookeville to New York City.

Before achieving an escape velocity from town, though, they first ran by Dana's apartment. Miles led them inside, his gun in hand. There was no one there; not in the closets, not in the shower. Miles peered unsmilingly out of windows while Dana packed two small bags.

Nearly the whole trip passed in silence. Miles periodically scanned out of the corner of his eye at the disheveled mop lying limp on the passenger headrest. He knew that he would surely protect that mop no matter what, and he doubled his resolve as the overhead lights flickered to life and arced by. Still, thoughts of their rendezvous – and the unknown quantity with whom they were to meet – simmered below his placid surface.

"Got it all taken care of," Miles said, attempting to reassure one or the other of them. "Wrote the guy. He was very reasonable; we agreed on everything." Dana did not respond. "A classic case of cooler heads prevailing. We drop this thing off, then spend a few days amusing ourselves in the city." Miles drummed on the steering wheel. "Guy seemed very reasonable. Bit of a computer geek, if I'm any judge. Somebody I can deal with. Rational guy. Albeit named after an operating system."

Another hundred miles up the Jersey Turnpike from Miles and Dana, a twenty-five-year-old dreadlock-festooned hipster sat in his remarkable digs, sucking on a cigarette and a quad espresso from the big bronze machine behind the bar. That device had cost him fifteen hundred dollars – and worth every penny, he thought as he slurped rhythmically, in time to the techno soundtrack that rattled the beads in the doorway and bounced the disco ball in the dim light.

A powerful voice rumbled up from behind him. "Boss. I can't get hold of Jean-Michel."

FreeBSD nodded his head in time to the beat and glanced around drolly, principally at the several half-naked teenage girls happily dancing about. One of them sat down on the couch and cuddled up. "Hey, baby, how do I look?" she asked.

"You make every other girl here," FreeBSD drawled, "look like five miles of bad road."

"No *Jean-Michel*, no *money*, no *product*." This was the annoyingly serious voice behind him again. A dangerously built black man, with a glyph shaved into the back of his afro, rounded on the younger, paler man on the couch.

FreeBSD couldn't avoid addressing the man now; he took up his whole visual field. "I swear you're coming down with the shits, the fits, and the blind staggers, Ace. Well, if Jean-Michel's run off, we'll just tear his limbs off and fling them into the middle of next week." FreeBSD jumped up, pulling the girl with him, and began to dance frenetically. He leaned over to stub his butt on the marble coffee table, hopped over it, and danced off with the nubile sixteen-year-old.

"But what the hell," he shouted over his shoulder, shuffling off into the disco-lit dimness, "he can pick them up on Wednesday! ON WEDNESDAY, HA HA HA . . . !" Ace took several deep breaths, then galumphed off.

FreeBSD – it stood for "Berkeley Standard Distribution", a popular flavor of Unix, though in certain circles it could also be expanded as "Big Swinging Dick" – started up a fair version of the hustle as the looping soundtrack shifted. FreeBSD – ex-chemistry student, ex-sysadmin, highly successful online narcotics salesman of late, all-around carefree and fun guy – generally preferred not to be in the business of giving a shit about things. In this case, though, regarding the disappearance of his courier, unfortunately he gave rather more of a shit than he cared to let on.

As far as Ace or anyone else knew, Jean-Michel hadn't had more than $50K worth of product on him when he left. And if he got nicked on his sales call, he wasn't nearly stupid enough to sell out his boss. But then, that was only the story FreeBSD had fed Ace. In reality, rather more money than that was on the table. And much, much more than money was at issue.

FreeBSD whirled wildly to the music, trying not to think about Jean-Michel's disappearance; or about the mind-wrenching shit he'd been reading on his laptop; or about this random bozo it seemed was driving all the way up to *return the disappeared bag*. It was an awful lot not to think about.

The Datsun rumbled rhythmically over the crooked bridge slats, and the horizon began to go fuzzy with the sunset on their left. Miles and Dana stopped at another silent tollbooth, paid, zipped off, and saw a sign for the Holland Tunnel – less than an hour from the city.

"Hey, you know something else," Miles added, apropos of nothing, after an hour-plus silence, "I've also got this new friend in New York, someone I wouldn't mind seeing. Maybe we'll drop her a note." Dana had drifted off. Their luggage, swept over arcingly and endlessly by the passing streetlights, bounced on the back seat. There were two overnight bags, Dana's backpack, Miles' laptop bag – and the red nylon duffel with all the liberated recreational chemicals.

The tunnel loomed.

Die, Punks

T'ien Ken stood in the hallway, waiting, right in the inset doorway. In addition to the door, the doorway held a card reader, a doorbell, and a little wooden plaque. The plaque read:

> There is left, there is right, there are theories, there are debates, there are divisions, there are discriminations, there are emulations, and there are contentions. These are called the Eight Virtues.
>
> Welcome to the POTEV

The doorway was otherwise nondescript, as was the hallway, which led to nine other doorways. Most of these other doorways had doorbells and a couple had card readers. None of them had graven wood plaques.

Commercial office space actually worked out well for the Angry Young Taoists, because they generally showed up in the evenings, a couple of hours after the other tenants had cleared out for the day. For all practical purposes they had the building to themselves.

The words engraved on the plaque beside the door came from the *Chuang Tzu*, the number two tract in the Taoist canon. POTEV was a not-entirely-unsayable acronym for Palace of the Eight Virtues, which was what Kenny wanted to get into, standing out there in the hall.

Some shouting came from behind the door. Kenny leaned forward. He could make out, through the very thick wood, the faint but emphatic intonation, "I'm going to kill you, bitch."

He squinted, unmoving, head bent forward. He heard, muted, "Sorry about your head."

He removed a white plastic card from his back pocket and swiped it through the reader. He'd already swiped it once. And he'd rung the bell three times.

Kenny wore black Levi's 501s which fell to the second eyelet of his black fake leather shoes. Tucked into the 501s he wore a Fruit of the Loom V-neck cotton T-shirt. Over that, a loose black genuine fake leather jacket hung open, down past his hips. On his smooth chest, in the V of the T-shirt, lay an emblem on a hemp loop which looked like this:

道

He continued to hold the white keycard gingerly between thumb and forefinger and to lean tentatively forward. He heard, "Fuck."

Shan sprinted to keep up with Abhijit. The hallway twisted sharply, then again. He was having trouble keeping his eye on Abhijit's frenetically moving ass. But the two emerged into the courtyard together. Stepping out, Shan pivoted right, panning the barrel of his shotgun across his field of vision. He knew to go right, he always went right. Abhijit would be going left, and would have that side of the courtyard covered.

All was clear.

They advanced, roughly side by side, to the archway at the other end of the courtyard.

"Go," he said and the two sprinted out in tandem, firing wildly.

A single figure appeared ahead of them, picking up something in the corner. As the shooting started, the figure turned tail, making for a nearby doorway. Shan watched as Abhijit pursued the figure at a flat sprint, spraying rounds. Shan paused. He couldn't see anybody else. He could only see the one guy. Where was the other guy.

Angelo perched on the open ledge. It was only one storey to the ground, and wouldn't hurt him a bit if he fell. But he did not want to lose this position before he made his shot. He lined up the tube of his rocket launcher; his target stopped dead in the open. Angelo adjusted his aim, lower, toward the feet of his target. One always wants to aim for the feet with a rocket because then even a near miss will do the job – the rocket will explode on the ground, doing almost as much damage as if it had hit the guy square. With a near miss on a head shot, the rocket might sail right by him and blow up a hundred yards away. Angelo smoothly depressed his trigger.

Abhijit cursed under his breath as the fleeing figure gained the doorway. He should have had him, out in the open, but he'd gotten anxious. A couple of his rounds had gone home, though. He'd seen the tiny splatters of blood.

Abhijit gained the doorway and peered in. He saw a narrow section of corridor, and flashed a big grin – because he had the freeze thrower. Still grinning wickedly, he put his chain gun away and pulled out the fearsome freeze weapon. He opened up, and dozens of shiny globules rocketed down the corridor, ricocheting wildly and tirelessly.

Shan screamed obscenely as he died, his body accelerating into madly hurtling pulp. The force of the rocket sent him arcing high and wide across the clearing, and as he flew he could see Angelo standing up on the ledge, and he could swear he could see him smirking his ass off.

When the front door at long last opened, T'ien Ken was greeted by Naja in person, who tried to voice her apologies for keeping him out on the stoop. But her little voice was no match for the explosions, gunfire, and smack-talk echoing through the suite.

"Die, punks!" Shan bellowed as he reincarnated, grabbed a weapon, and sprinted through the virtual texture-mapped corridors.

Video game carnage was in full swing in the POTEV.

"I'm going to set some limited hours on this shit," muttered Naja, shutting the door behind them. She, T'ien Ken, and Laylah were alone in the relative quiet in the administrative office. "I'm under some obligation to provide a safe and non-threatening work environment here."

"What?" Ken chirped. "You're kidding. Everything we do is unsafe. That's why it's fun."

"Oh," Naja shrugged. "I meant here in the Palace. Workplace harassment, that kind of thing. Somebody could sue me for having to listen to people shouting, 'I'm going to tear you a new asshole, you punk-ass bitch!' during work hours."

Laylah, seated at a computer station, and Ken, still standing, stared blankly at her.

"Never mind," she disclaimed. "How'd it go?"

"I was the bomb," Kenny answered in his stilted hipster idiolect. "I walked right in like I was the Maytag repairman. I got passwords, and planted the radio router tap in the machine room."

"Cool," said Naja, obviously pleased. Kenny had gone on-site at an uptown law firm. This firm had done quite well lately defending companies engaged in various environmentally disastrous practices upstate and in Long Island Sound. The strengths of this law practice tended toward tying things up in court, burying evidence of malfeasance and noncompliance, and paying off judges and prosecutors where possible.

T'ien Ken had been charged with doing a little digital bugging and he had showed up at the front desk of the law firm's offices claiming to be from Comp-U-Friends, the on-call, by-the-hour computer support service to which they subscribed. On the strength of this assertion – and a forged business card they'd Photoshopped and color laser printed in thirty minutes the night before – he'd gotten the password to their file server, unescorted access to their server room, and free glazed doughnuts.

Kenny glowed in the recounting of it. Before he finished, though, Laylah was back at her computer screen, scrolling through a page of text. Kenny sat on the edge of her desk and asked, "And what madness are you working on, chica?"

"Oh, a little greenmail," she smiled, her eyes glued to the screen. Her voice was thin, pretty, and mischievous. "Nothing nearly so exhilarating." She flicked her mouse, whipping its tail into Kenny's black-denim-covered thigh, which had encroached on her mouse pad. Kenny shifted out of the way. As she repositioned the mouse, the white tattoo on the inside of her wrist became visible for a second. It showed the same symbol as Ken's neck adornment, with the words "Tao helps you do great things" above and below the image.

"Good for you," he said. "Who are you working?"

"Movie producer."

"What do we have on him?"

"Oh, you know, the usual. Drugs, prostitutes . . . sleepovers in the White House." She walked Kenny through some of it, while Naja leaned tiredly against the inside of the door, absorbing with the back of her body the muffled sounds of weapons fire.

On the other side of the door, Mike and Angelo were down.

This wasn't, if you looked at the score, Angelo's fault. Angelo was a very solid player. It's not clear that military training is helpful in first-person 3-D "shoot 'em up" video games. But Angelo just did seem to have very good instincts, and a palpable coolness under fire. He seemed always to be in the right place at the right time, see you coming before you saw him, and make his shots in tight situations.

Mike was a bit of a problem player. He didn't have great control of the mouse and keyboard, particularly in crisis situations. If he was caught by surprise, or charged by an opponent, his aim would swing drunkenly from side to side as he manically overcorrected with his mouse movements. Also, he didn't really have the knack for "strafing", the side-stepping maneuver so crucial in shooters.

In the end, after Angelo's pretty good numbers got diluted by Mike's pretty poor ones, Mike and Angelo spent a lot of nights getting routinely clobbered by Abhijit and Shan. But they never could convince those two to mix up the teams. Abhijit and Shan just had to run together.

The pair had come up together, four years at Georgia Tech in Atlanta leading to a sometimes contentious but very committed lifelong friendship. Abhijit came there for a masters degree in computer science, from the University of New Delhi. Shan was on the home stretch of his seven-year undergraduate career in electrical engineering. They'd started speaking in the video arcade of the student center, where they frequently ran into each other around some of the more destructive games which they would share in two-player mode.

After graduation, Abhijit had ended up working in an insurance company in Connecticut, while Shan started doing six-month contracts overseas. Abhijit's job had been quite slack and he spent his days corresponding with Shan and his nights in New York City, exploring and carousing. Ultimately, he hooked up in person with some of the alt.religion.taoism.angry people. By the time he met Naja – and they began seriously planning their new enterprise – Shan had just finished another contract and was looking for something to do. The pair reunited in the city, now partners in crime.

"What up with the Manuscript?" T'ien Ken asked, when he and Laylah had run out of reports.

"Oh, that," said Naja.

"I thought we gave up hope on that last spring. I know I did."

"Well," sighed Naja, "we know at least two other people are out there looking for it."

"The TJC girl?"

"Yep. One Dana Steckler." Naja recounted from memory, "Twenty-three years old, graduate student, red hair, and pretty anorexic looking, ask me."

"You've got a picture? What, from a yearbook?"

"No. It was on the web. The Master's Program in Medical Ethics."

"Cool. We get her mail?"

"Not really. Shan did get into the box at TJC with her account. But she uses a POPmail client, so most of her mail is downloaded to some PC somewhere, where we'll never dig it out. But she did have a few interesting text files lying around, including one with her log-in information for another account, on a different machine. She's user 'dollface' on something called boatanchor.tjc.edu."

"Heh." Kenny laughed. "And she's looking for the Manuscript? Maybe she'll find something we missed. Or have better luck than we did."

"And we'll be there when and if she does," added Laylah.

"Not if we don't get off our asses and stop playing video games," amended Naja. She arched one brow and stared at the ceiling, pondering how to get Shan off his carnage crack pipe and into the admin office to plan next steps. "Do me a favor and go into administration for the router. If I'm not back in one minute, turn off all traffic to and from Shan's machine. I think he's .233."

Naja marched out the door and down the hall. She put a hand on Shan's shoulder. She could see him flying around with a jet pack, firing rockets at a figure on the street below, and cackling. She said, "Need you in the office, Shan. Need to talk about the Manuscript." Getting no response, she waited thirty seconds, at which point the fleeing figure on the ground disappeared into thin air, and a cursor prompt and "Out of Sync" error message appeared at the top of the screen. He'd been cut off, courtesy of remote network administration. He turned to face Naja, looking out of breath, uncomprehending, and vaguely hurt.

"Come on, Shan, it will be quick and painless. And afterwards we'll go out and have a nice dinner, some Thai or something. If you're really good, we'll walk back the bad way and try to attract some muggers." Shan got up mutely and followed her. Abhijit watched them go.

White, Black

From his office, Mr. White looked out onto the floor of Global Acumen. His door stayed open. This didn't mean everyone felt comfortable walking through it, but that was the suggestion, with the door being open. His office was larger than everyone else's, but not hugely so, and spare. A map of the world hung on the wall behind his chair. Laptop in a docking station, wired to a display and a network jack low in the wall. No window. Even the GA offices on the exterior of the building had no windows.

White tabbed through mail with the fingertips of his left hand. With his right he scratched his chin. He considered how well things were coming along under Celeste. Though it was transparent to Mr. White that what Celeste would really love, in her heart of hearts, would be for her staff to just leave her alone. But she was learning how to be in charge.

Mr. White had had to learn this himself. He had not had a whole lot of normal-person type experience out in the world. Running Global Acumen was only the third job he'd ever held.

From age twenty-two to age thirty-two he had worked for the United States federal government. He hadn't gotten into government work by any very exciting circumstances. He'd simply started talking to some guys at the CIA table at the campus job fair at the University of Colorado, where he'd just earned a degree in International Relations. Shortly after, he went off to Washington for ten years. Though in fact, he had spent little of that time in DC, or the US, or the Western hemisphere for that matter.

He hadn't, suffice it to say, ended up in a desk job.

On the night of the tenth anniversary of his federal employment, he sat in a candlelit and nearly empty studio apartment off of DuPont Circle, and stared at flickering shadows, looking back and forth between them and his hands, which didn't have any blood on them, but the candlelight and his psychological state were playing tricks. That night he realized he had a career problem, in two parts.

The first part was that he didn't know how to do anything other than what he did. He didn't feel optimistic that he could learn how to do anything else, nor that he could get a different job doing it. For all practical purposes he had a ten-year hole in his resumé. If he so much as made conspicuous reference to what he had been doing at the Agency all that time, and anyone in the Agency caught wind of it, they would come and lock him up in a room and throw away the room.

So this was the first part of his problem.

The second part was that he could not continue to do what he had been doing. He hadn't been killing or hurting anyone, not really, not directly. But he had personally and single-handedly made a great deal of killing and hurting possible. During his years there, the Company had been making bad things happen to people on a large scale, mostly in Central America. White never, or almost never, pulled the bad-things lever himself. But he often wired up the lever.

And on a June night ten years down the road, looking down at his red candlelit hands, he figured he wasn't going to wire up those sorts of levers anymore, after that day.

So that was his second problem.

The reason for his confliction about this decision was that – aside from the fact that he didn't have a whole lot of other conspicuous career opportunities – he *liked* what he did. He was, as his employers well knew, very good at it. He liked moving information, and operating in hostile environments, and figuring out how to make extremely dangerous casts of characters do his bidding. It made him feel alive; it made him feel capable, and powerful, and that he could rely on himself, even in a scrape. And it paid okay.

No, he liked what he did.

He just didn't like who he did it for.

The US might be the good guys in a global, and relative,

sense. But that was a very rough sense. There was just too much ugliness involved in US covert international activities.

When he thought of it this way, it slowly became obvious that there was really only one employer for whom he could do this kind of work, and maybe feel okay about himself and the state of his immortal soul on Saturday mornings, after a full week of wiring up bad-things levers.

So off he went to work for the Israelis for the next ten years.

Sure, the Mossad did almost exactly the same shit as the CIA. And he did almost exactly the same work for them. But the State of Israel happened to be surrounded by twenty-two nations of people whose stated and wholly undisguised aim was, and had been since 1948, to drive each and every Jew in Palestine – man, woman, and baby – into the sea. That pretty much justified any sort of covert ugliness or bad things you could think of, as far as White was concerned, and as far as the Israeli intelligence groups – the Mossad, and Shin Bet – were concerned.

Before going off on this career lark, White had been briefly concerned that the one club he could stomach joining wouldn't have him as a member. The Mossad didn't just hire anyone who knocked on their door with a ten-year hole in his resumé – particularly not non-Israelis, and particularly not non-Jews. But as it turned out, White's experience at the CIA proved invaluable to the Mossad, and, luckily, in a variety of ways that did not compromise US intelligence secrets.

So he'd sounded out his official Mossad contact, through the CIA, about making the switch. Within twenty-four hours, he had packed two bags and gone, without ever going in to work again. For all he knew, that U of C Bison coffee mug still sat on his desk at Langley.

Almost exactly ten years later, the Mossad dismissed him for no stated reason (probably something to do with US–Israeli relations), and he returned to the US as "Mr. White". He then co-founded Global Acumen with an American partner named

John Adams. Adams, ironically, worked for the CIA. The two had met through joint US–Israeli intelligence work (White on the Israeli side).

John was the one with the entrepreneurial and business skills. But unfortunately, he died six months after GA was launched, probably a hangover from his Agency work. White soldiered on – and learned quickly how to run the business. He'd long ago learned how to learn quickly; the trait of learning slowly would not have selected him for survival in his line of work.

White was thinking a lot about survival, and about Celeste Browning, and about his fondness for, and level of commitment to her, as he logged into the central file server himself to go over some documents. He sent e-mail to the new guy Celeste had recently welcomed on board. The firm still had fewer than a hundred people, and White was glad to be close to many of them – and gladder still to have offloaded most of the day-to-day management to people like Celeste. The new guy stuck his head into the office twenty seconds later.

"What's up, Mr. White?"

"What up, black!"

Theron Johnson reclined at a thirty-degree angle, in the accommodating hospital bed. A dauntingly large glass of water perched by his bed, half empty. His mouth still felt dry, due to the anesthetic, which caused awful dehydration. He'd been awake for a long time; they'd taken the tube out of his nose shortly after he'd come to. A paperback lay steepled in his lap.

Theron felt his breathing. Apart from a dull ache across the upper left quadrant of his torso, extending a bit down his left arm, and some tenderness, this all seemed pretty indulgent. He had nothing to do here except just be with himself, think about things. But he hadn't really ramped up the thinking too much just yet. He watched the air, a few dust motes, probably pollen from the flowers, floating in the thin sunlight that bled through the curtains. Everything in the room was white.

Everything except Theron, of course.

The flowers had been sent by the boys. Also a card, crowded on every surface by the signatures of every warm body on the Hookeville force – beat cops, detectives, SWAT, and secretaries. There were magazines, chocolates he wasn't allowed to eat, and books. His partner had left the books, knowing his literary tastes.

Getting shot, operated on, and hospitalized could really be, Theron considered, quite a relaxing experience. A good sleep, some quiet time. Sympathy flooding in from all directions.

And he wasn't angry. Getting shot, he considered from his very quiet and philosophical place, was just one of those things that happened sometimes. He'd figured it would happen to him eventually. Heck, he'd thought it would happen before he was even sworn in, in his youth. He felt pretty relieved, really, that it had been such a manageable episode of getting shot. Bullet in and out, cracked the collarbone as it breezed through. A little torn tissue. All the surgeons did was sew up the two holes and give him some blood and antibiotics. Wanted to keep an eye on him for a day or two. He was just a little sore, and dehydrated. And a little tender across his chest and abdomen. From all the other bullets.

He didn't think too much about how he might be feeling if the vest hadn't been between him and those other rounds. That's what the vest was for. That's why he wore it. Almost all of the time.

The hearty "What up, black!" had emanated from James' head, sticking around the corner of the cracked door. No James' body, just his head. James, of course, had originally been right by the bed when Theron had come to. He'd been in the hospital since Theron was admitted, until they had kicked him out. Theron had figured he'd be back for visiting hours. His head was back.

"Hey, man," Theron said, in a normal speaking voice, a little on the serene side.

"Got a surprise for you," said James.

"More books?"

"No." He stepped into the room. "The book on your shooter. And the shooter's boss."

"Word." Theron pulled himself more upright. "Anything on the mystery fed?"

"Nothing yet."

James stayed and talked until the other was nodding again, then tiptoed out.

Theron slept all the way through to midday, and then checked himself out – giving both his doctor and his boss no choice but to agree.

Gotham

"You know, we should go to the Statue of Liberty tomorrow," suggested Miles, as he and Dana shivered in a pool of darkness in a doorway at 86th and Central Park West, New York City, New York.

Miles had the red and white bag slung over his shoulder and he clutched Dana's arm, the mist of their breath mingling. It was midnight. Across the street, Central Park loomed black, empty, and terrifically menacing. In a few minutes, they would brave the menace in the altruistic act of giving a bag of drugs back to its rightful drug dealer.

"Get on the ferry, look back at the city, climb all the way up. You know?" He angled his watch toward the light and saw that two minutes had elapsed since he last checked. "What do you say?"

"Sure," agreed Dana dully.

Miles tried to smile at her. Suddenly he felt his age, very old – a few weeks away from twenty-five. He dazedly recalled the events that had led them from Hookeville, scene of their lives, to a pool of cold shadows across from the world's most storied urban park and into which, he remembered someone telling him at some point, in very forceful terms, one should never go after dark.

Four hours earlier, just after sundown, Miles and Dana in the gullet of the Datsun had poured out of the Holland Tunnel, awed by swooping patches of light and crashing waves of sound, Miles instantly overwhelmed by the crisis of driving in city traffic. They were practically on their way out of town on the Williamsburg Bridge before Miles reined in their stampede and pulled to an empty stretch of curb at the edge of the East River.

"Jesus Christ . . ." Miles muttered in regard to his twenty-minute intro to Manhattan motoring, as he rifled the glove compartment for the atlas, wishing they'd planned some trajectory through the city before arrival. As he folded back the page with the detail map, he heard the passenger door open. Miles yanked it closed.

"What are you doing?"

"Getting out . . . ?" Dana seemed nonplussed.

"Do you have any idea where we are?" Miles implored pedantically. He was obviously laboring under some characteristic Southern ideas about New York.

Dana relented and contented herself with swiveling her head around, craning through the windows. Light traffic rumbled by, between warehousey structures that hulked over the water. By overhead streetlight, Miles traced the pad of one finger on the map and quietly cursed.

"What are you looking for?" Dana asked. Miles shot her an annoyed look, but quickly realized he had no idea what he was looking for. Dana's question forced him to confront this.

"I suppose what we need is a hotel," he said.

"One close to Central Park," Dana added. She took the atlas and took up navigational duties.

After rolling north for twenty minutes, they did loops in a few-block radius bordered by Central Park West, until they passed beneath a *Vacancy* sign on a hotel that seemed like it might not bankrupt them. They parked, slung their luggage, repeatedly locked the car doors, and checked in.

Dana lay, bouncing, on the bed nearer the door. Miles smiled a bit despite himself. He dug into his satchel, uncoiled power and phone cables, cleared the surface of the desk, and arranged to turn Room 312 of the hotel into a node, albeit a humble one, of the global Internet.

"Not long now, doll," Miles noted, as he typed away, checking new mail, and reviewing an old one. "Soon we'll be rid of your albatross there," he tossed his head at the duffel bag, which had landed up against a headboard, "and we can relax."

"Okay, Miles."

For a final time, Miles read the last message from his mysterious correspondent.

From: an8465407@anon.penet.fi
Subject: Re: returning the goods
To: darken@boatanchor.tjc.edu
Date: Sat, 23 Oct 2004 23:17:23 -0500 (EST)

Fine, let's do the shit tonight. In Central Park, there's a round hill at the northeast corner of the Receiving Reservoir. Be there at 2am with the bag. We'll call it even.

And so Miles and Dana had a couple of hours to kill, sharing the long, quiet minutes with each other . . . and with multiplying rafts of anxieties . . . and with the dozen or so very sketchy strangers scattered all around the Atlantic seaboard who had all listened in on that e-mail exchange, and were gearing up to go to Central Park themselves.

"We should go," Miles said from the shadows across from the park, checking his watch a last time. The pair squared themselves up, and stepped out.

"Hang on." Miles halted. He pulled his Bersa out from his waistband, dropped the magazine and checked it. He cracked the chamber, checked that.

"You're scaring me," Dana whined.

Miles replaced the mag and the gun. "Sorry. Make sure and stay close to me."

They traversed a black path through the park, foliage menacing them from all sides in stumbling darkness, horror movie dark. Ultimately they reached what Miles gathered to be the right clearing, and emerged onto a wide, round, damp hump of grass and earth.

As they shed the encumbrance of the path and of the total darkness, the moon shook the clouds off, dousing them with buckets of light. Miles and Dana actually shielded their eyes.

Miles scanned the area, trying to augment the safety of his charges: the small auburn-festooned package of woman, and the large white packages of drugs. The area bore a lot of scanning: three hundred dark pointy bushes, five dozen wide trees, two dark grassy knolls, and one pale water fountain, not wide enough to conceal an attacker, but Miles gazed at it balefully all the same.

He was being overmatched by *a park*. Really unfortunate, a park. One must pine for Miles, as he stands humbled by a park, in consideration of the time when all of the bad men show up.

Sixty seconds.

Mark.

Back at the Ranch

"Gotta have rocks in your head the size of Gibraltar to go undercover. Want one of these?"

"Yeah. Gimme the bear claw."

"The what? What the fuck is a bear claw."

"Not important. Let's hear the end of the story."

"Agreed. So, you're in central Virginia's seediest bar, playing pool with the perp."

"That is correct."

12:15pm, and the group of Hookeville cops sat on the edges of their desks, bullshitting and swapping stories. During the lunch hour they could undo their collars, rest their palms on their pistol butts. Shoot the shit.

"So this perp's a big guy. Wearing boots and jeans and this leather vest, no shirt. Lots of jailhouse tats. I'm chalking my cue, getting ready to break. And this guy pulls a nickel .44 out of the back of his waistband, from under the vest. I hadn't seen anything on him. Totally caught by surprise."

"Did you draw down?"

"No. It was too late. I froze. I watch him thump this huge revolver onto the felt. I'm standing there holding my chalk on the tip of my stick."

No one said, "Caught holding your staff, eh?" Bad guys with big guns just aren't an acceptable subject of humor in law enforcement circles.

"But the gun's empty. The guy pulls this one big gleaming hollow-point out of his front vest pocket, pops the cylinder, and loads the round. Slaps it closed, thunks the gun back on the table. And he says, 'If you lose, I'm going to kill you.' No smile, just these black eyes. 'Now break,' he says."

"Please tell me you pulled your badge at this point."

"Nope."

"What did you do?"

"I broke the rack, and ran that goddamn table."

"You did not run the whole goddamn table."

"Bet your ass I did. Have you ever played pool for your life? Later, I got the perp in a buy outside, took him down without even blowing my cover. Went back for his pal the next weekend."

"You're an icy man with twelve-pound steel balls. Taking lessons from Johnson, clearly."

On cue, Theron T. Johnson came through the door and walked the length of the squad room, his arm sling under his leather duster. Conversations went out like spotty radio broadcasts as he went by. He was like a human sunspot. A blackout.

"'Sup," he said as he passed the group.

"Hey, T-Bone!"

"Whassup!"

"How's that shoulder?"

"I'll be fine." He did not break stride, just stretched his neck and smiled, continuing straight into the police chief's office.

"Hey, Chief. Gotta minute?"

"Afternoon, Theron. Come in. Door's always open."

The police station in downtown Hookeville sat about two miles from the TJC campus, where federal agent Stanley Luther was dodging more hay-seed cops. He walked from one end of the quad to the other, looking down, hands in pockets. He thought this pose made him look professorial; and it also poofed his jacket, so his gun printed less.

Uniformed officers and detectives swarmed in and out of Campbell Hall, ducking under yellow crime-scene tape. A crowd of gawkers was growing. An ambulance had driven right across the grass to the door of the building. A uniformed cop stationed outside returned Stanley's look grimly.

He reached the end of the grass and entered the structure flanking Campbell. Several upstairs rooms in this building, he'd noted, had windows overlooking the scene. Finding the stairs, he took two flights, circled back to the front, and picked an office lock.

Bingo. He yanked the cord of the blinds and found himself looking almost straight down on the ambulance. He peered, and pondered his next move. On his first trip after the shoot-out, to the girl's apartment, he hadn't found the girl there, and he hadn't found the bag. Now he found his plan B – to dig up the professor – thwarted by a goddamned police cordon. At the same time that he had gotten the girl's name and address, he also got the news that she worked for the professor. This being, yes, the same professor his Agency job had him chasing.

That is to say, his contract job had segued nicely into his real job.

Although nice was precisely the wrong word for it.

The Agency wanted him to surveil, for reasons unknown, this Professor Castrolang. And his other employers had hired him to snatch a bag from a drug deal; but the drug deal had turned into a Wild West show, and the bag had run off with a girl – which girl, it turned out, *worked* for the same professor. Peering through the glass, Stanley wished that someone, he didn't care who, would be kind enough to tell him what the fuck was going on.

He also really wished he could just find Castrolang; and as he thunk it, he watched two paramedics wheel a gurney out of Campbell Hall, fully covered. Dark streaks stained the white fabric, across the outline of a human shape beneath. Stanley couldn't know for sure the identity of this ex-person, but given the way things had been going – and given the building the gurney had rolled out of – he could certainly make an overeducated guess. It did not appear that the professor was going to be of any help to him, or to anybody, ever again.

Two minutes later Stanley sat beneath a tree in the corner of the quad, fondling his Blackberry. The mail he found waiting from his contract employers did nothing to calm him: instructions to turn back north, three hundred miles further north than he had started out. Evidently, everything that was going to happen in Hookeville had already happened. Next stop, fucking New York.

Stanley figured he was in it now. *Never should have cashed that advance*, he thought.

"So tell me again," asked the Chief, "what you're doing in the station house today?"

"Well, you know," said Theron. "Just trying to keep up with things."

"Keeping up with things."

"The investigation."

The chief looked eerily like a fifty-year-old version of Theron. Both had intelligent coal-black eyes, round close-cropped hair, and carefully trimmed beards. The chief had an extra thirty pounds around his midsection (Theron had just a few that seemed to be looking for company), some gray in his hair and beard, and a lot more care and tiredness in his face. But, otherwise.

"Our investigation is going fine. How is your disability leave going?"

"Can't complain. Got some physical therapy to do. Some video games to play." He paused to check out his shoes. "Any news on the federal agent?"

"No. We've queried DEA, FBI, everybody. No one had any-one working here."

"I hear we've got an ID on the connection. The guy I shot."

"Yes, we do." The chief paused and looked tired. "And I know you already know all of this, Theron – who he is, who he works for, where he's from, all of that. I can't stop your colleagues from talking to you. However – and I don't know why we're wasting my time having me point this out – if you do so much as *ruminate* on that information too intently, I'm going to bust your tail."

When Theron had gotten shot, in some ways it seemed as if the chief took the bullet. Perhaps he related to Theron too closely, just as Theron was too close to the investigation to work on it. Thus he was a few hours into a Chief-mandated four-week disability leave.

"I understand," Theron answered levelly. "Anyways, I just dropped by to let you know I'm going up north for the rest of my time off. Going home."

"Home New York home."

"Yeah. I'm gonna see my mom, get some food out of the deal."

"Why are you saying this to me? Do you think my kids don't talk enough smack to me? Is it your considered opinion that I don't get enough disrespect from the fine elected officials of the town of Hookeville every day?"

Theron, head lowered, had no response to this.

"The disposition of your leave is your decision. But I shouldn't need to note the ramifications for you if there is any police work involved while you are in New York City. Have a safe trip."

Theron left without meeting his gaze. He stopped in the squad room for a couple of quick conversations, notepad and pen held low.

Desperate Times

Miles and Dana strode past the hotel night clerk, he with his head buried in his collar, she smiling and giving the old man at the counter a cheery wave. The clerk, recognizing them from check-in a few hours earlier, returned the smile and the wave, then cocked his head in puzzlement at the red flecks on the girl's face.

Miles gripped Dana's elbow and steered her up the narrow stairs. Emerging from the stairwell, they turned down the dim corridor and reached their door. Miles fumblingly worked the key in the lock. He checked the hallway behind them, then pressed the door closed and locked it.

A mirror hung on the inside of the door. Dana stood looking at her reflection, making no move to clean the light spray of blood from her cheek.

It was all just like before.

In the mirror, she could see Miles clearing crap from the desk chair. He sat down and fired up the laptop. As it booted, the screen described varying levels of brightness, reflected on Miles' face. He pulled the cord from the phone and stuck it in the modem. All of this was reflected in the mirror on the door, in the undulating light of the laptop screen. *Bright; dark; kind of bright; scowl.*

She could see him regaining his composure as he manipulated the computer, jacking in. The familiar machine seemed to have a calming effect on him. She had never before seen Miles without his composure, his intent nonchalance. And that frightened her more than anything. More than the menacing city, more than all the men with guns, more even than her second shoot-out in three days.

She tried to replay the fantastical thirty seconds she and Miles had just lived, on that rounded hill, in that moonlight. But it was already turning to motion blurs, flickering tableaux, in her mind's eye. First a single man had appeared and Miles had stepped forward to meet him. Then, of an instant, there were human figures everywhere, running, converging on them – then diving, falling down. And the noise: shouts, and gunfire, fading behind her as she ran flat out, away through the park, Miles grip locked on her forearm.

She refocused on the hotel room as Miles' modem squelched, then hissed, through the room. Miles lowered the volume, and began typing at his usual frenzied pace, though the frenzy seemed a little more underscored tonight.

It seemed to Dana that she was growing oddly accustomed to all of the sudden blood-letting. She'd never really bought into the idea that people and the world were okay at bottom, and it was almost in some sense a relief for her to witness the facade crumble, within a few feet of her face.

Interestingly, to the outside observer – of whom there was only one, Miles – her manner had not changed with her acclimatization. In the day after the shoot-out at the fraternity house, her shock had kept her insensible, numb, and staring stupidly. Now, her resignation – and serenity from the validation of her vague, lifelong dread – kept her smug, quiet, and staring knowingly. This was a largely indistinguishable state from the first one.

Like smiling at the hotel clerk with her blood-flecked lips.

That was her smugness; nothing was shocking to her anymore, and nothing frightened her. She was all done being frightened and, though that is surely a form of madness, she was relieved. She preferred it to the prior form.

The difference between the two of them now was profound: Miles couldn't really believe any of this was actually happening, but coped as efficiently as he could. Dana thought it all made perfect sense, and didn't really care what happened next.

She flicked on the bathroom light, splashed water on her face, and sat down to urinate, not bothering to close the door. The tinny splashing mingled with the wooden keystrokes.

From: Miles Darken <darken@boatanchor.tjc.edu>
To: celeste@gloac.com
Subject: Re: Very Non-Urgent:
Date: Sun, 24 Oct 2004 02:29:32 -0500 (EST)

Celeste,

Wonder if you're still casting around for that ennobling act . . . ?

* * *

The only light in the bedroom came from the monitor glow, which turned everything blue. Celeste had moved from the bed to the desk when her phone had beeped her awake. Like people will do, she and Miles had continued to recycle the same subject line, and thus his mail continued to get forwarded to her phone. But she had gotten up to read it on the bigger screen. And to fret.

Half of Celeste saw her worst paranoia about the Net in general, and this e-mail dialogue in particular, all coming true. This guy was *in* New York? And he wanted to *come by*? She saw a stupid, not-very-cleverly-laid trap, set out for a Net-addicted operative with a little hollowness in her and a weakness for interpersonal contact. And she saw herself walking right into it. *Just unbelievable.*

But the other half of her still clutched that shampoo bottle in the fuzzy, white light of the corner store, feeling infinite sadness and compassion. In other words, she was experiencing the after-effects of her humanity moment, and didn't feel any too rational. She felt awfully like helping somebody.

Hope you feel like getting killed or kidnapped, she replied to herself. *Self*, she added, *you are a freaking idiot.*

From: C. Browning <celeste@gloac.com>
Subject: Re: Very Non-Urgent:
To: Miles Darken <darken@boatanchor.tjc.edu>
Date: Sun, 24 Oct 2004 02:57:03 -0500 (EST)

At 02:29:32 10/24/04 Miles Darken wrote:
> Seriously. I'm in your neck of the woods right now, New York,
> with a friend, and the two of us are in trouble. An emergency,
> really. I know it's out of the blue, but I need to ask for your help.

Well, what are total strangers for?

> I guess this isn't the ideal circumstance, but would you be
> available to put us up for a night or two? It's me and one
> friend. We can meet you, anywhere you want. Just name it.

There is a 24-hour espresso joint on Broadway at the corner of 62nd. I'll wander in there one hour from now.

Browning

* * *

"Why were you writing to your New York friend?"

"Well, you know, you can't buy a gun in New York. So I'm thinking maybe she'll loan us one of hers." Miles' Bersa was lost, somewhere in the tall grass in Central Park.

The lights were out and Dana lay on top of the covers with her ankles crossed, hands behind her head. Miles peered out through the blinds, where he'd stood for twenty minutes since putting the computer to sleep. Dana neither laughed nor protested at this comment, which unnerved Miles a little.

"'Cause, you know, people on rec.guns, we loan out firearms all the time." Still no reaction. "It's really like a communal armory." Dana *hmm*'d assent.

In reality (or in his internal reality), Miles wrote his mail to try and get the two of them out of that room, out of that hotel. He didn't *believe* anyone had followed them from Central Park. But the old dark building felt like a trap to him. It was too close to the scene of their recent betrayal and rout.

But he hardly needed to write Celeste Browning for that, a fact Miles might have admitted to himself in a more honest moment, one less monumentally panicked and paranoid. They could walk or drive twenty blocks, find another hotel.

Miles had his ostensible reason, getting them a new place to stay; and his put-on for Dana, about getting a replacement for his lost gun, hoping to make her laugh. But a third, deeper level of motivation had driven him online, and into the confidence of a near stranger. Down in that subterranean area of his volition, a bit of panic had begun to pool. More than a bit; in truth, a whole kettle of it. But within that cauldron of edgy near-madness there also floated a pale little ribbon of hope, and of faith. Miles found a feeling of reassurance, of confidence, in his new online friend. Their interaction had only flowed between them for a few days, but it had carried a lot in its course. Celeste also conveyed a palpable air of capability, and confidence – even across the wires.

The two huddled together in the closed room until it was time to leave. They packed up the laptop, the only thing they had ever unpacked. A different man sat at the front desk now. This time Miles said hi as he slid the key across the counter, and Dana kept her face covered.

The thick wind, cold like stone, fought with them with each step through the dark night, until they pulled tiredly on the door to a small and coolly lit coffee shop.

They huddled in the short line at the counter, while Miles scanned the half dozen faces around the room. He'd never seen Celeste before, but he felt sure he would know her. They ordered drinks and carried them to the window counter that faced the street. Before he had gotten his coat arranged around the stool, Miles felt a tap on his shoulder.

"Miles."

"Celeste."

They shook hands while Dana looked on.

"This is Dana. Thanks for meeting us. Particularly at this hour. I know it's all very strange."

"It's definitely that," said Celeste. "But I do like your Unix jokes an awful lot. So . . . what's going on, then?" Celeste sat and pulled her coat close around her.

And then Miles held forth with everything – everything he knew – from Dana's early morning phone call two endless days ago, all the way through the meet gone bad in the deadly bowels of Central Park. Celeste Browning fidgeted silently through the narrative, anxious and conflicted.

At the tale's end, she sat silent, staring at her untouched coffee. One of those awkward social moments had come upon them – one which Celeste was going to have to get over, one way or another, in the next few seconds. As she twiddled her coffee stirrer, and glanced through the glass at the streetlight shadows on the sidewalk, she thought she could hear gunfire, faint and distant.

(Escape From) The Can

"Jesus, he's taking a dump." The cop – a New York cop, not the Hookeville kind – loosened his already loose tie with his left hand and held a pair of binoculars with his right. He could see that the bathroom – through the window, across the street – was no more than four feet by ten. He knew from the floor plan, which lay half-covered in doughnut boxes and coffee cups on the table behind him, that the right side of the bathroom held a stand-up shower, and the left a sink. In the middle sat a chipped ceramic toilet, and this the cop could see for himself, because the toilet faced the window. Slitted horizontal blinds hung from the window; a bulky figure sat behind them, on the can, with his head tilted into a magazine.

"What is this clown reading?"

"Use the digital binocs," suggested another cop, at the table behind him.

"Why?"

"'Cause they're twice as powerful, that's why. If you'd use the other binocs, you'd see he's reading the *Times* Home Design section."

"You're kidding. We got an interior decorator here?"

"Yeah, he only goes on killing sprees as a day job."

The cop at the window pursed his lips and scanned the windows above, below, and to either side. He brought the binoculars back to rest on the original scene and blindly fingered the twelve-gauge Remington shotgun that rested on the window sill in front of him.

"Hope he's got the kitchen done." He picked up the mouthpiece to his radio.

When the meet had gone bad, when the meet in Central Park had devolved into a bullet festival, and then a charnel house, just a couple of hours earlier, there had been ways, and means, and difficulties, and cross-purposes. And misunderstandings – legions of those. And while our lanky systems administrator protagonist and his redheaded charge were not the *only* folks who escaped the shoot-out in the park, they were two of the very few. Miles and Dana had failed to accomplish the seemingly simple task of handing off a duffel bag. But they had, miraculously, made it out still breathing. Stunned, short a handgun, and scared completely witless; but breathing. They had done a lot better than the majority of folks who had shown up.

One other person who also left the scene in a single piece happened to have caused most of the others to *not* make it out alive. That was the Cleaner, of course. He'd gone to Central Park to clean, and clean he had. However, he had not only missed his primary targets of the evening, but he had also departed the site of the job with a tail on him.

Getting pinned with a tail was extremely uncharacteristic for the Cleaner. But then again, so was going to a putatively straightforward job, and finding himself in the company of *two* separate opposing teams of guys, of unknown origin, also trying to ambush the client – *his* client – and everyone armed to the nines and blazing away. It had been all, in fact, the Cleaner could manage to shoot six or eight of the unexpected guys, and get out with his dignity intact. Of course, he'd made sure that none of the guys in the clearing had followed him out. But his tail did not come from the clearing.

His tail – a highly flustered and adrenalized law enforcement type – had come from a patrol route on the edge of the park. He had heard gunfire, come running, and seen the last moments of the shoot-out. He saw enough to know that the big guy in black had been the winner of the contest in the clearing, and that everyone else had tied for last. And so this breathless and wide-eyed cop had proceeded to follow the Cleaner all the way home, something no one had managed to do to the Cleaner in the course of a very long, and highly storied, career.

And so of course this one cop had then done what cops invariably do: he called in scores more cops. Great throngs of additional cops, with heavy weapons, and serious dispositions. And these additional cops spent the next hour avidly encircling the Cleaner's apartment, and loading weapons, and finalizing plans for going in there and bringing, or taking, the motherfucker inside out.

Not that any of this would come to much, in the course of things.

"Roger that," said the SWAT team leader into his radio mouthpiece, to the cop across the street. "He's still unarmed?"

"I'm looking right at him. He hasn't moved from the toilet. I think it's a go."

Two rows of men in black, hung with weapons and ordnance, lined the dingy hall.

"All teams, we move in ten. Ten seconds . . . mark."

"*Uh, hold, team leader,*" the voice fuzzed out of the earpiece. "*He, uh . . . he closed the blinds. I don't have a visual on the target.*"

"Where'd he go? He can't leave the bathroom."

"*Yeah, I mean, he's there. He just, he kind of reached out and closed the blinds. Didn't look away from his magazine . . . just closed the blinds.*"

"We're going in." He flicked his wrist, raising three fingers. "He's there, we're going."

"*Yeah, we got you, be careful.*"

Crack, and the wood of the front door splintered. Across the street, everyone in the surveillance room jumped a foot as two shots rang out, then a hundred or so more.

The SWAT team leader held his H&K MP-5 submachine gun dead on the doorway, as two of his guys went into the bathroom. One thousandth of a heartbeat later, with wood splinters from the door still flying through the air, his first guy flew by the doorway into the shower in a red mist, and his second guy came right back out the door, landing at his feet.

Two handguns, and two hands, appeared around the door jamb and swept the entire room from left to right with muzzle flashes glowing in a doublestar supernova and brass casings filling the world like a tinny locust swarm. Somewhere in the haze of that frozen, exploded moment, the team leader felt a weight in his chest like someone had dropped a piano on him, and he fell backwards, depressing his trigger. The room came alive with noise and light from his H&K.

The wooden floor hit him in the back of the head and a black curtain dropped on his stage, then rose a second later, for an encore.

Shaking his head through the roar, he looked up to see the guy – the fucking guy – putting head shots into one, two, three, four, five of his guys lying on the floor around him. His H&K had disappeared; he pulled his sidearm and fired wildly. The guy shuddered as a round creased his shoulder. He fell back into the other room, the bedroom, and the scene went completely, unbelievably silent, just like that.

Across the street, the entire surveillance room cleared out in three seconds – except for the original cop, who stood frozen at the window, still staring through binoculars, jaw slack, breath caught. He watched from above as thirty cops sprinted across the street below him.

In the World

In the end, Celeste dashed all expectations, including and in particular her own, by bringing Miles and Dana home with her.

She'd spent a few minutes in serious interrogation, at the coffee shop counter. Miles elaborated where he could while Dana sat demurely silent. When Celeste had satisfied herself, as well as she figured she was going to, that a) they were telling the truth, b) they hadn't been followed, and c) they really were there out of desperation and terror, she made up her mind.

"You mean it?" asked Miles. "We won't be too much trouble?"

"That's a good one," said Celeste. "In-laws are trouble. I don't know what you guys are. Death on a stick, maybe." At least she still had her sense of humor. "You can at least come by and get your bearings. Put your things down. Get a few hours' sleep. And maybe we can try and brainstorm some solutions to your, erm, situation. You'll be safe, at any rate."

Celeste sighed aloud, trying not to think too much about what she was doing. She reached out and gave a squeeze to

Dana's arm. "It'll be okay," she offered to the young woman. It seemed to Celeste that she could use the reassurance.

The three rose, exited, and marched four blocks to Celeste's brownstone in tense silence, through the very middle of the black, dead night.

"I thought about shooting someone a thousand times," Miles said to their new and unlikely hostess. "I thought about every part of it."

Only a few minutes had passed since Celeste had admitted them to her first-floor walk-up, invited them to drop their bags on the floor of the living room, and dug out some extra linens.

The apartment took up 1,200 square feet, on a pretty block of 58th Street. It was done in dark woods and fabrics, the front door opening onto the living room, a dining area on the left. The kitchen looked out from over a butcher block bar. A hallway led past the bathroom to a single bedroom.

Miles and Celeste were rehashing the debacle in Central Park. They had already gone over the facts of the incident, most of them twice. Now, with a little time and space between it and him, Miles began to grope around fumblingly for his feelings about what had happened. Even if and when their other problems – legal jeopardy, survival issues, drug problems – sorted themselves out, Miles would probably be dealing with the emotional fallout for a long time.

He couldn't even be sure that he had hit anybody. He hadn't even been able to hang onto his gun after the mayhem started. Still, he had anticipated and envisioned such a scene many times before.

"It happened totally unlike I ever thought it would," Miles went on. "But I'm not really off of the idea, yet, either. Not even after having experienced it."

"The gun is very simple," Celeste said, returning to the dim light of the main room. Sunrise was still a couple of hours away, and only one lamp was lit. "Very reductionist. Point and shoot

– good on one side, bad on the other. Really, there's nothing to figure out – your aim just needs to be good. While a violent situation, or a violent life, is a terrible thing to contemplate, it's also terribly, wonderfully, simple. You need never agonize again. *Just don't miss.*"

Celeste turned and stepped into the kitchen, returning with two glasses of water. Dana lay curled on the soft corduroy surface of the couch, her boots angled off onto the hardwood floor, fast asleep. The strain of these days was making her cat-like; she slept through everything.

"That's the theory, anyway," Celeste added.

Miles frowned. "Do you ever have the gunfight-as-impotence dream?"

"Can't say I have."

"I have it a lot. Basically, I'm stalking an opponent, a bad guy. I've got a gun. I see his back and have a clear shot. I fire, and hit. But it doesn't kill him. He turns around, really pissed off, and starts advancing on me. I keep firing, but each shot has less power, first bouncing off the guy, then dropping right out of the barrel, flaccid. I usually wake up then, equal parts embarrassed that I got caught shooting the guy in the back, and terrified that he's going to kill me."

Celeste looked thoughtful. "I always have the one where it's final exams, and I've never been to class. And I'm not going to graduate if I can't figure out how to pass the final."

Miles smiled. "It's a big relief when you wake up and remember you graduated."

Celeste frowned now. "That's the thing. I never did graduate."

"Oh."

Miles sat on the floor now, laptop before him, logging in. A power cord snaked off behind the couch; his WiFi card blinked happily in connection. Celeste peered into the glare as she walked by and handed him a glass. "Be careful what you log into there, champ, okay?" She sat on the love seat and crossed her legs. She sipped her water and let out some breath, appraising the familiar and strange man on her floor. Despite the rundown of events in the coffee shop, and the subsequent psychotherapy, he had been somewhat sketchy on what he planned to do next.

"So . . . your plan of action involves making another attempt to return this bag?" She patted it where it rested on the arm of the love seat. She looked a little skeptical.

"Mmm," Miles assented.

"How do you intend to set up another swap? More importantly, what makes you think the next one won't turn into another blood-letting? Or that you'll get lucky and *survive* another one?"

"Hmmm . . ." he disclaimed, looking up at his eyebrows.

Miles had spoken very frenetically at the coffee shop. Having this sense of urgency leak onto her, Celeste thought, might have contributed to her bringing these two strays back with her without giving the matter as much critical thought as it probably deserved. Now, she felt deflated listening to Miles barely sigh in response to her questions. These were wild extremes of loquaciousness. In point of fact, Miles had simply grown very tired. He'd had a great deal of adrenaline earlier in the evening, and it had melted now into raw fatigue.

"You say you originally contacted this man by e-mail. Why don't you write him again?"

"I did," Miles answered, perking up slightly.

"When? Why didn't you mention that?"

"Tonight, after I wrote you. Before we left to meet you. Sorry, I forgot."

"Has he responded, and you forgot to mention that, too?"

"No. He has responded, and I just saw it this minute. Look." Miles swiveled the laptop on the hardwood floor. Celeste took to her knees beside him.

From: an8465407@anon.penet.fi
To: darken@boatanchor.tjc.edu
Subject: Re: returning the goods
Date: Sun, 24 Oct 2004 04:11:11 -0500 (EST)

Miles Darken <darken@boatanchor.tjc.edu> wrote:

>We didn't have anything to do with what happened tonight.
>And we still want to return your bag. Hell -- now more than
>ever. Please tell us where we can meet, or leave this thing.

Yeah, whatever. Don't contact me again. I might want my bag back, but I don't want to get in a body bag to do it. Enough is enough. I can't do nuttin' for ya, man; FreeBSD got problems of his own.

"Well," said Celeste, leaning back against the couch and removing her glasses. "That doesn't sound hopeful."

Miles looked near to sleep, though he still sat at the keyboard, bad dreams queuing up already. With his last strength, he forwarded Celeste the mail from FreeBSD, just for her reference. With that, Celeste tucked the two of them in for the night, scattering half-folded blankets on various surfaces. She then retreated to her bedroom and pulled the door closed tight. She undressed, laid a handgun on the night stand, killed the lights, and got into bed. She lay awake for a long while, examining her motives, turning them this way and that in that dark.

The Throne Room (Back to the Can)

"This throne room could use some redecorating," said the detective from across the street.

Now he sat in the bathroom itself, just about the most horrifying forty square feet of porcelain and bathroom fixtures one could envision. Most of the surfaces were brown with dried blood or blood spatter; a few thick pools, on the floor, in the shower stall, maintained a reddish hue. Much of the porcelain that was still white was actually black and gray with bullet holes. Insulation, stained concrete, and indeterminate building materials poked through everywhere. The section of tiling under the window had given way completely, and lay on the floor in ragged chunks, soaking up blood.

Some sorry asshole had earlier tried to draw chalk lines around the bodies. Substitution of a grease pencil had made it possible to mark the one in the shower stall, though the poor bullet-riddled, and glass-shard-lacerated fellow, doubled over in the tiny space, hadn't in silhouette produced anything remotely reminiscent of a human figure. The corpse in the main area of the bathroom had been surrounded by too much debris for its resting place to be marked. They took pictures instead.

The man sitting on the toilet did not look horrified when he spoke. He didn't even look tired. He didn't look anything. From his expression, he might have been sitting in a swivel chair at a conference table, waiting to begin an important meeting that would probably go long. He didn't even wear a poker face, because he had nothing to conceal behind it. With the toe of his shoe, he nudged a hunk of bloody drywall away from him, so that he could stretch out his leg.

Almost a hundred cops swarmed in and around the building now. A hundred living cops and, until a few minutes earlier, seven dead ones as well. Interestingly, no one had been wounded in the botched raid – every cop shot had died. The survivors had not even started trying to account for this fact. But that was because it was a secondary question, and not even a very interesting one, compared to the issue of how the guy had gotten out of the building.

The guy was so completely gone; he couldn't conceivably be any less there.

They hoped that the wreckage, and carnage, that remained in the dingy apartment would yield some clues as to where the guy might have gone. But many of the officers on the scene – in particular the ones from the original stakeout – were having difficulty breaking free of the fog of shock that surrounded them, and everything, on that early morning, in that place.

It wasn't so much that they didn't know what had happened.

In a nutshell, their suspect turned out to be the kind of extreme motherfucker who went to the can armed – heavily armed – and he had killed half the team that went in to get him, driven off the other half, and escaped.

They knew what had happened. They just didn't believe it. It was a little like watching a martial arts master wade through a dozen surrounding attackers. Yeah, you can see how he did it, but beforehand you would have bet the ranch that it wouldn't happen that way.

It was all so unthinkable that it shook everyone's faith that the NYPD more or less had control of things. Certainly, it played hell with their familiar assumption that they could always bring overwhelming force to bear, given time to get it assembled. It was just really jarring, this going in strong with almost twenty heavily armed and armored professionals, and getting their asses kicked into next month by a guy with his drawers around his ankles. It left them looking over their shoulders; jumping at loud noises.

If the guys who had been there all morning, some since 3am, were still fighting groggily through various stages of shock, the new officers on the scene exhibited livelier emotions. Most of them had responded to a call for "all available units – shots fired, officers down." They had arrived to find seven fallen comrades, no one to rescue, and the action long over. Moreover, they had found no one to shoot. All of this resulted in a serious surfeit of adrenaline, galloping heart rates, and a lot of seething bad attitude that would only get worse until the opportunity was had to make somebody pay.

The blank-faced man now sitting on the throne was a fortyish-looking detective in a checkered suit jacket, with graying auburn hair and deep lines in his sagging face. He had bushy eyebrows and his last shave had started to get a ways off. He was dealing with his numbness by being flippant.

"You could probably get a good deal on it as a fixer-upper," said his companion, a younger detective, unjacketed, moustachioed, and slightly more on edge. He leaned on the inside of the splintered door jamb, chewing on an unlit cigarette. He peered over his shoulder into the main room, where a lot of fingerprinting, picture snapping, and drawer emptying was going on. The gathering of evidence had begun in the bathroom, and was finished there for now. These two had occupied the bathroom possibly to get out of the way, possibly out of some gruesome fascination.

The two snapped from their reverie when a patrolman, leading a young black man with his arm in a sling, stuck his head in. "This guy wants to talk to you, boss."

"Detective Johnson. Narcotics, Hookeville Virginia PD." He held open his leather topcoat, which hung over his arm sling on one side, and lifted his sweatshirt, revealing the badge on his belt.

"Well, hi," the detective on the throne grunted, looking up from under arched and very furry eyebrows. "What are you doing here?"

"In New York? I'm from here. I grew up here."

"No." The detective neither nodded nor blinked. "What are you doing on my crime scene?"

Here we go, thought Theron. *Time to stop stepping on my dick.*

He raised his immobilized arm as Exhibit A and said, "Two nights ago in my jurisdiction, a perpetrator, based out of *your* jurisdiction, put a slug through my collarbone while I was working undercover. This perpetrator was killed, but the narcotics he carried were not recovered."

The two locals nodded in sync with each other, as if to say, *That's interesting.*

"This dead perpetrator," Theron continued, "was known to work for a large Manhattan dealer who was probably involved in last night's shoot-out in Central Park. Due to the large number of his employees found dead there."

As Theron spoke, a *boop*ing noise came from the main

room, followed by a hissy tape recording of a voice: the answering machine. The ringer on the phone had been turned off (or shot off).

"And you think," monotoned the detective, rising slowly and looking over Theron's shoulder into the main room, "that's strong enough for you to work this case in my back yard?" The dialogue paused while all three of them squeezed out. In the main room, a crowd had gathered around the phone. A whine issued as the tape rewound.

"I think," answered Theron, "the fact this seller is doing business in *my* back yard is enough for me to work it here." He craned his neck over the crowd as the machine *boop*ed again. "In any case," he added more quietly, "I heard the radio chatter from this scene, and since the guy who did *this*," he waved his good arm around the room, "came from the shoot-out in the park, I came by hoping it might help me figure out where the dealer is at. This 'FreeBSD.'"

"Hell, we coulda told you where *he* is," the detective grunted over his shoulder.

"No shit. Where?" But Theron got shushed as a voice began speaking to the machine, in urgent but measured tones:

"*Noel, this is Anthony. If you were there, I know you would pick up.*" There was a pause, and some indistinguishable background noise. "*I wouldn't normally leave work on your machine. However, the customers are very displeased about last night's job. You must meet last night's principal client again at his place of business, and you must complete the service package. The address again is 1062 33rd Street. Contact me at the mobile number when it's done.*" *Click. Whizz.*

The detective turned around, amid a wave of incredulous mumbling that washed across the room. "Why, he's at 1062 33rd Street, in the Garment District," he answered jovially. "We've known where FreeBSD's headquarters is for ages. We just couldn't go in there yet."

Now it was Theron's turn to arch his brows, eyes wide, lips

parted, head lowered. *This is spooky fucked up*, he thought, and almost said it out loud.

But the detective had already turned away, animatedly saddling up the posse. Ordinarily, at this point, he might be wondering why he'd not heard from this Johnson's department chief. But plenty more anomalous things were happening all around him, all demanding his attention.

Little Breakthroughs

Morning found Celeste Browning's apartment, as it does every other place. The two groggy and disoriented houseguests had just felt the first light when Celeste found them, right where she had left them. Everyone looked vaguely surprised to see one another. Celeste dispensed ritual inquiries after sleep quality while attending to the coffee maker. Without additional preamble she said: "Alright, then. Let's have a look at your ill-gotten gains." She came back to the living room, waving a mug of coffee near Dana's face, which had half-disappeared into the couch cushion.

"Won't work," Miles said from the love seat. "Try sitting on her."

"You sit on her," demurred Celeste, passing him coffee. She wore the same outfit as the day before – jeans, white cotton button-down, boots – but looked freshly showered. Her face did not betray any of the tiredness that Miles' did. She had long practice working crisply on no sleep.

Neither showed any enthusiasm for rousing Dana with body weight, so they started the day's business without her. Complying with Celeste's directive, Miles emptied the red duffel bag onto the dining-room table, stacking five small, white, blunt-cornered bricks into a pyramid. Wordlessly, Celeste produced a tool box, arrayed several sharp objects and little vials of liquid on the table, and went to work on the duffel bag.

Miles watched respectfully as Celeste sliced open the bag at various seams, and performed myriad drippy operations on sections of the fabric. She then produced a strange light and ran it over the surface, each time the light glowing a different color. Only when she came to a halt did Miles make so bold to ask her what she was doing.

"There's not really that much here," she answered, looking vexed and thoughtful. She sat hunched over the table, with her hands on the arms of her chair. "Maybe $50,000 worth, if it were cocaine cut to street-level, just at a guess." She looked out of the corners of her eyes, which suggested to Miles that she wasn't merely guessing. Then she seemed to have a burst of re-inspiration, and attacked the nylon straps of the bag with an Exacto knife. Slitting open the fabric, she continued, "Now, the original drug buy in Virginia you described, that makes sense – an undercover cop, two or three guys getting shot over a score like this. I could see that." She seemed to lose interest in the straps after turning them into wide frayed scraps of nylon; but then examined the scraps. She capped the Exacto, swiveled on her chair, and looked Miles in the eye.

"However, last night's shoot-out. In Central Park. If what you described happened the way you described it . . . well, that's a whole lot of guys blazing away. Including some who don't sound like entry-level shooters in the local narcotics industry."

"What do they sound like?"

Celeste looked away from him. "Sound like professionals."

This wasn't really Miles' field, but he was a quick study. "So you don't believe all those people shot each other dead over only $50,000 worth of cocaine?" His eyes widened in comprehension. "You thought maybe there was something else in the bag?"

"I did think there was something else in the bag," assented Celeste. "Still do, maybe. But in any case, it isn't cocaine."

"What?" Miles' look of comprehension ran away from him.

"I slit one of the bricks and tested it last night, while you were asleep. But the chemicals weren't necessary. It's talcum powder."

"What's talcum powder?" Dana's head protruded from underneath her blanket, sleep and bangs dancing in her eyes.

"Which brick did you test?" Miles asked across the table.

"That one, marked '238'." Celeste pointed with the sheathed Exacto.

Dana had lain stilly under her blanket as Miles explained Celeste's suspicion that there might be something additional, something hidden, in the bricks. She looked very thoughtful as Miles told her that the putative drugs were not drugs.

"238," repeated Miles. Small, black, greasepainted numbers marked the surface of each of the plastic-wrapped bricks. "That's the weight, right?"

Celeste didn't reply, she just tapped her tool on the *238*.

"But what's the unit? That's not nearly 238 ounces. And it's a lot more than 238 grams. Decagrams, maybe?"

Tap, tap.

"That's not right either. All the bags are pretty much the same size, but the numbers aren't even in the same ballpark . . ." Miles trailed off. Dana padded into the dining area in stocking feet, and peered around Miles at the mess on the table. She rested her chin on his shoulder.

Celeste unpiled the bricks, shuffling them on the table like a street hustler with a ball and cups. Four of the bags showed three-digit numbers in the greasepaint. These she arranged in a straight line. They read: "238", "142", "222", and "064".

Dana's bob of hair moved up and down as she spoke, her jaw flush with Miles' shoulder. She said, "Dotted octets. It's an IP address, right?"

A heavy silence sat on the table as Celeste palmed the fifth bag, and flashed it to Dana and Miles like a badge. On the bag was written, "4044".

"And a port number," said Miles. "Fuck me."

Slack-jawed, they all turned to look at the laptop sitting open on the floor.

"The address of the Manuscript," Miles breathed. Dana nodded in silence.

"What manuscript?" asked Celeste.

"We'll explain in a minute," answered Miles. "Mind if I log in?"

There are blessedly few ways to arrange four numbers, in this case the constituent numbers in an IP address. Celeste stood at the table doing her street hustler routine, lining up the bricks in various orders while Miles sat on the floor, trying to connect to each resulting address. Logged into his server in Hookeville, he sent pings – little sonar-like sequences of "Are you there?" messages – to one, two, three forms of the address.

The fourth combination answered back. Or, rather, something with that IP address, at the other end of a very long wire, answered back. Killing his ping, Miles attempted to connect to the remote machine. He tried a web browser first – no response. But he got the service right on the second try: good old command line FTP (file transfer protocol). Unfortunately, the machine stonily rejected his attempt to log in as "anonymous".

"It's prompting for a password," said Miles, trying to mask his excitement. "A username and password. Check the bricks."

As he stared at the prompt, Miles considered that he had no idea why anyone would bind an FTP server to port 4044. (The standard ports for it are 20 and 21.) But then, this perplexed him less than someone writing the address on five plastic-wrapped bricks of talcum powder and taking them to a doomed drug deal . . . though even that was slowly beginning to make sense.

"Check the bricks again," he said. "There should be a username and password."

"There's nothing else."

"Fuck. I would have expected a password."

"And how many nights will you be staying, Mr. Luther?"

"I don't know."

"Very good. Do you need help with your luggage?"

"No." Stanley shifted his bags, palmed the keycard, and made for the elevator. Tired and greasy after driving fifteen hours in three days – and sleeping one night in the car – he realized he also smelled strongly of sulfur from the gunfight in Central Park (where he had arrived just in time to nearly get his ever-loving ass shot off). He rode up twelve flights alone, trudged the length of the floor to his room, and fought a quick action with the keycard lock.

He dropped his duffel by the door and carried his laptop to the desk. At least the hotel had broadband. The laptop and puffy white plastic-wrapped brick he laid out together. He logged in and spent several minutes surfing the web to see if he could figure out the language scribbled on the brick. It turned out to be Arabic. He probably should have recognized that, he considered.

Stanley then took another risk by logging into the Agency's secure extranet. While the system verified him, he used a handheld scanner to suck the Arabic writing on the brick into an image file. The Agency ran a proprietary online translating system that recognized over three dozen languages, including many with non-ASCII character sets. With luck he might get a translation – without later having to answer any awkward questions about what he was doing in Manhattan, and which Arab nations were involved.

He chose "Arabic" and "Digital Image File" from pull-down menus, and uploaded the file. While the imaging system caressed the edges of the image, and as the dictionary churned, Stanley lit a cigarette. A long minute later the results screen came back, with the Agency logo, the time and date of his request, the scanned image of the Arabic script . . . and the translation. It read:

username: shastra
password: muezzin

Stanley had no idea what this meant. An online dictionary told him that a "muezzin" was "in Moslem countries, a crier, as in a minaret, who calls the people to prayer at the proper hours".

He did not feel this cleared things up in any significant measure.

"Shastra" had no definition at all.

He logged out again, and then back into his personal account, and composed some very pointed mail to his employers (the contract ones) to the effect that he needed timely and substantive intelligence support in order to reverse the debacles of Hookeville and Central Park and recover that bag. Furthermore, he needed help in locating the redheaded girl and her armed companion, and if he didn't get it, he would drive back to Arlington in the morning and file a report with the Agency.

This wasn't the first time he'd sent e-mail in anger. Nor would it be the first time he'd live to regret it.

Miles had started typing furiously again, but stopped speaking. He sat on the floor in a heavy mist of concentration. Celeste used the interval to make a quick phone call from the bedroom. Dana ducked out to the bathroom and returned looking more alert. Sensing their return, and the little wave of curiosity they pushed out in front of them, Miles answered their question in advance.

"I am whipping up a script to run crack on this thing."

Neither of the women said anything. In a moment or two, Miles noticed the silence.

"I wasn't actually making drug humor. 'Crack' is also the name of a password-cracking program." His typing and his speech moved in little parallel cross-currents, cresting and falling. "The problem with crack is that you're supposed to use it after you have gotten hold of an encrypted password file. And what crack does is basically throw the dictionary at them."

"I don't get it," admitted Dana, standing with her palms on the back of the couch.

"Well, what Unix does with passwords is it encrypts them into meaningless strings using a program called crypt. It's a one-way operation. You can take any string of characters, and run crypt on it, and get some gibberish. And every time you run crypt on the same string of characters, you'll get the same gibberish. But there's no way to reverse the operation; you can't figure out the original string from the gibberish. So, what crack does is take a 40,000 word dictionary, or whatever size electronic dictionary you have, and run crypt on every word. It then checks if the result matches the encrypted string in the password file. If so, it knows it's got a match. It's called a brute force attack."

"So you're trying to use crack to guess the password of the site?" Dana asked.

"Not precisely," Miles hedged. "Like I said, crack is great when you have the encrypted password file." He paused to move the mouse pointer with the trackpad, brought his fingers back to the keyboard. "However, I don't have that. I don't have shit. This machine – the one somewhere out on the Net, but with its IP address inexplicably written on these talcum powder baggies here . . ."

The three all sort of reverentially regarded the non-drugs on the table, getting used to the idea that they'd stumbled onto some sort of mystery.

"This machine seems not to exist," Miles continued. "Well, that's not quite accurate – obviously it exists, we've opened several connections to it. Something is giving us a log-in prompt. But that's pretty much the only evidence of this thing's existence."

"How do you mean?" asked Celeste.

"Well, it doesn't have a name for starters."

"You checked the InterNIC registry."

"Yep. 238.142.222.64 has no machine name, and is not a part of the Internet Domain Name System. Not that surprising, I guess. Further, suppose we try a traceroute to this thing. Traceroute goes out to a remote host across the Net and lists all the hops it took to get there."

"So you can see where in the physical world it is?" Dana asked.

"Right. If we try a traceroute to this thing, we see the first few hops – from boatanchor, to the local router, then the big backbone, then on to MAE East, which is the big transfer point on the East Coast." He paused to exhale. "Then it's gone. Just disappears."

"How could it disappear?" Celeste asked. "If you can get to it, there has to be a route."

"Right. There has to be, but there's not," he added somewhat stiltedly. This conversation was competing for cycles with the Perl script he was writing, and his conversational rhythm suffered. "Look for yourself," he added, swiveling the laptop toward the others. "The last dozen hops are just rows of asterisks."

Celeste looked thoughtful. "I think those are foreign hosts," she suggested. "I've seen that before. Usually it's these backwater third world nations that are sharing a single ISDN connection with about twelve neighbors. That's where this machine is. In Latvia. Or Chad. Or Suriname."

Dana looked to be deep in her own thoughts. Staying within earshot, she started packing up the few things she'd taken out the night before. She seemed to sense they might be going soon.

"Hmm, I suppose it could be," assented Miles, pausing his typing, and shaking out his fingers above the laptop, as if anointing his program. "I've never seen that before. But I'll take your word for it." He returned to the keyboard and began methodically debugging.

"So, the original point being that I don't have the password file to run crack on, and, worse, it doesn't look like there's any way I can get it. Normally, getting a look at the password file isn't that hard: all you have to do is get a toehold into the system. You can look for holes in sendmail; or mount a volume via NFS; or finger for user accounts, then find the inevitable accounts that have no passwords, or passwords that are the same as the username, or 'guest,' or 'secret,' or some such. Or you can call up on the phone and do a little social engineering. Most people will simply give you their password, if you pretend to be someone official."

Miles stopped typing, and spoke intently.

"Sendmail is not running on this machine. NFS is not enabled. Finger is not running. If there even *are* any user accounts, I can't figure out what they are. I cannot try and social engineer the owners, because with no InterNIC registration, there's no way to figure out who they are. And I can't even call their upstream provider because I don't know who that is *within eight fucking hops*." He rubbed the bridge of his nose. "In fact, this machine doesn't seem to be running any services whatsoever, other than FTP. It's like a total brick wall. I've seen secure machines before, hell, I've secured plenty myself. But this is ridiculous. It's like ripe fruit dangling at thirty thousand feet."

"Or," intoned Dana, "a Pandora's box, cemented shut."

"Which raises a vital question," added Celeste. "Whether you want to get into it at all."

"We do," said Miles. "Trust me, we really, really do."

"Why? And, moreover, how?"

Miles grinned and flourished at the laptop screen. "I've written a script to run crack – against the log-in prompt. Essentially, it throws the dictionary at the log-in. Actually, four dictionaries that I've plugged into it. Four languages. Forward and backward." Celeste and Dana looked impressed, realizing what he had been doing with all that furious typing the last few minutes. "The problem, of course, is that crack wasn't designed to run this way. When you have the encrypted password file, crack runs like a bat out of hell. All it has to do is keep invoking crypt, which Unix can do very quickly. What we're having to do here, though, is actually establish an FTP connection, and wait for the remote machine to respond with a login prompt; then reject our guess; then give us another prompt. Also, the remote machine disconnects after every five failed attempts, so the script has to reconnect."

"I imagine that will take much longer," ventured Celeste.

"Probably several orders of magnitude longer. And that's if they let us keep trying. On any normal system, some alarm should go off after so many failed login attempts. In the least case, the logs will show all the activity."

Celeste sprang to her full height. "So you're saying *the people who did all the shooting over this are going to know what you're doing?*"

"I don't think so . . . for two reasons. For one thing, I'm running the program from a machine across the country I happen to have access to. I'm running it as a user on that system, who I happen to hate. I've also connected through a half dozen machines to get there. So there's a good chance that anyone listening will think it's this other guy trying to breach their system, or at least won't be able to trace it back to my machine. Or to us."

"And the other reason?"

"The other reason is that I don't think anyone's listening. It's possible, maybe even likely, this machine is maintained as a sort of Fort Knox: battened down, and guarded by some serious guys down in Latvia, or wherever. That's one explanation. But I've got a feeling it's something else. I've installed and maintained hundreds of these systems, and I know them pretty well. And I think this one is stone-deaf for another reason. I don't think it's a Fort Knox – I think it's more of a Dead Sea Scroll."

Dana and Celeste listened on.

"I think it's just got this one service, just FTP – and if it's what Dana and I think it is, it's serving just one thing through it. And it's not being used for anything else. It's totally intuition on my part, but I'm guessing that no one administrates this thing. I wouldn't be surprised if no one had logged in for years." Miles scratched his neck, then went still. All three stared at the laptop.

"But you think," asked Celeste, "that your crack script will get you in?"

"No. I think it's incredibly unlikely that it will. Not for weeks or months, if ever."

"So the mystery ends here."

"Well. There's one other possibility."

"That being . . . ?"

"We contact the guy who owns these bags."

Celeste looked highly skeptical. "You mean contact him again. And, what, just ask him for the password? What in the world makes you think he'd help you? He wouldn't even talk to you about taking his bag back. "

"Because if this server is home to what we think it is, then Dana was supposed to have access to it." Celeste looked puzzled and frustrated. Miles went on: "I'm afraid we've got a little more explaining to do. But, even aside from that, what's in this site is pretty obviously what all those people were shooting each other last night to get their hands on. Aren't you just a lot curious to find out what could be that valuable?"

"I'm guessing you're about to tell me what could be that valuable." Celeste looked deeply troubled. "I need to tell you, however, while I'm thinking about it, that my assistance to you in this matter is provisional. That is to say, I'm not sure why I'm doing it, except that I think it has something to do with the novelty of meeting someone online and having him show up at my door a week later. And some strangely philanthropic feelings I've been having recently." She pushed her glasses up her nose and brushed a bang out of her eyes. "But. I reserve the right to abort this project, and put you out on the street, at any time. Particularly if I start to anticipate being shot as part of the deal." She sighed. "When I come back I want you to tell me what exactly we're getting ourselves into."

With that, she turned on her heel, went back to the bedroom, and opened the case with the guns in it. She had an unpleasant intuition that one or two should be at hand. The clacking of the keyboard in the living room resumed, flirting with the clicking of magazines and pistol slides in the bedroom.

And Celeste's muttering.

Yes, she was curious to know what could be that valuable. *God save me*, she grumbled in the privacy of her bedroom, the privacy of her head.

Bad Characters

From: <darken@boatanchor.tjc.edu>
To: an8465407@anon.penet.fi
Subject: black ink (was Re: returning the goods)
Date: Sun, 24 Oct 2004 10:09:32 -0500 (EST)

Dear FreeBSD,

That you have "problems of your own" is well taken. However, we still have the bag. And we've also deciphered your encoding scheme -- and have gotten so far as to connect to the site at 238.* . But we want the password. We're working on cracking it now, however, if you were to find it in your heart to, say, just send it on . . . I mean, we know Dana was supposed to be getting this thing in the first place. (Albeit, we do understand you haven't quite gotten paid for it yet.)

Your ever faithful servant,
MD

"Son of a bitch!" FreeBSD kicked over his coffee table, spilling two half-drunk espressos and a bowl of beer nuts. "What fucking bullshit!"

He didn't stay mad long – just long enough to scare off most of the hangers-on in the Crib, which was probably all to the good. He quickly remembered how glad he felt to still be alive after last night, a night in which lots of people – including several nice young fellows in his employ – had gotten slightly dead. He remembered, as he always tried to, that life could always be a hell of a lot worse.

After that, he also began grudgingly to admit to himself that this Darken guy was right. The redheaded chick was supposed to be getting the info on the Manuscript site. She was even supposed to have gotten the password, though God only knows what had happened at the original exchange in Hookeville. Also, FreeBSD was impressed that the guy had figured out the IP address thing.

Just his luck – his goods not only didn't go to the paying customer, but they fell into the hands of another geek, to whom his little encryption scheme proved transparent. Hell.

Over a fresh quad espresso, and a laptop, he poked around a little in the cooling ashes of his previously white-hot anger, and gave himself over to his frivolity. True, he *hadn't* gotten paid – by any of the people who were supposed to be paying him. Given that, the most this Darken guy was getting was a good solid clue:

From: an8465407@anon.penet.fi
To: <darken@boatanchor.tjc.edu>
Subject: black ink (was Re: returning the goods)
Date: Sun, 24 Oct 2004 10:22:00 -0500 (EST)

So you want to crack the product? Do your own crypto work, homey.

Oh, yeah: try plugging in an Arabic dictionary. Figure it out and the whole deal's yours. I'm done with it.

Peace and I'm out,
F*D

* * *

"That was quick," Celeste said, sitting cross-legged on the floor beside Miles. When she had returned to the main room, Dana had led her off to the couch, while Miles fiddled at the machine. Leaning in conspiratorially, Dana had given her the primer on the unlikely topic of the Manuscript. Celeste had listened for twenty minutes without interrupting. Now she read Miles' e-mail over his shoulder. "What does that mean?"

"It means, I do believe, that I didn't quite have the right dictionary plugged in."

In the Crib, Ace stood silent and motionless. "'Pack'?" he repeated. "We goin' somewhere?"

"Yeah. I mean no." FreeBSD adopted a scowl. "What the fuck are you second-guessing me?" He regarded the very large, very taciturn, and very black man. "Last I checked, I pay you to do shit for me, not give me shit. Now please start packing the product, the cash, the guns, and the backup tapes, or I'm going to tear your head off and beat you to death with it."

"What you pay me for," intoned Ace, in a quiet, very smooth basso, leaning down ominously toward his employer's agitated form on the leopard-skin couch, sliding his mirrored blades down his large pug nose, "is to keep this organization functioning, and to keep you out of trouble. If I go into the back and start putting tape and junk in boxes, everyone will go batshit. I'll do it; but don't be surprised if you come home later and find the whole posse standing around dressed up as the gang from *Clue*. Professor Plum . . ." he went on significantly, "in the Parlor . . . with the Candlestick."

"Yeah, bitch!" FreeBSD reached up and hugged Ace around the neck. "You know, that's the most I've heard you say at one time as long as I've known you. And a eighties cultural reference in it, too." He released the breadbox-sized head and smiled. "You're right. Send everyone home, make up some excuse. You're right as usual."

"Get the fuck out," Ace bellowed, straightening up. "5-0's coming by, all you boys with sheets clear out." The room emptied quickly and, without another word, Ace went behind the bar to look for packing materials. Watching him, FreeBSD reflected that he surely would have thought of these things before. He seemed less detail-oriented lately. And he must be out of his mind to be corresponding with the Darken guy. He had already changed in other unlikely ways, too. It wasn't hard to guess why.

One other detail tugged at the corner of his caffeine-, shootout-, and Manuscript-addled brain. He spoke across the bar: "One other thing, Ace. Why don't you take a look out there on the street, or send somebody, and see if you can see anything."

"Anything like what?" Ace froze, holding a roll of tape in one hand and a knife in the other.

"Anything like worrisome-like." FreeBSD deflated a bit. "Like maybe I got followed home."

"You mean, maybe sumpin' like a Caddy with tints sittin' on the curb down the block? Or maybe sumpin' like the hang-up phone calls this morning? Sumpin' like that? Better, or worse?"

FreeBSD didn't have to tell him to pack faster.

"I'm thinking," said Celeste, semi-authoritatively, over Miles' renewed clacking, "that there's no way for your drug dealer buddy to trace your mail back to this apartment?"

"No good way. He'd have to be a lot better at following tracks than I am at covering them."

Dana emerged from the kitchen with breakfast: juice and fresh fruit, a second pot of coffee, and instant jumbo biscuits from a tube – the popping sound of which opening caused everyone (including and especially Dana) to jump six inches.

"Anyway, after last night, I imagine 'my drug dealer buddy' will be too busy with other issues to spend a lot of cycles looking for us. He probably wants to put as much distance between us and him as humanly possible."

Celeste had shown only a placid expression since her talk with Dana. She put her arms on the bar ledge, and spoke now, brows furrowed, staring into the empty kitchen. "I think I want to hear more about this document you're looking for. But first, what I'd really love to figure out is who all those people in Central Park were."

Miles looked up at her. "Like I said last night, I hardly saw anything. Just blurred figures rushing toward us, and muzzle flashes all around. I think the first guy I met was the drug dealer. But everything happened too quickly. I didn't really get a look at anyone else."

Dana spoke up now: "Actually, I did. I saw one other." The other two looked at her. "There were all the guys rushing toward us. But there was one on the periphery. I froze when the shooting started, but I could make out this one figure, in the moonlight. I think he was wearing a skullcap."

Celeste's eyelids fluttered. Her head lolled a little to one side, lips slightly parted. But Miles was looking at Dana, and Dana was looking into the middle distance of her memory.

"He was on the edge of the clearing, circling. And shooting. I'm pretty sure he was the one who shot most of the people running up the hill, once all the shooting started."

Celeste piped up, seeming to gather herself a bit. "What did he look like, besides the skullcap and the shooting everyone bit?"

Dana: "He had two guns, one in each hand. And I think he was wearing round, or oval, glasses. They glinted every time his guns went off. And he was moving—"

"—really fast," Celeste finished for her. Her heart felt as if it were being licked by a cat.

"What, you know him?"

Celeste turned wordlessly on her heel, making for the bedroom.

"Where are you going?"

"To get more guns." She reappeared a few seconds later with a thick, rigid suitcase, clearly heavy. She laid it on the top of the bar and flipped the top up. Within, Miles could see gunmetal, nickel and blued, glinting unabashedly, magazines, a box of bullets. Celeste removed a large silver autoloader, dropped the magazine and checked it, then cracked the chamber and checked that. With this, she felt Miles' greedy gaze on her.

"No, you don't get one," she answered in advance. She paused. "I'm sure you know the rules of gun safety. What about her? Since I have these out . . ."

"Miles taught me," Dana answered quietly. "I know."

Celeste nodded. She replaced the silver autoloader, tucked her Bersa into her waistband, then produced another, much smaller gun in a nylon holster. She wrapped the strap around her ankle, and pulled her trouser leg over it. She put her palms on the bar top and gave a short, audible laugh, amused at her own dramatics. Miles and Dana looked on blankly. At this, Celeste's smile melted away, as she remembered that what had happened to these two last night was no joke whatsoever. And the "guy in the skullcap" – if there were any chance he was who Celeste suspected – was the furthest thing from a joke any of them would hear all year long.

Meantime, down Hookeville way, boatanchor busted ass. It had queued up Miles' script and now directed the assault on the remote FTP server, querying for Arabic terms and dumping them on the mysterious server just as fast as it could get prompts.

Boatanchor didn't mind the load – or notice it, for that matter. It wasn't doing anything else. Well, almost nothing else. It had been getting some unexpected finger, anon FTP, and other suspicious probes from a .gov host, and others from an unresolvable IP address. Boatanchor happily told them all to go to hell. It had been taught well.

But . . . no machine is an island. Not forever.

Boatanchor worked over the mysterious server, while mysterious others worked on it.

"I . . . can't say for sure," Celeste allowed, finally undertaking to explain why Dana's report had changed the mood in the apartment so completely. "But I'm thinking this might just possibly be, um, a contractor with whom my firm sometimes . . . contracts."

"What sort of work," drawled Miles, looking up at Celeste from his squatting position, "does this contractor do?" He looked a little ill.

"He does wet work," nodded Celeste matter-of-factly.

"A cleaner?" chirped Dana. Her tone and wide eyes indicated that she found this novel. Celeste's averted gaze – and the tone of *her* voice – said that she did not find this novel.

"*The* Cleaner."

"Huh?"

"Around my office, he's referred to as *the* Cleaner. The Cleaner."

"Holy shit. I thought you worked in consulting."

"Yes, but I never told you what kind."

* * *

Several minutes of silence passed after the discussion of which indefinite or definite article should be used in referring to their presumptive assassin. Then Celeste gave Miles and Dana the three-minute rundown, in general terms, of what sort of work she actually did at Global Acumen.

"Well, we sure came to the right place. But," Miles added, still clearly uncomfortable with the prospect of him or Dana being professionally assassinated, "what do we do now, knowing all this? Shit, I can't believe you know this guy. What are the odds?"

"Well, it may or may not be who I think it is. But it is a relatively small professional community. As for what you do now, well, I think the winning strategy is to turn off your script, log out, and never make another attempt to break into that site." She held Miles' gaze stilly. "If there are people out there who feel protective over what's in there – and who are also employing professionals of this quality – then trust me: you do not want anything to do with it."

"Who exactly is this professional?" Dana finally asked.

Celeste shook her head. But she couldn't resist talking up a workplace icon. "I've met with him twice. He's big, about six two, maybe two hundred pounds. Wears a topcoat. He never takes off his oval specs – though he did remove the black skullcap, when I entered the room. He's impeccably mannered, but in this strange, childlike way." She paused, not intentionally for effect, but just to swallow dryly. "He's said to be unstoppable and unkillable. He's killed a great many people."

"How many?" squinted Miles.

"Why don't you tell me," said Celeste, obviously keen to change the subject before she fomented hysteria, "about this Arabic dictionary. How does it work, and is it going to get you into this FTP site you really shouldn't be messing around with in the first place?"

"Oh." Miles glanced at the laptop on the floor. "Nothing to tell, really. It's a dictionary of Romanized Arabic terms. It's a private project, but I know someone who's working on it. So I have access. I told my script to suck as much of the Arabic dictionary as it could, and try it all on this log-in. As to whether it will get us in, I have no idea. However, if it's going to, it might do it more quickly now. I turned everything else off, and it seemed to be running pretty quickly, last I looked."

He sat back down at the laptop and typed for a few seconds. "Well . . . no breakthrough yet. But there is mail."

(FreeBSD is) Out Like a Scout on a New Route

"Yo, boss, you don't wanna see this, but you best take a look. The webcams are going down."

Ace was shouting, something of a cautious shout, out of the server room. He had gone in there to pack backup tapes, carrying them out in treacherous stacks. On the floor by the pool table in the rear sat three identical, huge, black sports bags. The two zipped ones contained cash and coke, respectively. The third was for data and was only yet half full.

FreeBSD sat on the divan with his back to the packing scene, flailing away Mozart-like at a laptop on the coffee table. He was trying to crack somebody's shit.

"Yo, *chief*. I say the *webcams* are going *down*." Ace stood in the doorway of the machine room, backlit by the fluorescent lights within.

One part curiosity . . . two parts vanity . . . and three parts thinking ahead to future possibilities (albeit remote ones) drove FreeBSD now. Drunk on this witch's brew of motivations, he endeavored to learn more about his trying correspondents.

So far, he knew this Miles Darken character had turned up in town with his package; that the redheaded chick had come with him; that they both had adopted a curious desire to *give the bag back*; and that their proximity seemed to increase, by a large factor, one's likelihood of being repeatedly shot. What possibly could have gone wrong in Hookeville to result in all this, FreeBSD couldn't for the life of him. And, moreover, he didn't know enough about the people to whom he'd been trying to sell that bag to even guess what in hell they might do now.

But, with a little savvy hacking, he figured he could at least gather some data about the pawns in this game – the crackers from Hookeville, the babes in the big city. Data such as their identities, backgrounds, and current physical location.

FreeBSD knew they were in the city, but the Darken character still wrote him from out of Thomas Jefferson College. He had already probed the mail host, boatanchor, a few hours earlier, but had found it locked down tight. He could have gotten in, given time, but he and time were not buddies at the moment. So he did it the easy way: he broke into a nearby router.

A few choice traceroutes told him that everything that went in or out of this machine hopped through the same two routers at TJC. So, a few hours earlier, he had dropped a piece of code into one of them – code which would sniff any mail packets on the way to, or from, boatanchor.

Now, squirming on the divan, he saw it had worked: a couple-three messages had landed in his crabtrap. Oddly, one of them was *his own* message to Darken from the night before, but forwarded to one <celeste@gloac.com>. FreeBSD would bet the ranch (though, admittedly, his general attitude was, "What the fuck, it's only a ranch") that <celeste@gloac.com> had a Manhattan street address.

"Yo, boss," Ace whispered solemnly in his ear now from a range of one inch. FreeBSD spun like a top from the shock of warm breath on his ear hairs, started to speak, then stopped. "*The webcams . . . are going . . . down.*"

"*Huh?*"

"Some *motherfucker*, is fucking *outside*. The cameras are going *down*."

FreeBSD rose and followed Ace into the server room, where the two hunched tensely over a twenty-inch monitor. Seen from behind, the two consisted of a big knot of sandy dreadlocks, on the left; an ace of spades carved into the surface of a short afro, on the right; and a whole bunch of tense back and neck muscles all around.

The monitor displayed a dozen grainy video feeds, in 200×200 pixel windows, laid out in an orderly matrix. Six of the windows displayed various urban scenes: a trash-strewn alley; an empty corridor with a door at the end; a service entrance on a rooftop, with steam vents jutting up in the foreground and papers blowing by. The other six windows were blacked out.

Now seven were black.

"Whup, there goes the rooftop."

"*Ohh, this sucks*," FreeBSD whined. He was watching his eyes poked out in front of his face. "Is it the guys in the sedan? Across the street? Why didn't you tell me about them before?"

"It's not the guys in the sedan," Ace said. "And I did tell you about them before; I put it in e-mail. Don't you read your mail?"

"How do you *know* it's not the guys in the sedan?" FreeBSD looked back and forth between the display and the side of Ace's head.

"Because those guys're still there, man," Ace said. "I checked two minutes ago."

Another window went black.

FreeBSD stole a glance at some of the other workstations in the room, not looking for anything in particular. "So then they've got to be doing this remotely somehow . . ."

"Not that either," Ace answered. "Those cameras ain't on the Net, neither is the box driving 'em. Ain't nobody gotten into the box, I checked that, too. Trust me. It's the *physical* cameras, being disconnected. Basically . . . somebody got a pair of wire snippers." He paused, the two of them gazing wide-eyed and transfixed at the monitor, trying to guess which camera would go out next. "I wrote you 'bout the sedan first thing this morning. Didn't you read the mail?"

"Yeah." FreeBSD twisted his neck to the left. "It must have gone in one eye and out the other."

Ace had bought, months previous, a dozen twenty-nine-dollar webcams and installed them at various points around the perimeter of the Crib. This precaution might have been excessive, but for the low cost. The only real expense had been labor – thinking of a dozen appropriate places to stick the things. Since then, their little gnats-eye-view images had projected into the server room, monitored sporadically by various employees – dealers, enforcers, coders – as they wandered in and out.

And now they were all going black. Not randomly; but in a sequence describing a rough arc around the perimeter of the structure.

Rousing themselves from their stunned vigil, the two young men turned to face each other for a moment, before both pulling handguns from their waistbands. Both were already thinking about breaking out bigger hardware, and considering which cannons they wanted at hand in a crunch.

This was looking increasingly like a crunch.

"Maybe . . . we shouldn't'uv sent the Crew home, after all," Ace offered quietly. "You want I should finish packing?"

"You bet," FreeBSD answered with a grin, as he cracked and checked the chamber of his black SIG Sauer semiautomatic. "But grab some more guns first. Oh, and—"

Ace turned back to face him, his bulk half out of the doorway.

"*—pick up the pace, Ace!*"

He'd wanted to say that forever.

"Did you ever meet yourself coming around a corner?" someone had once asked FreeBSD, admiring his caginess. Now, sitting in his besieged Crib, his only company Ace; a chopped M4 assault rifle with duct-taped reversed magazines; his SIG, with two spare mags, jammed in a pocket; the laptop, with purloined e-mail; three burgeoning bags of dope, cash, and data; and some deadly motherfuckers outside with wire snippers (and God knows what else) . . . FreeBSD calmly reflected on all of his good planning.

He was in really good shape. He really was. All he had to do was get out of the building alive. While he reflected on that exigency, he also did some quick online searching.

He copied the address <celeste@gloac.com> out of the mail snagged from Darken's router.

While doing this, he mentally reviewed the contents of the escape bag in his other digs, the studio four blocks away, where he sometimes went to sleep away from the 24/7 activity in the Crib. The escape bag contained a passport, a couple of changes of boxers, a toiletry kit, and $75,000 in cash. He'd intended this, in his contingency planning, to be merely enough to get him out of the country. But still, it made a significant supplement to the $400,000-some he had in the Crib, all of which Ace had piled into one of the black bags. All told, it added up to just about enough for a comfy third-world retirement. Or at least a shamefully long vacation.

Next, he grepped the newsfeed for <celeste@gloac.com>. A hit came up right away, in alt.quotations. There was a signature file tacked onto the post. There was a name in the .sig.

FreeBSD also thought, while doing this, about logging into his servers, and running the shell script which would wipe virtually everything, trashing the file systems of every Unix box in the Crib (and a couple elsewhere). Then it would trigger a piece of custom hardware inside the power supply which would blast the entire array of machines with enough juice to send motherboards shooting out through the roof like burnt toast.

He copied the name from the .sig – "Celeste Browning" – into a web-based white pages. He typed "New York, NY." He clicked on the Search button, and waited one second. A street address came up – just onc. It was in the 50s on the West Side. *Bitch is in the book*, he thought. He took a big bite of his one last quad espresso.

He watched Ace dance heavily around the main area with a Benelli autoloading shotgun in one hand and a red and silver gas can in the other. He splashed gasoline across the pool table and over the bar, sending fumes everywhere. Ace was bringing down the office. Soon the Crib would be a charred but pleasant memory. Just a matter of a few minutes and a heat source.

Only one of the webcams was still up. And the phone service had gone out. But the T3 line was humming right along. Must be some real old-school guys working this job – killing the *telephone service* for Chrissakes. Not the briar patch. FreeBSD carried on typing.

He copied the street address for Celeste Browning into a text file and transferred it to his smartphone via Bluetooth. That way he'd have it even after he blew up the server with his mail on it. Maybe later he'd feel like sending a dead fish to these guys, or something. More likely, he'd be busy drinking margaritas and drawing rainbows in the white sand with his sunburnt big toe. He drained his espresso, toasting that thought. He stood up, letting the laptop fall straight out of his lap. It bounced once on the coffee table and hit the floor with an ugly thunk. He gave Ace a big smile and a thumbs up, signaling that he should start the inferno, and that the two of them should make their run for it.

FreeBSD swallowed a huge lump of adrenaline and pinged what felt like every nerve on every surface of his body. The air glowed in front of his face. The deadly hardware, in his hand and in his waistband, felt like instruments of the Holy Sacrament. The espresso in his belly rolled like the ocean. The metaphors fell like rain in his head, and his eyes rolled back for an electric second. He'd never felt so alive as now – faced with the challenge of getting out alive.

Ace flicked his Zippo, arm extended. They both cocked their heads – they could hear engine noise outside, seeping into the eerily silent Crib. Traffic was approaching their normally deserted stretch of block. A strange thing to hear just then. Surely their senses were jacked beyond normal.

Ace lifted his eyebrows at his boss, asking if he should proceed. He fell down. Pitching forward, he showed a wet, red divot in the back of his head where the ace of spades used to be.

FreeBSD watched him fall, trying to register what he saw. He ducked his head reflexively, and his mouth formed an *O*, and his rifle came up and he emptied a fifty-round magazine into the back of the Crib. In two and three quarter seconds he fired it completely dry.

FreeBSD never heard the zipping sounds of collapsing air pockets cutting a channel over his head, plunking into the stereo behind him, shattering glass and circuitry. It all got erased, retroactively drowned out, by the roar of the full-auto assault gun in his hands, filling and shaking the room.

He never saw anything distinct, either – but he wasn't really aiming. He merely kept the trigger depressed as he lunged forward to grab the bag of cash with his left hand, then reversed course in a sprint toward the front door, while swinging the gun around to fire behind him.

Pushing his flailing and wild-eyed way out the front door, he was all but dumbfounded not to feel any bullets plunk into his back – a sensation for which every cell in his body had grown prepared. His surprise at seeing a half dozen police cars screeching to a stop outside was extremely minor by comparison.

He dropped the rifle, which clattered noisily on the sidewalk, and executed a hasty U-turn into the adjacent alley. He shifted the weight of the bag around behind him, to help his balance as he ran, and also in case anyone started shooting at his back. He thought he smelled smoke as he hit the next block – the coast there was clear, a miracle – and he thought Ace must have dropped the Zippo when he fell. If he made it through the next minute alive and free, he promised himself, he'd try to log in and see if anything remained up in the Crib. Still chugging full-out, lungs pumping, limbs flailing, a huge black bag bouncing on his back, he crossed himself in silent memorial to his deceased loyal henchman. Then he focused on those three remaining interminable blocks between him and that toiletry kit.

Unlike the driver, Theron waited until the squad car reached a complete stop before hopping out. He'd bummed a ride in the black-and-white the twenty-four blocks from the bathroom crime scene to the Garment District – and what was clearly about to become another crime scene. The first part of the ride hadn't been exactly leisurely, as half of the NYPD officers and detectives on the scene, and Theron, rolled south on Eighth Avenue toward the address from the incoming message on the answering machine. It didn't seem likely that the perpetrator – who'd escaped from an impossible trap, and killed a baker's half-dozen of SWAT team members doing it – would go from the scene of his hair-raising escape straight to a hit. But it was the lead they had.

They passed 42nd Street moving fast and began to circle around a drab, vaguely industrial couple of blocks, triangulating in on the address. As the caravan turned at last onto the correct block, an unmistakable peal of rolling automatic weapons fire rang out, causing the entire group of police cars to accelerate wildly for forty yards, and brake madly for an equivalent distance.

As Theron slid out of the back seat, his Colt in his good hand, a blithe dispatch came across the police radio: shots fired – at what was starting to seem like a very familiar address – and all units respond. *Man*, thought Theron, looking warily up and down the street, *these mugs must have 911 programmed on speed dial.*

As the crowd of officers scrambled out of their cars and across the street, pistols drawn, Theron thought he could see a figure blurred with speed rounding the corner into the alley. He must have seen it right, as several of the uniformed officers angled toward the alley at a dead run. He also saw smoke spilling out over the top edge of the doorway.

As he approached the vestibule it "flashed": smoke, ash, and heat blasted out of the open door with an audible whoosh. That was always, Theron knew, a pretty good time to enter a burning building, if you were going to – right after the flash. He looked around to see if anyone was watching. Unfortunately, a couple of uniforms, as well as Detective Eyebrows, were looking at him intently. Their facial expressions moved in synch from alarmed to indignant as Theron picked up his trot toward the smoking entranceway.

Fuck it, he thought, taking a deep breath and pulling his leather coat around him, *I'm not even supposed to be here.* He put his head down and charged inside.

Twenty seconds later he emerged back onto the street. Flames flickered from behind the second-storey windows overhead, and Detective Eyebrows did a little flame job of his own on Theron as he teared, blinked, coughed, and held his coat tight around him. Theron nodded humbly at the invective and meekly followed as a young white cop led him away to the end of the block.

Theron stood on the corner, sucking oxygen, and lightly massaging the warm laptop he clutched underneath his duster. Five minutes later, a yellow cab appeared and pulled over as Theron raised his hand, lowering his head. No one noticed when he ducked into the cab and drove neatly away from the shouting, burning, confusing scene. A few seconds later, Theron found the laptop still humming, with an open browser window showing a search query return. It still displayed a name and street address: Celeste Browning. Upper West.

I am a BADass, thought Theron T. Johnson.

"*Biatch!*" FreeBSD ejaculated into the small, and otherwise quiet, space of his studio. To his amazement, he had gained the apartment, winded, terrified, but all in one piece and uncaptured. He had tossed his pistol on the bed, and the satchel on the floor, then hauled on its heavy zipper.

It gave way to an expanse of white powder under plastic: the bag o' blow.

"*Fargin' biatch!*" he shouted again, for emphasis.

Ordinarily, in his trade, he could easily convert high-grade white stuff to the green stuff. Now, however, FreeBSD found himself suddenly out of business – and with *no particularly good fucking way to turn a quarter million dollars worth of coke into a quarter million dollars.*

"The *fucking cash*!" he loudly lamented, all red-faced and forlorn, and kicked the bag of drugs across the room. It knocked over a spindly-legged plant stand, which fell with a crash.

A thump sounded from his floor, which was some other guy's ceiling. "Knock it off, you asshole!" a voice floated up. FreeBSD clenched his jaw and proceeded to jump up and down with his full weight, six times in a row, dreadlocks grazing the ceiling at his apex, shouting, "HOW WOULD YOU LIKE TO EAT A BOWL OF BIG FAT DICK!!!" at the top of his lungs. He jumped twice more. "*AHHH!!!*" He snatched the SIG from its resting place on the bed and took aim at the floor. He pivoted left, then right, picturing the layout of the apartment below, finger twitching on the trigger.

But almost lighting up the downstairs neighbor brought him a bit back to his senses. He had some issues to deal with, and needed his full faculties to do so. He stood motionless, shoulders slumping, and considered.

He wasn't the first person in history to grab the wrong bag in the heat of the moment – but he was the latest. *Tarantino would appreciate this*, he thought sullenly. *I wish I did.*

But where did that leave him?

It left him fucking poor, after three years of drudgery in the computer business, and more than eight months risking his precious neck in the drug trade. Suddenly, he didn't even have six figures to his name. His exit strategy had turned into a receding horizon. This was bullshit.

Quickly enough, he realized what he needed now. He

needed the Manuscript deal; he needed it back. *Fuck enlightenment*, he snarled inside of his head. *I want to get paid.* He'd given up on that deal, given it away, really, afraid of the risk that had built up exponentially around it, and reasonably confident in his liquidity position. Well, the risk hadn't gone away – if you were paying attention to current events – and all his cash had. That was bullshit, too.

He'd given the deal away; but he knew who had it. And now he knew where to find them. He yanked his phone from his pocket. While jabbing at it with his thumb, he dragged the escape bag from under the bed and checked the contents. He threw in some more mags for the SIG.

He read this message from himself – correction, from his former self. Out of the trade, he guessed he was Paul Lineberry again. No, that didn't feel right, either.

You can never go home again.

"But, shit," he muttered, "I can go to Celeste Browning's home. Two tears in a bucket – fuck it." With his bag, his SIG, and the address glowing off the small screen, he tromped intently out of the door, and he didn't bother to close it behind him.

The Grace of No Meaning

"Mail from who?" Dana asked. "The dealer?" She was referring to the message Miles had found in his account, on logging in to check the progress of his script.

"Not this time," Miles replied. "This one's actually from boatanchor. Suspicious system activity. Someone's been trying to get into my box."

"Did they succeed?" asked Celeste, returning from peeking out of the blinds, worried.

"I don't think so. Most everything you could try to get into a Unix system, and which would show up in the syslog, has been tried. There are a few things that will trigger boatanchor to write me: too many failed login attempts, attempts to NFS mount certain volumes, whatever. But there's a lot more subtle stuff in the syslog."

"Does that mean your system has been compromised? Or your mail? What does that mean?"

"Uh, no. I don't think so." Miles typed zippingly. "Well, I wouldn't think so, except for one thing." He paused to arch his eyebrows. "My job is stopped. The one I had running that dictionary against the mystery FTP site. It's not running anymore."

"I think we can assume the worst here . . ." said Celeste, grimacing through tight lips.

"No, not so. Could have been all kinds of things. I wrote the script kinda quick. Sometimes processes just die, and you never figure out why. Might be joott."

"Jute?"

"JOOTT. Just one of those things."

A totally different hand-held electronic device from FreeBSD's – but fascinatingly with the same street address showing on it – lay on the passenger seat of a gray Camry going north on Varick Street. The usual pile of high-tech crap sat beneath it; but he'd cleared out the back entirely. At the corner of West Houston he came to a stop and leaned across the cabin to read an unlit neon sign on the front of a nightclub. Two men in neat but nondescript suits emerged from the doorway, smoothing the breasts of their jackets and not looking at anything in particular.

They split, one circling the car, and got in the back of the Camry on opposite sides. Both were Hispanic, wearing dark sunglasses and with closely cropped hair. The one who'd circled around was young, with a smooth dark jaw, brilliant teeth, and a light step. The one at the curb was older, a little stouter, and unsmiling. As they pulled the doors simultaneously shut behind them, they were surprised to see the driver exit the vehicle.

Stanley Luther swung around and took up a position bent

over the back driver's side door, a foot or so distant from it, one hand on the window sill, the other out of view.

"Tell me who you are," he said calmly, "and only your mouths move."

Fear, and then indignation, passed across the face of the man closest to Stanley, the younger one. He started to speak, but was cut off by the other, who removed his shades and placed his hand on his companion's sleeve.

"Salvatierre and Moreno. We're here at the behest of the Concern to help you recover a lost item and to retire a . . . a 'red-headed bitch'? Sound about right, friend?"

Stanley climbed back in and pulled away, grimacing. He removed the Blackberry from the seat and passed it over his shoulder between thumb and forefinger.

"Either one of you know where this is?"

"Keep going north," answered the older one, his sunglasses back in place. The younger one looked out the window, his right elbow on the seat back, left hand resting on his lapel. The sun came out and glinted on everything.

"How long has it been stopped?" asked Dana.

"No idea. But I'm restarting it."

"So, I'd really like to think through," said Celeste over the mouthpiece of her phone, "what exactly that means if your mail has been compromised." She was on hold with the GA Ops desk. The duty staff there were checking to see if Celeste's phones, home or work, had been tapped, and if her accounts showed any signs of being breached. They were also sending someone by to case her block.

"Well, they'd know a lot more about security advisories and ridiculous user support problems."

"I'm more interested in shit like – yes, Bob, I'm here. Thanks, I appreciate it – shit like my name, my e-mail address, and my invitation to meet at the coffee shop four blocks from here."

"Look, I'm sorry," said Miles, almost looking up while he

typed. "You definitely don't need this. I'm just gonna restart this process, and then we'll throw this bag in the river, and get a cab to my car. And I don't think whoever is after us will bother you after we're gone."

Celeste looked surprised, Dana fearful, and Miles resigned.

There was a knock at the door, and all these expressions melted into terrified blankness. Dana gave Celeste a "You expecting someone?" look. Miles hit Return, restarting his hack.

While he'd felt incredibly vulnerable hailing the cab, FreeBSD felt a hell of a lot safer inside of it, slumping in the soft seat. He'd recited the address without referencing his phone. The more blocks he got from the Crib, the more he felt himself sinking into the delightful womb of anonymity that was the city. He didn't relax, but he did smile nervously. He was able to remember that this shit was hilarious, just as everything always is. Life in the world is a slapstick comedy of massive proportions. To take it seriously would be absurd. He crossed his legs, and draped his arm over his luggage.

Cash out early and often, he reminded himself, for future reference. For now, his main chance – the next one, most likely the last – lay just a few blocks up the road.

"Hi, Bob." Celeste stood at the door for almost a minute, eye at the peephole, gun barrel pressed stiffly against the wood, before opening up. Miles and Dana hid in the bedroom. Celeste was committing that most American of abuses – using company resources for personal business.

"Didn't know what the trouble was, but I wanted to come myself," said Bob. He stood six feet, athletically solid, with gold-rimmed glasses on a clean-shaven face.

"Just you?" she asked.

"Busy day. In any case, I've already checked the alleys, the roof, and the lobbies across the street. If you're being surveilled, I can't find out about it."

"Did you check," she asked, peering over his shoulder, "the Caddy across the street?"

"Sorry?"

"The Caddy. Across the block." But she could already see, over his shoulder, that it was gone. He followed her gaze but she said, "Never mind. Thanks for coming out."

"It's my pleasure. I'm going to do another circuit, then have a nice leisurely take-out dinner in my car at the corner. If I see anything amiss, I'll jump right back here. Or give you a call."

"Thanks, Bob." Celeste couldn't help smiling as she squeezed his arm.

Bob tripped lightly down the stairs as early evening sunlight maneuvered through a crack in the skyline, slanting onto his shoulder. It would be getting cold soon. The street was empty. He unclipped his phone from his belt and brought it to his ear as he crossed the street.

"This is Brickhouse," he said. "I've checked in with Browning. All still clean."

"Roger."

"Got that security audit?"

"Yep," an efficient male voice answered. "I've just mailed it to you there."

Bob continued to walk the empty street, a few feet off of the curb, avoiding the sidewalk with its shadowed doorways and stairwells. A few lights started to come on in the other brownstones. The sun set into the city's skyline. As Bob approached the corner, where his car sat in the lengthening shadows, another man rounded the corner in his path.

"Got a light, friend?" the man asked, seeming nonchalant, suddenly only two feet from Bob. A smiling Hispanic in a suit. He extended an unfiltered cigarette and looked Bob in the eye.

Bob took a quick step back, scanning the street around him. "Don't smoke," he said. "Sorry." The man still stood between Bob and his vehicle; but then he raised his eyebrows and shoulders in a friendly way, put his gaze on the sidewalk, and continued down the block. Bob watched him go, while also watching every other spot in his view, at, and above, street level. He got in the car, started it up, and drove around the block, parking again on the opposite end of the street. When he killed the engine, the Hispanic man was gone.

"Okay, don't sweat it," said Celeste. "Everything's fine. The cavalry's here now."

"I still think," offered Miles, "we should get out of your hair . . ."

He stopped when he saw Celeste's expression. Her gaze was still aimed toward him, but her brow was furrowed and her focus well beyond Miles' position. She opened her mouth to speak, paused, and then looked at Dana. Finally, she spoke. "This manuscript you described. Am I alone in thinking this has *really* got to be some kind of a fairy tale . . . some sort of urban myth?"

"No," Dana said simply.

"I mean," Celeste went on, looking at nothing, "all the secrets of creation, just scribbled down in one place? It's not the kind of thing . . ." She trailed off, licked her lips, and looked again at Miles. "And you think this thing is at that IP address?"

"I don't know," answered Miles quietly. "Do you?"

"I think," said Celeste, seeming to come a bit back into the room, "there's something there that a whole bunch of people were willing to shoot it out with one another in Central Park to get a look at. Which makes me rather want to see it, too."

"Well, I'm glad you said that," said Miles, "'cause my script is running again."

"That's the spirit," said Celeste, with a slightly tired smile. With that, she disappeared into the kitchen and emerged with three tall bottles of beer. She handed one to Dana as she passed the couch, angling toward the center of the room. Dana reviewed the label, which was all in German.

Celeste handed off the other bottle to Miles and asked, "So, if you had to guess, how long will it take you to break into this site?"

"Oh, shit," Miles replied, before taking a long pull from the bottle. "Hard to say. Depending on latency, it might get likely in as little as a couple of weeks. In other words, I'll have to send you the results by e-mail." He smiled, and lowered his head, looking placidly at the bottle and computer in front of him, shifting his gaze from one to the other.

The room had grown dark with the setting sun. They'd been there all day.

Miles did a double-take at his screen; then a triple-take.

Some shouting sounded out on the street, but died away quickly as Celeste and Dana leapt to either end of the drapes on the picture window. Miles didn't move from his spot on the floor.

"What was that? What did you hear?" asked Celeste.

Dana said, "Sounded like 'Fuck.' And something else."

The laptop screen in front of Miles said:

```
Connected to 238.142.222.64.
230 User shastra logged in.
```

Miles typed:

```
ftp>ls
200 PORT command successful.
150 ASCII data connection for /bin/ls.
Manuscript.txt
```

And he boggled quietly at the filename.

Celeste couldn't see Bob anywhere on the street. She could make out his car at the end of the block, but no Bob in it. She pushed Dana aside to peer out the window from the other side. As Dana stepped aside, she saw Miles' expression in the laptop's glow. She padded quickly to his side.

"You got in . . ." she whispered.

Miles squinted deeply, then gave Dana a brief look. But he seemed to be looking right through her; she could see him furrow his brow and silently mouth, "Manuscript dot, " and something else. He looked back to the screen, and typed:

```
ftp>get Manuscript.txt
200 PORT command successful.
150 ASCII data connection for Manuscript.txt (32456 bytes).
```

Dana peeked over his shoulder now. Reading the text on the screen, her breath went out of her.

Celeste still stood at the window. She unholstered her Bersa, unsafetied it, and spoke over her shoulder: "Okay, guys. I think we're leaving. Be ready. When we go, we're probably going out the back. There's a door in the utility room at the end of the hall which leads—"

But Miles and Dana were transfixed by the screen and not listening very well.

```
226 ASCII Transfer complete.
32461 bytes received in 7.433 seconds
```

"—to the alley. I'm going out to check the street out front first. Be ready—"

Miles opened an FTP client to download the file from boatanchor in Hookeville, to the laptop in New York. He was getting a vague auditory impression they might have to log out soon.

"—to go quickly." Celeste turned to look at them. "Did you get that?"

"We got it," said Dana.

"We got it," said Miles.

Celeste checked the peephole again, yanked the door handle with a deep breath, and stepped out with her hand under her coat.

* * *

"Something's wrong," said Dana.

"She just left a second ago," responded Miles, glancing around now.

"No, with your download. It's only a 32K file. It looks like it's hung."

"Oh. Sure enough." The FTP client had frozen. Miles checked the wireless network connection. "Shit, it kicked me out. What crap timing; we got the first 2K of the file." He looked tired. "I'm going to see where Celeste is."

He stood and looked around the dim apartment, as if for the first time. Quiet had encroached along with the darkness; it seemed suddenly very crypt-like, particularly with Celeste not there. *I should be paying better attention*, Miles admonished himself as he went to the door. He looked through the peephole – nothing. As he cracked the door, Dana spoke from behind him, "Miles . . . look at this . . ." She had taken his place at the laptop.

Miles turned around again, and the sweep of the door revealed to his view a young, dark man in a suit trotting across the street directly toward him. His hand was in the small of his back, and he moved intently, smiling brightly. Miles slammed the door.

The Grace of No Meaning 2

Two kilobytes of text sat on the file system of the laptop – a small patch of crazily varying magnetism on a little-used corner of the hard drive. They had overwritten a note Miles had written to himself, long ignored, and deleted. They'd taken a long trip without papers or letters of introduction and, as quickly as they navigated the wormhole, it closed down behind them.

Dana opened up the truncated file. It said . . .

"Marines! We are *leaving*!!!" No, that was Miles. He was running through the room, and he was shouting, and looking at everything but Dana, who could feel herself not moving. Miles disappeared into the rear of the apartment, his frantic aura fading behind him. Dana shifted her gaze back to the screen. Words had appeared there, and they said:

> In the winter of 1868–9, with the companionship of one William Maxwell, and against a paroxysm of the Wanderer's chronic malady of Ennui, I bade adieu to consular duties in Santos, trekked overland across the Brazilian Highlands, and pushed through to the desolate Pampas of Argentina.

The screen was far too bright; it hurt her eyes. She also heard music – some Bach, or Björk, or something. An embedded sound file? She put her thumb to the button with the sun icon; some of the glare seemed to go away. She saw no volume button. She looked again to the screen. It said . . .

"Laptop! In the bag! We're going!" Miles pulled on her elbow. She came to her feet, and he draped her backpack around her shoulders, and tried to wrench the machine from her grasp. "No! I'll carry it!" a voice, hers, protested. In his left hand he held his satchel, and in the right the frayed and threadbare red duffel, and Dana's right hand.

As he began to jerk them both into the rear of the apartment, Miles pulled up short. He had caught sight of the black case on the kitchen bar top – the one with the guns, which Celeste had never put away. "Don't move," he said, and darted into the kitchen. He unbuckled the clasp on the case and pulled open its cover. In front he found the big nickel automatic Celeste had pulled out earlier – a Ruger, in .40S&W. Miles snatched it up, then began rooting jerkily through the other contents, coming up with a dual magazine pouch. He pulled one magazine out and dropped the mag from the Ruger; they were identical. He shoved the pouch into his pocket and returned to Dana, who still stood motionless, staring into the screen of the laptop. It was saying to her:

> In those remote heights, revelations were given to me – ones more fantastical than any held by any one of the world's revealed religions – or of the lot combined

Miles yanked on her arm, and they lunged the full length of the apartment. Her bag felt weightless on her back; she clutched the laptop in front of her. But then they ceased their headlong flight, as the back door, peeling paint and hinges creaking, opened before them. Thin light came in from the alley, and suddenly they reversed course, moving backwards, back into the apartment. An awful stillness came in with the dirty light. Dana saw a huge gun pressed against Miles' head, and an unsmiling man in front of him. The two walked backward in slow motion. The laptop screen said . . .

"Ah! Whatcha got on there?" No, the man with the gun had said this. He was bulky and blond and smiling now, with big teeth. "Maybe . . . some sports scores! Uh . . . Stock ticker? No?"

The screen said:

> These revelations left my mind in tatters. They were to do with: whence the soul comes and to where it goes; the string of our lifetimes, and the good deeds and foul that attach to each of us; the shape of time before any times – and how all times are only just beyond our sight; and what lies at the edge of space – a universal soul that longs to take us home.

And then the screen bled away its glow, and the music, real or imagined, faded into the other large and menacing sounds swirling in upon them. With a final glance downward, Dana saw these last characters fade into dead LCD gray:

> Most implausibly of all, these claims of a revealed wisdom,

> of a universal cosmogony, of a beautiful history of the cosmos and life within it, of a binding and final morality, of a living Godhead . . . have been demonstrated to me, beyond any question of doubt or disbelief, to be: true.

Miles' left hand still clutched the bags, and Dana. His right arm, terminating in the Ruger, lay at his side, ninety degrees away from being useful to him or her. He couldn't make his gun hand move.

Dana watched the screen of the laptop, waiting for instructions. But that was it, the end of the truncated file. It was the point at which they had lost their connection, for the uncommon reason of the physical link being severed (i.e. Salvatierre cutting the line).

And now the screen saver kicked in.

And now she could see the blond man's head bounce forward awkwardly, a look of pain and shock on his face. And the laptop said:

"Nice and slow there. Or I'll give you a way to talk shit going as well as coming." Actually, that was Celeste. She was standing a few feet behind the blond man, in the alley, with her Bersa held in a modified Weaver's grip, pointed at the base of the man's skull. Her sleek and indeterminately colored coat flapped in the light breeze. She'd conked Stanley Luther ungently on the back of the head to get his attention, then deftly retreated outside of disarming range.

Stanley mouthed *Fuck me*, which Miles could easily discern, facing him inches away.

Surprised from behind, Stanley now had a decision to make – but one which got easier as he caught sight of Moreno, standing inside, gun in hand, grinning up a storm, and covering Dana and Miles from behind. He had walked in the front door of the apartment under cover of all the strained silence. So Stanley spun around rapidly, showing his ass to Miles and his muzzle to Celeste.

The two stood squared off, eight feet from each other, in that most untenable of postures: the Mexican standoff. They looked each other in their steely eyes, each more resolute than the other.

Neither one fired.

They just aimed, in unspeakable silence.

While the small bits of street noise and city breeze float into the little alley; as the first lights of the evening spit to life nearby overhead; while Miles stares numb and misty at the back of Stanley Luther's big blond head and hopelessly wills his gun hand to move; while we're at this little pause in the action . . . now's as good a time as any to reflect on the anomaly of the Mexican standoff.

This erotic and breathless dance of two people pointing pistols at each other in close quarters evokes a thousand timeless themes: the ultimate fragility and nakedness of the flesh-and-blood human body; the infinite and seemingly easy capacity of people to inflict grievous harm upon one another; the galling interdependence of living in a world with six billion others; the icy resolve and quiet fearlessness of warriors who have passed beyond death, and the unstated and unemotional respect and bond between them.

One could babble on.

But beyond, or perhaps before, any of this symbolism, one wants an answer to a pragmatic question of tactics, one which dominates and galls the intellect: Why does neither pull the trigger? Is it for the theatrical purpose of inserting some deathless dialogue? Is it a wrong-headed delaying tactic to jockey for advantage? Is it hypnotism? All of these explanations offend the common sense.

Only two answers will do. For the amateur, the Mexican standoff novitiate, it is simple paralysis – a mind-killing wall of fear which stands invincible between the finger and the trigger; terror insurmountable. For the professional, on the other hand, it is an equally simple calculus of mutual assured destruction. For the professional knows that a handgun is not a magical switch for turning people off – it is merely a mechanical device for putting holes in them. And people with holes in them, even well-placed holes, can usually manage to squeeze an index finger. It's possible to *win* a Mexican standoff; but there's no reliable way to avoid getting shot as part of the deal. Hence the immensity of the impasse, the imbroglio of horns well-tangled.

Back in the alley, Celeste Browning did her best to look unwavering and resolved. Her hands did not shake, but her heart beat so loudly she worried it might actually interfere with her hearing. Stanley Luther pulled himself up to his full height and breadth, broadcasting intimidation and rebuke. His hands did not shake, but his armpits had flooded with acrid water, and the corner of his mouth had developed a sharp downward tic.

Neither fired. And neither dared speak. But someone else did, from inside.

"I don't think you want to go there, eh, friend?"

Just as, at the end of a long age, Miles had finally willed his arm to work, and to raise his gun to the blond man's back, a silky and smiling voice spoke from alarmingly close behind him. Moreno went on, "Why don't you lay the pistola on the washing machine there. And you and I can watch together how this thing plays out. Eh?"

Miles thought he could feel the hot beam of the man's smile on the back of his neck. He wanted to comply with the directive, but he'd lost arm control again. The fingers of his left hand bit into Dana's bicep, behind and beside him.

"Your friends," Stanley Luther finally said aloud to Celeste, damning himself for having to clear his throat, "have come a long way just to get you killed. Maybe you should choose your houseguests more carefully. In fact," he said, cocking his head,

"I'm thinking you should just, you know, just walk away right now."

Stanley stood just inside the door frame, facing outside, one foot on the hardwood floor, the other extended out to the dusty blacktop of the alley. Celeste stood directly opposite him, halfway between the exterior wall of her building and the next one over. To her right, the alley ran twenty yards to the street; to her left, it was five yards to an access path behind the building.

She answered, "Sure, we were just leaving anyway. But unless I'm mistaken, that's my brownstone you're dirtying up with your fat foot there. And unless you plan on subletting, you're really going to need to take your little panty raid back on the road."

While her attitude appeared unimpaired, Celeste's vision had begun to suffer from the tunnel effect that often afflicts those in violent contests. She could easily count the large pores on her adversary's nose. But visual details got blurry from there, in concentric circles out from the point of her focus. There isn't any such adage, but there could be, that – just as there are no atheists in foxholes – there is no peripheral vision in alleyway shoot-outs.

Stanley cleared his throat again, this time thoroughly and with relish. He relaxed his jaw muscles, and began to speak. "Okay. You know, I can see your point there. I can see maybe where we should just leave." The hairs on the back of Celeste's neck were going batshit, but she couldn't think of a likely cause. "Maybe I'll just put my gun down. And we'll call this whole thing even. And – no, on second thought, after all, I think I'll just have my friend Salvatore—"

"Salvatierre," the Latino said, stressing the subtle difference in pronunciation, and causing all hope and strength to immediately drain from Celeste's body. He spoke from ten feet away, slightly behind her and to the side, having walked right up the alley from the street.

"Yeah, sorry," said Stanley. "Just shoot her if she's holding that gun in five seconds."

Celeste pondered how many of her thundering heartbeats filled up a second.

At that moment, Dana shut her eyes. She remembered hundreds of hours spent picking over the eternal verities. She thought of the intellectual, clinical remonstrations of scores of brilliant and distracted philosophers; the soulful cries to heaven and declamations of clergymen from a hundred revealed religions; the evil silence of a single dead thinker in a tiny, book-lined office. She felt the battery of the laptop slowly going cold in her hands.

Miles thought about his inadequacy. He had first faced an invincible wall of mind-killing fear between him and the end of his right arm. Then, he endured the shame of watching his own hand place the gun on the top of the washing machine, where it sat heavily, and henceforth might as well have been a hundred miles away in a tree.

Celeste was pretty much just thinking one thing, to herself: *I fucking told you so.*

Then, as she looked on, frozen where she stood, Stanley Luther's facial expression went through a rapid series of transformations. It changed from smug dominance to mild alarm; then to panicked disbelief; and finally settled on amused regret. Celeste followed these facial convolutions and then watched Stanley put on an encore performance of his mouthing of *Fuck me*. And then a whole brand new, and pretty much totally unfamiliar, voice spoke aloud, audible through the alley, and into the interior of the building. It said:

"What's the rumpus, bub?"

Of the six other vertices in the deadly and increasingly complex polygon of this standoff, only one position – Stanley's – offered a view of the newcomer. Miles, Dana, and Moreno were inside the building. Celeste couldn't see much outside of a constricted visual cone centered on Stanley and the doorway. And Salvatierre, ruefully, had his back directly to the street. And as for Stanley, all he could really make out was a big pile of sandy dreadlocks, a single bloodshot eye, and a set of black gun sights, all peeking over the curve of Salvatierre's neck. The latter seemed to be losing his dark complexion by degrees.

"Let's not be too hasty," offered Salvatierre, speaking over his shoulder.

"You're not seeing everyone in this game," added Luther, thinking of Moreno hidden inside.

"Let's cut out all the smart talk and get to the stupid talk," said FreeBSD, striking Salvatierre savagely at the base of the neck. As the man crumpled, the drug dealer fired a half a dozen rounds over Celeste's nose. She fell instantly to the ground, and Stanley, back arched, hand over his head, scrambled a frantic retreat around the back of the building.

Instantly, Miles and Dana pulled each other into the alleyway, while Moreno stood stock-still and uncomprehending as he watched their backs disappear out the door.

Those two, Celeste, and the newcomer sprinted out to the street, skirting the prone form of Salvatierre underfoot. In the only rear-guard action, Celeste and FreeBSD fired a half dozen rounds at the few blond hairs that poked, briefly, around the corner at the back of the alley.

"Ooh! *Smooove*!" shouted FreeBSD, before squaring up again and sprinting flat out.

Out on the street, they immediately spotted a cab heading their way. Gun under her coat, Celeste jumped out to hail it. But it turned up occupied: a round-faced black man sat inside, swiveling his head as he passed, the whites of his eyes huge. As it passed them, FreeBSD grabbed an arm in each hand and pulled the group around the corner, where the cab he'd come in sat waiting, back door invitingly cracked. The four tumbled in, shoving FreeBSD's luggage to the edges of the back seat.

"Penn Station," said Celeste, picking a destination at random, just to get the car moving. The searing reek of ignited sulfur and cordite hung all over and around them. The driver, frowning, nose twitching, peered suspiciously at the rear-view as he pulled out and turned south.

Bob's Last Hit (A Negro Child is Born)

It was the last group of search terms – the one with all the hot-button terrorist and drug references – that got all the hits for Bob. Not at first; not immediate, dramatic, voluminous results. But, soon enough, Bob – the friendly anthropomorphized computer program – began snaring esoteric documents in its fine-mesh search net, and grabbing Paul's elbow, and poking his ribs, at all hours of the day and night. "Hey, Paul, take a look at this," Bob would prompt. "It's some trippy shit."

Now, FreeBSD attempted to relate this history to his new acquaintances, Miles, Dana, and Celeste. Slowly finding his narrative rhythm, he continued: "It had been over six months since I'd quit the Media Lab, when the fateful e-mail came in. Triggered by Bob's last hit." He paused, looking rueful. "Everything's always in the last place you look for it."

The four sipped coffee in a corner booth of a greasy spoon in the Bowery. They were no more than ten blocks from FreeBSD's torched place of business, and his dead friend and colleague. But the woman in the coat had directed the driver here, during their sensationally tense cab ride, and FreeBSD hadn't felt like contesting it. It had already been a long day.

Celeste, Miles, and Dana didn't yet have any response to his jumbled tale. They were occupied shifting their postures around the guns tucked in their waistbands, trying to be inconspicuous. The four of them concealed a small arsenal – and a less-small aggregate level of paranoia. The booth oozed with adrenaline and borderline panic.

One can only imagine how this group might have reacted if they'd had any way to recognize Theron T. Johnson when he walked in five minutes after they did and sat down at the counter. Dana certainly should have recognized Theron. She'd not only met him, but seen him get shot, as well. But memory is fickle – and that goes double for bad memories.

Theron, however, had immediately recognized Dana, when his cab had rolled by them, during their sprint from Celeste's alley.

FreeBSD went on, speaking to Miles, Dana, and Celeste, while Theron listened in, picking up snatches of the conversation while trying not to crane with the same inner agony one uses to hold off a sneeze. FreeBSD spoke deadpan, head gliding from side to side on his neck. He stared at the table top, occasionally scanning the other customers, and faces passing on the street beyond the glass.

He paused to bum a cigarette from Miles (a clove) and went on with his story, still avoiding eye contact. He had just given them the eight-minute version of how he'd come to search the Net for the literal meaning of life. The next eight minutes would be the show stopper.

"How did your program crack through the password, when it hit the site?" Miles asked. "Did it do that with every authenticated server it hit? Just brute-force the log-in?"

"No," FreeBSD shook his head. "I mean, yes. But that's getting ahead of the story." He waved his cigarette vaguely and eyed the man behind the counter, who was visibly trying to decide whether they could smoke those in here. "The meaning of life was just an afterthought. Well, okay, it was the main thing. But there was some other pretty damned interesting shit going on out there." He paused to drag. "Underground economies. Electronic black markets, running day and night. People buying and selling information."

"What sort of information?" asked Celeste.

"This." He bobbed his head. "That. Lots of corporate data, trade secrets, new technologies not in the news yet. And tons of stolen code – fragments, entire development projects . . ."

Miles found this talk unbearably exciting. He sat rapt, gazing across the table.

"Then there was the government stuff." Sitting across from Miles and Dana, and beside Celeste, FreeBSD spoke more emphatically now. He gestured with his crackling cigarette, causing Celeste to shrink, and reminding her of Christmas hams past.

"What," Celeste said, stifling a cough, "kind of 'government stuff'?"

"Well, let me put it this way. Anybody who thinks federal agencies are slow adopting Internet technologies is looking in the wrong place." Celeste seemed keen for more detail and FreeBSD elaborated: "NSA sites. The foreign service. CIA, too. They're all using the Net, I'm guessing, to keep in touch with agents abroad. Hell, maybe they've been using it that way since 1973. Maybe that was the whole idea behind ARPAnet. Anyway." He paused to flick an ash. "I found a bunch of these services running in some very obscure spaces. I couldn't break into most of them, but even the front doors – though obviously intended to be opaque – made it clear that Uncle Sam was behind 'em. I managed to get into one or two. Scary stuff."

"What makes you think," chided Celeste, "that you got out without being detected?"

"I'm still here," FreeBSD laughed. Then his smile went cold. "Though, considering recent events . . ."

Celeste looked knowing. "You should consider recent events. Do you know who all those people in the Park shoot-out were? We don't."

Miles thought FreeBSD looked and talked much whiter than he seemed online. Miles felt vaguely guilty to have assumed FreeBSD was black. But the guy had paraphrased a Public

Enemy song in his mail the day before. Then Miles remembered that he too quoted PE.

While pausing and clinking his coffee cup for a refill, FreeBSD caught Miles' look. He interpreted it correctly because he had seen it before. He said, "I'm not as white as I look."

He elaborated. His maternal grandfather had been of African descent. But he had never considered himself such, not until late in life. While it wasn't technically necessary to be black to sell drugs, he had convinced himself that it might be helpful. In any case, Paul firmly believed that it was every man's right to reinvent himself – America stood for that, if anything. His prior transformations hadn't bought him much – chemistry undergrad to chemistry grad student, grad student to slacker sysadmin – but he'd be damned if he didn't do it right this time. If moving from genteel Cambridge to the back alleys of Manhattan wasn't enough; if changing careers from computer professional to organized criminal didn't do it; then perhaps a quick change of ethnicity would put him over the top.

"But I'm getting ahead of myself again," he noted. "Back to the drugs."

Through the vast spaces where the wayward, the forgotten, and the buggy Net services floundered; past the digital bazaars where industrial spies and code brokers traded compileable baksheesh behind filmy curtains of basic authentication and kerberized logins; beyond the dusky virtual corridors in which feds and spooks passed each other unblinkingly, handing off encoded and digitally signed binary packages; further into the reaches of this non-space, there resided the crown princes of the virtual deal: The Drug Kingpins.

"Right, the drug guys," FreeBSD intoned. "They were in crazy big – and they were smooth. Shipment scheduling, inventory management, surplus leveling, security. I saw it all. As far as technology goes, the narcotics industry adopted early – and often. The Net turned out to be the perfect enabler for the underground economy. And the barriers to entry were mighty low."

"Surely you didn't find all this just sitting out in the open?" asked Miles.

"No, no, no. It was all authenticated. But it wasn't locked down very tight. If the Feds had known where some of this stuff was – and who knows? maybe they did – they wouldn't have been long getting in. I'm good, but anything I can claw my way into, the NSA can pop like a twist-off forty. The point was the security by obscurity. *Serious* obscurity."

"So, what," asked Miles, "did you just like subscribe to the NYC drugs list, and that was it?"

"Not exactly." FreeBSD chuckled, spinning his coffee cup. "I started by bidding on a shipment. Coming into Boston, from Toronto. I withdrew some cash, took out advances on some credit cards. Showed up at the deal quakin' and shakin'. I bought the lot, arranged to sell it at a tidy profit two days later. I pocketed the cash, and went to bed drunk on adrenaline. Called in sick to work the next day, then sat by the water for two hours reliving the whole deal. It was the tits."

He smiled now, misty-eyed. "A couple-three more deals like that and I said, 'Fuck it.' I was hooked. Another ten weeks doing deals, making contacts, buildin' a web site and database back-ends to drive transactions, and I was *never* going back. But by then I figured out NYC was where all the action was. I made a deposit on a space in the thirties, and relocated. Hired a couple of people, some good fellas. Of course, they're mostly dead now. And I got the new name."

"Great name," said Miles.

"I never fooled myself," FreeBSD went on, more serious now. "I never thought thug life would be all laughs. But, on the other hand, that's where the money was. And I figured I was smart enough to keep a step or two ahead of the odds." He paused and sighed. "Mainly, it was something to do."

He continued, sounding resigned. "I always thought it would all end in a DEA raid, maybe bloody, maybe not. Or a federal marshal with a fistful of warrants. Or one of my own employees getting ambition – or getting paid more by a competitor."

He shook his head. "I never thought a ghost from my past would flit down into my new life and wake me from the dream." He looked up from the table top. "And it *was* like a dream. Unimaginable cash – trashbags full. Total autonomy. Yeah, running the business had its demands. But I ran it my way. And then the undeniable rush, the ego trip, of having triggermen, genuinely dangerous individuals, on my payroll. Ah. Humbled by a stupid philosophical bent. And by my own weakness in following where it led. Toppled, by Bob's Last Hit."

He paused. "It's all true, you know. I think it's all true." Miles, then Celeste, had read the first 2K of downloaded Manuscript, on the laptop, back in the cab. They'd seen enough to know what FreeBSD was talking about.

After his change in locale, profession, and lifestyle, FreeBSD still took a mobile phone everywhere – a de rigeur tool of both his new trade and his old. (Old joke: Only two industries refer to their customers as "users.") However, the Media Lab phone had long since gone into the drink, and Bob didn't know about the new one. It never occurred to FreeBSD to tell the script the new number.

He had cleared out of Cambridge quickly; and if he thought about Bob at all on his way out, he assumed the next sysadmin in the queue would find him and kill him. But he'd over-esteemed his successor. Bob had continued to run quietly and diligently in the background for those eight months, sucking cycles from that back-corner Media Lab machine, quietly and remorselessly exploring the cyberspace badlands on MIT's nickel. Looking for the meaning of life.

When it found it, it sent out a text message, which went to the bottom of the Bay. But Bob also blithely and unblinkingly sent mail to <paull@media.mit.edu>. This got forwarded immediately to the anonymous remailer in Finland, and thence to FreeBSD's account, in the Crib.

"It took Bob over five months to get in," he whispered into the booth. "Totally hung up on the one site, working day and night, trying to crack the password. That's why I didn't hear from him that whole time; that's why I forgot. Then, out of the blue, he rang. Imagine my surprise when I found what I thought I'd stopped looking for. Especially when I didn't really believe it existed. Especially when I thought I'd found the answer somewhere else." He laughed ironically.

"So," asked Celeste, getting at last to the money question, "do we get a look, or what?"

"Yeah, okay," FreeBSD replied. "Got a copy in my pocket." He slid out of the booth. "You wanna get the check? I'm not as rich as I was two hours ago. Let's get the fuck out of here." He strode across the floor and out the door, obviously expecting the others to follow.

The Manuscript

The city did loops around their path, lunging at them with the soot of bus exhaust, and the streetlight shadows of cold buildings, and indifference. The four walked in the lethe field of the Otherwise Occupied, staggering a slightly unstraight path, unable to recall twenty minutes later the route they had taken. Caffeine, and nicotine, and adrenaline darted up and down their circulatory systems, quickening blood flow, sharpening senses. They stopped in a semblance of a park, a quarter-block patch of green and gravel, because it was there, and because their path ran to it.

FreeBSD walked ahead and they found him holding up a peeling dogwood. The others formed a protective tribal circle around him; he fired up his phone, handed it over, and its glow illuminated them.

* * *

The trio leaned around each other, in front of the sliver of a device, contesting intermittently for control of the buttons, and the scroll bar.

They read it straight through.

And then again.

And a third time.

When they had finished, the last spark of the setting sun had gone out. No one spoke for a while.

"Well, I guess that settles things," said Miles, finally.

"Remember those, uh, those . . . important problems . . ." Dana stammered, trailed off.

Celeste remained silent.

Bob's Last Hit, Redux

The cells of four bodies cried for flight: a wilderness forest with a muffling pine needle floor; a small New England town, on the Sabbath; a gravelly, loudly windy mountain top; the mirror surface of the middle of the Gulf of Mexico. Anyplace but the city. Four bodies, every nerve screaming, "Bail! Just get the fuck out."

But how to get out of sight? FreeBSD no longer had a home; Celeste's had been jarringly compromised. Miles and Dana had a room in a hotel where the day manager was most likely inspecting bloody footprints in the carpeting on the third-floor hallway; the police were probably involved. The streets swarmed with sedans with dark tints. A million alleys, windows, corners, and shadows dripped menace. The city sang a song of persecution, of conspiracy.

Finally, some atavistic but apt instinct drove them underground.

A subway car wasn't bugged. It wasn't staked out. No one was circling in on it with drawn guns and malevolent beaming smiles. There was nothing on board to ping, traceroute, or NFS mount.

There *was* Theron, who had trailed them from the diner, and then ensconced himself in the car just behind theirs – but they had no good way of knowing that.

In their subway car, the four talked about cashing out. Like a thousand fugitives before them, they needed traveling money.

"No, I didn't advertise it," answered FreeBSD, explaining how he'd first come to put the Manuscript up for sale. "I didn't do shit with it, initially. I didn't quite know what the fuck it was."

The rocking car shook the cigarette from Dana's hand. It rolled down the aisle and underneath the opposite bench, irretrievable. She shifted her gaze to her shirt front.

"Okay, I figured out what it was. I mean, I'd been looking for the thing. But you don't just take in shit like that right away. If you're out looking for the meaning of life, it takes a while to sink in that you've found it. As for what I did then: I didn't advertise it. But I did respond to somebody else's ad."

The four sat huddled in the rear of the shuddering steel canister, shaking.

"I spent all night, and then some, reading, just reading, the thing. I didn't know what to think. I went back where I started, lurking on some of the religion groups, hoping to maybe catch wind of something that might help me sort it out in my head." He paused, looking even more tired. "And you know, it was funny – right away there was a post in alt.religion.misc, someone asking about what had happened to alt.religion.taoism.angry. The newsgroup where I originally read about this thing."

"Dana's post," said Miles.

Dana only shrugged.

"I did keep looking around," FreeBSD went on. "I hadn't read any of those groups in ages, so I checked the archives to see if anything had come up. Sure enough: there's an archived post from this guy, on alt.religion.misc, about three months old." FreeBSD's expression changed to amusement. "He was pretty ham-handed. He was like, 'Hello out there, I hope I'm doing this right.'" FreeBSD spat thinly on the floor. "*Any*way, sure enough, he was describing the Manuscript, or something damned like it. Said he's looking for a rare religious document by Sir R.F. Burton, thought to be lost."

"Jim," said Dana, half-hidden behind her bangs.

FreeBSD appeared to grow weary of historical narrative. His voice told the tale, while his body made little let's-get-on-with-it gestures.

"I responded." He lolled his head left, then right. "I said I might have heard of such a thing, and how much was it worth to him? He offered me five thousand. Of course, that meant nothing to me, so I told him thanks but no thanks. And I went back to work I could conduct on a profitable basis.

"And, of course, thinking about what I had read. Little hard to just get back to the grind after reading sump'n like that. Leaves you on edge. Thinkin' 'bout eternity. Wantin' to know if there's any truth to it. Trouble, was: Castrolang was *not* the only party getting my mail." With this comment the rail line noise seemed to fade to the background. "And I guess I wasn't the only one getting his."

"It was the spooks," said Celeste. "The Federal Government. Right?"

"No. Oh, no."

"Oh, yeah? Who, then?"

"Trust me, it wasn't the Feds. Some scary motherfuckers, but not the Feds. And what they were communicating, if I might continue, was a counterproposal. Their mail copied the original offer of five thousand, and my mail where I said, 'Thanks but no thanks'. And then it said, 'What do you say to five *hundred* thousand?' It was signed, 'A Concerned Party'. Well shit, I was concerned, too, if a half mil was on the table."

Theron had ridden a different line than this one to school, in his youth. But he wasn't far from his old stop. The familiarity, the pleasant nostalgia, formed a soothing bubble around him. But he kept that emotion, and every other, far away from his face.

He sidled up to the door at the end of the car, and peeked through the porthole Plexiglas. His four new best friends were still on board.

"'You got it,'" FreeBSD had said, in regard to the second, rather more generous, offer. "'You want it by mail?' But they weren't having any of it. I wrote back that I had *found* the thing online. They replied, saying they wanted the address of the FTP site. Didn't want a digital copy of it. Didn't want it by mail. They obviously didn't trust the networks."

The four sat blankly while the train shuddered to a stop. Passengers trundled on and off.

"What were the headers on the mail?" Miles asked, when the train and noise resumed.

"It was forged, of course. From <foo@bar.com>. I traced it upstream, naturally. It had been forged from a machine at cert.org."

"Holy shit. They sent forged mail from CERT?" Miles could tell from Dana's expression that she didn't recognize the acronym. "The Computer Emergency Response Team," he clarified, speaking breathlessly. "The guys who investigate computer break-ins."

"Yeah," said FreeBSD. "I think they were trying to tell me I wasn't going to figure out who they were. I took it at face value. Of course, they were writing to me through my remailer, so they didn't know who I was either. I hoped. What they told me was: do the deal with Castrolang."

Celeste: "Who is this Castrolang?"

FreeBSD: "Academic type. Professor of philosophy. Down at Thomas Jefferson College." He spoke the last words in stentorian tones, sounding for a moment like the college professor he himself might have become. "The 'Concerned Party' wanted me to sell *him* the Manuscript. But they had two requirements. One, that it not be the document itself, just the IP address of the site where I found it. And, two, I had to go to the deal myself.

The implication was, they would take it from there. They didn't say how they would take it from there.

"I was beginning to wonder who the fuck I was dealing with, and whether doing so was a good idea. But, you know, I had a retirement figure in mind, and was anxious to get to it. A chunk of change of that size would put me right over the top. Plus, how does one put this . . . I felt more anxious than ever to be on a beach somewhere, pondering the mysteries of the universe. Or, as things turned out, critiquing the solutions. I had a lot of shit to think about."

"Like the Complete Divine Magisterial Secrets of the Entire Universe," said Miles.

"Right."

The three listeners seemed deferential, and thoughtful. They had a lot to think about as well. The silence stretched out as the train decelerated jerkily into another station.

"Giving up the IP address, and the port number, and the password – I had no problem doing that. And the second requirement – that I go in person – didn't bother me either, 'cause I figured, hey, they have no idea what I look like. I can send anybody. I wrote back to Castrolang, telling him, on second thought, you know, my rent was due, and five thousand dollars actually sounded great. And I knew just how to make delivery. As it happened, I do some business in Hookeville, now and again, and I could stop by his office on my next trip. Drop off the item, take the cash, and how would that be?

"Castrolang wrote back – and, again, I'm sure it wasn't just me getting the mail – that this would be fine. But he was gonna send someone else to do the deal, and not in his office. He was very firm about not going himself. So we arranged for a meeting at the fraternity house, which is practically my local sales and distribution center. And Castrolang told me who I'd be meeting. Redheaded chick. About five foot three. Hundred pounds." FreeBSD stared levelly at Dana.

"So I slapped the numbers on top of these bags of what

looked like product, and sent them on down south with one of my fellas. His instructions were to meet with his regular connection, then wait for the redheaded chick to show up." FreeBSD looked again at Dana, whose gaze was locked with the floor. "Only, I guess it's a good thing I didn't go myself, because I never saw my guy again. But strangely enough, this bag," and he patted it, "has come right back like a homesick puppy."

This was getting too weird for Celeste. She considered getting off and putting distance between herself and all of this. The words she'd read in the Manuscript, though, were doing strange things inside her head. The idea that things could actually be so clear, after all this, was intoxicating. Also, she had a lot of accumulated leave time, and she could use it any damn way she wanted to. This wasn't the only leisure activity that could get one killed, she considered, even if it was the oddest.

Theron, watching moving lips through the glass, only managed to pick up scraps of this conversation. No sound passed between the cars except rattles and hums. *Wish I was that lip-reading SWAT guy.* He stood up at every stop to make sure the four hadn't gotten off. This twitchy behavior went unnoticed, due to the fact this was the New York subway.

He eyed the redhead. Recognizing her on the street, as his cab had approached the address, had made his already hammering heart skip a beat and a half. He'd felt like an asshole, a speechless one, craning around to follow the four figures as they trotted by and jumped in the next freakin' cab. Regaining his composure by the end of the block, he had barked over the top of the headrests, "Turn it around. Follow the other cab. But don't get too close."

"Yeah," complained his Jamaican cabby, twisting around, "and I suppose you want me to drive real fast and run all the red lights, too."

"No," said Theron, pushing his badge to within two inches of the man's face, "you can drive the motherfucking speed limit, and stop at the lights. But you lose that cab, I'm gonna beat your ass and personally piss on your livery license."

Now, on the train, Theron was fully prepared to beat the ass of the train conductor, too, if it came to that. For the time being, however, he just cooled his heels and kept watch. It wasn't his first stakeout; merely his strangest.

Dana, chin on her chest, voice catching, said, "It was my research project." She paused to wipe away tears, and shook her bangs back in her face. "It was a project for my advisor, Jim . . . He asked me to look for it. He'd been looking for it for years. But he, he'd given up on finding it, because it was thought to have been destroyed." Dana paused and gulped. "And now he's dead." She began to sob.

Miles reached to comfort her, then startled. "Did you see that?" he said. "Someone was looking in the window. A black guy."

"Oh really," said FreeBSD, "a black guy on the New York subway."

"In the next car. I'm gonna go look." In the next car, five rows down, there was indeed a black guy, in a black leather duster. He stared at his feet and didn't look up. Miles walked back.

"There's someone there. I don't know, he's probably nobody."

"Maybe," said Dana, grabbing at the opportunity to change the subject, "it's time to get another room." Everyone agreed, as the train pulled obligingly into 75th Street. They exited.

Strange Bedfellows

"I don't think," said Celeste, in the elevator of their new hotel, "we thanked you for saving our asses. We were one player short of a team before you showed up."

"Don't worry," FreeBSD responded breezily, following the elevator lights. "It was pure self-interest. Needed this bag back."

He patted the well-traveled red duffel hanging from his shoulder. Homeless, they were all slung with numerous small bits of luggage.

"I thought you gave us the bag," said Miles. "And the deal."

"That was then. This is now." He lanced Miles with a suspicious dart of his eyes, then looked back to the panel. "I seem to have fallen on hard times."

"And the other thing," continued Celeste, "is you didn't mention how you came to drop by my home. Or why."

The elevator door opened and the question floated out with them as they exited. Eight eyes scanned the corridor. A few minutes earlier, six of them had blinked in the shadows of the lobby, while Celeste checked them in. She paid for their first night in cash, and registered using a spare name and credit card.

As they strode down the empty hallway, FreeBSD said, "How is easy. I hacked into homeslice's router here," he pointed an elbow at Miles, "and grabbed some mail with your name on it. And – maybe you wanna think about whether this is really a good idea – you're in the book."

Celeste reddened at his smugness.

"And I'm happy to tell you why." Reaching their door, he put his hand over his shoulder without looking back. Celeste pressed the keycard into his palm. He opened the door for the others, entered behind them, and pressed it closed with his back. The three stood in the entry, turning to face him. The room was dark and quiet, and smelled clean.

"Two hours ago some motherfucker came by my place of business, killed my best friend, and burnt the building down. This would have been okay, you know, 'cause I was ready to leave anyway. Only, in all the shooting and arson and whatnot, a big bag of cash – my retirement savings – got slightly confused with this." He swung his satchel, jabbed a thumb at it. "This huge bag of drugs.

"So, the point being," he continued, pushing past and flicking at a light switch, "is that I'm a little light right now, and need to get back in on the ground floor of that five hundred thousand." He plopped on the far bed, reclining on his elbows. "The *bad* news is, I got a ugly suspicion that the motherfucker who tried to kill me today *works* for the bitches I was trying to sell the Manuscript to in the first place. Here's the score so far: Jean-Michel, the guy I sent to Hookeville as me – dead. Castrolang, the guy who wanted to *buy* the Manuscript – dead. All the guys I brought with me to meet you in Central Park – dead. Call me Chicken Little, but it look to me like the motherfuckin' sky comin' down."

He sat up, his tone businesslike now: "So, first all of us are gonna compare notes on this ongoing clusterfuck, starting with Miss Professor's-Little-Helper here, and see if that clears things up any, which I'm thinkin' it's going to. *Then*, we're gonna contact our friends the 'Concerned Parties,' and arrange another sale." He stood and walked to the window, pulling the edge of the drapes, taking a look. "We're going to jump into the fire, and see if we can't get back into the frying pan with the cash. Then we're going to get the fuck out of Dodge.

"At least, *I* am. Y'all can do what you want."

As the luggage hit the floor, and the four collapsed around the room, Dana stumbled into her narrative. She sat on the bed near the door, her back to the headrest, legs crossed Indian style, fingers working nervously in her lap. FreeBSD perched the wrong way on the desk chair, clutching its back with one hand and a burning clove with the other. Miles and Celeste lay on the other bed. For several minutes, Dana spoke at her lap in a quiet monotone, detailing the shoot-out in the fraternity house.

"Well, that explains where my guy went," sighed FreeBSD. "And why I never got paid."

Dana said, "It doesn't explain why the shoot-out happened. Or who the T-Bone guy was."

"Probably a narc," said FreeBSD. "That kind of shit happens a lot in this business."

Dana paused, looking up at him. "Do you want to know where it came from?" she asked.

"Heh," FreeBSD laughed. "It never occurred to me to ask. Why? You know?"

"Captain Sir Richard Francis Burton," Dana recited, "1821 to 1890. English explorer, soldier, anthropologist, eroticist, swordsman, linguist, translator, writer . . ." and off she went.

Several minutes later, the room had grown silent again, as they paused to let FreeBSD absorb this volume of biographical data. Finally, he spoke up, brightening: "Hey," he said. He had kicked something with his boot, and paused to kick it again. "Mini-bar."

"Right on," said Miles. "Let me in there."

They'd all just had, they realized now, the kind of day that called for a drink – or several. Their moods brightened at the unexpected bounty, and someone turned on another light.

Over a single malt, FreeBSD asked, "If Burton wrote this thing, then what happened to it?"

Dana sipped her Bailey's before answering. "His wife. After his death, she burnt everything."

"Then, yo, what the fuck have we been reading all week?"

"We don't know for sure that the original got burnt," Dana replied. "It just seems likely. But we think maybe he sent a copy to someone. Possibly to his friend and collaborator, F.F. Arbuthnot."

"Oh yeah?" replied FreeBSD, draining his drink. "Well motherfucking F.F. Arbuthnot didn't put it in his motherfucking FTP site."

"I'll drink to that," said Miles, raising his glass.

"How do we know Burton even wrote it?" asked Celeste, rolling her Chianti gratefully.

"We don't," Dana answered. "His name's on it. And it reads like him. Also, Burton's fortunes changed a lot for the better after the time in South America. Even his attitude seemed to change. But," and she scanned the room, "does it even matter?"

With that, each of the four of them called for another round, and began putting handguns on various surfaces – so that they could get to them more readily, and so they wouldn't shoot themselves in their respective crotches, in their progressing inebriation.

"Hey," said Celeste to Miles, accusingly. "Is that my Ruger?"

"Um. Yeah, it is."

She exhaled and looked at the floor. "Cool. Just don't shoot me in the ass." She turned back to Dana. "Earlier, you said Jim was dead. Castrolang."

Dana darkened. "Before I called you Saturday morning," she said, looking at Miles, "I went to his office. I have a key, and I wanted to drop off the bag." She shrugged, her face disappearing behind her hair. "Jim was at his desk, the phone receiver in his hand. His chest was all bloody. He always looked so child-like, like he was slightly surprised by everything. He looked just the same dead. That's when I called you," she said, and began to cry again. Miles reached out to touch her arm. "I'm sorry I didn't tell you about that, Miles. I didn't know how to talk about it."

"Shit, I need some air," grunted FreeBSD, after a respectful pause. He shook his head wearily. "And some normal cigarettes. I think these things are making my lungs bleed." He got up and slouched toward the door, patting his pockets.

"I need to make a call," said Celeste, hopping off the bed and falling in behind him.

"Uh," stammered Miles, "is that a good idea, to go out?"

"Donchu worry 'bout me," said FreeBSD weakly, waving a gun reassuringly with his free hand as he turned the locks. He absently replaced the gun as the door opened.

Celeste said, "We'll be fine. You two just don't go anywhere. And stay on your toes."

Miles waited a moment, smoothing Dana's back. "Am I to understand," he asked, "that your advisor was killed for this thing? The same night as the thing in the fraternity house? The same morning you called me? I guess you saved the very worst news for very last."

"I'm sorry, Miles. Please don't be mad."

"I'm not mad. I'm just trying to get my mind around it all."

The two sat in silence and stared into the shadows at the corners of the room.

Two strangers stood in a hallway, sharing the cordial but uncomfortable silence that augurs an imminent elevator.

"How, I tremble to ask, *did* you get involved in this?" the man asked the woman. "You must go way back with those two."

"I hardly know them," she answered.

"Figures." He shook his head resignedly, as the elevator dinged.

"They came here," Celeste said to the closing doors "because they were afraid of you."

"They shouldn't believe everything they read on the Net," replied FreeBSD.

"Should they believe what we read today? Maybe this is your own private practical joke."

"What do you think?" he countered. "And if that's what you think, why are you still hanging? Why are you here *in any case*?" He looked down and across her, monitoring her mid-section.

"I think someone believes in it enough to pay a half a million dollars for it." She stretched her shoulders back, then relaxed them and exhaled. "And I want my hundred and twenty five thousand."

"Oh shit, a four-way split. We're *definitely* going to have to up the price . . ."

"And I'm going to spend the next couple of years in Bali rereading the Manuscript. So, all *you* have to do is not get anti-social on us, and go running off with that bag." She pinned him with her eye. "That's why you and I are going to the smoke shop together."

The doors opened, and Celeste stepped into the cool air of the lobby. Following her, FreeBSD thought, *MAN, this shit gets more whack every minute ON the minute. . . .*

Grand Designs (The Last Deal)

Miles let Celeste and FreeBSD back into the room after an extended review through the peephole. The two swept in in their dramatic coats, and FreeBSD began addressing the group before the door had closed behind him.

"So let's get one thing perfectly straight," he said. "I am not on a mission of mercy to save y'all from death at the hands of bloody-minded and ruthless seekers after truth." He paused and twisted his neck. "I'm here for the money. Show me the motherfucking money."

Celeste stood by the door. When FreeBSD paused, she said to his back, "I find it hard to believe that all of the money you claim to have made was in one bag, which you lost. Didn't you put anything away?"

"What, in a bank? Yeah," FreeBSD said, turning to face her, "with a joint savings account, and maybe a motherfucking IRA, too. What the fuck, did the War on Drugs end while I wasn't looking? Or did the IQ composite drop rapidly today?" He shook his head and exhaled. "Actually, I did have an offshore account. And I had been meaning to get around to actually putting some money into it. Now, if we could get down to the affairs at hand . . ." He moved to shrug off his coat.

Celeste still wore hers. She held her right hand in the coat pocket, and stood in three-quarter profile to FreeBSD. Miles and Dana looked on, motionless.

"First," Celeste said significantly, "you and I need to have a quick Q&A." FreeBSD froze, halfway through taking off his duster.

Dominant themes of this tableau included tension and brinkmanship. Miles hoped to God neither of them drew down. All he could think was that he had zero desire to find himself playing the part of Nice Guy Eddie in a re-enactment of the climactic scene from *Reservoir Dogs*. Dana found herself experiencing massive déjà vu, from the fraternity house. She wondered if she should grab floor. She hated to think she wasn't learning anything from all of this.

"One," began Celeste. "Why are you here?"

"Told you." FreeBSD rubbed his thumb and first two fingers.

"Two: why did you give up the bag, and the deal, in the first place? I don't buy into philanthropy. And Miles never would have gotten into the site if you hadn't told him how."

FreeBSD shrugged slowly and dramatically.

Celeste glared at him icily for as long as she could. But FreeBSD won the stare-off. Celeste smiled. She understood his gesture. If he were to ask why she had helped these two, she could only answer with the same shrug. They were partners in a perverse altruism.

"Three: why do you need us at all? Why don't you take the bag and do the deal by yourself? And why do you even need the bag? All they want is the IP address, which you've got in your head."

FreeBSD's expression softened. He said, "Don't wanna die."

"How's that?"

"I need to do this deal," he continued. "As for why use the bag . . . yeah, maybe I could do a new bag, or give them the address in some other form. But the bag is what they recognize. It's what they're looking for. But that's not even the important point." He drew breath. "These guys with the money, and the e-mail hacking, and the philosophical bent . . . I think they want me dead. They've tried to kill me, I think, at least twice already, probably three times. What I'm hoping is that y'all can make the sale for me, and we can all get out alive. I don't need the bag so much as I need y'all. I need your help." With this he went quiet.

Celeste didn't seem to quite buy this. FreeBSD had one last

pitch: "Plus, you know, I'm kinda gettin' to like y'all. Miss Eager Beaver Net Researcher over there. And Miles, too. Boy's got some chops. You know I couldn't break into your machine? Boatanchor? That's why I had to do the trick with the router. Your shit was pretty tight." Miles smiled. "You'll just have to take my word for it that I am very clannish. If I'm in with y'all, then I'm in with y'all."

"I believe him," said Miles.

"I believe him, too," said Dana. "I think he's being hunted as much as we are."

Celeste frowned and said, "Too true. Maybe they want to kill everyone who's read it. Maybe they want to be the only people to read it."

FreeBSD didn't answer.

"If you turn on us, I will put you down," she concluded.

"*Fuck* you," he shot back, spinning to face her. "I can have you fucking killed."

"No, you can't," Celeste said. "You can't do shit anymore."

FreeBSD laughed. "Yeah, well, I guess that's where you're right." He tore his coat off in a rapid motion. No one reacted. His SIG Sauer stuck out of his waistband. He reached for the satchel with Miles' laptop in it and started unzipping. "Don't mind," he asked, seeming to ignore Celeste, "if I use your machine? Actually, I've got another office on Long Island. If anyone's still there, I can still have all y'all bitches killed if I need to."

"Help yourself," said Miles.

Celeste shook her head resignedly, as she had countless times that day, and took her hand out of her pocket. It had her Bersa in it, which she holstered.

"I been meanin' to do this anyway," FreeBSD said, typing. "There should be a couple of fellas in the satellite office who I can get down here to back us up. 'Course, if they found out the Crib got taken down, they're probably both up in a tree – or, rather, different trees – in New England somewhere, by now."

He logged in and opened a web browser. "They won't hang around long if they think things have gone bad."

"What's all this?" asked Miles.

"Web-based messaging and texting. Allows me to swap messages with my staff."

"It's just basic authentication?"

"That and SSL. But with Anonymizer, me and the boys can leave and pick up messages from anywhere, even in dire catastrophes like this one. Totally secure and anonymous, in every direction. Always thinkin' ahead." He tapped his temple, typing one-handed for an instant.

The two men hunched over the screen. The women hovered at the fringe. Celeste returned to the mini-bar, and retrieved the only alcohol left. "Chardonnay, or Rolling Rock?" she asked.

"The white, please," answered Dana.

"Check it out," FreeBSD said to Miles. "Click here, a chime goes off in the office. If anybody's in, they'll come running and we can do a Java-based chat."

"Cool," said Miles. "Nice app."

"Thanks. Had some time on my hands early on, when business was— All right!"

Text scrolled across the window, and FreeBSD began typing rapidly in response.

Shit! What's up at the Crib, boss? Where you at?

I'm intown. Everything a'ight out there?

We're fine. What's up at the Crib? Nobody answer the phone, no machines responding, nothin. It ain't 5-0, is it?

Worse. It's the competition. The Crib's down.

Oh shit! We're out, then.

Not so fast, Rufus --

How you know it's not William writing?

Never mind. Trust me, I know y'all. Hold up, there's one last thing I need y'all's help on. It'll net you $50k travelling money. You down?

The text stream paused for a disturbingly long interval. Finally it scrolled back:

There's one other thing. Someone dropped by today, looking for you.

Someone *came by the Kitchen*?

Yeah.

Who?

Someone serious.

FreeBSD removed his hands from the keyboard. He pulled a Camel from his new pack and fumbled for a light. Dana tossed him her lighter.

Can you *elaborate*?

Big guy. Heavy accent. Skullcap.

"Tell them to bail," Miles said. FreeBSD looked at him quizzically. "Just tell them to get out of there. I'll explain in a minute."

When we couldn't get the Crib on the line, we locked the office down. Had this guy on camera, all five locks and both guns on the door. He went away when we told him no one here by your name.

Yo, Rufus. You and William get the fuck out. Don't go home. Stay light, check this dropbox. I'll get back. FreeBSD out.

Yo, we're in the wind, boss. Rufus out.

"Well, I guess it's not looking so good for our backup," FreeBSD announced, over the ember of his cigarette. "Oh well, on to the next debacle. Yo, Red, you're on." He pinned Dana with his eye. "You wanna explain the skullcap guy thing?" he added in an aside to Miles. Miles made a short but sobering story of it, while Dana ambled around to the desk.

FreeBSD opened a telnet client and planted Dana at the laptop. Miles gave her instructions in reassuring tones. "These guys know we have the Manuscript. So they shouldn't be surprised if we try to sell it to them. But they've already tried to kill FreeBSD, and he knows it, and they know he knows it. So, it just makes more sense for us to be contacting them. What did they call themselves, Free?"

"The Concern."

"Kind of pretentious. We're the ones with the fucking Manuscript."

"You said it."

"Why me?" Dana asked. "Why not you?" She stared at Miles pleadingly.

"They know who you are, Dana. They don't know who the hell I am."

"Look," said FreeBSD curtly, "all you gots to do is log in and post to alt.religion.misc."

"Don't you have an e-mail address for these guys?" Celeste asked.

"I did. Another remailer. But I tried it two nights ago. The mail bounced. They've shut it down. The only way I can think to get their attention is the same way I did the first time."

"Isn't posting to Usenet a little public?" Celeste demanded.

"Just exactly who do you think is going to read it," replied FreeBSD, "who isn't trying to kill us already?" He turned again to Dana. "You know how to use a newsreader?"

"Yes," she answered.

"OK. So, just post that you're looking for some 'concerned'

people in regard to a 'manuscript' you've stumbled on. Then stay logged in. My guess is they'll send you mail in, like, ten minutes. When they do, you just tell 'em you got the red bag, and you want the five hundred thousand." He paused, looking across the room at Celeste. "Plus another half mil for incidentals."

Celeste peered into her glass, and spoke up softly. "Incidentals like almost being gunned down in Central Park? Or like having my home invaded? No, I think we'll call it a nice round two million."

No one took issue with this unforecast inflation.

"We'll take it from there," Miles said. "Don't worry."

Hands shaking, Dana logged in. She zipped through her list of subscribed newsgroups, posted as instructed, then quit the newsreader and leaned back. Everyone sank in their chairs.

"Now we wait," said Miles.

Ten seconds later the machine beeped. On the command line they could see the message:

$ You are being talked by ⋕" " Press 'y' to accept.

"Talked by nobody?" Miles boggled, locking eyes with FreeBSD. "How the fuck can they be talking as 'no user' at 'no host'?"

"If the shit fits wear it," FreeBSD answered. "Scoot over, goddammit." He took Dana's place at the machine. He typed:

This is Dana. Who is this?

"It's not going to work," said Celeste, stepping forward. "No one with half a brain is going to mistake you for her. Let her back in the chair."

We're authorized by the Concern to pay your asking price for the red bag. Where are you?

"Get the fuck out of the chair," repeated Celeste, stepping closer. "You can *tell* her what to say. But she writes it out." FreeBSD didn't move. "Look, Bob Marley, even your fucking *typing speed* will give you away. Beyond that, your natural language is a dead giveaway. Professionals aren't going to fall for your half-assed impression of a twenty-three-year-old female graduate student. I know, I do this shit for a living. Now get up." He still didn't move. "How did you know it was Rufus a minute ago?"

FreeBSD startled, and gave up the chair. Celeste sat Dana down and said, "Now, you two guys do your worst. But Dana, put it in your words."

> Where are you? Are you still there?
>
> --------------------------

"Tell him you're still here. You're in the city. You have the bag."

> I'm right here. I'm still in New York, that's plenty for you to know.
>
> --------------------------
>
> Are you alone? Who are you with?

"Tell them you're alone. Tell them you ran off with the bag, and you're alone."

> It's just me. You're dealing with me.
>
> --------------------------
>
> Ah, but, Miss Steckler – you left Miss Browning's house in company: your friend Mr. Darken, and our mutual friend Mr. Lineberry.

"Fuck me," muttered Miles.

"*Fuck* these guys," spat FreeBSD.

"Who the fuck is Mr. Lineberry?" asked Miles.

"Tell them," intoned Celeste heavily, "you will meet them in a public place and trade the red bag for two million in cash in another bag."

> Whatever. I'll give you the bag, in a public place, for two million in cash. Show me the money first, and you'll get the Manuscript.
>
> --------------------------
>
> We accept. What is your public place?

Dana smoothed her hair, then replaced her hands at the keyboard. She drew breath.

A series of six sharp knocks issued from the door.

Dana froze, and the others grabbed weapons. Celeste crouched behind the bed, her Bersa in both hands. FreeBSD stood behind Dana, SIG held out stiffly in his left hand, his profile a thin line to the door. Miles crouched in front, feeling for the safety of Celeste's Ruger. Its barrel drooped toward the floor as he fiddled with it.

Six more knocks. Then: "NYPD. Could you come to the door, please? Open the door, please."

"Looks like," whispered FreeBSD, drawing his hammer back, "the jig is up."

Celeste held up the palm of her left hand in a gesture of restraint, and advanced on the door. "Just a minute, officer," she said loudly. "I'm coming."

Dana stared at the screen. She couldn't bring herself to break the silence, even in a stage whisper, even as her interlocutor wrote again, and then again, asking for a response. Finally, she put her fingers to the keys and delicately pressed out a letter at a time in answer. The other three had developed combat tunnel vision and didn't see or hear Dana's typing.

Celeste put her gun in the back of her waistband, motioned for the others to clear out of view, and worked the locks on the door. Behind it stood a uniformed officer of the young, stout, and curly-haired variety. He did not smile. His hand rested on the butt of his holstered sidearm. He had just begun to speak when Celeste interrupted:

"Thank you for coming so quickly, officer," she said, sending little ripples of confusion across his face. "I only called five minutes ago. What time do you have?"

The policeman raised his watch toward his face, and Celeste grabbed it with her right hand. She locked his wrist, turned it ninety degrees, and jerked him flailing into the room.

When he looked up a second later, he had been disarmed, the left side of his face was pressed into the carpet, Celeste sat on his back, and two men were pointing handguns at his head.

"Speak quickly," said Celeste. "Why are you here, and did you call in on your way?"

"I called in," he answered immediately – the too-quick answer Celeste had hoped for.

"That's the second question," Celeste chided. "Take first things first, please, Officer Friendly. What brought you up here?"

When he paused, Celeste pushed his face more firmly into the floor, and FreeBSD, holding his gun sideways with a twisted wrist, adopted a very impatient and wild-eyed look.

"Her. It was her." The cop gestured across the room at Dana with his nose.

"I set up the deal," Dana chirped, as everyone in the room turned to look at her.

Under further interrogation, the cop confessed that a photograph of Dana had passed around at his shift's roll call a few hours earlier. Moreover, his beat passed outside their hotel. Stepping into the lobby at the beginning of his shift, he'd recognized Dana as she boarded an elevator with the others.

"What the fuck about me?" interrupted FreeBSD, giving his gun hand a few additional menacing degrees of twist. "I'm the gangster here. Ain't nobody lookin' for me?"

"I see pictures of ten guys who look like you at roll call every day." Also, the girl was wanted for questioning in connection with the killing of seven SWAT team members in the early hours.

"Where would the police get a picture of Dana?" Miles asked aloud, squinting at the curtains as if someone with the answer might be hiding behind them.

"That's probably my bad," answered FreeBSD. "I had a picture of Dana in the Crib. The Professor sent it, so I'd recognize her at the meet in Hookeville."

"I thought the Crib burnt down?" contested Miles.

"Papers survive fires," answered Celeste, still on her policeman piggyback ride. "Sometimes better than the structure they're in." She waved off this digression and spurred her steed to proceed.

Officer Friendly had gotten their room number from the front desk. As he rode the elevator up to their floor, his radio crackled with an all-units call, an armed robbery four blocks away.

After two hours of crime scene work and paper shuffling, he had gone back out for the remainder of his shift, walking right by the hotel before remembering the redhead again.

Then he came straight up – after calling in, he added gravely.

"Who's got duct tape?" Celeste asked procedurally. Five minutes later they'd taped up the cop, wrists and ankles, gagged him, and deposited him on the bed. Miles rifled admiringly through the gear on his duty belt.

Dana, in the corner, looked like a very pale cat who had eaten some bad canary.

"Congratulations," FreeBSD smiled at her. "You're a wanted man."

"Great," Dana muttered. "What about the deal? I can't go to Rockefeller Center now." The others turned from the hog-tied figure of New York's finest. Their expressions betrayed complete ignorance of what she might be talking about. This gave way to a vague memory of Dana saying something about a deal. They also belatedly recalled that she had been chatting with the Concern when the cop showed up. Miles and FreeBSD raced to the computer. But the session was dead and cold.

"Rockefeller Center?" asked FreeBSD. "Whose idea was that?"

"Theirs," Dana answered.

"When?" asked Celeste.

"Tomorrow," answered Dana. "Noon. There are some other details. I saved the session."

"We shouldn't have let them pick the location," said Celeste. "But too late now."

"Well, shit," said FreeBSD. "I guess the deal got done, while we were fucking around with Ole Bill here. Now all we gots to do is get another room, figure out how to pull off this caper, and get some damn sleep. And then get to the gig." He began shutting down the laptop. "And get paid."

Wordlessly, they all started packing again, using the surface of the free bed, and the space around the prone form of the cop on the other. And then they were on the street again.

Celeste directed their cab driver toward a one-star hotel twenty-some blocks away. When they arrived, she checked them in using a third identity.

In the new room, the four could barely keep their eyes open as they put together a plan for the next day. Finally, sleep came, with morning hot on its heels. Miles woke up first. Lying awake, alone, he tried to put away the night's bad dreams, and think instead of the money, and the Manuscript. The latter brought a flood of anxious questions. As his mind raced, a vestige of the old buzz of thrill, of possibilities, of being alive in the world, echoed inside his chest. Shuddering slightly, he savored the giddiness, lying on top of the covers.

The End of Waiting

"*Two damn hotels in one night*," Theron muttered into the lapel of his coat. His breath rose up white around his black beard and frosted the steering wheel, over which he hunched, shivering. He tugged at the edges of his coat and glared at the climate-control panel.

"Damn *heat* takes all night to *warm up*." He pushed on the temperature control, which was already all the way on the red side. The streetlight picked out the dust on the dashboard controls.

Theron had planned to leave the car parked for the duration of his stay. But when he found he had to stake out a hotel for the night, he retrieved it from the deck where he'd deposited it. He then parked illegally across the street and got busy watching the door. After two hours of that shit, he had just decided to go in and have a chat with the hotel management when the foursome loped out of the revolving door, looking spooked and urgent.

So instead he followed them to the next hotel, this one smaller and cheaper. There, he found he had a view of their room from the street. The other woman, slightly older and more serious looking, stepped to the window and peeked around the curtains, a few minutes after they checked in.

When the lights in their room went out, Theron huddled up and got busy sitting. He prayed for heat, and nursed the dull, cold ache in his shoulder.

A little after 4am, he awoke with a sudden and panicked confusion. He didn't know where he was, or what he was doing there. When his senses returned, he exited the car, now almost warm, and quietly pressed the door closed behind him. Looking in all directions, he dog-trotted down the block to a phone booth, and dialed his partner at home.

"James," he said in response to the muted cough of a hello on the other end. "It's Theron."

"What's wrong?" He could hear the man on the other end rub his eyes. "Where you at?"

"I'm still in New York. I found the girl from the frat house. And I found the dealer."

"Oh, man. You working with NYPD?"

"Sort of. I'm alone right now."

"Whatchu gonna do?"

"I don't know, brother." Theron shivered violently, scanning the purple stillness of the street around him. The voice of his friend did a great deal to reassure him, but it made him feel weak, as well, just to connect with someone who cared about his welfare.

"Why don't you bring them in?" James asked. "Take 'em down, get on with your vacation."

"I thought I should take 'em. But . . . something else is going down. I can tell. They've been on the run, all over the city."

"So what? Let NYPD worry about what the fuck goes down up there. Grab the collar on these two, and let the rest sort itself out. I don't like you messin' around up there. And the chief is going to mount your ass on his wall, he find out you're working this case."

"Yeah," sighed Theron. "You're probably right. I'm not gettin' paid by the hour, anyway."

"That's *right*. You call me when you get back. We'll go kick it for a weekend at the beach."

"You got it, James."

"Okay. You take it nice and easy, T-Bone."

"Will do. Peace, and I'm out, brother." Theron softly replaced the receiver.

In the cold glare of sunrise a few hours later, he willed his stiff legs to move naturally as he followed on foot. The four did not grab a cab. They hoofed it instead, moving quickly. They didn't have all their bags with them, either. Theron was tempted to search the hotel room; but he didn't dare lose them. He followed behind on the wide boulevard, inconspicuous in the morning crowd.

James' advice weighed heavily on him as he walked, shoulders slumped, head down.

Stanley Luther had spent the long evening hours back in his room, mulling over unpleasant e-mail, getting heartburn from too-spicy takeout, flipping channels, and polishing to a high sheen his anger at those Latino guys. They had made certain disrespectful and impolitic comments after their failed caper of the afternoon, before he dropped them off.

He managed to catch a few hours of afflicted slumber. Then he showered, dressed, armed himself, and headed off to what he hoped would be the final act of this highly amateur production.

As he drove through the empty pre-dawn streets, he tried to

grab his mental reins, and get his head back in the game. He even resolved not to kill Salvatierre or Moreno. Not unless he got a really good opportunity to do so.

He pulled to the curb beside the same nightclub. He entered, ascended to the loft office, and found the Latinos sitting silently, loading magazines. Five minutes after Stanley sat down, the front door banged open again, and half a murderous football squad pushed by the doorman and up the stairs. Luther, Salvatierre, and Moreno stood blank-looking as the knot of newcomers bobbed up the stairs. The men wore casual clothes and looked extremely grim. Some were very big. On inspection, Stanley could see that all concealed weapons.

A man in the fore, obviously the leader, said to Stanley, "We're here to assist you today." He paused and changed tone slightly. "Except that I'm in charge."

Stanley could only exclaim stupidly, "All these guys to make one exchange?"

The other man looked off into various corners of the loft. "Our group isn't making the exchange," he answered coolly. "We're juuust backup."

Noel sat upright in a corner chair in the near dark. The room held the chair, a bed frame with bare mattress, and a dresser. A picture window with a white shade would keep out much of the light of the rising sun an hour or so later. A clunky, cubical piece of brown leather hard-luggage sat at his feet. He'd retrieved this – a backup set of weapons, a hot spare – during a quick trip by Anthony's. He'd had to do this after checking out, unexpectedly, from his last residence.

On the counter top sat a thick manila envelope, stuffed with hundred-dollar bills, and a single typed page. This detailed his assignment for the next morning.

Noel breathed evenly and looked out of the corners of his oval sunglasses.

In another sixty minutes – exactly sunrise – he would stand

up, open the case, remove three guns and numerous accessories, and go to work.

In the wee hours, Mike pulled duty at home. He had lost the knack for sleeping during the night, and now felt that a sunrise was a delightful thing to view just before going to bed. Lately, he'd also discovered he could get a lot of side work done while pulling night duty for the AYTs.

He liked to sit in his safe, dry, comfy loft, and keep his fingers on the pulse of things, online.

On this night, the newsmonitor.pl script had sent him mail at precisely 10:15pm.

Their automated script had detected a post in the same newsgroup, alt.religion.misc, and from the same chick, Dana Steckler. Mike stubbed out his cigarette, twiddled down the volume on his headphones, and opened a new telnet window.

Ten seconds later, he had logged onto boatanchor.tjc.edu as user "dollface." Sixty seconds later, he had tapped into her talk session. He did not accomplish this feat of online legerdemain lightly, and felt proud to have managed it so quickly. Still, he caught only the end of the session – luckily, the important bit. He got the place, and the time, for the Last Deal.

He began sending mail to mobile addresses – and lots of it. The messages all read:

Manuscript in play. Kickoff at noon tomorrow. - M.

* * *

A desk phone rings in the squad room.

"It's me. Guess who disarmed one of my patrolmen last night and left him gift-wrapped on the thirty-second floor of a hotel on 75th Street?"

"Not the guy?"

"Not the guy. The other guys. The dealer and the redhead."

"No shit."

Ecstasies of Agonies

The bills outmaneuvered Dana's fingers, her hands going numb in the cold. A few minutes earlier, she and Miles and Celeste had marched up 48th Street, to the corner of Rockefeller Plaza – the street that borders the other Rockefeller Plaza, the one most people think of. The sunken plaza. With the flags and shit.

Right down Rockefeller Plaza, the street, Dana had marched. And right down into Rockefeller Plaza, the sunken flag-ringed court, she had descended – alone, after Miles and Celeste left her. Shoulders hunched, bangs protectively in place before her eyes, she walked with the red duffel bag clutched under her arm, the strap slack on her shoulder. With each step, her trembling had increased.

The Plaza, and the surrounding Rockefeller Center, teemed with humans – something like 240,000 people use the Center each weekday. Dana, on her long, lonely walk to the bottom of the Plaza, passed by an awful lot of them. Each seemed to her to radiate menace. Every eye she caught seemed to pin her. Every face that looked away did so too quickly. Some people were obviously moving out of her way, others were sticking too close. Half of them pressed fingers to ears, the other half had their hands inside of their jackets. The crowd was Dana's personal paranoiac's fantasy.

But unlike the paranoid, Dana was not imagining things. As it turned out, rather a lot of the people who seemed to be out to get her actually were. They'd come for a special event: The Last Deal.

Dana took the ice skates from the clerk and moved to a bench, shaking and looking at her feet.

Miles and Celeste sat on a patio overlooking the Plaza from the next building over, not drinking two cups of coffee. They were close enough to monitor Dana's progress, hopefully far enough away to avoid being seen themselves. Dana was supposed to make the drop alone.

"She's got the skates," Miles narrated.

"I can see that," Celeste agreed.

"Those guys in line don't look like recreational ice skaters."

"I can see that, too."

"Do you see the guy with the money? Anywhere in the rink?"

"Shut up, Miles. And stop grimacing. You'll be ten times less easy to pick out."

Miles pulled his lips across his teeth and literally sat on his hands.

Dana's fingers, trembling and numb, were now giving her trouble with the quick-pull knot Celeste had taught her – the one that could be undone with a single pull. Dana managed it, but excess lace hung down beside her blades. She tucked them into the boots. She shifted the pen, the one Celeste had given her, from her back pocket to her shirt front. She pulled the duffel bag strap over her head again, slung it behind her, and stood up.

The bag felt light on her back and the pen fragile. But a pistol sat heavy and solid in her waistband, an extremely comforting weight. In their last minutes in the hotel, Celeste had equipped Dana with her backup gun, a little Beretta Tomcat in .32. Ripping the Velcro from her ankle, she'd handed it over butt first, with a lot of advice and instruction. Now, Dana resisted the urge to touch it with her hand. She sort of felt it with her waist, moving her pelvis against it.

And then she skated out onto the ice. Merging with traffic, she began to circle. And to look for the guy. He found her first. Before she knew to be surprised, a man skated up alongside her, perfectly in stride. She took in his physical particulars with a horrible fascination. He was big and solid, about six-two and two-twenty. He wore a black nylon jacket, blue jeans, and a black baseball cap with nothing emblazoned on it. He carried a backpack, as Dana expected, black as well, and puffy full.

He smiled at her sidelong, attractive lines creasing in the corners of his mouth and eyes, and motioned Dana over to the wall. The two screeched to a stop and the man grabbed Dana's elbow, as she nearly lost her balance. He pulled her in to him, gently. She gasped, looking the man in the eye from twelve inches away. He said, "Hello, Dana. I'm the man with whom you're meeting."

Tears leaked from the corners of her eyes and she worked to breathe.

"You're going to be fine," he said. "Why don't you sling your bag around so I can open it up, and I'll do the same." Dana nodded epileptically. She fumbled for the pen in her pocket, pulled the cap, and stood there with the felt tip pointing upward stupidly.

"I want to know what's going on," Miles said urgently. "Give me the radio."

"Not on your life," said Celeste. "You'll look like Max Smart with that thing out."

On their way, they had run by a novelty shop specializing in amateur spy gear. They couldn't risk going by either Celeste's home or her workplace, but they did need a couple of items of specialist gear: for instance, the counterfeit-detecting pen which Dana now held. And hand-held radios.

"It would be nice to know what the fuck's going on down there."

"Then use your eyes. Everything's fine. They're making the trade."

Dana and the man stood inches apart. They probably looked like lovers to the other skaters scritching by, and to the hundreds of spectators up top – but not to the several dozen people there for the special event (of which group Miles and Celeste were only two).

The man opened both bags and rooted through the white bricks in Dana's. Dana, steeling herself, began marking bills at random in the backpack. They were all hundreds – thick, indulgent stacks of them. Each of her marks came up golden. Gold or yellow meant they were okay; black or dark brown would indicate a counterfeit.

Dana marked fifteen bills, while her counterpart searched among the bricks and spoke into his cuff. Dana realized he was trying to get the dotted octets into order. The username was straightforward, and the password too. FreeBSD had scribbled them on the back of the brick with the port number, by way of giving the customers their money's worth. But those three-digit numbers had become jumbled.

"Two thirty-eight, one forty-two, two twenty-two, sixty-four," Dana recited. She had memorized it, and had a personal interest in making this go quickly. "Port forty forty-four."

The man held her bag, and her gaze, and said into his left cuff, "238, 142, 222, 64. Port 4044." Then he read off of the final brick: "Username shastra, s-h-a-s-t-r-a; password muezzin, m-u-e-z-z-i-n." Five seconds passed in silence while Dana and the man breathed condensed breath at each other. A voice sounded, too faintly to make out; the man nodded. With a dexterous motion, he switched their straps. Suddenly, Dana wore the backpack, and he carried the frayed red bag.

Dana turned and made for the entrance to the rink.

Theron paid for his slice of pizza and took the end off with his teeth. He'd been out in the cold an awful lot lately, and hadn't eaten in almost twenty-four hours. So he had left the redhead in line for skates and the other two ensconced at the cafe outside, while he ducked into the mall to grab something. The dealer, FreeBSD, he'd lost entirely. But he couldn't follow everyone when they split up. And he had a feeling they'd all hook back up before the day was over.

He held the greasy paper plate with his bad arm and tried to curl the mammoth hunk of pizza with the other. He began fast-walking down the underground mall, back toward the entrance to the Plaza. That's when he heard the first shots. He looked lamentingly at the slice, dropped it where he stood, and took off running down the echoing corridor.

Stanley watched the leader of the backup team, who drummed his fingers on the casing of a laptop as he listened to the radio chatter. This guy still hadn't done so much as introduce himself since his group's dramatic entrance at the bar, and his insolence did nothing to palliate Stanley's normal difficulty in working with others. On top of that, they weren't even doing any work; they just listened to the radio, and waited for something to go wrong.

The group, nine in all – Stanley, Moreno, Salvatierre, and the six ringers – were holed up in a bare basement room in one of the Plaza's buildings. They weren't more than sixty yards from the ice rink, but neither did they have a window, being underground. Stanley considered that they could have gotten something with a window, so as to at least see what the fuck was going on. But, as it was, they monitored things in an auditory fashion, making Stanley feel distinctly mole-like. They could get to the Plaza in a few seconds, up a flight of stairs and down a service hallway. But at the moment, the radio served as their only window on the action outside.

The room held two folding tables, a number of folding chairs, and plaster dust in the carpet. On one table sat the laptop, power cable snaking across its surface, GPRS modem card blinking serenely. Also, a hand-held radio, standing upright and making noise.

Stanley and Moreno fidgeted, and the guy in charge tapped his fingers. The others sat motionless and stared at the room's horizon – the dusty white lines where the wall met the floor.

The bag guy came through on the radio. He'd found the girl; none of the others in sight. Then he was making the buy, and babbling some numbers, which brought the leader upright. He positioned his fingers over the keyboard. The leader started typing, surprisingly quickly for a guy with ham hands. Then he was scrolling and reading through slit eyes, as the others in the room looked on expectantly. Finally, he reached for the radio. Depressing the bar on its side, he said, "It's the thing."

"Roger," the voice came back.

"Give her some space," the leader continued. "Then you and the team follow her to the others." He replaced the radio and slumped back in his chair, his features slackening.

Stanley wanted to ask if that was it, then, and could he leave. But the atmosphere in the room did not convey that that was it; or that anyone could leave.

Then the voice came back through the radio, urgent now in tone.

"Uh, I've got two. Darken and Steckler." There was a crackle. "No, I've got three. Darken and Steckler and Browning, inside of fifty feet."

The leader furrowed his brow for one second. Then he snatched the radio back up and said, "Take all three. You're hot." He put the radio down again, and just had time to say, to no one in particular, "We'll dig up the fourth later," before the distorted sound of gunfire fuzzed out of the radio, overloading its little speaker. He twiddled the volume knob down.

Thirty yards of ice stretched out before Dana like a limitless arctic horizon. The other skaters weaved around her pell-mell. If fear had shaken her going in, it just about debilitated her coming out.

It was all because of the hope.

Dana had started to think that just maybe she would get out of this, not only alive, but with the cash. Before, when planning, when walking in, she'd felt already dead, and had enjoyed that special peace of hopelessness. But now she'd gotten hope again, and it was not her friend. Making for the edge of the ice, she expected at any second to be shot, to be tackled, to be vaporized, as she skated woodenly away. Every nerve in her back fired, every muscle spasmed, her skin cold and her breath gone. Strands of dead hair waved before her face. The weight of the backpack pulled her down.

Miles could see Dana flirting with collapse, and he ran for the Plaza, with Celeste hissing at him to stay put. But off he went. Dana's toes hit the edge of the rink, and she fell into his arms, sobbing, near to fainting, useless, all the way gone.

"It's okay, doll, I got you." And then Miles saw him – the bag guy, only a few skates behind, stepping off of the ice. He locked eyes with Miles and grinned. There was an odd snapping sound, and the man shrunk two inches. Miles looked down, and saw that the blades had fallen off of the man's skates; he stepped forward off the ice without them. And still he grinned, and whispered into his sleeve, and bore down on them.

Miles went ice hot with anger, and his muscles swelled with fury. He envisioned himself punching the guy, drawing down on him, shoving him to the ground. But he merely pulled the other skate from Dana's limp foot and helped her up, readying her to flee, or himself to fight.

But the moment had passed. The man walked past them, with the familiar tatters of the red duffel slung over his shoulder, and the fingertips of his right hand pressed to his ear. Miles swiveled and followed with his eyes. Over the guy's right shoulder he now saw the swirling topcoat and brown silken hair of Celeste, who stood on the stairs, right in the man's path. She had followed Miles down.

The bag guy stopped dead and put his wrist to his mouth. He looked over his shoulder, pinning Miles and Dana in place with his gaze. And then he drew a black handgun from under his jacket and sighted in on Celeste – who now tried to clear her Bersa from under her coat, but wasn't going to make it. She fumbled it, caught by surprise.

Miles shot the man four times between the shoulder blades with the Ruger.

The bullets didn't fall out of the barrel; they didn't successively lose power; the man didn't turn around angry and indignant to humiliate and destroy Miles. The man just pitched forward, dead, onto the concrete, and Miles didn't even really stick around to watch him do it. He pulled Dana, in her stockinged feet, by the hand, and they and Celeste ran for cover.

Behind the falling body, behind Celeste, a press of bodies mobbed the stairwell. Scores of panicked citizens ran up, away from the pitching corpse, but ran headlong into another group, many of them waving badges, coming down. Beside them, another urgent motion erupted from the rink. That left one direction to flee – into the mall.

None of the three had noticed that when Dana and the bag guy exited the rink, fully half of the other skaters had moved, with varying degrees of speed and urgency, to follow them. Fully half of the ostensible recreational skaters were really not there to skate at all.

It was hard to miss, though, when the exodus from the ice turned into a shoving match, and then a shooting match. The last thing Miles saw, over his shoulder, was a tumult of bodies near the skate rental booth, and gracefully arcing droplets of blood as several of the skaters inexplicably fired at each other from point blank range. He heard crackly gunfire thicken and accelerate like an engine revving up, and two shouts: "Drop it! NYPD!" and "Son of a *bitch*!"

Celeste reached the other two and led them at a dead run into the underground mall.

Rules of a Gunfight

The two cops, late of the Throne Room, and a dozen or so of their fellows, stood around a well-appointed corporate conference room directly overlooking the Plaza. The room held a large boat-shaped table, swivel chairs, and an overhead video display. The younger detective stood at the glass exterior wall, peering down to street level, a dozen stories below, with digital binoculars.

"This view is great. Are there any more bagels?" A uniformed officer hustled out of the room and returned with another platter of bagels and assorted cream cheeses. "Because there isn't a frickin' thing going on down there."

Detective Eyebrows shook his head in a slow, wide arc.

"Officer Friendly's sure they said noon?" the other asked, using their sobriquet for the cop they'd found tied up. The poor bastard had made the mistake of noting Celeste's pet name for him, and it had stuck. Despite the joke, the NYPD's stakeout of Rockefeller Center was predicated on his strange and sketchy report.

"You want to ask him again? Pass the bagels," said Eyebrows. The younger one still peered, nearly straight down, with the binocs. "I said, pass the bagels. I don't feel like circumnavigating this table again. I'm old and tired."

"It's her." The tenor of the younger man's voice had snapped back to humorless sobriety. "The redhead. She's in the rink."

Everyone in the room moved toward the window.

"The others?"

Now, chatter filled the room from the radios. It was all about Dana.

"Give me a second," he said, panning the binocs as the radio chatter crescendoed. And then the distant popping of gunfire floated up, muted through the thick glass. The officers in the room gaped at the scene below, as the radio chatter chilled their blood where it flowed.

"*Officer down! Officer down! Requesting backup! Son of a BITCH!*"

From the entrance at the skating rink, the underground concourse made several sharp turns – a good layout for guys on the run. Dana didn't think about the boon of the floor plan. She was concentrating on not sprawling on her ass, running flat out on linoleum in stocking feet.

Miles, while he did spare a look or three over his shoulder, mainly tried to calculate how many rounds he had left in his gun. He was beginning to develop some sympathy for the movie hero who drops his hammer on an empty chamber – when everyone in the audience already knows the gun is empty. From inside the movie, he had a whole different perspective: if you could manage simply to aim, and continue to breathe – much less count off your rounds as you fired them – you were a world champion, as far as Miles was now concerned.

Only Celeste said a silent prayer of thanks for the layout of the mall. The angular twists of the corridor would keep any pursuers from drawing a bead on them as they sprinted headlong.

They only knew for sure they'd been followed when they did hit a straightaway – one of two long, straight corridors running to the Rockefeller Station concourse. In pursuit were two men – the only ones to escape the savage gravity well of the melee in the rink and get to the mall. Two strapping and well-armed badasses, employees of a nameless Whomever, they were brethren of the deceased skating bag guy, his like and his measure – confident, adroit, and remorseless.

They made their pursuit known with a volley of gunfire, pausing to send a group of slugs down the hall at 1,200 feet per second, chipping up glass and drywall as they impacted. Miles heard a fluorescent bulb explode, then felt shards of glass tickle his scalp. Everything slowed to bad-dream speed and he saw filament dust on his eyelashes. Only after did he hear the shots.

Nothing stood between Miles, Dana, and Celeste and their pursuers but empty hallway. But these first rounds fired at them missed, as first rounds often will. The 4th Rule of a Gunfight is to watch where your shots fall and correct your aim. Shooting is a sport of adjustment; even the best marksmanship depends on the alignment of the sights, and the physiology and breathing of the shooter, and the winds. A corollary, Rule #4a of a

Gunfight, says that when scared you will tend to shoot high – so adjust accordingly. Reaching the long corridor, and spotting their prey in the open, the pursuers took aim and began yanking their triggers. They did not watch where their rounds fell, and they didn't adjust. So they shot out, mainly, the ceiling panels and lights over the heads of their targets.

Which was the last break the pursuees were going to get for a while, so they had better take advantage of it.

Safety's off, Miles confirmed. *Hammer back.* He didn't have time for this. But neither did he have time to fuck it up. *How many rounds left? How many rounds?* The gun felt heavy and wobbly, its barrel trying to droop as he lined up the sights. And he had a wicked case of tunnel vision. But, then again, he was looking down a tunnel.

Miles crouched inside a hair salon. This is where his headlong dive had landed him, out of the corridor, to the right, after he identified the sound of gunfire to the rear. The scent of styling gels and conditioning creams enveloped him. Two stylists hid beneath their chairs.

Celeste knelt directly across the way, in a bookstore where she had dove to the left.

Dana, in the democracy of anarchy, had not taken a shop, but instead made flat out for the end of the corridor, for the T intersection at its terminus. She had dove neither right nor left. She appeared to be going for the endzone.

Neither Miles nor Celeste could see her touchdown run. Both of them, within seconds of getting under cover, turned back to face the way they had come. They leaned around the portals of their respective American mall icons, brandishing arms.

This, what they were about to do with the guns, was part of Celeste's job. In her life, her profession, she had to be prepared to shoot at people. This considered, Miles accounted himself more impressively. He remembered – after checking the gun, and checking its wobbling – to draw a deep breath, release half of it, use his sights, and to gently squeeze, not jerk, the trigger. He remembered to look where his shot landed, to adjust his aim, and to fire again. Miles could have been forgiven for simply yanking his trigger as quickly as he could. (Rule #19: You can't miss fast enough to win a gunfight.) But he didn't – he carefully placed his shots. And Celeste did as well.

The pursuers stood exposed at the end of the corridor, realizing their peril too late. They found themselves reconsidering things, and running for cover, under the relatively precise enfilade that bore down on them. They didn't enjoy the good fortune of shop fronts readily at hand – only the bend in the corridor behind them. Both were lightly wounded when they reached it.

Despite popular perception, most people who are shot don't die. But a light wound will pretty much do the job. Real people, unlike action heroes, do not clamp their palms over gunshot wounds and soldier on. More commonly, they fall down, moan, lose bladder control, pass out. Maybe yell for help.

Miles felt like yelling for something as he watched the two figures spastically react, then disappear. He stopped firing and gaped at the device in his hands. He had moved a metal lever an eighth of an inch, and human beings forty yards away had yelped, had stumbled . . . and had certainly undergone much worse. This was like puppetry in hell. Miles' breath was utterly gone; and something dry and heavy rolled over in his gut.

Celeste sent a few more rounds down the hall to keep heads down. By the time she and Miles earned their breathing room and stood up, adrenalized and unsteady, Dana was nowhere to be seen.

The airy building lobby into which Dana emerged appeared safe. Far enough away from the nightmare at the skating rink, it had not yet caught the hysteria. Such was the epidemiology of the Rockefeller Center shoot-out, and Dana rejoiced that she had escaped the hot zone. People in suits walked around like any other day, getting on and off of escalators, stiff-arming their way through revolving doors onto the avenue. Two beefy security guards sat behind a large desk.

Dana took all this in, then turned back toward the stairway from which she'd emerged, knowing she could not muster the courage to go back down. This was problematical as, even then, Miles and Celeste ran beneath the lobby of the next building over, having gone the other way at the end of the corridor.

Dana turned again to face the room. She saw glass, and statuary, and three other levels of lobby, and Manhattanites, scores of them. She could see no bad guys, but no one conspicuously good, either. No one familiar. She sidled toward the wall of doors and looked out onto the street. Nothing there suggesting shoot-outs, the concluded kind or imminent. She looked back toward the stairwell door, through which Miles and Celeste were still conspicuously not emerging.

She shrugged her shoulders under the weight of the backpack, the presence of which had somehow slipped her mind. She was wearing two million dollars on her back. And no shoes.

While she had her back to the doors, Moreno entered from the street via revolving glass. He made Dana from behind – her hair and backpack gave her away. He began walking her down.

Something had indeed gone wrong with the deal, causing the underground backup team to stalk off in various directions to get into the action. The lead team, in the rink, had reported via radio the escape of Miles, Celeste, and Dana into the mall. So, back at the ranch, the guy in charge sent his guys out to try and cover each exit from the underground complex. Most of these were inside the outlying buildings of Rockefeller Center.

Moreno had been dispatched to the two buildings to the north, which spread him pretty thin, but there it was. He had exited the underground lair and sprinted up 49th, then ducked into the lobby of the first building – and bingo.

Keeping half an eye on the security desk, Moreno grabbed

Dana's elbow and smoothly steered her in a ninety-degree arc, back toward the stairwell. He knew where this lay, and where it led. He'd had nothing to do all morning but stare at floor plans.

Dana jumped three feet, inside her head, then sagged all the way down, captured and done for, in relief and exquisite despair. Blessed hopelessness, returning at last. She didn't even think to scream or fight or balk. When they reached the doorway, she'd go back into the dark place where thought couldn't occur. Moreno looked satisfied but wary, feeling okay, thinking ahead a few moves. When he heard Theron shouting at him to freeze, from behind, he made the mistake of wheeling around without drawing his gun. That was ill-advised.

Rule #12 of a Gunfight is: *Action beats reaction in close quarters with no cover*. In other words, Westerns may frequently depict main street shoot-outs where the bad guy goes for his gun, and the good guy gets his out first – but don't bet on it. Creatures with less intricately evolved information processing systems, insects for instance, can react and, say, bite down, in less than a millisecond. But any human reaction which has to get routed for any kind of neural processing (as opposed to autonomous stuff like jumping off a hot stove) is going to hit you for about eighty milliseconds right off the top. And that's just the overhead. Decode and process the raw visual input of a guy's hand moving ("It's a man reaching into his jacket"); translate the symbol into a meaningful information value ("I'm probably about to be shot"); formulate a plan to deal with it ("Draw, aim, and fire my gun"); and prod the old corpus into action; and you've already fallen behind at least a third, maybe even a half, of a second. You're not going to catch up.

Theron's left hand held his badge, painfully pulling on his sling; his right rested on the butt of his Colt. He stood about twenty-five feet from the perp, and the girl. Twenty-five feet is the shortest distance one practices at the range – the definition of close quarters. And nothing but air and floor – no cover –

stood between Theron and the perp. Who would act? Who would react?

Theron's hand stayed on the butt of the Colt. For some reason, this crowded lobby made him reluctant to pull his piece. Maybe he just knew New York: one guy pulls out a gun, never mind a black guy, and pretty much anything can happen. However, when the Latino turned, Theron immediately saw something in his eye that said he wasn't coming quietly. Most perps, when cornered by the police, immediately throw in the towel – and they all wear the same towel-thrown-in look. Theron knew that look, and this wasn't it. So he drew the Colt after all, and won handily by virtue of Rule #12.

Sprinting from the abandoned pizza slice to the Plaza had bought Theron only a dead end and a good view of a bad scene. The gunfire and shouts grew audible long before he got to the rink. But he had to peek around the corner, gun pressed to cheek, to get a real feel for things. On the periphery, hundreds of citizens fled or cowered, and dozens of cops tried to fight their way down to the rink. On center stage, on and around the ice, the half dozen or so undercover police officers skating on stakeout, and the half dozen or so guys skating in support of the bag boy, were fighting to the death.

Blood flowed on the ice, much of it around three bodies. A wounded man, on hands and knees, tried to locomote himself out of the open area beside the rink. Another, who must have dove over the counter into the skate rental booth, fired over the top of the wounded man's crawling form. Two pairs of men wrestled on the ice, holding each other's gun hands by the wrists. Shots went off, unaimed. On either side of the rink, several combatants had escaped the open killing zone, and now put out rounds across the expanse.

Theron peeked out from the edge of the glass door and winced sharply at the carnage. He wanted to get in there and help. But he faced two problems, the same ones faced by the officers up top. First, rounds were coming in all over the place, many of them near, or actually through, the glass doors of the mall. Secondly, and more vexingly, Theron didn't know who the fuck anybody was. All of the officers down low wore plain clothes. So did the bad guys. Theron might have recognized one or two of the cops from the crime scene of the night before – they were some of the same guys – but only under less mad circumstances.

Even the backup officers, who could presumably recognize their colleagues, and maybe make some shots from the upper level, couldn't fire into wrestling bodies. And they couldn't get down close, due to the panicked crowds and wild gunfire. Within a roughly two-minute window, the combatants in the rink were just completely on their own. They survived, or not, on their skills, their ferocity, and the cold, cruel, random luck and geometry of this gunfight. That was it.

Theron couldn't do anything but turn around, backtrack, and try to get above ground some other way. Sprinting, panting, he took the first stairwell he found and emerged into an office building, finally bursting out onto the avenue just in time to see Moreno round the corner onto 49th. So he followed him, all the way to the building lobby. Initially, he gave chase because he marked the guy as a perp escaping from the shoot-out. Only a minute later in the lobby, when Moreno spun, did Theron recognize him – from Celeste's the day before. Theron's cab, before he'd turned it around to follow the other cab, had rolled right by Moreno as he emerged from the alley.

Now, in the lobby, drawing first, Theron placed his shots into Moreno like brain surgery – because Dana stood only a few inches away. Moreno went down, actually less quickly than the rest of the crowd, who covered their heads and dropped to the floor electrically, while Moreno only obeyed gravity, and flailed and staggered backward from the force of the rounds.

When Moreno did hit the floor, only Theron and Dana were left standing. Dana stood stock-still with her lips trembling and eyes slitted. Theron advanced on her, and the dead man, with his Colt held stiffly forward, one-handed. With his other he waved his badge crazily at 270 degrees of the lobby. He shouted, "Police officer, everybody stay down, police officer!" with dry lips, louder than necessary, into the silence of the room, hoping to God nobody took it upon themselves to light him up.

Nearing Dana, he growled, "Get your hands out, away from your sides!" Dana didn't look threatening, or even functional. But this dubious redheaded person had been right there – and in up to her neck – when Theron got his ass all shot up; and he wasn't going to let the shit happen again.

Theron kicked the automatic on the floor – Moreno had gotten it clear of leather, at least – away from the still and outstretched hand. Glancing down, then back to Dana, then out at the room, he decided the guy looked pretty dead – hit in the center of mass, four or five or six times, Theron forgot. But he did remember to raise his badge and gun when he then spun around at the sound of the lobby door whooshing open.

In through it walked a blond guy in a sport coat with a drawn gun.

Stanley Luther had been a couple of doors down the block, checking another lobby, when he heard the gunfire. Sprinting a long stretch of sidewalk, he drew a deep breath and charged in. Seeing Moreno dead on the floor didn't surprise him, but seeing the Hookeville cop alive and on his feet, and in New York, certainly did. He also felt very pissed off, and cursed under his breath, to find himself in another fucking Mexican standoff. Well, he'd deal with this one a little differently.

His back to the room, and to Dana, Theron drew a bead and shouted, "Police officer, drop the gun!" The blond guy, who'd drawn a bead right back, shouted, "Federal agent, undercover!" Theron tensed as the guy went for his ID. When it appeared, Theron slacked his trigger finger, and lowered his barrel forty-five degrees. He expelled breath heavily through puffed cheeks, and thought to himself, *Jesus Christ, that was close.*

Stanley Luther thought to himself, *Jesus Christ, that was close.* And then he lit up Theron T. Johnson, who hadn't worn his vest because the weight of it made his wounded collarbone hurt like hell. Theron collapsed to the lobby floor and didn't have time to be surprised, afraid, or sad.

And then Dana found herself moving toward the stairwell again, going underground, this time with a blonder bad man gripping her arm.

The Death of Hope

"I feel like I've been chasing you all over the fucking East Coast," hissed Stanley, jerking Dana alongside, toward the backup room. He was afraid he'd find the underground corridors crawling with New York cops. On the other hand, they'd probably give him a medal if he turned up with the redhead – he knew the NYPD were also avidly seeking her.

But ideally, he'd make it back without giving her up. They had the bag now; and they had the girl. This fulfilled Stanley's responsibilities in the matter as far as he could tell. If there were others to round up, the guy in charge and his damned wrecking crew could take care of it. And, God willing, he'd be out of the city inside of the hour. Checking his bank balance from the car.

Pulling Dana along, watching fearfully ahead, Stanley fairly wilted at the thought of going home. This job, he decided, sucked. It would probably all seem okay in the soothing glow of memory, and a cleared electronic funds transfer. But right now he'd give almost anything to be back in Arlington. No New York, no cops, no anonymous mercenaries. Particularly no cops; he was beginning to feel that all he did anymore was dodge local gendarmes. With that thought, he readjusted his grip on Dana's elbow and rounded a sweeping corner of hallway. And that was when the radio chirped up, from inside of Dana's pocket. He stopped them both dead in the hallway, and looked at the girl long and hard before patting her down.

A sleek shadow moved within a larger shadow – right in the bright part of the day, in the broadness of daylight. But the slant of the light did not make this shadow a shadow; it was in the way the shadow moved – with speed, and an efficiency beyond efficiency. It had that go-anywhere, do-anything, the-axe-is-now-falling sort of assurance of movement, reminiscent of evaporation, or of lights going off in sequence, or very heavy doors closing softly.

The shadow moved from within one shadow to another, from the lee of one service structure to another. The shadow's feet moved across crunchy roof tarring, but it may as well have been goose down; shadows don't make noise.

The shadow wore an intricate leather harness. The harness held two large sheath knives, a stiletto, a pair of garrottes, a set of lockpicks, a small general purpose tool kit, four explosive canisters, three handguns in two different calibers, and two dozen spare magazines. But shadows don't clink, sway, or come loose; a shadow has no parts or divisions, merely a continuous, undifferentiated area.

This shadow also wore a black skullcap, oval sunglasses, and a black topcoat over the harness. And stubble, black.

At the other end of the rooftop stood a distinctly human non-shadow, one which seemed all too fallible and fleshy, juggling a SIG Sauer, a radio, and a pair of binoculars. It squatted at the edge of the roof, making crunchy noises as it shifted from foot to foot, pulling at the ass-crack of its boxer shorts, and peering over the precipice at an awkward angle. It was perched like a gargoyle, defenseless like a blind infant. Twitchy with agitation, it seemed still to react to the sounds of gunfire that no longer floated up from two hundred feet below.

The shadow rested a couple of service structures from the edge of the roof and the twitchy gargoyle. The shadow, more commonly known as the Cleaner, didn't do anything so prosaic as take a deep breath, or steel himself. But he did pause to swivel his head, to gather in a little more visual data. As he did so, the radio on the gargoyle by the precipice started making noise.

It said, "Dana."

This disyllable froze the Cleaner where he stood. For the next few minutes he listened puzzled to a great deal of odd radio chatter, shouts, and – ultimately – gunfire, come into and go out of the radio clutched by the gargoyle, more commonly known as FreeBSD, at the building's edge. After a while, Noel concluded that he'd heard enough, and that none of this had any bearing on his job there on the roof of the building. He began to move again, when a last dispatch came in over the radio. A woman's voice said, "FreeBSD. Come in."

Below ground . . . hundreds of feet above ground . . . now Miles and Celeste had gotten precisely back to ground level. As through a particularly tricky level of a video game, they had overcome one obstacle after another. They'd escaped the shoot-out at the rink; navigated the underground maze; eluded the dogged pursuers; and gained the stairs leading out of the catacombs. But the level had not ended just yet – or if it had, the players had not gotten their just rewards. They had no money, no girl; no weapons, power-ups, or extra lives awaited them here.

Pushing through the crowd in the building lobby, both Miles and Celeste knew they had gained one thing by making it this far: a respite, a modicum of temporary safety. They intuited that the men trying so unrelentingly to kill them would not do so in this place, in front of all these people. However, intuition is a faculty of limited utility. The bad men had tried to kill them in the middle of the Rockefeller Plaza skating rink, not ten minutes ago. But one does not like to think of such things.

And there did at least seem to be a bit of distance, spatial, temporal, between them and the bad men. They'd gotten a little buffer between them and death. Unfortunately, they'd also gotten a little buffer between them and Dana. (And the money, Celeste added mentally.) Miles spoke in an urgent whisper as they walked.

"Where else could she have gone? How many exits are there from the mall?" Celeste kept walking, and thinking. Miles, brow furrowed, stayed on her arm. "There was a T at the end of the hall. We turned right. Dana must have gone the other way. I don't think there were any other turns." Then Miles tugged at her topcoat-covered elbow, trying to reverse course. They reached an alcove of pay phones, and Celeste yanked him roughly into it.

"Can't go back down there, Miles. Bad guys down there. Get dead down there."

"Then how do we get Dana back?"

Celeste merely stared at him. Miles looked down into the narrow space between their bodies: in the gap, she held the radio with two fingers.

"Holy shit. Silly me." Miles grabbed at the device. Celeste didn't let it go.

"So, Darken," she said grimly. "We assume Dana got out of the mall some other place. We find a spot to meet, out on the street." Miles nodded his understanding and pulled on the radio, which didn't budge. "Here are some possible problems. One, this radio has crappy range, so we may not reach her at all. Two, she may still be in the mall, and we'll have to talk her out. Three, she may have gotten caught." Miles' expression went hard and black, and more so when Celeste added, "If she has, our chief obligation is to avoid getting caught with her. Finally, she could be dead. Oh, yeah, and anybody could be monitoring this – the scrambling on this thing is a joke. Now ring her up, champ, time's awasting."

Stanley looked at the radio, then at Dana. He shoved the Beretta Tomcat, recovered from her waistband, into his. The Tomcat had stayed safely under her shirt through both of her recent captures, and her brief rescue. She had considered going for the gun – in the same way one considers stepping off of high ledges, or jumping out into traffic. Merely having the thought in her head terrified her.

"Dana," the radio entreated again. Stanley gave the device a little toss in his palm. He thought.

The radio repeated, thin and distant, "Dana. Are you there?" A man's voice, urgent.

In the end – only a few seconds later, all the time he had – Stanley scrapped together a little plan of ambush. He coerced Dana into going along with it by putting a pistol to her head. He also told her he only needed to ask her friends a few questions. So she said what Stanley told her to, terrified, speaking stiffly into the radio pickup, while Stanley depressed the transmit bar.

And a few minutes later, in the backup room, Stanley tossed the backpack of money to the guy in charge. He pushed Dana wordlessly into a chair, and commenced digging into their reserve armory, which consisted of a couple of lumpy bags of larger guns in the corner.

"What are you doing?" the leader asked Stanley.

"I'm putting down the carrot," Stanley grunted, pulling out guns, "so I can swing the stick with both hands."

"No, Miles, fuck that," said Celeste. "Guide her out. We're not going down there."

"You heard her, she's too scared to move."

"I heard her. She's under duress."

"What are you saying?"

"They've got her. And they're using her to bring us in."

"No, that's bullshit," said Miles. He shook his head. "I can find her. If you don't want to come, I'll get this back to you." He lifted up his shirt and checked the chamber of the Ruger. He was really just stalling to get his courage up, though in fact it seeped away as he delayed.

Celeste considered asking him how he planned to get him

her share of the money, in the unlikely event he emerged with it. But that issue lay too far down the road. At the moment, she had to decide whether or not to let Miles go alone. She'd be an idiot to go down into the mall, into an obviously laid trap. In the end, though, when Miles took off at a trot, she found herself following. They found a pile of brochures at the lobby information desk. One had a floor plan of the complex.

"There." Miles jammed a finger at the map as they made the stairs. "Under the next building over. We can get there easy from here." Celeste felt too somber and resigned even to shake her head as they ducked in; she just grimaced.

At the bottom of two flights of stairs they broke into a run, sprinting the long corridor again, this time in reverse. It was empty, but they could hear noises around the bend, the sorts of noises police made. Radios. Orders. An edgy, businesslike tumult. They took a service door just short of the bend. The noise of the door brought two cops around the corner with guns drawn, but they had gone.

More stairs lay at the end of a service corridor; they went up one flight, then through another heavy door. If their navigation was sound, and Dana's report accurate, she should be beyond this door.

And if Celeste's assessment proved accurate, they'd find the ambush behind the door.

"Go right," she said. "And remember: it doesn't matter what you believe, only that you believe."

Miles tried to smile, but failed, those muscles in his face not responding. He pulled open the door and dove in. He saw an empty corridor, ending in a T-intersection. No Dana – and no ambush. He turned to verify that Celeste had followed him.

And then he heard Dana's voice, calling for him, from somewhere around the corner. Suddenly Celeste stood beside, and then beyond him, as the two reached the end of the corridor, the T. Dana's cry must have come from the left, as Celeste turned in that direction. Miles glanced the other way, to the right, where the hall continued ten feet, to some inset doorways and a dead end.

"Miles," he heard her yelp one last time, suddenly cut off – her tone very different.

And then the shooting started again, more of that terrifying roar of large-caliber handguns in a confined space. Miles could see Celeste flat on her belly on the thin carpet, and he could see the slide of her Bersa lock back – she had emptied the gun from first round to last. He watched the heads at the far end of the corridor disappear under this onslaught.

Miles remembered, in this fraction of a second of an interregnum, this heartbeat of echoing silence, being told what one should do in an ambush. A high school classmate had joined the army and later come back from basic training. He had told them that, in an ambush, the ambushed soldiers are assumed all but lost. The whole idea in setting up an ambush, the logic goes, is to create an area where the ambushees are totally exposed, and the ambushers are not at all exposed, and escape is unlikely in the extreme. The only question is whether someone happens to walk into it. Once they do, the conclusion is nearly foregone; those in the kill zone are screwed.

Given that, American soldiers are trained to fall flat, expend all their ordnance – including and in particular grenades – and then get up and run *straight through* the lines of the ambush. If they make it alive, they can then turn around and shoot at the rear of the ambushers. A gambit, an only chance.

Miles, in this half second he had here, couldn't help but notice that Celeste seemed so far to be following the US Army line on ambushes – falling flat, and unloading all her ordnance. When Celeste went dry, though, that's all the time he had for thoughts of strategy. And running forward seemed out of the question. Heads began to pop out at the end of the corridor, and Miles and Celeste were both open and exposed. And Celeste was empty.

Just before he began egregiously to yank his trigger, Miles thought he recognized one or two of the heads down the hall.

One, blond and ruddy, was pretty obviously the guy Celeste had faced down in her alley. He could see three other heads, or maybe four, all sighting down gun barrels.

Then Miles unloaded, sweeping his fire from one side of the corridor to the other, while Celeste scampered back beneath his broadside. Almost amusedly, Miles caught himself backing away as he fired – the classic technique from Doom: retreat down the corridor, making shots and strafing to dodge fire. In this case, though, three problems with this strategy presented themselves: 1) You usually didn't have to reload in video games; 2) you can't sidestep out of the way of real bullets; and 3) Miles found himself, suddenly, at the rear end, the dead end, of the corridor, with not another inch of retreating left to him.

When Miles went dry, the opposition came back yet again, going hard, and Miles took an inset doorway on the right. He could make out Celeste ten feet ahead of him, in the other hallway, the one they had originally entered. Cowering deep in the inset doorway, he shouted out to her, "Well, goddamn, you were right. It is a trap."

"I thought I already told you I do this for a living," Celeste shouted back, leaning out to squeeze off a couple of rounds, then adding under her breath – and the withering return fire that came back – "you dilettante son of a bitch."

An immovable object sat atop another immovable object – and this in the middle of a day when every force seemed irresistible. The contingencies of the day's forces did not make the object immovable; it was in the way the object comported itself, with businesslike resolve, and loyalty, and an untouchable dignity. That not-going-anywhere, doing-the-job-at-hand, the-doors-are-now-open-for-business kind of assurance of bearing, reminiscent of heavy mass, or mesa walls absorbing desert sunlight – or veteran soldiers carrying out orders.

The immovable object, Angelo, had perched on the roof of the other immovable object, another building overlooking the

Plaza, for almost three hours. All but two minutes of that had passed unremarkably. The balance had offered mainly frustration, with no time or opportunity to take even a single shot at the chaotic scene below. But Angelo quickly put his frustration aside and went back to business. The time for action would come, or it wouldn't, and the immovable object would be right there and ready. And sharp.

The thin air blew cold, but the bright sunlight reflected off of the tar surface onto Angelo's face. He'd been on his belly the entire time, scanning the expanse of the Plaza tirelessly through a thirty-two power optical scope. His pivoting movement from left to right, and back, seemed mechanical, with little smooth variations in the sweep as he picked out corners of the activity below. The scope sat on top of a Dragunov sniper rifle, Russian-made. The US Marine 1st Lieutenant (ret.) preferred American hardware. But he had to take what he could get on the secondary market.

Angelo scanned the Plaza for signs of the girl, or the guy, or their new friend, the woman in the trench coat. Or for the bag. When the time came, he might play a role in grabbing one, or all four. He might even help get them out alive. A good man with a long-rifle in a high place can do wonders.

"Angelo," a voice came through on the radio. He lifted it with his left hand, not taking his right from the grip of the rifle, nor his eye from the scope.

"Roger," he answered, in a normal speaking voice.

"Whatcha got, Marine?" Naja asked through the scratchy radio transmission.

"No sign of the targets." He paused briefly to pivot the rifle. "Fifty or so more cops, uniformed officers. They're still pouring in."

"Okay, guy," Naja answered. "Sit tight for now. I've got everyone else in vehicles now, working a five-block radius. I'm not that optimistic about us getting out on foot – half the NYPD is here already. If it looks like the promenade is going to get roped off next, you withdraw from the roof, but stay in the building. Can you spend the night there?"

"Roger that."

"Good. Don't get made, and don't be playin' war hero. If things get hot, find a broom closet and sleep it off."

"Roger that."

"Maybe we'll get one last look at our kids. Never can tell. Peace out."

"Roger that, out."

He switched to a police channel. A great deal of frantic chatter came over it.

Detective Eyebrows paced the sidewalk, the Plaza's flags fluttering madly and distractingly in his peripheral vision. He harangued into a phone: "Right, just make sure SWAT knows how many . . . how many plainclothes are here. They're how many blocks away? Patch me through. Okay, never mind. Just tell them the area's secure. I don't want them coming in here guns blazing. Yeah." He snapped the phone away from his head. "Fuck."

He looked to his compatriot for sympathy. "Have we not had enough of a bloodbath? We need more EMT, not more shooters." He shook his head; the other remained silent, palms on the concrete balustrade. All the uniformed officers darting about brandished arms. Many still pivoted to and fro, covering the entrances to the mall. The detectives had their guns holstered, like generals pacing the lines. They knew there was more danger now of an accidental shooting. The big show was over, and they had mucked it up.

"We're going to have to go room-to-room, aren't we?" the younger detective asked.

"Yeah. Every office in every building in the Center."

"Think we'll get anybody?"

"Nope."

"What was this all about?"

"Don't know. Not my job. As of now, we're janitors. We clean up."

"Bad mess."

"Yep."

Back at the OK Corral, the Dana Recovery Operation had almost ended. Never even mind Dana, Miles and Celeste – cowering around their corners, shooting around the edges without looking, ducking zinging bits of plaster and splintered wood, deaf – had both come to realize that while Celeste could still escape, Miles was pinned down in the dead-end corridor. He'd zagged when he should have zigged. And now he was trapped.

They had both reloaded. But they almost couldn't even lean around to pop off a shot now. Their ambushers had them zeroed in. And, much worse, they were advancing by inset doorways, walking them down. In another minute or so, they'd be there, and the end with them. When they reached the doorway immediately before Celeste, she'd have to abandon Miles. She'd have to go. And that would be that for him.

Celeste stole a longing glance behind her at the stairwell door, and the elevators. She nearly dropped her gun when the elevator bell clanged and the doors slid open. She didn't know whether to cover her corner, cover the elevator, or just shoot herself in the head and have done with it. Her reaction, when she laid eyes on the men who exited the elevator, was beyond chronicling. It was precisely as if they had stepped from the world into her bad dream.

Miles had just dropped the slide forward on his last mag, when three guys in body armor with submachine guns spilled into the corridor and opened up, putting the various heads at the other end under cover. Miles worked his jaw, and blinked hard, when one of the guys curled his gloved fingers at him, and shouted, "Move!" It was Bob, from Celeste's place. Miles grabbed his hand, got pulled around the corner, and just like that six of them stood panting in a climbing elevator.

"So," said a man in a suit, unrumpled under a Kevlar vest. "You must be the fellow who's gotten my Miss Browning into this execrable mess."

"Miles Darken," said Celeste, slumping weakly against the railing, a pair of hot tears at the corners of her eyes. "Meet Mr. White. My boss."

From Betrayal, From Heartbreak

In a crowded elevator, six people rode with adrenaline. No one spoke. Celeste and Miles did that gulping, dry-throated thing, where one needs to say something, but has let the silence drag on too long. The elevator lights floated upward as if in a silent film.

"What are you doing here?" Celeste finally managed.

"I might ask the same of you." Mr. White spared her a fleeting and proper sidelong glance. "And by that, I mean not, what are *you* doing here, but what am *I* doing here, rescuing you?" He unswiveled his head. But he also put his hand on her upper arm and gave it a squeeze. She took a while formulating her next question. In the interim, Miles held forth with his particular burning issue.

"What about Dana?"

"Yes, your auburn-haired friend. Don't worry, we'll gather her up as well. It will just take a little time. This whole area is lousy with members of the local constabulary." He actually checked his wristwatch. "Relax, Mr. Darken. First we need to get a little altitude." The elevator still climbed.

"Hiya, Bob," Celeste said weakly.

"Hi yourself, Celeste. Nice day for it." He pointed his submachine gun at the juncture of wall and ceiling with gloved hands. Miles imagined that Mr. White tensed slightly at this exchange. Oddly, there was now this social tension in place, fifteen seconds after a life-or-death gunfight. Humans can be awkward absolutely anywhere.

A scant few floors from the top, and thus, necessarily, from their stop, Celeste remembered something she'd forgotten, and she remembered it out loud: "Oh shit, FreeBSD."

White looked at her noncommittally.

"A, uh, friend of ours," she explained. Silently, she noted that she probably had a great deal of explaining to do.

Mr. White nodded and said, "Well, bring him up, by all means. He'll be safe with us. You can phone him?"

"Radio," she said, producing it.

"Capital," White replied. Miles squinted, trying to make out a glint in White's eye. He gave up; everything had grown white and fuzzy. He was near collapse from exhaustion and shock.

As their motion ended and their bodies decelerated against the carpet of the elevator floor, Celeste said, "FreeBSD. Come in."

"Celeste! 'Sup!" came back a welcoming voice, small and faint.

The doors opened. "Sixty-fifth floor of the RCA Building," White said, exiting. "The whole floor. If he's quick, there should be any number of ways he can make it up without incurring arrest or death." Celeste issued terse instructions over the radio, stepping onto the sixty-fifth floor of the RCA Building, the whole floor.

The elevator – elevators actually, two ran side by side – opened onto a large, sparse suite. A few desks stood in the main room, which was bordered on the right by a glass wall. Beyond that, sky. On the left was wall, and corridors going away. Also a water fountain, and restrooms. At its far end, the room bent to the left. The right-side glass wall followed the sweep gently around and out of sight.

A number of people, more or less conspicuously armed, stood or sat around the desks. They pored over laptops, or studied papers. One of the tables had what looked like floor plans spread out on its surface. One of the computers, wired to a display panel, projected onto a bare wall. Two of the people stood before it, fists on chins. In all, a half dozen or so figures occupied the room, when the half dozen from the elevator joined them.

White continued walking, though more slowly now.

"Bob," he said, and the man darted to his side. "Go back to the office, please. I'd like you to brief the staff in the situation room, and coordinate from there." Bob arched one brow slightly before snapping a "Yes, sir," and reversing course. He gave Celeste a smile as he passed, and strode back onto the elevator the group had just exited.

White still stood with his back turned. Just as Celeste warily took in the details of the room, and as Miles wet his lips to ask again about Dana, the elevator, the other one, dinged. Miles and Celeste turned to see the doors open, and behind them stood Dana, behind her bangs.

And behind her stood Stanley Luther, and Salvatierre, and four members of the wrecking crew, all looking as grim as Judgment Day, to Miles' and Celeste's bulging eyes. The guy in charge strode though the glass doors and intoned, "Are we glad to be back up top. Gettin' hot down there."

Miles could see Celeste going for her radio, not her gun. She was going to wave off FreeBSD from coming up. Such was loyalty, earned and bestowed in a day.

"Don't touch that dial," said Mr. White behind her, significantly.

When she and Miles turned, everyone in the room had drawn down on them. They stood naked and afraid right between the millstones.

Somebody disarmed them both. Dana was shoved back into their ranks. And Stanley Luther dropped the black backpack onto one of the tables.

Things were not looking good for our heroes.

* * *

Celeste and Mr. White, now alone in a tiny conference room, no windows, no table, two chairs. White stood behind one chair, lightly gripping its back. Celeste sat in the other, upright, good posture – but still slumping. The slump was behind her eyes, in the air around her; much of what she thought of as her had leaked right out.

And it had left an empty place – on the inside of her waistband. She pined for her Bersa . . . the cool molded rubber of the grips . . . silky light trigger pull . . .

She was alone. Alone in the sense of being physically separated from the others; and alone in the company of a friend, one who had been a rock to her throughout her adult life. Now gone strange.

"Your question," White began, finally, looking her in the eye, "was, 'What are you doing here?'" He drummed his fingers silently on the chair back. "Of course, you had no way of knowing this . . . but I've always been here. From the very beginning."

Celeste raised her chin and met his gaze.

Miles' ears rang painfully. Muscles in his legs and lower back ached keenly. His right wrist and palm were sore and chafed from rapid-firing a large-caliber pistol. He was suffering from the effects of adrenaline burnout, extended shock, sleep deprivation, hunger, dehydration, and post-traumatic stress disorder – which was flooding in before the original stress had drained out.

He was saying shit like: "You should have seen when I put down that fairy friend of yours, the one in the ice skates." Grinning and half-lidded, he scanned the other faces in the room. "Couple of double taps right between the shoulder blades. Yeah, that was like the motherfucking Cap-in-Your-Ass Ice-Capades. Ha, ha."

The level of ire in the room was going through the roof. The others – Global Acumen employees, contractors, federal agents? tough to tell – pretended to work on whatever they were working on. But they couldn't help listening to Miles. He held the floor.

"And those guys who chased us into the mall!" Miles snorted, a violent motion which moved both his chair and Dana's – they, and the chairs, had been tied together. "Those guys shoot like ass! Man! They shoot like little girls. We lit them up pretty good." Dana banged the back of her head into the back of Miles'. "Say? Are those guys okay? They around here?" Miles twisted his head around, looking for wounded guys.

Dana popped him in the back of the head again, then twisted around as far as she might. She whispered, "I want you to shut up, Miles. Please."

"Shut up? Why should I shut up? I'm just talking about all those punks we shot earlier."

"You sound," Dana hissed, "like FreeBSD. Just shut up."

"What's wrong with FreeBSD? I *love* FreeBSD. That guy's the tits."

"No," Dana said, facing forward, and losing her fear again, "you just idolize him because he used to jockey computers, then went out into the world and *did* something."

This did shut Miles up then. Too late, though: Stanley Luther was choking on bile, and approached Miles for a word.

The room Celeste shared with Mr. White lay deep in the middle of the suite, off of the main area. It had been a long walk for Celeste, listening to Mr. White's perfectly creased slacks swish behind her. And listening to Miles and Dana being tied up behind that.

"Let me back up," White said. "No, let me preface. You're really not going to believe this."

"Global Acumen was hired to get the Manuscript."

White stopped short, something Celeste had never once seen him do. He swallowed a smile on its way up and he said, "That's my girl." He backed away from the chair and leaned against the whiteboard with his hands behind his back. "How did you know?"

"It's obvious," Celeste answered, without any evident pride. "The Manuscript is the ultimate trade secret. If it existed, and somebody wanted it, they'd come to us to get it for them." She looked him in the eye, keeping her sarcasm measured and thin. "That's what we're good at."

FreeBSD made it to the ground with little trouble. After high-tailing it off the roof, he'd had to exit the building all the way on 49th. But no cops in sight. After that, he moved quickly.

In his few months in the city, he hadn't spent a lot of time in this neighborhood. But the RCA Building was hard to miss, being four times taller than everything else. He circled it, keeping wide of the Plaza. Through the cross streets he could see police barricades and flashing lights. The entrance to the big building seemed open for business, though a few uniformed cops darted to and fro.

He ducked in, keeping his gaze low and his gait confident.

Shortly, he found several different elevator bays, though most didn't seem to go where he was going – all the way up. He took a few minutes finding the right one. When he entered it and looked over his shoulder, he saw a boy in blue watching from across the lobby. He made a production of reading the map on the wall, shook his head and doubled back. The cop seemed to lose interest. But FreeBSD realized it wasn't the cop that had him so spooked.

He felt keenly as if someone else was with him. The hairs on the back of his neck waved.

But he didn't see anyone. He circled the lobby for a little while, trying to be sure.

"I don't know who they are," Mr. White said. "In our client database, they're listed simply as 'A Concern'. They pay their bills promptly. And they were accommodating in regard to some ethical issues I had about certain aspects of the job."

Celeste figured she could guess half of this anyway.

"I tell you about the client," White went on, "because it bears on your situation, directly and immediately. These clients don't just want to have the document. They wanted to be the *people* who have the document. The only ones. They're concerned with the disposition of anyone else who's read it. That was one or two people, initially. But you seem to have expanded the circle."

"More's the worse for us," said Celeste.

"More's the worse for you."

"Look, boss," she said with a hint of a sneer, "all I really can't figure out is how you manipulated me into bringing Miles and Dana in, with the bag in hand. That, and why you didn't take the three of us anytime yesterday; like when Bob was standing outside my apartment."

"Why didn't we grab you? Left hand didn't know what the right was doing," White answered. "And for good reason. Do you think Bob would have grabbed you? Bob loves you. That's why he isn't here now. As for the first question: we didn't manipulate you into anything."

"Yeah, sure."

"I already told you that you weren't going to believe this. Didn't believe it myself. At first, I figured the client had hired you out from under us. Hell, I did the same thing to NSA when I hired Stanley Luther, the blond spook you met."

"Why did you hire an NSA guy?"

"The NSA had some good intelligence on the Manuscript, probably the best. When we started running into dead ends, I contacted a friend there. He couldn't get at the intelligence, but he did arrange to get Luther assigned to go to Hookeville and investigate the people looking for the Manuscript. Then we simply hired him on the side. Luther likes contract work."

"You were saying something about not manipulating me."

"Actually, the subject was 'unbelievable coincidences'. That is to say, we didn't have anything to do with your involvement in this. Any of it. You met Miles Darken – and then Dana Steckler, and Paul Lineberry, aka FreeBSD – on your own. And you let them drag you into it, on your own. Like I said, I didn't believe it myself. But we went back and read all of your mail as soon as we realized you were involved. And there it was. You just stumbled onto these people on your own."

Celeste just shook her head.

"You have a lot of commentary," hissed Stanley to Miles, "for a guy tied to a chair."

Reality presented itself briefly to Miles and he eyed a patch of floor.

Stanley worked his jaw, waiting for a fuller head of steam, when the guy in charge appeared at his shoulder. He said, "Thanks, Stanley. I'll take it from here." He said, to Miles, "Why don't you tell me who else has seen the Manuscript? Make me look good in front of my colleagues, and make it easier on yourself. We just want to know who else has read it." He grinned conspiratorially. "Who else is in on the little secret."

"Hey," said Miles, head rolling, "it's just between you, me, and the crack dealer on the corner."

"The crack dealer's on his way up now," the leader said, nodding and missing the joke. "But I don't believe you're telling me everything."

"If there were alien visitors here with a ray gun to my head and a rectal probe to my ass, I couldn't tell you any more."

"You should *be* so lucky."

Stanley turned to leave. "This is highly pointless," he muttered.

"We spent months digging everywhere, including online, following the tracks of this thing," White said. "We were chasing ourselves in circles, and there was no movement on the project. Then, out of the blue, someone popped up on a discussion group, also looking for the Manuscript. This was a professor at Thomas Jefferson College."

"Castrolang. Dana's advisor," Celeste said.

"Yes. Well, stumbling onto someone else looking for the

same thing we were was odd enough. But imagine our surprise when he found it. When he got a *response* to his inquiry. From your FreeBSD character." White shrugged. "I don't know why we didn't think to post about it ourselves."

"You're not Net-savvy. Otherwise you'd know that you can find anything on Usenet."

"Touché. But find it we did, regardless. Castrolang and FreeBSD of course took their correspondence to private e-mail, but only half of it was private to us. We never could hack into Lineberry's mail, but Castrolang's was transparent; and half of the correspondence was enough.

"I wanted simply to set up a deal in the city, and get the item. But the client was concerned about the others looking for it, namely Castrolang, and his lovely assistant. They wanted to set up the deal in Hookeville, to get all the players in one place. It was fairly clear why they wanted everyone in one place, and that brought the issue of the wet work to a head. But I was a little too enthusiastic with the financial figures involved in the project – very large ones. Also, I have to admit I was intrigued by the document in question. They'd had to give us a reasonably detailed description of what it was they wanted us to find. So I was never prepared to let this one go. Even when I should have."

He rose from his reverie a bit. "So I referred them."

"To the Cleaner," Celeste finished for him.

"Yes. The referral was the first big mistake. But I did it in service of my conscience. We sent Luther to Hookeville to grab the bag from Lineberry at the meet with Dana. And the Concern – by way of the Cleaner – would take care of FreeBSD, Dana, and Castrolang as they saw fit. But even that first bit spun completely out of control. First of all, Lineberry didn't go to Hookeville himself. Then, the grab in the fraternity house turned into a bullet festival, due to the very surprising and even more depressing fact of there being an *undercover cop* in the room at the time. By the time the shooting stopped, the bag had disappeared. Who had it? The last person we expected: Dana. As for the rest, well – talk about the right hand not knowing what the left was doing . . ."

"The Cleaner got the Professor," said Celeste.

"Yes. But that was just a light warm-up. In Central Park, he got a couple of FreeBSD's kids, and two of mine. Because I didn't know he was going to be there. He wasn't working for me, he was working for the client, for the Concern. And they were playing all of their cards at the same time, and have continued doing so. In fact, the Cleaner got almost everybody in the park *but* his three targets, namely Darken, Steckler, and FreeBSD."

"That I don't understand," said Celeste. "I'm unaware of him ever having missed before."

"Yes, well, such is celebrity. But everyone misses some time."

"Am I on his list?"

"No. You would be, to be sure, since you've read the Manuscript, but the Cleaner has been unreachable since the Central Park incident. And that's one of our big problems. After the initial two debacles, the client chose to throw money and bodies at the problem. Global Acumen isn't the only source of contractors they can hire and half of those men out in the room don't work for us, as I'm sure you've guessed. First they brought in the two Hispanics you met at your place, to work with Luther in getting the bag back. There was no way I could protest; we had failed to get the job done ourselves. And after you slipped out of the grab at your place, they brought in that whole lynch mob out there. And I've had no choice but to try and work with them."

"It looks like you've done okay," said Celeste. "You've got the bag, and you've got us."

"No," White said. "You don't understand. I've been working at cross-purposes with them. For the last two days, I've been trying to save *you*."

Celeste slitted her eyes at this. The corners of her lip turned down and began to tremble.

"Just now was the first chance I've had to grab you, with my own people. Right now is the first time we've gotten to be alone. And these next few minutes will be the only chance you're going to have to get out of here alive."

FreeBSD had now circled the lobby three times. He made one more swooping pass at the elevator bay. He pressed the button. It lit up, and he waited, tapping his foot. The elevator on the right opened; though the one on the left was descending as well. He still felt paranoid, hunted. But how not?

"They're hell bent on seeing me dead?" Celeste asked.

"Oh, yes. It was never explained why they wanted to be the only ones who had read the Manuscript. But one can imagine. One doesn't like to think about people who not only want to be enlightened, but also want to keep enlightenment from the world. It is worse yet to think that they are prepared to kill to accomplish that. I don't know why." He paused, changed tone. "We only have a few minutes. But I have to ask: Is it what they say it is? Is it the thing?"

"Who knows? It looks pretty good to me. How much time did you say we have?"

"Until FreeBSD gets here. When he does, they'll interrogate him. They're interrogating Darken and Steckler now. Then they're going to dispatch the three – and you with them, if you're still here."

"I take it you're suggesting I don't be."

"I assume you'll have some sympathy with the suggestion." White drew himself up, businesslike. "I think you're going to sucker-punch me – do draw some blood, please – and I'm going to fire a couple of rounds down the hallway. And you're going to escape down the back stairs."

Celeste looked at him coldly.

"It's going to be a close thing. They'll be right behind you. But I trust you'll be quick enough to evade them. Also, they'll be looking for you after today. But I'll arrange for your body to turn up."

Setting her jaw, Celeste said, "I'm not leaving without the others."

"I don't see how that's going to happen."

Neither do I, thought Celeste.

"You do this," White said, drawing himself up, "or you'll force me to turn you off myself, which I will do before I let those crackers out there take one of mine." He leaned over her, menacing – and Celeste was well menaced. She had lived in awe of this man every day for years. "Get out of my building now or else, Browning," he said. They glared at each other, the silence hanging thick and ugly for a full ten seconds. And then the shooting started again.

Ding, the first elevator dinged and when it did, and the doors opened, they opened on a mostly empty, large expanse of room. From inside the elevator, across the small lobby, through the glass doors, FreeBSD could see the room. He could see Miles and Dana, sitting.

Nothing seemed amiss; but clearly everything was amiss.

His left hand was wrapped around his SIG, under his coat, as it had been for the entire, interminable elevator ride. He drummed his fingers on the butt, readjusted his grip, and stepped to the juncture of elevator and lobby. He stood in the path of the beam of light which, broken, prevented the elevator doors from closing. He didn't walk any further.

Miles and Dana looked at him wide-eyed now. Something was no-fucking-shit wrong.

That was when they started coming out of the shadows, synchronized, covering him, the room filling with maybe a dozen guys, a couple of them women, and they all had the drop on him. It happened too quickly and completely for FreeBSD to react. He cursed under his breath and gripped the concealed pistol with bloodless fingers.

He must be tired, he thought. His reactions were better than this. They had been better when he got out of Central Park alive. They had been better when he escaped the hit at the Crib. They had been spot on when he rescued these jokers at Celeste's place. Now he'd gotten trapped right with them, and men in black were walking him down.

He didn't freeze up; he just paused to berate himself. But either way he didn't move for a few seconds. Later, he'd like to think he'd already decided to go for it, by the time the other elevator dinged – but in fact he was still debating. When the other elevator, next to his, did ding, all decisions got much easier very rapidly.

From FreeBSD's point of view, he couldn't see into the other elevator. He only saw a dozen gun barrels smoothly pivot fifteen degrees, from covering his center of mass in his elevator, to covering something in the other elevator.

He could hear the doors of the other elevator open.

And he actually got hit by two or three empty shell casings, from the two guns that started going off in the next elevator, sweeping fire across the main room. Those two guns extended just outside of the elevator doors; and FreeBSD stood just a bit in front of his elevator, so he caught a couple of flying casings on the shoulder.

But then he was swinging his arm up, and his body down, hitting the deck and opening up himself. The dozen or so guys in the big room all appeared to be firing into the other elevator, not at him, but he did not give a shit. He opened up, with all vigor.

The operatives in the room fired wildly at a dual pistol-wielding shadow in the next elevator, the one on their right. As they did, several took hits, and went down jerkily. The rest went for cover. And all of them fired nonstop. But the shadow had already gone from the elevator, slithering forward and off to the left, into the corridors on the interior of the building.

In front of FreeBSD, the glass doors of the lobby sparkled all over the carpet, a brilliant lake surface of shattered glass.

He could also see one of the dozen pop up from cover, as if to pursue the shadow. A pistol appeared around the corner of one of the corridors on the left, no head or body, just pistol, and knocked the pursuer to the ground with two rounds. The others hunkered back down.

FreeBSD crouched on the floor, behind the lip of the elevator doors, breathing crazily. He decided to stay put, and his elevator doors closed again. A few shots rang out, decreasing in frequency. Just when FreeBSD had warmed up the decision-making process about which button to push – *Open Door* or *Lobby* – the shouting and rapid firing started up all over again.

Scylla, Charybdis

Dana and Miles lay side by side on the floor, still tied to each other and their chairs, immobilized. Miles had relocated them there by violently rocking their lashed-together, landlocked junks when the shooting started. They lay with their cheeks, her left, his right, on the scratchy carpet. They were unhurt. They saw shell casings lying all around them. And bodies.

The room was much darker now. Most of the overhead fluorescent lights had been turned off in preparation for the ambush of FreeBSD. The remainder, in the lobby area, had been shot out in the initial enfilade. (Rule #4a again.)

The gun battle had slackened and now proceeded on a desultory and one-sided basis. Some of the dozen continued sniping at the other end of the room – at the hallway on their right, at the elevator, at that general direction. But even from his prone position, Miles could tell that no one returned fire.

Miles had immediately recognized FreeBSD in the first elevator. And he had a pretty good idea – though good was not at all the right word for it – of who had come up in the other one.

"Are you all right?" he whispered at Dana, beneath the noise of the sporadic sniping.

"Yes," she said. Miles didn't follow up. The last thing he

wanted to do was to draw attention. They were in something of an exposed position.

Members of the allied dozen began to strafe out into the open, sidestepping in modified Weaver stances, gun barrels sweeping the dangerous end of the room. No longer firing, they stepped around bodies, and around Miles and Dana. Some of them did quick tactical reloads. They found the elevator lobby empty, the hallways on their right dark and quiet.

Miles and Dana still went ignored.

As the group moved forward, the guy in charge motioned for two of his team to reverse course and check the back of the suite. These two turned and followed the curving sweep of the glass, out and away from the main room. A second later, one of the GA employees (Miles could see he had the body armor and H&K of the group that had "rescued" him and Celeste downstairs) cut out, jogging down one of the hallways into the interior.

As the remainder of the diminished group continued moving toward the elevator lobby, two silenced shots chugged out from behind them, from the bend in the back of the room, where the two-man rearguard had gone. As the group in the room wheeled, they heard fifteen unsilenced shots, a shout, one second of silence, then two more silenced shots.

Miles could practically smell the freaking-out pheromones gushing out of the group of operatives like musk, as the entire group bolted for the rear of the area. "He's coming around the back!" someone shouted, massively redundantly.

So it was that they all faced away from the elevator bay, rushing to the breach in the rear. But Miles and Dana had faced forward when they fell, so they alone could see the doors of the first elevator open again, and FreeBSD emerge. His gun extended, his face damp and shiny, hair wild, he visibly shook as he moved. Miles and Dana could see the whites of his eyes shining prettily in the partial darkness, as he ran stiffly toward them – maybe twenty-five yards behind the retreating backs of the operatives.

As the eight survivors of the original dozen reached the

bend and began firing again, shattering the outer glass and letting in the wind, FreeBSD reached Miles and Dana. He hooked the backs of their chairs with his right hand and, not looking down, dragged them out of the room into the nearest available cover – the women's bathroom. As he dug at the knots of their rope bonds, he tried to speak above the renewed gunfire, asking about the money.

"What now," White griped, in response to a knock on the door. He held a gold-inlaid .45 automatic in his right hand, which he had produced from the small of his back at the first sound of gunfire. He trained it on the door, keeping one eye on Celeste, and pulled on the handle.

A GA guy, wearing body armor and a very agitated expression, stepped inside and pushed the door closed behind him.

"Mr. White," he nodded. "Hi, Celeste," he added, pointing his H&K at the floor.

"Hi, Carl," she replied. "Trouble in paradise?"

"You shut up," White said, looking from one to the other. "You tell me what's going on."

"It's him," Carl said simply. "He's loose on the floor."

"Son of a bitch," White said, shaking his head. "Didn't he *recognize* anybody? I mean, you've worked with the guy on five different occasions."

"Didn't really come up," Carl said grimly. "He must have been working the drug dealer, and followed him up to us. He got off the elevator, saw the crew armed to the teeth, and he started cleaning. That's what he does."

"That's what he's good at," Celeste added. She slumped in her chair, looking tired and hopeless. But this was a ruse. She was just waiting for her moment.

"I told you to shut up." White looked at Carl again. "How many down?"

"Only four or five so far. But like I said, he's moving. He'll most likely take the team, if we give him a few minutes."

"Can we get his agent on the phone? Turn him off?"

"I tried this morning; I'll try again." Carl pulled a phone from his duty belt.

As he flipped the mouthpiece and hit a speed-dial button, White narrated to Celeste in an aside, "As I alluded to a minute ago, we've been trying to get this guy off of this job since the Central Park debacle. But we haven't been able to contact him."

Carl locked his thumb on the volume button, turned the phone out into the small room at the end of his black-clad arm. In an Italian accent, clear and undistorted, the phone said, "*This is Anthony. I may be in town at the moment, and, again, I may not. Ciao.*"

White grimaced at the message. Carl grimaced as Celeste locked his outstretched wrist. She put the locked wrist over his shoulder and moved in a blur to stand behind him, simultaneously drawing his sidearm with a rip of Velcro. She disengaged the safety and pointed it over Carl's shoulder at Mr. White in a single motion. She peered at White around Carl's right ear, from four feet away.

White pointed his gold .45 right back.

Looking down, Celeste realized that Carl was pointing the stubby barrel of his H&K straight up at her chin. *Hmm*, she thought, *I missed that.*

The sound of gunfire started up again outside, good and loud. They had to speak over it.

White said, "I believe this is very nearly how we began our professional relationship."

Celeste ignored that. "Your parole," she said simply.

"You're not in a perfect position to demand it," White answered, lowering his gun. "But you have it. You always have." He nodded to Carl.

Celeste released him. "Sorry about your wrist, Carl," she said. She safetied the handgun, reversed it, and proffered its butt to him.

"Keep it," the man said, shaking his wrist out. He shifted the

H&K to his left hand, removed another, identical, nickel-finish Beretta from an ankle holster, and slipped it into the empty spot on his belt. Celeste took the safety back off of hers, and reached out to crack the door.

"You on the clock?" White asked, hopefully.

"No," she answered. "But good luck."

"Do I *always* have to be bailing you motherfuckers out?" FreeBSD wanted to know, tossing the coiled ends of the rope to the floor.

"What I want to know," griped Miles, rubbing his wrists, "is why we've been risking our necks for this money, if we've already discovered the meaning of life."

"Enlightenment don't pay the motherfucking rent. Now where's my money?"

"It was outside," answered Miles. "On a table."

"No," Dana contradicted. "Somebody picked it up."

"Somebody picked it up? Who?"

"The blond guy."

"Son of a bitch," said FreeBSD.

The three still stood in the ladies' room, free, poised for action, debating how to get paid. They agreed to focus on salvaging their hides first. But they also felt disinclined to have gone through all this for nothing. Particularly when they almost certainly stood less than fifty yards from the two million dollars. The sounds of the gun battle still drifted in, though growing more distant.

"I'm gonna check the room," FreeBSD said. He killed the lights, put a palm to the door, and peeked through the crack. "Looks clear." He let the door mush shut. "Well, shit. If we can make a break for it, I guess that's what we do." He appraised Miles and Dana. "I guess you two aren't strapped." He tossed his head at the door. "Lotsa guns on the floor out there. Grab some, and we'll make for the elevator." He spat. "Without the money."

He pushed the door open with his back and covered the

room, as Miles and Dana made for discarded arms. They had just begun hardware scavenging when Celeste appeared, darting in from one of the side hallways.

After almost shooting one another, the four retreated hastily to the sanctuary of the bathroom. There they traded notes on their status, and the disposition of the cash.

"The blond guy has it?" Celeste asked, incredulous. "Fuck. Well, I'll get it," she declared, as if she thought this unproblematic. Miles looked at her fearfully as he checked the magazines of a pair of Glocks he'd found.

"Get out of here," Celeste said. "I'll make a go at the backpack. When I get it, I'll radio you and we'll meet up." She paused. "Oh, shit, where are the radios? Never mind, I'll e-mail you."

"How do you intend to keep that private?" asked Miles.

"She can use your PGP key," said FreeBSD. "It's on your page."

"I don't have PGP," Celeste disclaimed. "I don't even have a fucking computer anymore."

"We don't have time for this," urged Dana.

"Post to Usenet," said Miles.

"Which group?"

"Uh . . . alt.barney.purple.dinosaur.die.die.die."

"Christ," spat Celeste, stomping out the door. "Why does everything have to be so geeky with you people?" She disappeared, making a sharp left back into the lethal labyrinth of hallways.

Miles, Dana, and FreeBSD quickly realized they should have followed her out, but they had hesitated. Now they heard gunfire rising in volume, and a couple of shouts floating closer.

FreeBSD checked a huge Desert Eagle .50 he had picked up, with his SIG in his left armpit. "You ready?" he asked.

"I gotch'er back," said Miles, a little theatrically.

"Yeah, and I got your fucking nose," FreeBSD replied, tweaking Miles' proboscis with his index and middle fingers. Between the two, he held up his thumb triumphantly. "What are you going to do now, huh?" He made a display of putting the nose in his pocket, then palmed the other handgun and held both in front of him.

Miles held the twin Glocks.

Dana clutched the little Tomcat, the only one of their original belongings they'd recovered.

The voices and gunfire grew louder, which made additional delay seem suicidal.

"I feel pretty good," Miles said, sucking breath. The fog of exhaustion was off of him.

"Yeah, well, forget how you feel," FreeBSD said, "and get the fuck on with it."

They burst out of the bathroom in a tight knot, not entirely unselfconsciously in a Butch and Sundance motif. For better or worse, the frame didn't freeze, and the credits didn't roll. Neither did the entire Bolivian army await them. But there were a couple of guys outside. Two or three very spooked and edgy surviving wrecking crew guys.

Fuck this bullshit, Stanley thought, with finality. *Enough is enough already.*

He had two million bucks on his back, and he'd already gone way over and above the call on this one. Also, it appeared that his contract employers would soon be way too dead to fire him. And he was rapidly losing faith in the prospects of this bullshit room-to-room action.

He'd managed to drift to the rear of the group; a fine spot from which to slip out the back.

Two million, plus his previously banked fees for this job, would take him a long way. All he had to do was get out of the building.

He stood still and let the team advance without him for five seconds, their black garments fading into the greater blackness. He then reversed course and slunk off in what he hoped was the right direction. He padded down a long hallway, which he imagined led toward the elevator lobby.

He could just see the glinting of the outer glass wall, when he stopped dead at the renewed sound of gunfire and profanities coming from up ahead. He could swear he heard something about daddies and bitches. But he definitely heard gunfire.

Fuck. There were stairs in the back of the suite. He could take those instead of the elevator. All he had to do was circle around the team, evade the hit man who was killing everybody, not run into White, and blow this taco stand. He reversed course.

Celeste spotted him a few seconds later, in one of the cross hallways.

"*Who's* your daddy?!" FreeBSD shouted, leading their charge. "*Who's* your daddy?!" He held both guns up and out, blasting away like the world's deadliest crane.

Miles followed his histrionic lead: "Suck on this, bitch!" he belted out. "Suck on these!" He triggered off the Glocks, thrusting them at the scrambling and blurred figures on the far side of the room.

They both fired two-handed, running drunkenly, shouting like maniacs, Dana following.

Their opponents fired wildly as well, diving for cover, taken by surprise.

It was all over in thirty years and two seconds: two seconds to get to the elevators; ten years for the doors to open; and another two decades for them to close again. The three huddled in the corners and fired around the lips of the doors, willing them to close. When they finally oozed shut, and started ringing metallically with bullets hitting the outside, the kids inside felt like their parents' ages.

"You shoot like ass! You shoot like a little girl!" Miles shouted, as they began to descend. "I think I winged that guy," he added, standing up, visibly shaking.

"Good job," FreeBSD muttered in reply. Only then did Miles

realize the other man still huddled in the corner, on the floor. He looked paler than usual, and held one of his guns over his mid-section. His black T-shirt showed a darker and wetter black around the gun.

By the time they reached the basement, all three of them were pressing down on FreeBSD's stomach, and he was crying quietly.

Tracking Stanley Luther, trying to convince herself that each second was the right second to take him, Celeste wondered why she risked all this.

Much of the training she had undergone involved how not to get into situations like this. The best conflicts, she'd been taught, are avoided entirely. Failing that, shoes are the best defense – run like hell. Finally, in the very worst case, one should resolve mortal contests this way: *Kill or incapacitate your attacker as quickly as possible*, ideally in a completely one-sided contest. The only dirty fight is the one you lose. This wisdom did not make Celeste feel any better about the idea of shooting a man in the back. She slid into a doorway, behind a wall of thin plaster, keeping in mind Rule #27 of a Gunfight: "Remember the difference between cover and concealment."

They'd almost reached the rear of the complex, and the stairs. Stanley paused, peering left and right, before passing another cross hallway.

Celeste was still grappling with the issue of shooting the away-facing, when Stanley obviated the problem by looking over his shoulder, and wheeling to face her. They pointed, once again, their guns dead at each other, from a few feet away. Stanley cocked his head and said, "*Oh*, no, not this shit again," and he pulled his trigger – but the shot went wild, for the unlikely reason that a knife had appeared, pressed against his throat. The knife came with an arm, from his side, from the cross hallway, and then also a large, warm body, which pressed against Stanley's back. Finally, a second arm appeared and pointed a handgun over his shoulder, inches from his cheek, at Celeste down the hall. Stanley felt breath on his ear.

Peering straight down his cheeks, Stanley could see the huge knife at his throat. The gun out in front of his head was enormous as well. He let his pistol roll over his index finger on its trigger guard, going limp and pointing at the ceiling. After all his annoyance at the inconveniences and indignities of this job, he now for the first time – for the first time in years – experienced good old, bare, helpless fear. Death hunched over his back, that much was obvious.

Celeste had frozen, too.

The Cleaner, standing motionless behind Stanley, for all the world like the other's shadow, fingered his trigger, then squinted down his sights, showing a stubbly look of inquiry.

"Celeste?" he asked in an accented basso profundo.

"Hi, Noel," Celeste answered slowly. "How are you?"

He nodded barely and quickly in answer. "You know this guy?" he asked, darting his eyes at the side of Stanley's head.

"No," Celeste answered, and winced sharply as Noel flicked the knife, opening Stanley Luther's throat, and let him slump to the floor. *Oh shit*, she mouthed.

"What are you doing here?" Noel asked suspiciously, sounding mildly befuddled, and still pointing his gun at her. (She had lowered hers immediately, that was an easy one.)

"Oh, I was just leaving," she answered carefully. "You mind if I take that?" She pointed to the bag on Stanley's back.

"Eh? No, take it. Just go. Quickly." And he turned to disappear. As he did, Celeste had a thought, hopefully not her last, steeled herself and said, "Noel?"

"Yeah?" He looked over his shoulder, halfway around the corner.

"You remember Mr. White, and Carl, who work with me?"

"Yeah, I remember them."

"Well, they're up here, too, so be careful."

"Yeah, okay, I'll look out for them."

And then he was gone, off looking for a drug-dealing client who had already gone. Celeste jerked on the straps of the backpack, which had only a little blood on them. Then she and it descended those much-sought back stairs. Forty-plus flights of them.

Getting Handed Your Ass

Miles and Dana, empty-handed, sprinting down the wide expanse of the Rockefeller Center Promenade, like a final drizzle of photons emitted from the dying supernova of the ice rink shoot-out, flashing toward Fifth Avenue at something less than the speed of light.

The Very First Rule of a Gunfight is: "Bring a gun."

But Miles and Dana and FreeBSD had all been empty, or nearly empty, by the time those elevator doors closed and so they had left the guns when they left FreeBSD in the elevator. A good thing, too, else they might have found themselves in a short and one-sided gunfight with the two dozen or so uniformed NYPD officers who now chased them at a dead sprint, shoving pedestrians and leaping over bums and poodles, down the Promenade.

The cops, much less tired than Miles and Dana, were gaining. The ghosts of recently deceased colleagues animated them. But the fact that the sprinting suspects did not appear to be armed did keep the madly sprinting officers from opening fire. Barely.

Miles and Dana had left FreeBSD in the elevator in the RCA Building because he couldn't run; and because he was, at a rate about which they could not be at all sure, dying; and because, as he pointed out laughingly, he hadn't really done anything wrong.

"What the fuck are they going to nick me for?" he laughed, wincing from the pain of his belly wound, and from his mirth. Miles and Dana launched into another refusal to leave him, but he cut them off. "I'm a drug dealer. But ain't no drugs. My whole joint went up in smoke. And I shot at a couple of hit men, which was self-defense – like any of those spooky bitches is going to show up in court." He paused to labor for breath. "Oh, yeah, and I discovered the meaning of life. Motherfucking sue me."

Miles and Dana didn't like FreeBSD spending his strength on this rant, but they caught his meaning. The cops could likely save his life, and he could almost certainly beat the rap (if anyone could figure out what to charge him with).

So they'd dropped the guns in a dumpster in the basement, wrapped their friend's mid-section tightly with a belt and a shirt, and pressed the button for the lobby. Dana kissed him, and Miles tried to administer a hug, but his target lay on the floor, and in pain, and was steeling himself for some last thing he had to say. He seized Miles by the lapel.

"Hey, man. Miles."

Miles squinted down at him, serious and expectant, their faces a few inches apart.

"One other thing—" FreeBSD curled up over his own stomach, coughing weakly. "Somethin' I meant to tell you. I need to tell you."

Miles steeled his jaw and whispered, "Go ahead, man." Dana held the elevator door.

"The Central Park thing. That was me. It was my fault. It was me."

"It wasn't your fault," Miles answered. "It was the bad guys."

FreeBSD shook his head. His lids were low and his breathing shallow. "It was me. I led 'em there. Listen. When you wrote me about bringing the bag back. They read that mail, too. The Concern. They read the mail." Miles remained silent. "After you wrote saying you were in town . . . they wrote me a minute later. They told me I could still get paid if I set up to meet you and take the bag back. And if I went myself. They told me to meet you in the park." Miles still looked at him skeptically. "Why else would I bother goin' out to get a bunch of talcum powder back?"

Miles' expression softened, and he said, "I was actually wondering about that." They both paused in silence, still practically nose to nose; FreeBSD hadn't loosed his grip on Miles' collar.

"But listen, man. You gotta know: I never, *never*, would have set that thing up—" and he averted his head to cough, "—if I'd had *any* idea—" and he swallowed hard "—they were gonna kill me too."

Miles laughed aloud. "You bastard."

"Yeah," FreeBSD agreed, releasing his grip on Miles, head lolling. "Pretty much every day. Just take care of the money," he said, beginning to shiver with shock. "And I'll drop you a note . . . or something . . . when I'm back on my feet." He hugged himself, head falling back against the wall.

Miles squeezed his arm, and stepped backward with Dana. And the doors closed.

From there they took some stairs up to the street, and once above ground made it about two steps before getting made by a couple of the hundreds of cops in the vicinity. Which precipitated the foot race. Which, to reiterate, they were losing.

Dana had almost run out of breath (damn the cigarettes). Miles thought balefully about prison – life in a cage. But his pumping arms and legs were so tired. That awful, discouraging, psychological thing had started to happen where his body began to instruct his mind that it should start caring less. Neither had reached the point of giving up; but they could see it out there.

Before they reached that point on the horizon, however, chips of cement and bits of foliage began to fall around the feet of the pursuing cops. This caused the more savvy and levelheaded amongst them to leave off their chase and dive for cover. But the point was too subtle apparently for some. So the hand of Miles and Dana's guardian angel on high ceased firing and unscrewed the silencer at the end of his barrel, still calling out updates into the open channel of the radio on the blanket beside him, and he began firing again, but much more loudly now.

This time the near misses – underscored by the staccato rifle reports from the rooftop – caused even the most stalwart brother officers to stop running and get under cover.

"Shooter! On the roof!" one of the late-adopting cops shouted unhelpfully.

"God*damn* now it's gonna be hard to get off of this building," Angelo cursed. He held his position for another few seconds, until he saw Miles and Dana reach the street, and saw the van screech to a halt in their path. And then he pulled his rifle away from the lip of the roof and slid on his belly away from his overlook, as the police started to take some serious potshots.

"Miles Darken, Dana Steckler," said the dark, young, serious man with the beard and the ponytail, out of the passenger side window of the van. "Please take advantage of our courtesy shuttle service." Or that's what they thought he said; his accent was very thick.

Miles and Dana couldn't even begin to know what to think about this. It had been all they could do to keep from hurtling into the side of the vehicle – it and they had reached the same spot of curb on Fifth Avenue at virtually the same time. Angelo had single-handedly gotten them all there, with his radio and with his rifle.

Miles spared one look back down the Promenade, where police advanced under cover.

They got in.

The driver, more nondescript than the striking passenger, squealed the tires and they accelerated south, Rockefeller Center receding behind them. The Indian twisted in his seat to face them. Miles realized he had a laptop on his lap.

"The IP address," he said.

Miles and Dana both stared at him stupidly.

"Quickly! The address of the Manuscript."

The driver added, flatly (and more intelligibly), "Look, we're not out of this yet." He tossed his head at the rear-view mirror.

Miles and Dana looked out the back and saw two sedans gaining on them, moving up angrily. "What if we're killed in the next minute?" the driver posed. "You want the Manuscript to be lost for another hundred and thirty years?"

The driver made a squealing right turn.

Dana recited, "238, 142, 222, 64. Port 4044. Username 'shastra'. Password 'muezzin'."

The guy with the laptop typed blazingly as Dana spoke.

Miles craned out the back window.

The city caromed by them; the Hudson River loomed. And still they went faster. But the two pursuing cars were on them. They weren't police cars. They were, Miles realized, the wrecking crew. Maybe not the same exact guys. But basically the same guys. From the same camp.

The two pursuing vehicles split and accelerated to pull up on either side, boxing them in.

Miles and Dana were unarmed.

The dark passenger was typing furiously; he didn't even look up from the laptop, at the impending danger, or at anything else.

The driver said, "Duck, please."

Abhijit, in the passenger seat, leaned into his own lap. The monitor of the computer angled radically backward, and he continued typing with his nose inches from the screen.

Shan released the steering wheel and picked up a second handgun from the seat with his left hand. (Miles hadn't noticed the first one get into his right hand.) His head darted left, right, then bounced back to center, his even gaze straight ahead. He crossed his arms, sticking the gun in his right hand out the driver's side window and extending the gun in his left over the curve of Abhijit's back. The car filled with a staccato roar, and then a huge number of hot brass casings. The brass bounced off the upholstery, the dashboard, the passengers. Shan fired out of both front side windows of the van, his arms crossed over in a sort of "Polish Gunfighter" configuration. Miles, peeking between the front seats, could see that Shan steered with his knees while he fired.

"Here's your ass," Shan shouted as both guns went dry, their slides locked back, breeches wide open like the mouths of hungry baby birds. "Now cool it a while." The car on their left careened onto the sidewalk, obliviated a thin tree, and spun into a shop front. Both of the men in the front seat were extremely dead of head shots from Shan's right-hand gun.

The car on their right exploded – not in spite of, but because of Shan's crappy left-handed shooting. The passengers in the cabin had gone unscathed while all sixteen rounds plunked into the front-left quarter panel. One of them must have found a fuel line. Flames and thick black smoke engulfed the front of the car and the driver locked up the brakes in an effort to stop and evacuate.

"Hah, hah, motherfuckers," Shan said to the Chinese fire drill in his rear-view mirror. Miles and Dana peered out the back, over the cracked bench seat and through the cracked glass.

Shan wheeled the van into the Lincoln Tunnel, gunned the big engine, and started reloading with one hand and his free leg.

"Welcome to New Jersey," Shan said.

"Who *are* you people?" Dana asked wide-eyed.

Abhijit, proud of his friend's handiwork, couldn't help grinning widely as he answered.

Celeste on the street, in a cab, and then in a netcafe. While the cab meter ran outside, she paid in cash for an hour on a machine, fabricated a username and mail address, and posted a message to alt.barney.purple.dinosaur.die.die.die:

> Article 34976 Subject: CB to MD. 1 of 1
> From: Rich Girl <cb@foo.bar >
>
> Pick me up where we originally met (IRL); 10pm, day after tomorrow.

Post, log out, and exit. Then, in her slickest move since recovering the multimillion-dollar bag, Celeste swung by their last rented room and recovered their cached luggage, including FreeBSD's drugs, $75K, and toiletries. Pushing her luck, she went by her place as well. In through the back window, big duffel on the bed, and a few cubic feet of her life got to come with her. Happily, a number of these cubic inches were cash, in a couple of different currencies. Such was Celeste's world, even before this week, that she kept traveling money on hand. A few letters, a few pictures, passports. Toiletry bag, laptop, a couple of changes of underwear. One last gun and spare mags.

And goodbye Manhattan.

Finally, a couple of days to get lost in the city before hooking back up. Don't get killed; don't get arrested; and definitely don't get mugged. She had 2.105 million dollars on her back.

Celeste felt as if she were really hitting her stride.

Miles, Dana, and the two Angry Young Taoists circled back into Manhattan and back to home base. Miles felt at home in the POTEV in about five seconds. They held introductions, and an all-business debriefing by Naja. The three of them sat alone in the office while everyone else – literally everyone, the full group was in the house – sat at their machines, slack-jawed, reading and rereading the Manuscript.

It was like the second coming of crack to New York.

Miles fiddled with an ashtray on Naja's desk, which was inscribed with the puzzling admonition to "Smoke an empty bowl".

The AYTs

"I'm not going to keep y'all in suspense," Naja informed them, "because I don't care to make a production out of it. So say it."

"Why are we here?" Dana asked obligingly.

"You are here," Naja answered, "principally because we have

spent the past nine days reading all of your mail and posts. Albeit we weren't the only ones."

"Might we ask why?" Dana asked.

Naja sat motionless on the edge of the desk, her palms on its edge, her back against a computer monitor. She wore black jeans and a loose black pullover that concealed her bosom and her gun.

"Why? Because we've been looking for the Manuscript a lot longer than Jim Castrolang . . . or FreeBSD . . . or either of y'all, dear Dana. It's not exactly a point of pride, because y'all *found* the thing before we did." As she paused, the door knocked and Abhijit and Shan entered.

"We're here to help," offered Abhijit.

"Explain things to our new friends," clarified Shan, nodding to Miles, grinning at Dana.

Thanks awfully, said Naja with her expression.

Mike typed furiously and announced to the others in the room, "More stuff." Snitch and T'ien Ken crowded in.

"You got in deeper?" Snitch asked.

"A little," Mike disclaimed. "Got one new file."

"What is it?"

"Binary, no file type," answered Mike, as he poked around the bowels of the FTP server. "But," Mike dragged the word out, fingers flying, "looks like a bitmapped image."

Two minutes later, and one desk over, they panned across a graphic of a map, scanned from paper, originally drawn in black pencil. It showed Argentina, and some of Chile, with a route drawn near what was marked as the Uspallata Pass. And a thick, black "X" at the end of the route.

Nobody spoke. Laylah walked in; she had a couple of trade volumes cradled in her arms.

"It's him," she intoned serenely to no one in particular. "Either Burton wrote this, or I want to meet the impersonator who did." Laylah was the resident Burton expert.

* * *

Miles and Dana sat wide-eyed, though their heads had gotten wobbly on their necks. Naja pondered how to proceed. She decided to take advantage of her meddling staff members.

"All right," she sing-songed tiredly, "who wants to give Miles and Dana the six-bit background?" Abhijit raised his hand but Shan launched in.

"Miles, Dana, I'm sure you're wondering who the heck are these Angry Young Taoists. Well, we're just a dozen or so precocious and brilliant twenty-somethings who have a great deal of potential, but don't play well with others. We have fun, pick up beer money, and make the world a better place by means of hacking, industrial espionage, blackmail, infiltration, and other fun strong-arm tactics."

"But we only strong-arm people who deserve it," Abhijit added in his rapid-fire Bombay brogue. He and Shan had reverted to their habit of trading spoken lines, like an old married couple.

"That's right," Shan said in sequence. "We're mainly concerned with doing people who need to be done. To put it in mythical terms – which everyone seems to want to do – we steal from the irredeemably corrupt, and keep the bulk for ourselves. But we leave the world a better place."

Abhijit added, "Like Superfund contractors: making a profit as we clean up the landscape."

"Enough," Naja interjected. "Does that make sense? I can see from your expressions that it doesn't. But come to think of it, I don't care either way right now."

"I hate to conk out on you, but I've got to ask," Miles hazarded, "could we take a nap?"

"I was about to ask the same thing," Dana sighed.

"I was about to suggest the same thing," Naja assented. "We can fill each other in more after we've caught up on some work, and y'all have caught up on some sleep." She looked back at her dynamic duo. "Could one of you show our guests to the comfy couches?"

* * *

Miles and Dana got deposited on a pair of a raggedy, cloth-covered couches in a back room. The lights were out, and a nightlight glowed from a socket low on the wall. As the door closed on their repose, they both went out like flashlights with dead batteries.

They awoke two hours later when a tired-looking black man in black fatigues entered from the other room, letting in light. He tossed a gun, then another, onto the larger couch.

"Y'all know how to use these, right?" he asked.

"Can I get a spare mag?" Miles asked, blinking, picking up the gun and racking the slide.

"Sure, Sergeant York," Angelo answered. "Yeah, I might got one you can have."

"You must be in heaven," Dana deadpanned, sitting up. She looked to still be in her dream.

"Oh, yeah, I love shooting at people all over New York," replied Miles, scratching the back of his head, and considering the surprising number of people he kept running into with rafts of handguns in a city where no one was actually allowed to own one.

"I'm grateful for the gun," he said to Angelo, "and don't want to look a gift strap in the mouth. But why exactly are you arming us? You don't even know us."

"You're right I don't know you. I'm arming you because that's what Naja told me to do. She asked me to do it because we still don't have the 411 on the opposition. They found you once, might find you again. And if they find you here, we'll need all the help we can get."

"Do you think they'll come here?" Dana asked, looking askance at the other gun.

"I'm sorry, I'm not the designated thinker today," Angelo replied, his hand on the doorknob. "But if there's any more shooting, I can tell you what my next designated position is going to be. It's going to be up in the top of the big tree out in the courtyard across the street. Local news van is going to come by afterward, and they're going to have to stick a microphone up into the tree to get my eyewitness commentary, "Uh, yeah, that's right," he recited in a thick man-on-the-street voice. "I saw it all. The bad guys showed up and started shooting, which was when I took up my current position . . . which is right here . . . up in this tree." Miles and Dana got his meaning. He'd seen enough shooting.

He pulled the door shut behind him.

Five minutes later, Naja entered. She stared stilly into the dark room.

"So. We're going to South America," she announced flatly, but with a faint, undisguisable underbuzz of excitement. She bent her knee and put a hand on her hip. "Y'all wanna come, or what?"

Part Three

Do you imagine that the universe is agitated?
Go out into the desert of the night and look up at the stars
This practice should answer the question

— LAO TZU

The Movement of Return

They couldn't leave that minute. Even the Angry Young Taoists had not the power to get good fares on fewer than seven days' notice.

Day One: Some were bonding

"Die, punks," had just formed on Shan's lips, as he lined up a rocket shot on a figure in the middle distance. Unfortunately, he was already hurt, and wasn't watching his radar – and he died, put down by a pair of popping pistols.

"Silly Shan!" Miles clucked, running over Shan's crumpled corpse, scooping up weapons and ammo. He switched to the rocket launcher and advanced on the remaining opponent in the courtyard.

Hmm, dark blue uniform, considered Miles. *I believe that's Mike.*

He trotted right up to him with a pair of rockets ready to go.

"Oh, it hurts!" he empathized, as Mike catapulted across the arena overhead.

Miles checked the score. He held the lead, but he didn't have time to gloat over it: Shan had returned to the courtyard, and Miles was taking some near misses with long range grenade fire – that would be Angelo. Hiding out up high somewhere.

But then time expired, and all of the players moved into the same room. They smiled and shuffled and recounted the memorable bad-ass maneuvers of the game just concluded.

"Man, you really owned the middle," said Angelo to Miles.

"I had you *dead* to rights at the end," Shan said to Mike. "Then *this* bastard," and he tossed an elbow at Miles, "gunned me down with *pistol* fire." Everyone laughed, sloughing tension.

Day Two: Someone was returning

Celeste waited in the gift store across the street from the appointed coffee shop. She had spent the past two days nursing her paranoia, thinking about her very public post to Usenet, other ways she could be tracked down or dug up. So she waited across the street from the meeting place and watched for familiar faces entering the coffee shop.

Shan's and Abhijit's faces were not familiar to Celeste, though they had committed her description to memory. They sat and drank coffee and watched the door for forty-five minutes, from the very same counter where Celeste had first met Miles and Dana.

All three gave it up and left at the same time. Celeste spared a last look across the pavement expanse – and Abhijit caught it. "It's her," he said, pulling Shan into a treacherous jaywalk.

Two ominous-looking strangers heading right toward her was just exactly what Celeste had hoped not to see. She clutched her gun, her last gun, inside the pocket of her topcoat. Her instincts told her to bolt. But she wasn't going to outrun anybody with all the shit slung over her shoulders. She took two steps forward, to where she could crouch behind a parked vehicle.

The paler man stepped up and drew something from his pocket: a box magazine, tiny and empty. He stood only a few feet from Celeste, presenting her with the little gum stick of blued metal. It was one of the spare mags for her Tomcat (or somebody's).

"A redheaded gal asked us to return this to you," the man said, looking her in the eye. "She says she's sorry, but she lost the gun."

"Tell her not to worry about it," hissed Celeste, backing away.

"'Tell her yourself,'" said Shan as the AYT van rolled to a double park beside them. Celeste thumbed her safety under her coat as the side door slid open. Dana peered out from inside.

"Hi," she smiled. "These are friends. Get in, it's okay."

Celeste had no good way of knowing whether they were friends or captors. But she had seen Dana under stress, and this didn't appear to be it. And every second she stood out on the street put her in more danger. So she raised her gun up inside her coat pocket – the significance of the phallic protrusion obvious – and backed into the van beside Dana.

"Get in, keep your hands in the open, and start talking," she said to Abhijit and Shan, keeping half an eye on the driver. She could see he was young, thin, bespectacled, and cute. Abhijit and Shan complied and the van pulled out.

Dana clutched Celeste's arm and said, "We decided that Miles and I shouldn't stick our faces out. We're kind of popular lately."

"And whose faces *did* you stick out?" Celeste asked, eyeing this motley crew.

Day Three: Someone was forging

"What do you mean you don't have passports?" Naja snipped. "How can you not have passports. Jesus." She walked out of the room. Thirty seconds later Snitch walked in.

"Hi," he said cheerily. "I understand you have a paperwork problem."

Snitch sported white spiky hair and wore a black "Free Tibet" T-shirt and black jeans with a silver chain swooping across the thigh. He stopped in the middle of the room and smiled.

"Have *you* come to the right place." He patted a black valise under his arm. He opened it on a desk, revealing an array of art supplies.

"We do have a little raw materials issue," he admitted. "Generally, we're *altering* a passport. Making a few little changes to the picture or name. On the other hand, pulling one out of thin air requires, oh, a certain paper stock, a certain polyurethane billfold . . . These will take a bit of time to dig up." He had begun to rezip the bag when Celeste entered, her presence filling the room and drawing heads.

"I heard a deplorable rumor," she announced, "that someone was looking to falsify passports." She produced a full poker hand of them. Snitch went to work with digital camera, color laser printer, glue and Exacto knife, and in sixty minutes, Miles and Dana were good to go.

Day Four: Someone was healing

The hospital room didn't look like the one Theron T. Johnson had occupied in Hookeville. It didn't sparkle nearly as whitely, being a city general, rather than a university medical center. And it was not private. A large, middle-aged, and gastroenterologically afflicted person shifted endlessly in the next bed, watching daytime television overhead.

Nor did piles of flowers cover the bed table, nor books, nor candy from concerned colleagues. FreeBSD didn't really have that kind of colleague. He didn't have any kind of colleague anymore, unless he counted the new ones. Amongst his old crew, only Ace might have sent him flowers. Ace would have gotten him anything he needed during his convalescence – laptop, decent coffee, girls. He would have taken care of business in his absence and given him good-natured shit until he convalesced and dragged himself back to the Crib.

There wasn't any more business, the Crib was embers, and Ace was not going to be giving him any shit ever again.

Paul, or FreeBSD, made a brief and desultory attempt to keep from thinking these sorts of self-pitying thoughts; but he quickly gave it up as hopeless. Here he was bedridden, with round-the-clock talk show narration, the beached post-operative whale floundering heavily one bed over. To distract him: only a couple of dated *Scientific Americans*, scored from the candy-stripers, and twice-daily visits from certain endlessly inquisitive members of New York's finest.

No shit he was going to be thinking about Ace, and everything else he had lost.

Very little else contended for space in his head. There were his new friends, the new money – if they had got it – and whether he'd see either again. And the new understanding, of course. Couldn't take that away from him, he'd near memorized the thing. Whether any of it was true or not . . .

The morning and afternoon police interrogations tended to break up the hours in the day, so he didn't mind 'em. Although it did get a little repetitive, sticking to his same "bullshit story".

That was how the lead detective, the one with the eyebrows, referred to his narrative – the one he had come up with on the fly during their first meeting and had recited several times since. It explained how he'd come to be gut-shot in an elevator in the RCA Building, as well as what he'd been doing for the eight months prior to that. But there wasn't that much to the bullshit story, so he digressed a lot.

"You are once again talking about something," the detective would note, "about which we do not give a shit."

"Oh, I'm sorry," FreeBSD would respond with mock surprise. "What was the question?"

On this particular morning, his third since regaining consciousness, he had an hour before their first visit of the day – and that was when the unanticipated flowers appeared. He assumed they were for his roommate's already overgrown bed table, but instead they hit his bare one.

He found that the card had once been sealed, but ripped open subsequently. He whistled at the orderly on his way out and flashed the opened mail and an inquisitive look.

"The officer in the hall," the man in white said. FreeBSD didn't know there was a cop in the hall. But he might have guessed. "He read the note and copied it into his notebook.

They're allowed to. He left the money – all of it, I watched him." He shrugged and left.

In the envelope FreeBSD found new hundred-dollar bills, thirty of them, inside a gift card. On the front of the card: a nighttime shot of Rockefeller Center. *Bastards*, he thought, smiling.

The inside of the card had no pre-printed message, just block-lettered handwriting.

> HEY HOMEY,
> WE WERE DANCE-AROUND EXCITED TO FIND OUT YOU MADE IT TO THE HOSPITAL—AND NOT THE BASEMENT PART, IF YOU KNOW WHAT WE MEAN.
> WE HAVEN'T FORGOTTEN ABOUT YOU.
> THE MONEY PROBABLY WON'T COVER THE HOSPITAL BILL, SO YOU SHOULD SKIP OUT ON THAT. USE IT FOR TRAVEL MONEY INSTEAD. WHERE ARE YOU GOING, YOU ASK? TELL YOU LATER: <ANON34897@PENET.FI>.

It was signed "MD&C".

And so there FreeBSD found himself weeping for the second time that he could remember, and not from the pain in his stomach, which he almost couldn't even feel now, but from something he felt higher in his chest. A flood of frantic gratitude washed over him, to suddenly find that he wasn't alone here, that he hadn't lost everything, and that something did wait for him.

It could have been the drugs talking. But at that moment he would swear that he had found meaning, and it wasn't in the pages of the Manuscript. It was in the thread – Ariadne's, or electronic, or floral delivery, or whatever – and in what lay at the other end of it.

He wept with gratitude, and with fullness, and with sadness, and with some powerful and inexorable sense of something bigger than himself. He wept not to be alone in the world.

Day Five: Someone was dealing

"Can we move that, Snitch?" asked Naja.

"Sure, we can move that. We know some people," Snitch added for the benefit of Miles, Dana, and Celeste. They referred to the coke, FreeBSD's coke. They sat around a large pile of that, and cash.

"How much can you get for it?" asked Dana, wide-eyed.

"FreeBSD said it was worth three hundred thousand," noted Celeste.

"On the street, or wholesale?" asked Snitch.

"Well," sighed Naja, "I'm sure we'll get whatever it's worth."

Snitch added, "We know some *honest* drug dealers. Uh, 'people'."

"So that's the two million in the bag," recited Naja, doing math, "plus your FreeBSD's seventy-five thousand, plus Celeste's thirty K, and maybe another three hundred large for the white stuff. Nearly two and-half million."

Celeste and Dana grinned with greedy energy. Miles was internalizing – after all the distraction and the madness – that he seemed to have made bank. But he looked thoughtful as well as jubilant, and he said, "Dana and I wouldn't be here to enjoy it without you folks. What do the AYTs normally charge for rescue services?"

"No, thank you," disclaimed Naja. "You brought us the Manuscript. That's what we've been waiting for all this time. Anyway, we're all at or near our retirement figures anyway."

"You've been doing pretty well?"

"We do all right."

"At least a tip?" persisted Miles.

Naja shook her head slow and dignified. "Y'all can buy the first round when we get down south. Speaking of retirement figures, I'd say you all are in pretty good shape. More than six hundred thousand each, four ways – if you split it that way. Take you a long way, particularly if you have a taste for the third world."

"Third world?" Celeste asked.

"Oh, yeah," smiled Snitch. "It costs a fucking fortune to retire in this country."

"The money'll go farther than you think, in Cabo or Jakarta," said Naja, with the easy authority of someone who'd researched the issue.

"Or Belize," added Miles.

Naja eyed him, not responding to this. "Anyway, it's not like you can't make more. You've got skills." She looked thoughtful for a second, then tossed her head at Snitch and said, "Go." Wordlessly, he darted out of the room with the bag. "And be careful, sweetcakes."

Snitch came back later with $265,500 in cash, ragged bills. Their next and last payday.

Day Six: Some were dusting

"We're on it," Shan boasted.

"Yeah, 'we're' my ass," answered Mike, laughing. The two typed mechanically, and very quickly. A crowd looked on; this had become another friendly competition. "I've got the cancel order on Celeste's and Dana's last posts," Mike said.

"Meet my cancel-bot," rejoindered Shan, tight-lipped. "Dana and Celeste have never posted."

Damn, mouthed Mike. But he had a hold-out exploit; he'd been working on the Google Groups database server in his spare time. With a couple of minutes of inspired effort, he leveraged the access he'd gained earlier. Stealing a glance at the next monitor over, he saw Shan trying to work the same site from scratch. He chuckled quietly.

The room was quiet and dark, lit by monitor glow and the glare from the two hackers' damp foreheads. *Color me impressed*, thought Miles, looking on.

"Oh, look at that," cackled Mike. He flipped to a web browser from the terminal window where he'd been issuing rapid-fire SQL commands to a violated database. "According to

Google Groups, no one from the tjc.edu domain has posted to Usenet in the past year. Isn't that odd?"

"Okay, okay," Shan said measuredly. "That's nice. Too bad the opposition already has access to Dana's account. But, uh, you know, at least now Dana Steckler doesn't have any mail . . . or files . . . or accounts . . . on any systems within tjc.edu."

"You deleted my accounts?" Dana asked in dismay.

"We could have given you that password," said Miles.

"Oh, no need to bother," said Shan, already working on Miles' accounts.

In the end, much to Miles' delight, boatanchor proved invulnerable to both Mike's and Shan's attacks. Miles had to log them in himself, to wipe incriminating mail.

In the end, they smoothed over the digital footprints as well as they could with the palm fronds at hand. And in the end, whether due to these efforts or something else, the bad guys never did come over the hill to the POTEV. Maybe it was the dusting, and maybe it wasn't; maybe there just weren't very many of the bad guys left after the day in Rockefeller Center. Maybe they had taken their licks and had lost their taste for the game. Or maybe, just maybe, they had all read the Manuscript and their small Grinchy hearts grew three sizes that day.

Day Seven: Some were calling home

Miles and Dana at a pay phone, a good twenty blocks from the POTEV. The twenty-block trek was mandated by Naja, due to the likelihood of their phones – and the phones of everyone they'd ever known – being tapped. Mobiles were of course out of the question.

One after the other, they deposited the better part of a roll of quarters and placed short, emotional calls to the people in their lives, mainly to the effect that they were not dead. But they couldn't allow themselves to be a whole lot more forthcoming than that. It was difficult.

On the walk back, Dana broke the melancholy silence by

asking, "What about Belize?"

"What?" Miles had been preoccupied scanning the street, and replaying his phone calls.

"When Naja was talking about third world countries, you mentioned Belize."

"Oh, right. That. It's a, uh, tiny country between Mexico and Guatemala."

"You've been there?"

"No. Just been reading about it. It's got the lowest population density in Central America. Most of the land belongs to wildlife – jaguars, howler monkeys. The people speak English, and are supposed to be friendly as all get-out. And it's cheap, with the Belizean dollar tied to the US dollar at two-to-one. And pretty – it's got rainforests in the central highlands, savanna in the north, Mayan ruins all over, and a barrier reef on the Gulf Coast."

They kept walking, hands in pockets against the cold. Miles went on.

"Inside the reef are like two hundred atolls and islands, called 'cayes'. Most of them are uninhabited. The biggest one has a proper town on it. But the smaller ones are isolated and accessible only by charter boat. At the very end of the chain is South Water Caye. It's this little Robinson Crusoe strand of white sand and palm trees, like fifteen acres, in an hourglass shape. But you can get lodging – there's a place that rents cabanas, mainly for the few hard-core scuba divers who make it out there."

"Was there some special motivation for you doing all this research on Belize?"

"Um, yeah. An embarrassing one – the old sudden-wealth fantasy. You know, you find a huge bag of money dropped in a bank robbery getaway. Or otherwise come upon a pile of cash and need to get it out of the country. I was bored at work, and fantasizing, and thinking about where I might go. Should anything like that happen."

"Jesus, Miles. It did. It just happened."

Miles laughed aloud. "One other thing about Belize. Very liberal banking laws."

They walked the rest of the way back in daydreamy silence.

Going There, Being That Guy

The unlikeliest group of air travelers in the whole world stepped off an underground train, electric doors humming open and closed before and behind them. The Cylon voice of the tram said, "*Doors are closing and will not reopen.*"

Under his breath, Miles said, "Sounds like life."

The sun shone on the group with that particular muted intensity conferred by thick glass. They were flying through Miami – as did pretty much everyone who would take to the air to get from one to the other of the Americas. This was a layover, two hours. Long enough to get to their gate, get a coffee, watch some CNN, maybe check their messages or mail.

In the lounge, Naja sat with Miles and Dana, in silence, breathing in some of the sound an airport makes. Security advisories, a couple of passenger pages, and the endless stepping and chatter of people going, forever going.

At length Dana spoke up. "Why are we going, actually?"

"Oh," Naja sighed. "Couple of reasons. We'd like to see if any of it's true, of course."

"How will we know?"

"Well, if we make it all the way to the end of the trail on the map, and find the people there we're expecting . . . that's a pretty good start."

Snitch wandered up with a black courier bag slung over his lean torso and a pair of insect-eye wrap-around shades on his face. He held a bottle of spring water low by the neck with one finger and a thumb. "You want anything, boss?"

Naja smiled and shook her head. She waited until Snitch had

wandered off again before continuing. "There's another reason. If the so-called Concern was so keen on taking you out just for having read the Manuscript . . . there's reason to think they'll be just as keen to take out the main characters in the story. And they have the same map we do."

"Oh, shit," said Miles.

"We're going to warn them?" asked Dana.

"Something like that. Though I don't really have the feeling that these are the kind of people who will worry much about danger or death."

The PA announced boarding for Gold Medallion Club members, the critically wounded, and those with colicky babies. Three hundred or so pieces of carry-on baggage shifted audibly.

"Who were those guys, Naja?" Miles asked, solemnly.

"You mean the Concern, I assume," Naja said, staring straight ahead, out the glass toward plane and runway. "I had Mike and Shan try to track them back. But they got nothing; not a trace. Just blanked – which I've never seen happen. So all we have are guesses."

"Such as?"

"They could have been sent by the church."

"What? The Catholic Church?"

"Any church. Any one that wants to stay in business. And religion can be big business."

"Oh, shit," Miles allowed. Dana merely nodded.

"Or the government," Naja went on. "Especially one that depends on control of people to stay in power: the PRC, any fundamentalist Islamic country. Who knows? They were bad men." She shrugged her shoulders as if that were explanation enough.

Dana sat by Laylah on the plane

"Did you read McLynn's book?" Laylah asked over the engine noise.

"I skimmed the chapters on exploring Argentina. I was a

little pressed for time." They referred to a biography covering Burton's travels in the Americas. Each of the women had hoped this book would shed light on what Burton might have done or discovered in the Andes in 1868 and 1869. But it had merely raised more questions. Such as:

If Burton discovered an unknown civilization up in the mountains, how come he didn't write a single (public) word about it? And, if he had just discovered the keys to eternal bliss, how come he was in such a bad mood immediately after, when he and Maxwell reached the coast at Valparaiso which he described as "that drab-coloured wooden abomination . . . where fire or ruin by earthquake is purely a question of time"?

"Perhaps he didn't know whether to believe it or not," Laylah suggested. "He was trying to come to grips with it."

"Could be," Dana said. "And what about that purported shoot-out? Did it happen? And why would he lie about it if it hadn't?" Burton had claimed, on at least three different occasions, that he had spent Christmas Day 1868 in a running gun battle with bandits, in which he had killed four opponents and been badly wounded himself. In other accounts of his time in Argentina he made no mention of it.

"The shoot-out wasn't all he never made mention of." Laylah pulled a pair of Blowpops from her carry-on bag. Dana accepted one gratefully. She had started to wonder how bad the penalties could possibly be for tampering with, disabling, or destroying a bathroom smoke detector. Particularly as compared to the penalties for the other shit she had been doing lately.

Celeste sat by Mike on the plane

"Are you single?" he asked.

"You don't meet many women . . . ?" Celeste responded, not unkindly.

"I don't meet anybody," Mike admitted.

"What do you do for a living?"

"I fiddle around with computers."

"That," said Celeste, "is just what Miles told me he does, when we met online."

"Yourself?"

"Oh . . . intelligence. Counter-intelligence." The words tasted strange on Celeste's tongue – not dissembling about what she did, for the first time in her professional life. "Do you think that odd?"

"I don't know what's normal," he said.

"Do you believe it?" she asked, referring to everyone's favorite topic.

"What's not to believe?" he countered. "Truth is supposed to be self-evident, right?" He looked down at the clouds, as they shared a moment of mild awkwardness.

"Yes, I'm single," Celeste said. "And I don't really meet anybody, either."

"No one I know meets anybody," added Mike, in a resigned way.

"But you have all of these people."

"Yes. Wouldn't trade 'em." Mike smiled and glanced over the headrests before and behind him. He looked back at Celeste, "Do you have a group?"

"I did," she shrugged. "But I'm not sure I'm welcome with them any more."

"I'm sorry."

"Oh, don't be. A lot of them were kind of assholes. And anyway, it was just a job."

"That's a sound attitude: 'Just a job.' You can always get another one, if you need it."

"Are the AYTs hiring?" she asked, half-mockingly.

"I'm not sure the group exists anymore," Mike admitted. "I think we might be done."

Miles sat between Naja and T'ien Ken on the plane

"You've read the Tao Te Ching?"

"Sure," Miles answered. "Though Dana's read, like, four different translations."

"Which one have you read?"

"Stephen Mitchell."

T'ien Ken nodded his thrust-lipped approval.

"Do you see how it fits with us? With what we do?" Naja put to Miles.

"Nope."

"No one ever does," laughed T'ien Ken, going back to his copy of *Adbusters*.

"Basically, our job is to take the Power of the Way and apply it in very focused ways – all for good, naturally. This is, of course, at odds with the spirit of Taoism. But the world's kind of fucked up, you know? Somebody has to do something. You can't just sit around regarding the Mystery all day."

"How does what's in the Manuscript affect your outlook?" Miles asked.

"Basically, it looks like the Way of Lao Tzu turns out to be like the geometry of Euclid, or the physics of Newton." She looked Miles in his dark eyes with hers. "An elegant, immensely useful, metaphor. But it's just not the way the universe actually happens to be shaped."

"Okay," Miles nodded. "I can see that. Someone figured out what Lao Tzu insisted was beyond intellectual comprehension. Suddenly the questions that have eluded poets, priests, politicians, and philosophers for five thousand years all get sorted out. Which makes mysticism – the rejection of rationalism, non-explanations – seem like a much less attractive property."

"Too true," said Naja.

"On the other hand," and Miles had suddenly started squinting like a man possessed, "there was that one line in the Tao Te Ching I never did understand."

"Which one?" asked Naja absently.

"He kept talking about 'the source' but he never did explain what the hell that was. That always kind of ate at me. The line was, uh, 'If you don't realize the source, you stumble in confusion and sorrow. When you realize where you come from, you naturally become tolerant, disinterested, amused, kindhearted as a grandmother, dignified as a king.' Something like that. It always seemed to me like there was something important he wasn't telling us."

"Holy cow," said T'ien Ken, looking at Miles now.

"You don't suppose he, uh . . . he knew? But he just didn't want to spill the beans?"

"Or he didn't think people were ready to hear it," said Naja.

Touchdown: Mendoza, Argentina

The tarmac radiated heat. Summer had just begun in the grassy plains of the Pampas, and in Mendoza, at the foot of the Andes. But the exit door of the plane faced in the other direction, away from the peaks. The passengers descended a steep, steel ladder. Dark-skinned, moustachioed men in oil-streaked jumpsuits pulled bags from the belly of the plane, as if digging in a beached whale. Big tuna duffels and chub backpacks fell around the blacktop beach.

Miles noticed his compadres, instantly wearing dark sunglasses to the last, looked for all the world like a crack mercenary team arriving in Laos for some dicey extraction work. Man, they looked cool. And he couldn't fault them. This was their moment – what they'd been waiting for.

Miles smiled into the sun and light breeze, squeezed Dana's elbow, and moved forward with her as their bags hit the ground. As Miles leaned over for his, he could see beneath the belly of the plane, to the other side. Pulling along his bag, but forgetting Dana, he circled the plane in a slack-jawed plod, and stood silent and alone on its far side.

Of all the isolated ground Miles had seen, the Pampas was

the most barren and trackless region by far. Snow-covered mountains rose up in the distance; unspeakable flat distances surrounded them, and him; he could see forever. The foreboding and unreachable mountains, and the silence, made the scene feel uncomfortably like a level from Doom.

As was never possible with the Doom scenery, however, the group could and ultimately did reach those mountains. Soon they would climb them. Just a quick hike through the Andes separated them from their destination. If it existed.

Laylah dealt with the guides. When the plane had landed, these two, a man and a woman, already stood waiting at the corner of the terminal building. They had with them two covered flatbed trucks filled with gear and provisions. Two days of hard hiking awaited them, if the map could be believed. After clearing passport control and customs, the group piled into the trucks and began rolling west toward their jumping-off point.

Miles drew back the burlap flaps on the back of the truck and watched the airport recede.

Behind him, hunched over, avoiding the field of view of the driver, Naja, Mike, and Angelo began digging gear, including guns, out of their luggage. Angelo checked the chambers of a stainless steel .44 revolver with black rubber grips and a six-inch barrel. Miles stared, obviously in awe.

"Are we expecting more trouble?" Dana asked.

"Nope," replied Angelo, slipping the .44 in a belt holster. "But we're not in Kansas anymore."

They then passed around insect repellent, trail rations, water bottles, floppy hats, sturdy shoes; and Mike let Miles play with the handheld mapping GPS. Its color screen showed a topographical representation of the whole region, with waypoints programmed in for the path they intended to take.

The gear was locked down and ready to go when they reached base camp, a cluster of blockish, Spartan huts nestled in the shadow of steep, shale-covered hills. They dropped their gear and luggage on their narrow cots and emerged into the clearing between the structures. An evening meal was already being prepared over and around a five-foot circular pit of embers.

The cookout came with the tour package.

Naja and Laylah sat apart with the male guide and maps. Laylah translated for Naja.

"He says there's no village there that he knows about. But he never goes to that area."

Naja looked troubled. "Ask him why not." Laylah traded words with the man, sitting cross-legged on the dirt. Firelight licked at the three of them.

"He says all of the guides in the Pampas, most of whom have spent a lot of time billy-goating around this part of the Andes, steer clear of it. There's some strange talk about that mountain."

"What sort of strange?" Naja looked back to the body of the group while Laylah asked. The AYTs caroused around the fire, teasing, laughing, passing around mugs of a local beer.

"Tall tales," Laylah said. "Stories about mountain men who fly through the air, witches who move without sound. That come into your dreams, read your mind."

"Sounds rather like our guys," said Naja.

"You're right," Laylah smiled. "Apparently, these stories do more to keep the locals away than anything else, even the rough terrain."

"*Gracias, señor*," said Naja, nodding solemnly, and retired to the campfire.

They spent a happy night on the Pampas.

The Pass

They rose with the dawn. They had ground to cover, and things to look at.

In the Uspallata Pass, near the border which separates Argentina from Chile, a sculptured figure of Christ was erected in 1904 to commemorate the peaceful settlement of a quarrel. The inscription reads, "Sooner shall these mountains crumble into dust than the people of Chile and Argentina break the peace, which they have sworn to maintain at the feet of Christ the Redeemer."

The views from the heights proved breathtaking. At their stopping point, the group milled around, contemplating the statue, and the horizon. Miles stepped away from the group and took a position at an overlook. He couldn't see the Pacific, but felt that it was only a few steep rises from view. Back to the east, the plains of Argentina swept beige and endless.

"Bet you didn't think, two weeks ago, you'd be in the Andes today," Celeste said from behind.

"I've given up trying to predict the future. I'm just glad to not be at my desk."

"Yes, me, too." Celeste drew breath. "Hey, Miles," she said.

"Yeah?" He turned from the sun to face her.

"I'm glad you wrote me when you did. And almost got me killed and whatnot."

"Hey, no problem. Somebody had to turn up with an ennobling act for you to perform."

Celeste's eyes went wide. "*An* ennobling act? More like the twelve trials of Hercules!"

They both smiled. Naja called out to everyone to saddle up.

Mike said to Naja, "I'm telling you, this is the spot. The satellites don't lie."

Four hours of hiking later, the sun long gone behind the

mountain and sinking into the Pacific, the group and guides stood in a large clearing in the forested mountainside. The area was clear of trees, but heavily blanketed with underbrush. No village. Mike and Naja stood together looking at the screen of the GPS. The others stood slightly apart, in silence.

The failing light and the wind in the trees had begun to generate atmosphere.

Naja sighed heavily. "Okay," she said. "Sweep the area. Four groups, one with each radio. Go one mile out in the four cardinal directions, turn clockwise, circle back. We meet here in one hour."

No village was ever found. The overgrown clearing of trees was evocative, but hardly conclusive. All four groups returned from their sweeps without incident. In the very last light, they cleared a central area of underbrush and pitched tents.

The mountainside was black now on all sides, a dozen yards out from their campfire.

Exhausted from the day's trekking, most of the group wolfed down food before hitting the sack.

Miles, sharing a tent with Angelo, tumbled into his sleeping bag, and into sleep, like a man falling off a pier.

The Darlings of God

"Conquer thyself . . ."

Miles heard this voice in the night, in the dark, from somewhere outside. He tried to stir.

"Till thou has done this, thou art but a slave."

Miles couldn't recognize the voice. He couldn't see. Faint light bled in from outside. He rose and followed it out. The voice came again, from beyond a break in the trees.

"Do what thy manhood bids thee do . . ."

Miles followed the path, mesmerized, pushing at branches that swept at his head.

He emerged onto a grassy overlook, beyond the tree line, the mountains now towering before him. Further, at the edge of a precipice, he saw a single figure, shrouded in night mist and lit by starlight. Miles wanted to approach, but was afraid. He felt at his waist: no gun. No nothing.

He swallowed dryly before finding his voice. "Where is everyone?" he asked.

"They've gone on." The figure spoke without turning.

"Gone on where?"

"To the next place."

"They're dead?" Miles suddenly felt terror for his friends. But then he realized the man was not talking about his friends.

"There is no death. There are only tides. Rolling forever."

The man's voice was strong, remorseless, with an English accent.

"Why can you see these things," Miles entreated, "that none of us can?"

"What can you not see?"

Miles thought. "Our past lives," he said. "Other universes. The map of space and time."

"What else?"

"Our true selves. Where we come from. Where we go. What we should be doing. What is real."

"Why do you think it is you cannot see?"

Miles paused. He thought back to Dana's lectures. "Our minds," he said. "Six million years of evolution made them, to solve problems: hunting, gathering, surviving. On the African savannah."

"You did survive." The man rested his hand on the butt of a revolver, Miles saw now.

"But what use did we have," Miles went on, "for understanding space-time? Or how free will works in a mechanistic universe? The enigma of consciousness? We needed food. We needed fire."

The back of the man's head nodded. "You do not know your place in the universe."

"No," said Miles, feeling sad. "We've been trying to find it. For five thousand years."

"Poets," the man said. "Priests. Philosophers. Naturalists. Seers."

"All failed."

"I have found it," the man said. "They showed it to me."

"Who showed you?" Miles asked, stepping forward.

"Those who used to live here. I found them. Here. On the mountain."

"How did they know?" Miles pleaded. "How can *I* know?"

The man paused for a long interval before answering. "I can show you," he said. After another pause, he turned around to face Miles. His dark eyes glinted fiercely in the moonlight; a ragged scar traced one cheek, above and to the side of a sinuous forked moustache.

Miles took a step backward. "I know who you are," he breathed.

The man put his hand out. Before he realized it, Miles had taken hold.

He felt himself tumbling. Into the man's eyes. Falling off of the surface of the Earth.

The clearing shrank beneath him, and then the mountains, and then the continent as well.

Miles looked up, then down again. The Earth spun below him, gauzy and blue and silent.

"We've left the planet . . ." Miles breathed.

"There's no leaving," the man answered. "We are always home."

Miles gazed around at the endlessness of stars.

"And we are always now," the man said. "The past is that way," he said, pointing toward no place. "The future is that way," he added, pointing in the opposite direction. Miles tried to move in the second direction, ninety degrees to the X, Y, and Z axes of Euclidean space. The man followed.

"Space-time is real," the man said as they traveled. Extruded worm-slices of Earth, and the sun, and the stars, and the box that contained them, roared by along the time axis. "The past is but a place you have left, the future someplace you have yet to go."

Reaching out toward the worms, Miles caught sight of his own hand. It glowed with a swirling light, blue and red. "What is this?" he asked, making whorls in space.

"That is you," the man said. "You are your acts. They attach to you, forever."

"Everything we do matters . . ." Miles breathed. As he spoke, the blurring of their movement slowed, then stopped. The worms went away, becoming spheres and twinkles of light and rectilinear spatial boxes again. Miles felt himself being pulled down, cutting through the clouds, the Earth's surface coming into focus. The glowing light from his fingers extended out, circling the planet, flowing into six and a half billion other lights.

"We are all one," the man said. And Miles knew it to be true.

They continued to descend, cities coming into view, lines of light receding, silver and brightness. "What's all that . . ." Miles didn't know whether to call it buzz or glow. It was like voices in his eyes. Before the man could answer, Miles said, "I know. That's the global consciousness. It's the Net."

"The next stage," the man agreed. "After the first great gatherings, the cities, and nation-states. Finally, all are nose to nose. There is no longer any way to maintain the illusion we are different. You and your friends will speed the process."

"With the Manuscript?" Miles asked.

"You will give it to the world," the man said, turning away, shrinking with distance.

"Wait," Miles pleaded. "Can you show me the Godhead? Can you show me the Source . . . ?"

Faintly, Miles could hear the man say, "I am only the Father of Moustachios."

"The what?"

"*Soy El Padre de Moustachios*. I am the Father of Moustachios . . ."

Miles rubbed his eyes, twisting at the waist. He squinted as light leaked in all around him, as through cloth. Now it was a female voice saying the words, from beyond the walls. He tried to sit up. His sleeping bag was soaked. He heard Laylah's voice.

When he emerged from the tent, he could hear voices outside the clearing. Running barefoot, he found most of the group gathered around the gnarled truck of an ancient hardwood. At the periphery, he yelped, "What? What is it?" Celeste grabbed him by the elbow, still slick with sweat.

"There's carving on the tree trunk," she said. "Shan found it, relieving himself."

Miles craned to try and see. "What does it say?"

"It says 'El Padre de Moustachios' – the Father of Moustachios."

Miles stood stunned.

"Laylah says it was another of Burton's nicknames." Celeste paused. "He was here."

Miles fought with his breath, his dream still only inches beyond his sight.

Publish or Perish

"Well," said Naja. "Only one thing left to do now . . ."

Dana finished for her: "Publish the Manuscript." Naja smiled at her warmly.

They were back in the sky, now – not on the mountain, but far above it – two hundred miles northeast of Santiago, in the open area at the back of an airplane. Miles sat by Naja, who stood by Mike, who stood by Celeste, and Dana and Abhijit and Shan and Snitch and Angelo and Laylah and T'ien Ken, all in a tribal circle.

The plane had no broadband. But it did have air phones, with data ports.

Miles drove one of the hand-helds they had packed for the trip; a cable drooped across his lap to a seat-back phone. He tapped with a plastic stylus while the others milled and laughed. And drank.

"Another round first, I think," replied Naja. "It's a long flight. We can toast each submission. Stewardess?" They ordered more drinks and huddled up.

And they proceeded to register the address of the Manuscript server – complete with username and password – with every web search engine and index anyone in the group could think of, which was quite a lot of them. They got through two more rounds of drinks before finishing.

And just like that, the illuminated cat was out of the two-million-dollar bag.

It was a few days later that Miles went back to see if the registrations had taken; and to see where the Manuscript ranked, with which search terms. He went to Google and saw the listing come up. Very pretty. *Just let those Concern guys kill a billion web surfers.*

He went to click through, as he had before.

The hypertext flashed to red for the duration of Miles' mouse click, then calmed back to blue. The icon churned serenely in the upper right corner of his browser. *Contacting 238.142.222.64*, the status bar reassured him.

He watched, and waited for the sacred text to flow in regally across his screen.

A minute and most of its neighbor later, Miles still waited.

And then the connection timed out. *Host or gateway not responding*, his browser informed him, with what could only strike Miles as a very irksome casualness.

And so. If you could follow a whole burst of IP packets, a group of packets that cohered on reassembly, into something like a request for a document, on their way from – to pick a couple of spots at random – where Miles sat at his laptop in a bamboo beach cabana, to wherever it was that the Manuscript server physically resided . . . if you could follow along at the speed of light, as conducted by fiber, you might undertake their pilgrimage along with them, supplicating for illuminated data. You might ring at the palace of heaven; but you would find no one home.

And so, headers hanging, all the robustness and redundancy gone from their step, they turned around and returned to the machine of their provenance – a few inches beneath Father Miles' hand and solemn gaze – to report their failed crusade.

Miles couldn't even shoot the messenger in this case. These IP packets had long ceased to exist by the time Miles' eyes took in their report and sent some apologist packets of their own to Miles' brain, relaying the bad news. Thusly ephemeral is the physical transport of data.

Miles sat in his bamboo chair chewing on this one for some time. What happened to the site? Where did the Manuscript go? Who slammed the temple doors and stole their gift to the world? Or – to borrow the perennial words of untold frenzied sysadmins across the ages – "*Why is the goddamn fucking server down?!*"

Miles figured there were two ways you could go with this. The most likely culprit was load. A "Dead Sea Scroll" of a server, one no one administrated, might stay up on its own for years, no complaints, no hiccups, if nothing much were asked of it. On the other hand, if out of the blue this machine got hit with a few hundred (a few thousand? hundreds of thousands?) connections in a couple of hours, it might react badly. It might even crash, or get badly wedged, as servers sometimes do.

But . . . it wasn't the only possible explanation, and it wasn't the one Miles was thinking of. He was thinking about shell escapes . . . and known holes in wu-ftpd . . . and arbitrary command sequences to the shell . . . and denial of service attacks . . .

and the mere sixteen characters ("shutdown -y -g 0") a Unix person could type in under a second, if he could break in and get a shell in which to type them. Miles himself hadn't managed to get toe one inside of that box, the Manuscript server – and not for lack of trying.

But that didn't mean he couldn't *imagine* someone who could. For instance, the kind of people who could put two million dollars in crumpled bills in a backpack, and have people killed, and whatnot, could conceivably own or rent the kind of hacking talent that could get into, and bring down, a Fort Knox of an FTP server.

So maybe the Concern had shut the world out, after all.

Miles slumped into his trademark sitting slouch, snorted, and eyed the monitor of the laptop balefully. *Well, that's the end of that*, he thought.

He continued to regard the monitor, squinting.

And then he remembered something: that the site *had* been up the first time he had visited, a couple of days earlier. And he considered, correctly, that he *couldn't* have been the only person to have visited in that brief interval of the Manuscript's public life.

And he knew – he knew as surely as he knew all these other new astounding facts about the shape of the universe – that somewhere out there . . . in places separated by thousands of miles of physical space, and a few hops of Internet . . . out there was somebody, or most likely a dozen somebodies, or maybe ten thousand somebodies, who had already downloaded the Manuscript. Somewhere out there on a dozen or ten thousand C: drives, and MacOS desktops, and home directories, and microbrowser caches . . . were a dozen or ten thousand copies of a few thousand words that happened to accurately describe the shape of their shared universe, and the essential nature of the six and a half billion flitting souls who inhabited it.

And as surely as the logarithmic organic growth of the

Internet had turned fifty web servers in 1993 to something north of fifty million a mere ten years later, those few thousand words would find their digital, pulsing, speed-of-light way back up onto *other* servers all across the Net. Servers not password protected, nor sequestered in the Internet's backwaters, nor vulnerable to maintenance problems or hacker attacks by fearsome gun-toting salvation-craving cabals. Very soon, Miles had every reason to expect, the Manuscript would be leaking out all over.

To get things started, he put a copy on his own web server. Boatanchor wasn't going anywhere.

With that happy thought, Miles planted a big smooch in the middle of his browser window, and closed the laptop cover.

Epilogue: The Beach

The tiny cabana had one window and one door. It had only a composting toilet and a gravity-fed shower. But it did have a working phone line. The late afternoon light bled in through cotton drapes, settling on the still scene within. A pair of duffel bags lay at the foot of the bed. A lanky figure sat hunched over a cramped desk, peering into a laptop.

Miles surveyed his barren mailbox. He didn't get a heck of a lot of mail these days. But, strangely, the lack of that New Mail thrill no longer seemed to bother him.

He gathered up his sunglasses and wallet and stepped out the door, which had no lock. He emerged into the shade of a grove of palm trees. The next cabana, to the south, was a hundred yards away – out of sight and, happily, out of hearing. (It was the one Celeste and Mike shared.) Paul's new crib was the next one on.

Twenty steps took him to the tree line at the beach, where he turned north. The sun hovered ten degrees over the water to his left, very bright. It made glare and shadows of Miles as he loped half the length of South Water Caye. The breeze blew off the water onto the side of the face.

After a few minutes, he reached a short, wooden-slat pier. Palm trees and stunted palm bushes guarded its base. He stepped out over the water and took a seat on a wooden bench at the pier's end. He faced the setting sun, out past the Belizean barrier reef.

Miles considered the odd fact that he now knew how things worked. He had no way of knowing if his certitude was delusional; it certainly could be. But he figured it didn't matter. Belief was always conditional. Was his dream real? It was real while it lasted. It was real to him.

He wore the expression of a man who'd seen Heaven and remembered what it looked like.

The reflection of the sun on the water seemed about a mile wide – just like the first time he saw it, and just like every single evening since he had arrived. He felt sure he would never grow tired of it. He came here every day at this time.

Two hands squeezed his shoulders, and a pointy chin came to rest on his scalp.

"Hi, doll," he said, looking skyward.

Dana rounded the bench and curled up beside him.

"I really do like the results of your Belize research, by the way."

Miles smiled. "I could say a few nice things about the results of yours."

They sat quietly as the sun went down, again.